T0196243

A CLOSER TOMORROW

MATT CAFFREY

iUniverse, Inc.
Bloomington

A Closer Tomorrow

Copyright © 2013 Matt Caffrey

iUniverse books may be ordered through booksellers or by contacting:

iUniverse
1663 Liberty Drive
Bloomington, IN 47403
www.iuniverse.com
1-800-Authors (1-800-288-4677)

ISBN: 978-1-4759-4665-9 (sc)
ISBN: 978-1-4759-4666-6 (hc)
ISBN: 978-1-4759-4667-3 (e)

Library of Congress Control Number: 2012915866

Printed in the United States of America

iUniverse rev. date: 1/11/2013

This, my first novel, is dedicated to my family...past and present.

I would like to acknowledge the sacrifice made by my wife Yuliya during the years in took to complete this novel. Thank you for your serenity and patience when I sequestered myself, for days on end, in a room strewn with espresso cups, crumpled paper and ranting madness!

Thanks to Amy McHargue, Sarah Disbrow and Traci Anderson at iUniverse for all their guidance and assistance.

Thank you to Dan Varrette, my Toronto-based editor, for weeding my botanical garden.

And a special thanks to California-based artist Lori LaMont for granting me permission to use her stunning artwork on the cover of this novel. ('Cockfight No.2', watercolor on paper 40"x26" 2011)

CONTENTS

Hope is a waking dream.
—Homer

Seldom do people discern eloquence under a threadbare cloak.
—Juvenal

PART ONE

THE OUTCAST OF JIMANÍ

Jaragua sparked up a hand-rolled cigarette and rested his shaved head against the concrete wall behind him. His new skinhead look had nothing to do with fashion or politics; he just hated lice. His six-foot frame carried a lean muscularity that spoke of skipped meals and endless push-ups. He had brooding features and olive skin, a mulatto attractiveness that required constant proof of toughness.

He took a deep drag of the tobacco, blew a thick plume of smoke out his nostrils and silently wished himself a happy twenty-third birthday. He looked down in disgust at the red bumps covering his tattooed forearms. He wanted to rip the infected meat from his bones. He had picked up a nasty rash during his six-month stretch inside Higuey Prison, and so far he had received no medical attention nor been charged with any crime. He thought about the hundreds of inmates he had met over the years with the same story. Some men had spent many years inside without ever facing a judge.

He shifted his weight and stretched out the grimy towel he was sitting on, redefining the fragile borders of his territory. Squatters beware. He stubbed his cigarette out on the back of a loitering cockroach, using his thumb to push the hot ember through its back. Mustard-coloured goo squirted out of the bug's ass. It smelled like burned hair.

The jail crawled with rats, translucent scorpions, spiders, stinging ants and mutant-sized bugs. The air pulsated with shit-eating flies and disease-sickened mosquitoes. Lime-green geckos darted up the stained walls and stuck to the ceiling. They enjoyed looking down on the chaos, grinning amiably and bobbing their heads to a tempo only they could

3

hear. Some inmates passed the time by killing things all day, becoming the cellblock's self-appointed exterminators.

The stress of incarceration no longer bothered Jaragua. The overcrowding, the vermin, the constant tension—even the incessant noise became tolerable, nothing more than the drone and babble of an angry and occasionally violent news anchor. The only aspect of prison life that he had never adapted to was the relentless stench of the place. The unwashed bodies, the floor-pissers, the overflowing toilet, the festering wounds, the fear, sweat, blood, vomit, rotting teeth—a malodorous stew the sweltering heat simmered into a rancid meal, which Jaragua choked down with every breath.

He watched a short muscular Colombian strut about the joint, conducting his business. He felt angry that such a little troll of a man had the power to evoke envy in him. "Fucker," he mumbled, and spat on the floor.

The man had arrived less than a week ago and already had two double bunks and a spacious area around them, and in case anyone took exception to his comfort, he had hired members of the prison gang Tio Muerte as his bodyguards. Everyone knew the man was connected to El Guapo. Before the Colombian had even begun to stink, his pampered ass would be waddling out the front gates and into the air-conditioned luxury of a growling Hummer.

Jaragua wrapped his toes around the sticky wad of pesos he had jammed into his canvas sneaker and considered whether he would rather eat or get high. He told himself that his woman would be visiting soon and would bring him some food and that the drugs would alleviate his hunger until then. He told himself whatever he needed to hear until his addiction won the argument.

He stood up and pushed his way through the crush of convicts, a surly mix of Dominicans, Haitians, Puerto Ricans, the occasional Cuban and a couple of very unfortunate Canadian gringos. He ignored the lecherous stares he received from some of the inmates as he made his way towards the Colombian's turf. In any penal system, news spread like malaria, and there were no second chances. Once someone exposed a weakness, they were fucked—literally and figuratively. Alternatively, if someone had slit some ass-raping freak's throat in a La Vega lockup a few years back, he maintained a measure of respect.

He took his time while buying his dope. It was an oasis inside the Colombian's domain, and he was enjoying the atmosphere. He watched the man speak angrily into his cell phone and wondered how someone obtained such a lofty position in life. Was it luck? Hard work? Dedication? Whatever it was, he was determined to find out.

"Why you staring at the boss, cuero?"

Jaragua looked over at a heavily muscled Dominican who was lying on one of the bunks and thumbing bullets into a silver handgun.

"A maracón who wears gold eye shadow shouldn't be calling anyone a bitch," Jaragua said, and laughed.

The gang member slammed the last bullet into his gun, slapped the cylinder closed and lunged from his bunk. "You gonna be laughing from the grave, puto."

Another gang member stepped between the two men and handed Jaragua a small paper wrap of cocaine. "I know this guy from long ago. He's solid, not some punk, and you're making a mistake to treat him like one. So puff on that puffer fish and sit da fuck down."

Jaragua touched fists with the other man. "Gracias, Diego, but I had him."

"I consider you a brother, but you fight one, you fight us all, huh? You know the life," he said.

"I remember when a hombre had to *have* eggs instead of *eating* them to get into Tio Muerte," Jaragua said.

"Open invite for you, amigo. Whenever you get sicka sleeping wit da dogs, come and see me. You know what's up. Ain't your first vacation."

Jaragua had his reasons for not joining a prison gang, reasons he was finding harder to justify with each miserable day spent locked down. "Maybe, before I catch fleas."

"You know where I live."

Jaragua reluctantly simmered back into the cesspool. He felt insulted by his anonymity. He believed that he was destined for something better. He remembered what an old con had said to him once: "If a person lives like a sewer rat, at some point they should either eat the poison or become king of the rats."

He was already feeling hostile by the time he noticed another prisoner sitting on his towel, claiming rights to the space. "That's my spot, amigo. Maybe you didn't know," he said, offering the young Haitian a chance to avoid what was coming.

The boy flexed his skinny arms and tried to conceal his fear by spitting at Jaragua's feet and shooting him a crazy stare.

Jaragua switched from Spanish to Creole and tried to reason with the kid. "Last time, because you're new. Now get up."

"My place. Zaka's place. I kill you."

He was too loud and it was too late. Their minor drama had attracted an audience, and Jaragua knew the boy could not back down now.

Jaragua stepped in and slammed his knee into the boy's face, shattering his nose and bouncing his skull off the wall. Before the stunned Haitian could recover, Jaragua smashed his knee into his face again and then again. Each vicious blow decorated the wall with bloody impressions. They resembled Rorschach inkblots.

"And don't bleed on my towel!" Jaragua yelled. He grabbed the groaning boy, dragged him a few feet away and dropped him on the floor. The crowd howled their approval and jeered the battered newcomer.

Jaragua ignored them, sat down and rubbed a hand over his knee. There was nothing in the world that he could call his own except the rags he was wearing, a woman who loved him and a piece of jailhouse real estate the size of a hand towel, all of which he was willing to kill or die for.

When he was no longer the centre of attention, he unwrapped his cocaine and gratefully snorted a thick pinch up each nostril. He savoured the chemical taste of the mucus that dripped down the back of his throat. He closed his eyes and rolled his neck from side to side.

After a few minutes, the drug reached his brain and bullied any weak emotions it encountered. Pain, fear, anxiety—all bitch-slapped into submission. Hunger, thirst, exhaustion—bound, gagged and stuffed into vacant crevices within his frontal lobe. Traitors one and all. The microscopic crystals roared down his central nervous system on turbo-charged Ducati monsters, gnashing their titanium teeth, slicking back their laser-cut diamond pompadours and popping wheelies. Jaragua enjoyed the ride.

"Hey, man, you like tattoos, huh?"

Jaragua looked up at a small thin man standing before him and scowled at the interruption. His dilated pupils glistened with a black menace that would have stilled the tongues of most men.

"I don't want no problems, okay?" the man began. "I'm an artist. If you like, I make a nice tat."

"You Puerto Rican?" Jaragua asked.

"That's right. Straight from San Juan, via Miami, to this Dominican hellhole," he said, and flashed a quick smile. He was about thirty, had emotive eyes and a toothy grin and wore expensive shoes—and because he was still wearing his fine Italian leather shoes, Jaragua knew that the man couldn't be as frail as he appeared.

"You think I'd trust a spic with a sharp instrument around me?" Jaragua said, and smiled back at him.

The man's eyes went flat, and his smile twisted into a sneer before he answered. "Maybe you're right. Forget the tattoo, man. I don't want your AIDS blood on my needles no how."

Jaragua smiled at the man. "AIDS blood? That's original."

"That's right. You like that shit?" the man said, the tension in his face draining away.

Jaragua extended his hand. "Jaragua."

"Manny Rios."

The two men shook hands and grinned at each other.

"Yeah, I'd like a new tattoo. I got something special in mind, but I got no money," Jaragua said, and shrugged his shoulders.

"Yeah, but you got yayo, huh? Give me a bump or two an' I'm going to make you a nice tat. Just something to help me grin at nothing for a while."

Jaragua unfolded his wrap of coke and shifted the remaining powder around with his little finger. He looked at the jailhouse tattoos on Manny's arms and thrust his chin out. "That's all your work?"

"The ones where I can reach are," Manny said, running a hand over one forearm. "Here and here and this one…and this one too."

Manny's work was much better than most of the amateurish tats Jaragua had seen scratched and hammered into the flesh of so many other convicts—crucifixes that looked like lower-case Ts, hearts that resembled puckering orifices, attempts at tribal work that left the human canvas permanently disfigured.

"Okay, we got a deal. Just so long as it turns out better than this one," Jaragua said, and pointed to a misshapen blob of black ink on his arm. It looked more like a discoloured mole than body art.

Manny leaned forward and squinted at the blemish. "What the fuck is that?"

"A spider."

"A spider? Fuck no. That looks like something I saw swimming in the shitter this morning."

Jaragua laughed and self-consciously rubbed his arm. "So better than that one then?"

"Oh yeah, my friend, much better than that one. Even if I were a blind epileptic suffering a hangover better than that one."

Jaragua tossed Manny his cocaine. "So you say. Now back up your big mouth."

"Right on, brother…Right on."

Manny shovelled a fingernail's worth of the blow up each nostril. He pinched his nose closed, snuffled, snorted, sighed, opened his eyes really wide and slowly blew his breath out. "Okay, okay, yep. I got all my shit right here. Gonna make you a real one. One you can be proud of. Hey, nice stuff you got there. Very nice."

He fished a small tin box out of his pocket and rattled it at Jaragua. "See? All my shit. Right here."

He pulled the lid off a tobacco can and shook needles, tape, matches and cellophane-wrapped beer caps full of black and blue inks onto the floor. He winked, nodded his head vigorously and ran a quick tongue over his cracked lips. "What you want? And where you want it?"

Jaragua snorted another pinch before answering. He ran two fingers across the back of his left hand. "I want it right across here. I want it to say 'Estrellita Luminosa' in capital letters."

"Okay. Got that. Estrellita, huh?" Manny bit his lower lip and moved his hips back and forth with the gusto of an amateur porn star.

"Relax, stud. That's the girl I'm going to marry. She's a singer, and that's the name of her favourite song. Well, it's her name too, just not the *Luminosa* part. It's a nickname. Oh fuck. Never mind. Just do it."

Manny ceased his comic gyrations. "Hey, no problema. Estrellita Luminosa. No problema. I'm just fooling around. She your woman?"

"Yeah. She's coming to visit me in a couple a days. I want to surprise her, so make it nice. Right across there." Jaragua held out his fist.

He closed his eyes as Manny began to work on his tattoo. In his memory, he could see Estrellita's face, her opal black eyes looking up at him. For him, her eyes were the essence of her beauty. It wasn't their glimmer or strength, nor their colour or depth. It was what he saw in them that had won his heart. He saw something that frightened him. He saw belief.

RISING TIDE

"Noah's ark for insects," Maximo said. He used a twig to flick a venomous centipede off his soggy bed. He then pulled his knees up to his chest and shuddered.

Whenever the rains came, every creeping, crawling, twenty-legged and seven-eyed insect in Jimaní viewed his bed as higher ground. It didn't bother him that much. After all, he was a man of fifteen years. However, he felt sorry for his little sister, Lourdes, staying awake as long as she was able, defending herself against the apocalyptic swarm until her exhaustion conquered her fear. He felt as if they existed precariously on the lip of a drain, a great depression in the ground into which everything flowed.

He mashed a sodden New York Mets T-shirt into a lumpy pillow, eased his head back and scowled up at the ceiling, a rust-weakened sheet of corrugated tin that amplified the sound of the relentless rain better than it kept the rain itself out.

He sighed and pushed his straight black hair off his face, a face his Dominican mother had told him would break many hearts, a face that other boys wanted to punch in but could never say why. The other boys called him blanco: "white boy."

When he was younger, Maximo had held his own tanned arm up against his father's and sulked because his skin wasn't as dark. His father had sighed and pushed his panama hat up onto his forehead, a sure sign that the conversation had turned serious.

"When I look at your mami, I no see her clear skin; I see her clear heart. Anyone who judges one a you by this," his father had said, pinching some loose skin on the back of his own hand, "and no by this," he had said, touching his son's chest, "they is a prisoner of they own fear. They rot in a cell they may unlock with two words: *brother, sister*. Hate will always find a reason. If your skin is the same, they will hate you because your god laughs instead of cries, or because you fold your hands differently when you pray. If your faith is the same, they will hate you because your shoes are not as new as they, because you babble a foreign tongue, because your eyes are brown and no blue. Hate is a demanding master, my son. Don't ever be a slave."

Maximo listened to the rain with a mounting uneasiness. Its intensity seemed deliberate, a punishment. He watched the muddy water swirling around the interior of the wooden shack. He couldn't recall it ever having risen so high before.

He looked up at the sombre crucifix his mother had nailed over the doorway, and he scowled. After all his family had suffered, he considered his mother's resolute faith disturbingly delusional. He was certain that God despised the poor, the wretched. Perhaps *despise* was too strong a word—maybe they just embarrassed him. Maybe watching humanity— his greatest creation—scratch and peck their daily sustenance from the stony earth like soulless goats reminded him that he was fallible, that his opus was flawed.

Despite all the Bible stories his mother had read to him, he still preferred his father's religion, an eclectic mix of voodoo and Santería. He worshipped gods who drank and smoked, lusted and cursed, imperfect deities who flaunted their vulnerabilities, their egos sated with chicken blood instead of human subjugation.

Maximo looked over at his sister and thought that she looked small for seven years of age, like a porcelain doll with flawless radiant skin, huge eyes and implied characteristics. He gently tucked a corner of the sheet over her bare shoulders and watched the slight rise and fall of her thin chest. He remembered when she had taken ill recently. His parents couldn't even afford candles to ease the gloom and shadows from her fever-slick body.

Something moved

He raised his head and stared in disbelief, watching as a hand wove its way through his sister's mass of dark curls. It paused and then rested two long hairy fingers against her cheek. He squeezed his eyes shut, hoping that he was imagining it. He opened them again and suffered a jolt of adrenaline. His eyes widened in terror, and a scream caught in his throat.

Tarantula

Before Maximo could react, Lourdes' eyes snapped open, and she bashed the spider off her face, knocking it into the dark folds of the bed sheets. "Maximo!" she squealed, mashing herself up against her brother.

Their father, Solomon, emerged from a dark corner, splashing through the floodwater and descending on them like a witch doctor, his machete held high and his broad Haitian features scowling his intent.

"Papi, tarantula, here, there," Lourdes said, and pointed at the blankets.

Solomon cursed in Creole, took hold of the bedding and shook it vigorously. "Where him at?" The veins in his forearms twisted over his hard muscles like scorched earthworms. He badgered the linen until the panicked spider emerged from its sanctuary and dashed across the bed. His long blade whistled through the dank air and thumped down onto the bed, cleaving the tarantula in half. Its shocked remains continued to ooze and claw their way towards an escape its brain still believed possible.

Solomon sucked his teeth and scraped the spider's grisly remains from his children's bed. They plopped into the rising waters like a forlorn turd.

Maximo could smell the rum and tobacco of his father, smells that were as much a part of Solomon as his strong work ethic and easy smile.

"I was going to kill it, Papi, but she woke up. I was ready," Maximo said, trying to squeeze some hardness into his soft features.

Like any father, Solomon knew who and what his son was long before the boy felt the need to prove it to him. "I know, boy. You always watchin' over your sista.

"Come on, Palomita," he said, calling his daughter by her nickname. "You gonna sleep wit Mami and Papi tonight." He scooped her up with one arm, kissed her cheek and sloshed through the water towards his own bed.

Maximo watched them go, the machete dangling loosely by father's side. It was the same one Solomon used in the fields to cut sugarcane from dawn until dusk, earning just enough pesos to keep a leaky tin roof over his family's heads, rice and beans over the fire and a bottle of rum to help him forget that he had once dared to dream of something more.

Maximo slammed his fist onto his bed, its saturated surface stealing the power from the blow. I will escape all of this one day, he thought, and not the way his older brother Jaragua had—not with a gun. He looked up at the two posters he had tacked on the wall. One was of home run king Sammy Sosa of the Chicago Cubs, his bat in full swing as it connected with his 500th home run. He was the first Latino to achieve such a milestone. The smack of that wood had echoed throughout the Americas, throughout the world. It sounded like hope whispered into the ear of every boy who had ever used a stick to smack stones across a dormant riverbed.

Sammy was a legend in the Dominican Republic. However, Pedro Martinez was Maximo's true idol for two reasons: He was the best pitcher in the world, and he played for the New York Mets.

Maximo looked at the poster of Pedro on the mound, ready to unleash frustration upon another nervous batter. Sluggers averaged just .204 against Pedro's intimidating pitching style.

"Velocity, location, movement, deception," Maximo whispered.

Maximo possessed all the necessary skills to succeed as a pitcher. He was a sandlot star, and scouts from the island's Tigres del Licey were already pursuing him.

"Number forty-five," he said, speaking Pedro's number with reverence.

Yes, he thought, one day he would escape the bleakness of his birthright. He would make his parents proud. His sister could sleep the whole night through in a dry bed, with nothing lurking between the sheets to harm her.

He would change it all.

And Jaragua?

He frowned at the thought of his older brother, whom nobody had heard from for so long. He knew that their mother cried for him, wondering if he were hungry or even alive.

Maximo pushed his thoughts away and allowed himself to drift into his favourite daydream for the countless time. He is up on the mound at Shea Stadium, his New York Mets pinstriped uniform shining like a beacon, like a suit of armour.

Invincible

The batter is faceless, just another hulking demigod, one who thought his bat capable of humbling the newest sensation to have swaggered out of the Dominican Republic.

The Mets slogan "Ya Gotta Believe!" flashes across the JumboTron, inciting Maximo's fans to ever-greater levels of hysteria, his name a hypnotic mantra on their lips.

The pitch

A knuckler

The swing

The strike

You're out!

Crowd goes wild

Maximo's face shone from the glory of his fantasy, and his eyes sparkled with a certainty reserved for those who believed in dreams. A serene smile spread across his face.

"No. Not with a gun. The way that Pedro did; the way that Sammy did."

Like a legend

Like a hero

MAMBO #5

LONG BEFORE THE CROWING of his roosters invaded his workers' sleep, Ignacio dos Santos began his day's labour. He found that the best time to tap his trees was just before dawn. It was a peaceful time, suspended between light and dark, a hushed moment when all of nature grew still, anticipating the vermillion rush of another Caribbean sunrise.

He moved through the knee-high grass with a fluidness and grace that even twenty lost years on the oldest streets in the New World could not cripple. He was of average height and fine-boned and possessed a vitality that spat in the face of old age. He wore his chalk- and tin-coloured hair slicked back against his scalp and had a face that the combat boots of pain and loss had not completely kicked in, leaving it, if not handsome, at least stamped with a handsome word.

He walked into his strand of Castilla rubber trees and savoured the deep green smell of the woods, thankful that he lived high above the exhaust- and noise-choked streets of Puerto Plata. His trees were more than just a source of income to him; they were living beings, entities that had been instrumental in helping him maintain his sobriety, and he respected their wisdom.

Ignacio ran a calloused hand over one of the tree trunks.

"Good morning, ladies."

He winced when his palm glided over a patch of scored bark—raised scars where the tree had previously been milked. The wounds always reminded him of a boy he had shared a doorway with once; he had wrists like that.

Ignacio slung a burlap sack from his shoulder, laid it at his sandalled feet and took out some tools.

"Breathe in," he said, speaking to the tree.

He used a bone-handled knife to carve a deep V into the trunk. The blade sliced through the bark without damaging the wood—a surgeon's scalpel, splitting skin but not muscle. Next, he used a wooden mallet to drive a steel funnel into the base of the incision. He entrusted nobody but himself to tap the trees. It was a subtle and gentle art that, if done improperly, could result in the tree's destruction.

He hung a red pail from the spout and inspected the creamy latex as it bled from the gash and dripped into the bottom of the container. The liquid was a mystery to botanists the world over. The rubber tree, like all trees, received its nutrients via the circulation of its sap. However, latex was unique to the species, and its reasons for existing were still obscure.

The complex substance consisted of water, sugars, resins, hydrocarbons, oils, acids, salts, proteins and caoutchouc, the last being the key ingredient in the manufacturing of rubber.

Ignacio shuffled his feet over the ground, performing the cha-cha-cha on his way to the next tree.

Because all work deserved respect, he had decided to learn as much as he could about the history of rubber. He learned that even though it was a relatively young industry, it could rival the spice trade for its romance and cruelty, its wealth and corruption, human destinies forever altered.

He was fascinated to discover that the strange stuff had initially received little interest. They called it rubber simply because it was capable of erasing pencil marks from paper, and it wasn't until 1839—when Charles Goodyear discovered vulcanization—that its true potential was unlocked.

Ignacio tapped one tree after another as the wilting cool of the morning slowly offered its throat up to the hunger of the midday heat. He unbuttoned his faded green work shirt and merengued his way over to his last tree.

He had been born in the Cibao region of the Dominican Republic, in an area regarded as the cradle of merengue. It was a place where the musical soul of his country lived in the blood, the breasts and the hips of its people. He had grown up in Esperanza, and he always enjoyed telling strangers that he used to live in hope, grinning to himself when they asked, "In hope of what?"

When he finished tapping the final tree, he removed his sweat-streaked shirt and mopped his brow with it. He closed his eyes and listened to the wind as it tousled the leaves high above him, an affectionate father's hand through his son's untidy hair. To him, it sounded like music. He could hear the excited pulse of a tambora roll, the breaking crystal of a German accordion, nutmeg grated on the guiro—the soundtrack of a life he mourned and one that had nearly killed him.

He raised his arms up, embraced his imaginary partner in the classic vals-like position so popular in ballroom merengue. He shot one leg out to the side, performing the paso de la empalizada. He swivelled his hips and dragged one limp leg over the forest floor, the toe of his sandal furrowing the earth like an ox-driven plough.

Of all the stories he had heard over the years regarding the origins of the dance's stiff-legged posture, the one he liked best was that of a wounded soldier returning home a hero from one of the country's many revolutions. The legend said that, out of sympathy for the handicapped man, an entire village had felt obliged to drag one leg behind them during the victory dance, giving birth to the unusual posture.

Ignacio surrendered to the rhythm of movement and memory. He dropped his hands and began to mambo. Performing the dance always reminded him of Marilyn Monroe, of the time they had mamboed together. He remembered how the famous screen idol had smiled at him—that breathless squinty-eyed smile—a smile that could evoke lust in one man, love in another, a desire to protect, a need to possess, and beneath it all, a haunting sadness, that inexplicable kind that could come over a guy whenever he watched the sun set after knocking back a few too many highballs.

It had happened in Cuba.

The fusion of swing and Cubano music had created the wild new dance, a craze that had burned through Cuba, New York and Miami, a juggernaut that had shaken up such renowned clubs as the China Doll, Birdland and Havana Madrid.

Ignacio smiled at the ghost of his youth, at the handsome young man grooving to a rhumba beat. His heart had been about ready to quit on him when Marilyn had spun around him and laughed—a sound like ice being cast from a wind chime, a sound that told you all you would ever need to know about her, even if your eyes denied the information.

She had been wearing a red satin dress, and he could still smell her perfume: Chanel No. 5, her favourite.

A crowd of tuxedoed stiffs had encircled them, watching as Ignacio offered instruction and encouragement to his iconic partner. He had felt like a peacock among the penguins, scowling frozen birds with glacier-blue eyes and flexing jaws, men who detested spics, especially ones who wore purple silk shirts and danced with American movie stars. He had rubbed their arrogant beaks in it.

It was 1953, and Marilyn had just finished shooting *Gentlemen Prefer Blondes*, Castro had just been imprisoned for leading a failed coup and Ignacio had been a flamboyant merenguero, the leader of an up-and-coming merengue band called Hacienda de Ritmo.

Long after his wise old trees had stopped applauding, Ignacio danced with the mummified beauty of his past glories. He shuffled his feet through the shade and brambles with the same panache as if he were cutting a legendary rug with a living doll on the polished marble dance floor of a Havana nightclub.

AND THE LEVEE SHALL BREAK

MAXIMO AWOKE FEELING TERRIFIED. His heart was bashing its bleeding head against his sternum as if it were seeking martyrdom. He ripped the sheet from his body and gulped down mouthfuls of dread. His bed was quaking, and the walls were vibrating with a seismic energy that felt like living thunder.

He jumped from his bed and plunged up to his waist in a frigid pool of black water. He could feel the quivering mud beneath his bare feet. He could feel it right up into the frozen marrow of his shrinking bones.

He lunged towards his parents' bed. "Wake up. The river...it's coming for us!"

The noise of the approaching flash flood grew louder by the second, filling the tiny shack with its violent shriek and drowning Maximo's silent prayer. He had just enough time to look at his mother's startled face before the Rio Blanco kicked in the door and set upon them like a curse. He was swallowed whole, wolfed down into the darkness of the river's gullet. He somersaulted through its churning intestines and felt desperate hands grasp at him and half-eaten prey collide with his body.

He was deep, and the pressure threatened to rupture his throbbing eardrums. He wanted to swim but could not tell which way was up. He was desperate for air; his lips puckered and trembled. In another second, he would breathe water and die.

Something hard smashed into his stomach, forcing the remaining air from his lungs. He was done. He flailed his arms impotently, his body twitched in agony and he inhaled—

Air

Maximo clung to an uprooted tree, retched and coughed some life back into his limp body. He was a chunk of gristle ejected from the throat of something that had deserved to choke to death.

He barrelled downstream at gut-wrenching speed.

Objects surged past him like patrolling sharks—cars, gas stoves, refrigerators, struggling animals and the surreal image of his neighbours clutching bits of flotsam as they washed by him, their bodies rigid, eyes staring off into the distance towards a safer place, a place they would never see again.

He hauled himself up onto the tree, straddled its trunk and held on tight. It was all happening so fast that he wondered if he were dreaming. Maybe he and his family were still in their beds, snuggled into their sticky discomfort within the fragile walls of their cozy dilapidated shack.

He watched in fascination as the roof of a house swirled gracefully by him as if it were waltzing with the river. Someone was clinging to the roof, someone small, someone with a shock of rebellious dark curls.

"Lourdes!" he screamed.

Maximo stood up, rode the tree surf-style and waved frantically. He screamed his sister's name over and over again, fighting to be heard over the screeching wind. He watched in panic as the floodwaters took her away from him. She was a desolate figure with her oversized T-shirt and exposed legs, her tiny hands clutching at some loose roof tiles and the brooding sky vomiting its disdain down upon her.

It all reminded him of a story he had read once. The one about a house in a hurricane, a house that landed on a wicked witch in a place called Oz.

Maximo leapt from the log, plunged back into the dark water and was once again at the river's mercy. His head broke the surface just as the chassis of a truck tumbled past him and smashed down on top of a riderless horse, ending its struggle.

He struck out towards Lourdes' higher ground. He pinwheeled

his arms and lashed his head from side to side in a woeful imitation of someone who actually knew how to swim.

The power of the water shocked him. He felt so insignificant, so puny, just another scrap of human refuse being swept along the gutter of circumstance towards extinction.

He could not see Lourdes anymore. He could not see the land or sky, hope or salvation. All he could see was water, black and white, wet and cold, giggling and cursing.

Maximo screamed in pain as something in the water sunk its teeth into his leg. He grasped at everything that floated past— trees, furniture, dead bodies—but it was hopeless. He was no match for the strength of whatever was dragging him under.

He took a deep breath and dove down to face the water devil. He reached for his lower leg, expecting to encounter the long boney digits and calcified fingernails of a mythical Ciguapa, its silky hair flowing over his hands like kelp, its globular eyes shimmering with mischief, its backwards feet like broken paddles behind it.

Instead of an evil creature, Maximo encountered the wood and barbed wire of a mangled cattle fence. He pried at the wire with all his waning strength. He tore the skin from his fingers to free himself, but he was held fast. He bolted for the surface and felt his hands emerge from the cold water. He could feel the wind over his arms and then could go no further.

The river had allowed him within inches of deliverance before tightening his chain. He would die with the water chortling at its own black humour. He would die not knowing if Lourdes had survived. He would die.

He was blacking out. His body ached for a breath he could see, could touch, life and death separated by a thin film of bubbling liquid. So close, he thought. Just to that star up there, that single luminous star, just there, not so far... See? I can touch it.

A huge dark shape surged over him, blotting out his celestial solace. His hands encountered something solid, and he latched onto it. He was pulled from the water by the hand of a powerful giant. He sucked new life into his lungs for a second time and hugged whatever had saved him to his heaving chest.

He was being drawn and quartered. He screamed as his body stretched to the limit of its endurance. He was in a medieval torture chamber.

In his agony, he imagined that Simbi, the voodoo water spirit, and Changó, the god of fire, lightning and thunder, were disputing ownership of his soul. He slurred his plea as the creaking structure continued downstream, his leg still attached to its tenacious anchor. He felt the barbed wire slide reluctantly down his calf. It gouged deep wounds into his flesh, shattered his ankle and broke the bones in his foot before it finally relinquished its prize.

Maximo hung from the beams of a partially submerged house. He looked like a flogged seaman. He dangled above the undulating river, exhausted and naked. He moaned loudly as his grip began to slacken. He tried to haul himself up into the trusses above him, but he didn't have the strength.

It would be so easy to quit, he thought, and nobody would ever know. All he had to do was let go, and the effort and anguish of surviving this would be over. His grip loosened some more as he inched ever closer towards the seductive mouth of surrender.

"Changó, give me the bravery to die," he said, and laughed at his own words. The mirthless sound resonated eerily within the cavernous wooden shell.

He couldn't hold on any longer, not to a shuddering timber or a tentative life. Everyone he loved was gone anyway—he had nobody, no reason. He hung by one hand, his limp body twisting and swinging from the beam like a butchered hog at a border town market.

It was then that he first heard the angel calling to him, a melodic sound so full of sweetness and love that tears immediately began to fall from his closed eyes. Simply by speaking his name, or, more precisely, the inflection in her voice, he knew that all his sins would be forgiven and that she would fold him within the heat and terror of her wings and he would be saved.

"Maximo," she called to him again.

He raised his head and looked up, searching for his divine oracle, sure that he was already dead.

There

He could see her, high above him, no more than a silhouette framed by the pale blue light of her halo, serene and ethereal.

"Maximo."

The sound of his sister's voice punched a gaping hole through his hallucination.

"Lourdes?"

"Yes," she said, and began to cry.

Maximo hauled himself up onto the beam and collapsed over it. Pain pulsated through his body in nauseating waves. He ignored it and began climbing.

"I'm coming, Palomita. Hold on."

"Are you hurt?" she asked.

"No. I'm fine," he said, sliding through the broken rafters.

Lourdes gripped his bloody hands and helped him squeeze through a jagged hole in the roof.

"You are hurt. You're bleeding," she said, a note of accusation in her breaking voice.

"No, not really. Shh—" was all he managed before collapsing beside her.

"Maximo," she said, pressing herself against him and crying.

"Gonna be fine. Jus' a minute…okay?" he slurred, his body leaking adrenaline like a busted hydraulic hose.

CELLBLOCK SLAUGHTERHOUSE

JARAGUA AND A GROUP of other inmates huddled around an ancient radio and listened to a report concerning the disaster in Jimaní.

"Many hundreds dead, many more missing..." the radio squawked in its static choked voice. "Whole neighbourhoods washed away..." it continued. The newscaster stripped varnish from Jaragua's soul with every word. He clenched his fists and leaned in closer, trying to hear the report over the mumble and grumble of the cellblock.

"Shut up. My family is from Jimaní. I'm from there," he said, his eyes searching the crowd for a reason to lash out.

"The Red Cross and a U.S.-led multinational force, which includes Canada, Chile and Spain, are hard at work distributing aid and trying to reach isolated villages in Haiti that were buried beneath tons of mud and rock..."

Jaragua had heard enough. He shoved his way through the boisterous mob and vented his rage on the only thing stopping him from going to find his family. "Guards, I have to get out!" he screamed, kicking and slamming the bars with all his strength.

"Let me the fuck outta here!" Jaragua gripped the metal cage and shook it like a terrier with a rat clamped in its locked jaws.

Four guards clamoured down the narrow hallway, the sound of their military boots leaving little doubt as to their state of mind. The first guard to arrive at the gate rammed his baton through the bars, striking Jaragua in the solar plexus and dropping him to his knees. They unlocked the gate, and four uniforms pounced on him.

Jaragua tried to defend himself. He threw wild haymakers,

landing as many as he missed, screaming his frustration and brawling mindlessly.

It was over quickly.

Jaragua fell to the floor beneath the onslaught of sticks, fists and boots. He curled into a protective ball and took his beating in silence until one well-placed blow made him taste metal and lose consciousness. With all eyes upon them, the guards continued to pummel him, each gratuitous blow a warning to the rest of the prison population.

No shit taken

They left him bloodied and convulsing on the floor. The last guard to exit the cage delivered a final vicious kick to the head, one that transcended callousness and bounced Jaragua's head off the bars with a sickening clang.

"Fuck it. Let's kill him."

"I'll cut his balls off and play Ping-Pong with them."

The conspirators' words filtered their way through the cotton-batten nausea of Jaragua's concussion and poked inquisitively at his will to live. They dragged him from the shriek and lightning of his injuries and forced him to acknowledge his pain.

He gave no indication that he was conscious as he struggled for a breath his lungs refused to appreciate. He couldn't remember what had happened to him, but he knew that it wasn't good and that it wasn't over. They were all around him. He could hear their shoes scraping over the gritty floor as they shuffled about so close that he could smell the rank odour of their feet.

They were plotting his murder. Each uttered threat slapped him about the face until he was fully alert. He remembered where he was and that he had suffered an attack, but by whom he was still unsure. He surreptitiously flexed the muscles in his limbs and curled his hands into rocks, testing their strength and assessing his injuries.

"That Colombian's nothing more than the latest member of El Guapo's petting zoo."

"Uh-huh, and who wants that freak show calling the shots in here anyway? Disfigured blue-eyed prick never spent one hour inside, yet he thinks he owns the joint."

El Guapo?

The drug lord's name slashed a jagged path of clarity through the dense jungle of Jaragua's recollection. Suddenly, all his memories came scuttling and wiggling back into the light like unloved amphibians. It must be the guards, he thought.

He remembered everything—the radio, the flood, his loss of control, how the guards had bludgeoned him stupid and tossed him in a dark corner of the cellblock. Live or die, sink or rise. Either way, nobody cared. He tried to open one eye but found that he couldn't. It was sealed shut with dried blood. He cracked the other one open a slit and searched for an answer to his confusion.

Jaragua could see the squatting figures of the three conspirators, their foreheads nearly touching as they huddled together and sealed a man's fate. The filthy rags on their backs and their worn leather sandals told him all he needed to know.

The men were convicts, and they weren't even talking about him. They were members of a rival prison gang, a pack of steel-toothed piranhas who had little to live for and a hunger for anarchy. He imprinted their faces in his mind and closed his eye. He tempered his sense of relief with the knowledge that the plotting gang members wouldn't hesitate to include him in their plans if they realized that he was eavesdropping.

He continued to feign unconsciousness long after the men had skulked away. When he could no longer abide the swarm of flies that were greedily exploiting his open wounds, he achingly pushed himself up to a seated position and groaned some life back into his protesting body.

He ignored the snickers and irreverent comments hurled at him by some of the other inmates. He knew that most of the men weren't as cruel or as hard as they pretended to be. Inside, empathy equated weakness, and a lamb masquerading as a lion barred its papier-mâché fangs with a frequency that belied true ferocity.

Fuck 'em

Jaragua got to his feet and made his way to the toilets. He grunted in pain as he relieved himself. His urine was dark brown from the blood in it. He cleaned caked blood from his face and pressed a wad of wet newspaper against a deep gash on the back of his throbbing head.

The crowd parted for him as he walked back to his stake of ground. He was pleased to see that his towel was still where he had left it and that there was nobody on it who required a lesson in jailhouse etiquette.

He slumped down the wall, closed his eyes and sighed with relief. His thoughts returned quickly to his family. He recalled the bitter disappointment he had seen etched in his father's eyes the last time he had seen him. It was the shame a hardworking man feels for having raised a son who viewed honest toil as the legacy of donkeys, one who would rather kill than bend his back to the fields and would rather die than kneel in the dirt.

He thought about the hope his mother still harboured for him, for her firstborn. It was a faith he knew he didn't deserve and one that would leech the youth from her face with every swallowed tear.

There was also the adulation on his little brother's face that had always made him feel uncomfortable and the sweetness of his sister's smile that never had.

Jaragua thought about escape, a dangerous option that had seen many runners end up face down in an irrigation ditch by the side of a country road. He suddenly wished that he were somewhere else, anyplace where tears didn't smell like wool.

"Hey, my man. Wow, the swine really fucked you up, huh? I thought you were gonna die. Everyone did."

Jaragua opened his puffy eyes and grinned weakly at Manny. "Takes more than they got to kill me. Besides, where were you when the shit went down?"

Manny laughed and slapped his leg before answering. "My brother, I got your back but not against a guard dog attack. I'm not suicidal, you know. Anyway, I'm prettier than you are, still got plenty of hearts to break. I couldn't risk messing this shit up." He ran a hand over his jawline and smiled.

Jaragua laughed and instantly regretted it. "Fucking ass-clown," he said, and pressed a hand over his ribs.

"I got something to help with your girlie pain. I been busy. You know, working and banking. Here, bump a bit of that. Some coca leaf love, huh?" Manny laid an open package of cocaine on Jaragua's leg.

Real lions could afford displays of kindness.

"My saviour," Jaragua said. He snorted a thick pinch up each nostril. "Got a cigarette?"

After a few minutes, a slow wide grin seeped across Jaragua's face. He dragged on his cigarette.

"Better?" asked Manny.

Jaragua blew a smoke ring at the ceiling. "Getting there. Thanks, Manny."

"What made you lose it like that, man? If I can ask that of you."

Jaragua shook his head back and forth and frowned. "My family. They need me, and I'm trapped in this shithole… You know, just everything…so fucking useless…just all of it, and then some mudslide stinking flood takes them out, and they got nothing anyway, never have. Just their lives, I guess, so take those as well. Why not?" he said without opening his eyes.

"I'm sorry for them…for you. Family is all that matters at the end. Blood, and maybe sometimes water, but mostly blood."

"Water?"

"Yeah. You know, friends."

"Mmm, yeah. Sometimes, I guess. If they're like a brother maybe."

"That's what I mean—like family. Hey, how's that tattoo looking?"

Jaragua stared down at his hand, letting his gaze drift over his girlfriend's nickname. "Looks cool. Too bad I couldn't show it to her when she came to visit, after she travelled for hours on a bus just to be told that she couldn't see me. And you know those bastards wouldn't give her no explanation."

He slammed his fist onto the floor. "I got to get out of here, Manny." His dilated pupils darted around the room. He felt like a claustrophobic trapped inside a coffin.

"Take it down, bro. We're stuck, you and I. You're going to go crazy if you think about everything too much. Maybe your family is safe. You never know."

Jaragua didn't even hear him. He was too busy staring at his way out. It suddenly seemed so obvious to him that he wondered if he had suffered some brain damage during his beating.

"How did I miss that?"

"What's the story?" Manny asked.

"I don't know what the story is, but I do know that I'm about to rewrite the ending, or at least the chapter where I rot in here for the next few goddamn years."

Jaragua was watching the three gang members whose plot he had overheard. He could recognize the signs of imminent violence, a skill that had saved his life more than once. They were about to make a move.

"What's a man's life worth, Manny? A powerful man's life. What do you think he would owe someone for saving it?"

"Life for a life, man. The algebra on that one's easy."

"Exactly," Jaragua said, and looked over at his friend. "You got a shank on ya?"

"Thought you didn't trust spics with sharp weapons."

"I don't, but in your case, I'll make an exception. Now you got one or not?"

Without another word, Manny slid a homemade blade out from the waistband of his pants and passed it to him.

"You deadly little sprick," Jaragua said. He looked down at the shank. It was as ugly as the deeds for which it had been fashioned: a no-nonsense spike of sharpened metal with a wad of cloth taped over one end to protect the assailant's hand.

"This works out for me and I'll be walking out of here pronto," Jaragua said. "If it doesn't, they'll be carrying me out. Either way, I'm leaving." He touched his fist to Manny's.

"Respect," Manny said.

"Respect, brother."

Jaragua stood up and advanced on the closest of the three gang members, concealing the shank in the palm of his hand. He watched the men moving towards the Colombians' inner circle. They were using a classic trident formation, a three-pronged attack that improved their chances of making a successful kill. Only this time, the element of surprise was not in their favour.

Jaragua felt his stomach flutter in anticipation. His vision narrowed, and he could hear his heartbeat thumping a war song on his eardrums the way it always did when he was about to do something exciting, whenever he was about to taste the freedom of no longer giving a fuck.

He saw a small calibre revolver in the hand of the assassin he was flanking. Timing would be everything. He twisted the shank in his hand and bulldozed his way towards his first target.

The first assassin stepped out of the mass of nobodies, crossed over the invisible segregation line and raised his gun.

Jaragua stepped from the crowd, shoved the gunman's arm to the side and plunged the blade into his throat. Once, twice, three times he slammed his blade into his victim's neck, severing his jugular vein and spraying the air with red blood and blue language.

He saw the rest of the battle in slow motion. It was a survival response, a gift from the adrenal glands. He saw the fear of the Colombian, who dropped his cell phone and lunged for his own weapon. He saw the second assassin rush forward and level a sawed-off shotgun at the floundering kingpin.

A member of Tio Muerte stepped between the two men and swung a machete at the attacker's head. The shotgun exploded, sending its payload through the chest of the bodyguard and killing him instantly.

The machete fell from the dead man's hand, skidded across the floor and bumped up against Jaragua's feet.

The man with the shotgun pumped his weapon, ejecting a smoking shell into the silent air. Jaragua snatched up the long blade with both hands, raised it over his head and brought it down with all his strength. The machete severed the gunman's arm at the elbow, sending his limb and his weapon spinning into the air. Just as the gun completed a 180-degree arc, the wounded man's finger carried out its final command and squeezed the trigger. The man died by his own hand, his brains raining down on the cowering convicts behind him.

"There's three!" Jaragua yelled.

The last assailant charged forward, armed with nothing more than a sharpened wedge of Plexiglas and a heroin-fuelled madness. He made it within a few feet of the Colombian before his body suffered a storm of bullets. He collapsed to the floor in a leaking heap. Wisps of smoke rose from the barrels of at least four handguns.

It made Jaragua smile to see the way the Colombian stared over him. Gratitude looked a lot like freedom.

Without warning, canisters of tear gas whistled through the air and clattered across the floor. They hissed and spewed their noxious fog like tin goblins suffering paralyzing flatulence.

The prison erupted in chaos.

Projectiles rocketed through the smoky air. Fist and teeth and steel and flesh collided with one another as brooding tempers and shackled tensions erupted.

Jaragua dropped to the floor, cupped his hands over his nose and mouth and rolled towards the perimeter wall. He tensed his body against the random kicks he received and continued to roll until he thumped up against the cellblock wall.

He yanked his T-shirt up over his face and waited for the body count in cellblock slaughterhouse to stop rising. Surviving a prison riot was easier if you played dead.

THE APPRENTICE

IGNACIO OBSERVED HIS MEN with a critical eye. It was imperative that the latex be free of impurities. When it came to his work, he was a perfectionist, and he could never understand people who were satisfied with mediocrity.

He inspected the milky liquid as it passed through a series of fine mesh strainers, frowning and nodding at the trapped offenders—at the bark, leaves, dirt and the inevitable monstrous insects.

"Nice work, you. Screen it clean. Catch all the bad stuff now," he said.

He squeezed the shoulder of his newest worker, a skinny Haitian teenager named Marco. The boy had turned up on his doorstep a few months earlier, offering his sweat in exchange for food and a safe place to lay his head.

Ignacio ran a small operation, nothing more than a few rustic shacks, his trees and a handful of men. However, he had felt sorry for the boy and had taken him in, a kindness Marco repaid every day.

Ignacio walked across the smooth wooden floor and squatted in front of a bunch of rectangular steel molds. They were filled with white coagulated rubber. He poked an appraising finger into the first one, judging its jiggle like a chef admiring the set of his award-winning vanilla pudding.

"Marco," he said, waving at the boy.

The boy came at a gallop, his lanky body and spindly limbs at odds with each other. He collapsed beside his mentor and grinned at him. "How am I helping?"

"You have been carrying, stirring and straining since you arrived. Now I'm thinking it's time for you to learn something."

"I learned plenty so far, sir. Plenty more to know."

"'Course you have, but now we go to the next stage."

"Okay. Yes." Marco's eyes darted between Ignacio and the rubber-filled vats. He was anxious for his lesson to begin.

"After the straining and filtering of the raw product, we pour the latex into these casks," Ignacio began. "Rubber tree milk is an emulsion, just like a cow's milk. If let stand, the caoutchouc will separate from its water…like it has gone on the curdle. You know, soured up. Follow that?"

"Following all a that."

"Thought so. What we do now is add lime juice to the vats. This makes it jell up—coagulate some would say. Nobody knows why this happens. Just does. Same way blood will clot, I guess. Follow that?"

Marco nodded his head vigorously and worried a piece of twine between his fingers.

Ignacio stood up, arched his back and rolled his shoulders. "*Polymerization*—it's a stupid long word that could have been a lot shorter. It's what people smarter than you or me call it when something changes from a liquid into a solid. More than you wanted to know perhaps, but there it is. Now let's go chat with the bull."

They walked over to a brooding antiquated chunk of machinery. It looked to be in no mood for conversation.

"This is he," Ignacio said, placing a hand on the gnarled black iron rollers that crowned the beast. He took a long boning knife off the heavy wooden table supporting the machinery and went to work on a waiting cask of shimmering rubber.

"First we loose the sides, free up the jelly. Like this. Watching me now," he said as he slid the sharp blade around the sides of the mold.

"You're going to work the crank there." Ignacio jutted his chin towards a metal handle that stuck out of the bull's neck like a kinked matador's sword.

"Just wind it as hard and fast as I can?" Marco asked, seizing the handle in a stranglehold.

"No, not at all. Temper your vigour with patience. Finesse is what I require from you, what the rubber requires from you. The bull will provide the muscle."

"Slowly then?"

"Yes. Slowly, evenly. Now turn on that spigot there."

Marco opened up a brass valve, and clear water gushed over the machine's dormant mandible.

"Nice," Ignacio said. "Now start cranking when I feed in the cake."

"Yes, sir."

Ignacio coaxed the wobbling mass of latex between the squealing rollers. "That's it, Marco. Steady like that."

Marco watched in amazement as the raw product entered the rollers as a fat wet slab and exited them as a flat perforated ribbon.

"See how all the water is pressed out of it?" Ignacio asked. "See how the fresh water washes away all the impurities?"

"Uh-huh."

Marco continued to turn the handle until the entire cake flopped out of the press and into Ignacio's hands. It looked like a huge wedge of salted cod.

"There it is, boy," Ignacio said, holding it up for Marco's inspection.

"There it is," Marco mimicked. He peered intently at the rubber. For show, he wrinkled his brow in concentration, actually having no idea what distinguished good rubber from bad. "There it is," he repeated, his voice full of wonder and emotion. They were feelings he didn't need to fake.

"This is called crepe now," Ignacio said. "Follow that?"

"Crepe." Marco's eyes widened with excitement. Finally something he could relate to, he thought. A French word he knew. "Yes, it does look like a crepe. All him need is some sugar and lemon," he said, and laughed.

"I don't think you would like the taste of it, even then."

Ignacio threw the rubber over Marco's shoulder as if it were a saddlebag. "Good work. Now it's up to the smokehouse with this one. Come on."

The pair trudged up a steep incline together, following a goat trail through the long grass. They arrived at a sun-bleached wooden shack. It belched grey smoke from a myriad of fissures. Only the roof looked sound.

Ignacio opened the flimsy door a crack and waved Marco inside. "Hurry. In you go. Don't want to let all that sweet smoke escape."

Drying rubber filled the cramped space. Hundreds of black and tan slabs hung from suspended bamboo poles. They looked like animal hides. In the centre of the floor a smoldering fire hunkered down into its earthen pit like a disgruntled demon spewing its smoky venom. The room smelled like ammonia.

Marco coughed, fanned the opaque air in front of his face and looked longingly towards the exit.

Ignacio gave him an encouraging slap on his bare back. "Yes, it's sharp at first, but don't worry, soon enough it will be your cologne of choice. This is where we cure our product, the final stage. You can add an antiseptic during the jell-up phase, like creosote, or you can smoke the rubber, the way we do. Remember, impurities and moisture are the enemies."

"The smoke kills 'em?" Marco asked.

"Not exactly. We smoke it to prevent any proteins that may still be present in the latex from decomposing, from rotting. One way or another, rubber must be cured, and I believe that a smoked product is superior to just adding some creosote... Where's the magic in that?"

Ignacio took a dry piece and held it up to Marco's nose. "Smell that there."

Marco inhaled deeply and instantly regretted it. "It smells like a dirty old goat's piss."

"Are you crazy, boy? That's pure ambrosia."

"What's that?" Marco asked.

"What? Ambrosia?"

"Yeah, that."

"It's a tasty dessert, like a flan."

"Oh. Never had it."

"No? Well, believe me, it smells delicious. Like my rubber."

Marco laughed, slung the wet crepe from his shoulder and laid it in the spot vacated by the dry piece.

"Now feel this finished one," Ignacio said, offering up the same piece. "That's some good stuff, aye aye, boy. Finest Castilla rubber in all of Quisqueya, in all the world." He winked and grinned at the boy as if he were a merchant presenting his finest bolts of cloth for a trader's approval.

"It feels better than it smells," Marco said.

"Okay then. Lesson learned."

Ignacio threw a piece of wood onto the fire. The pit demon spat and moaned its displeasure.

They left the stifling smokehouse and stood quietly together in the sunshine for a moment, both enjoying the fresh air.

"Thank you for everything. For teaching me, for giving me a chance," Marco said, and smiled at the old man. It was a smile that life's backhands had so far failed to diminish. Ignacio found himself hoping that they never would.

"You're welcome, son. You're doing well here, learning fast. I hope you stay on."

"I'm going to do so. I'm going to make good rubber for you, the best rubber I can make."

"I believe you will. Now hurry and help the boys down in the woods."

Ignacio leaned against the warm wooden wall of his smokehouse and watched Marco run down the hill in his odd galloping style. He watched him until the sheen from his sweat-slick back merged with the sun's glare and he vanished into the grove.

Ignacio closed his eyes and slowly slid down the wall until he was squatting. He tilted his face towards the warmth and energy of the sun and smiled at its hedonistic caress.

"Humble dreams," he said, thinking of Marco. "God blessed those closest to his heart with humble dreams."

And cursed others with ambition

"You make a fine product, Ignacio," he said aloud. "You got good work, a good life. More than you deserve. It should be enough. Goddamnit, enough."

However, it wasn't enough.

He still harboured fantasies of one day returning to his music. He thought about what might have been, if what had happened had never happened. Whenever he felt strong, he was certain that it wasn't too late. He had the knowledge, the passion, the stamina to at the very least shake a pair of maracas or ratchet a guiro.

He sighed and ran a hand through his hair.

"Only a fool still chases dreams while staring his own mortality in the eye. Nothing to look forward to now but the grave, old man," he said, attempting to convince himself that his fear of trying was somehow wise. However, he knew the truth. He deserved nothing, less than what he already had, and still he had the audacity to dream.

His selfishness had taken from him all he had ever loved. He had committed an unforgivable sin, the guilt of which had driven him to alcoholism and the ranting edge of insanity. It had nearly cost him his life, and whenever he felt weak, he wished that it had.

Ignacio could hear in his mind the rapid fire of well-struck bongos as they echoed through the catacombs of his haunted past. A wailing blast from a crazy sax dragged him deeper into a place he didn't want to go. The sound mutated into a screeching phantom bearing rusty chains of regret.

He was back at the Palladium, the throbbing heart of Latin jazz in a city that claimed to be heartless. There was no crazier daddy-O place to be on a Wednesday night in the fifties. He could still see the legendary Machito and his Afro-Cubans as they pressure-cooked their set, steaming the joint up with Cuban-dipped jazz riffs. As proud as

Ignacio was of his merengue, as a musician, he loved many different styles of music, and there was no inoculation against the mambo fervour that had gripped America at that time.

Machito shook his maracas with religious zeal, the ruffles of his fluorescent lemon and lime shirt spreading out around him like the wings of a narcissistic bird performing its mating dance. And the chicks had swarmed, competing fiercely for the briefest of glances from their mambo king.

On any given night, Ignacio might have passed James Dean or Sammy Davis Jr. on their way to the men's room or smiled at some of the Copacabana chorus girls—girls such as Raquel Welch and Joan Collins—dancing to the blazing horns of the two Titos, Puente and Rodríguez. And that was before any of them knew what legends they would become, before they became immortals.

Music had transformed Ignacio. It had taken him from the humble fields of the Dominican Republic and transported him to the flash and scream, the buzz and thrill, of Havana, Chicago, Miami and New York. It had replaced the shy country boy with a confident bandleader, and it had gifted and cursed him with the greatest love of his life.

Don't think of her

The agitated crowing of his roosters dragged Ignacio back to reality. He swiped a fist under each watering eye and told himself that it was the smoke. He blinked his memories away and pushed himself back up the wall. He slapped the dirt from his pants and set his jaw.

"I make rubber, and I train my roosters."

He walked towards the sound of his hungry birds.

COW SANCTUARY

LOURDES' SCREAM SHATTERED MAXIMO's sleep. He bolted upright, disorientated and wild-eyed. "Mama?"

"Maximo, your leg," Lourdes said, clamping a hand across her mouth. Her eyes were wide and wet.

He hoisted himself up on one elbow and took his first look at the price the Rio Blanco had exacted in exchange for his life. He stared in horror at what used to be his leg. It was an unrecognizable slab of minced meat and exposed bone. He turned his head and vomited his revulsion. He could feel Lourdes' hand rubbing his back, and he loved her for it.

"It always looks worse than it is. When the swelling goes down, it's going to be strong and fine," he said, and then did something that she would remember for the rest of her life. He smiled at her.

Maximo looked up at the sky. It was all grey and white, pockmarked and withered—the face of an old man who had guarded a shameful secret for too many winters.

The river was flattening out, spreading and thinning.

He ignored the procession of corpses that rolled past. He was terrified that he might recognize one of their puffy discoloured faces. He could see the shimmering expanse of Lago Enriquillo in the distance, an immense brackish lake that was home to hundreds of saltwater crocodiles. A logjam was forming where the river bottlenecked—vehicles, trees, mattresses, boulders and dead things piled up like the building blocks of a demented beaver.

"Put your arms around my neck," Maximo said. "That's it, Palomita. Tighter. Now listen to me. We're going to have to go back into the water.

We're going to jump from this house, and when we land, you're going to swim…as fast as you can. Get up on something, anything. Just get out of the water. It's very important. Don't look for me. Just swim. Can you do that for me?" He braced himself as the frame of the house caught and stuttered across the shallow bottom.

Lourdes moved her head up and down and said nothing. Any protest she may have had in her died when she heard the fear in her brother's voice.

There was no gradual capsize. The structure they had found refuge on virtually imploded upon impact, and the children were catapulted from the roof. They spun through the air and splashed down into the infested lagoon like panicked baitfish.

As soon as his head broke the surface, Maximo yelled at Lourdes. "Swim! Get out of the water!"

He could hear splashing, but he couldn't see her. The reptilian eyes and warty snouts of half a dozen crocodiles began to move towards him.

"Maximo, here! Hurry!"

He swam in the direction of his sister's voice, blindly slapping the water out of his way. He could sense the crocodiles closing on him. Tired of feasting on corpses, they wanted a hot meal.

Somewhere up ahead he could hear Lourdes screaming, her voice shrill and omnipresent. He braced himself for the attack he knew was coming and churned away at the muddy water. He felt Lourdes' tiny hands clawing at his arms and back.

Maximo was unable to gain purchase on the slimy jiggling thing in front of him. He felt something touch his good leg, and he kicked at it savagely. He could hear the menacing snap of prehistoric jaws beneath him, and he scrambled higher. He could hear Lourdes whimpering.

They were huddled on top of a dead cow, both of them splayed out across its blotchy pungent abdomen. There was nothing but a sagging bag of bones and guts between them and the hungry crocs. The children held onto each other and watched in dread as several crocodiles nudged and sniffed at the cow's decomposing hindquarters.

"Don't look. We're safe now," he said, hoping that she still believed everything he told her.

Maximo scanned the water as their bovine raft drifted further and further from shore.

THE CALM AFTER THE STORM

"Thirty-seven dead, over sixty injured," the Colombian said. He tossed the newspaper onto the floor.

"How many of those were guards?" Jaragua asked.

"Not enough."

After the police had carted the bodies away, the prison had quickly settled into a semblance of normal. The most noticeable difference was that the place felt peaceful, the inmates subdued.

The Dominican Republic, if not the world, had at least acknowledged the existence of some severe problems within the penal system. For once, the men's screams had reached beyond the prison's walls. The politicians had primped and pimped for the media, looking and sounding suitably outraged at the injustices and the vile conditions. They said that they were formulating plans and building more jails, that food was coming and that a new health care system was in the works. Detainees would have their cases heard in a timelier fashion, sentences would be passed down without delay and blah, blah, blah.

Nobody believed a word of it.

Jaragua stretched his knotted body to its full length and revelled in the luxury of his new bed.

A couple of days after the riot, the Colombian had introduced himself as Juan and hitched a thumb over one shoulder. "There's a bunk free," he had said. It was the very bunk of the man who had called Jaragua a cuero. He had been one of the first victims of the violence.

"Who's the cuero now?" Jaragua said softly, and smiled to himself. "Who's the dead cuero now?"

He flipped onto his stomach, opened up a wrap of cocaine and snorted a couple of pinches' worth. It was even tastier now that it was free. As the drug began to sink its teeth in, Jaragua's thoughts once again returned to his family and escape.   The coke and comfort were nice, but he figured that the Colombian still owed him. A bribe or two was all it would take, and his cell door would swing open magically.

The reports that had trickled in regarding the disaster in his hometown had grown increasingly morbid, and the more he heard, the crazier he felt. The latest news was that the death toll had exceeded two thousand. The unfathomable number bounced around inside his volatile brain until it fell, unexpectedly, out of his mouth. "Two thousand. Fuck!" He drove a fist against the concrete wall.

He instantly regretted his outburst. Men who couldn't control their emotions were a liability. He wanted to earn respect in a manner that would eclipse his violent tendencies. He rubbed his skinned knuckles and pretended not to notice the Colombian approaching him.

"Problema?" the man said, lighting two cigarettes and offering one to him.

Jaragua accepted the smoke and mumbled thanks. "No, it's nothing. Just stoned, I guess."

They smoked their cigarettes and silently appraised one another, each man wondering how he could continue to profit from their new relationship.

"I'm going to be released tomorrow," Juan said. He tilted his head back, blew a lungful of liver-grey smoke towards the ceiling and turned his lifeless eyes on Jaragua. "And you are going to be out of here a day or two after that. Go to Jimaní. See about your family," he said, and blessed himself. "After that, you call this number."

He scribbled on a ten-peso note and passed it to Jaragua. "El Guapo wants to meet you. No promises, you know. Just wants to get a look at you. Have a chat. After that, who knows?"

He tossed a fat wad of American dollars onto the bed. "Here's a grand. Consider it partial payment for services rendered."

Jaragua picked up the money and stared at Juan. He could feel his mouth working but no words would come out.

"Yeah, that's what I thought you would say," the Colombian said. "By the way, thanks for saving my life. Now I have done the same for you. I hate being in anyone's debt."

"Consider us even. As soon as I see about my family, I'll call you. I don't know how long—"

"Don't matter. Do what you have to and then come and see us. Family first."

"Thanks, man. You have no idea what this means to me." Jaragua offered his hand.

"Sure I do," Juan said as they shook hands. "Gotta make a call, and yeah, it's about you."

Jaragua pulled his shoe off and stuffed the money up into the toe. There was a lot of excess room in there, as the shoes belonged to a man with much larger feet.

He would have had to work for half a year to earn that much money. Six months of labour beneath a tropical sun just so he could afford to buy enough food to squash the rebellion in his stomach.

"Yeah. Haitians and mules… Fuck that," he whispered, and sunk back into the comfort of his pillow.

He was determined to make a positive impression on El Guapo when they met. Whatever he had to do, he was willing. Nothing and nobody could stop him from becoming who he was supposed to be. He was going to take what he wanted out of life, grab it by its bony neck and squeeze until its tongue lolled and its eyes bulged in surrender.

Fucking life

ESTRELLITA

THERE IS A SWEATSHOP in Puerto Plata called Don Camino Shoes. It squats in the hot sun like a Machiavellian toad and wrings perspiration from its workforce with callous hands.

Estrellita could feel her energy evaporating within the humid confines of the factory's cinder-block walls. She looked at her watch, sighed and eased yet another jiggling slab of rubber into a pool of superheated sulphur. She could smell the rotten-egg stench of the liquefied chemical right through her cotton mask. That the stench seemed to bother her less with each passing shift bothered her more then the nauseating odour itself. She had been vulcanizing rubber at the shoe factory for a little over three months, and it was on days like today that her dreams seemed so utterly unattainable, so ludicrous, that she felt embarrassed by her need to cling to them.

Estrellita was the type of girl who wore her beauty like an afterthought, her dark eyes gazing out at the world from beneath restless shadows of mistrust and longing. She had copper-brown skin that glistened with youthful promise, and her lips absorbed the heat of her blood with a greedy passion. She was tall enough to model and possessed Latina danger, a look that had finally eclipsed the heroin-addicted waif as the new chic du jour.

She hummed a melody she had composed and watched the rubber cure in its 140-degree bath. Its polymer molecules were cross-linking, changing the soft vulnerable material into something more durable. The chemical process created a rubber that had a greater resistance to abrasions, made it tougher and enabled it to withstand extreme temperatures.

She sometimes felt as if life were nothing more than one long steamy soak in a vat of bubbling brimstone. Slowly but inevitably, a person's skin toughened up until the abrasion of compromise no longer wounded, their hearts hardened and no longer bled so easily. They became impervious to the chill of rejection and, sadly, indifferent to the waning drumbeat of their passions.

She yanked the claustrophobic mask from her face and impatiently shoved loose strands of her long dark hair behind her ears.

I'm only nineteen, she thought, too young to be fading beneath fifteen-hour shifts in a stinking factory.

Her looks had always afforded her the option of a different life, the kind of life that had seduced many of her childhood friends. However, the price of surrendering her body to a man whose touch she couldn't stomach was simply too great, and she knew that afterwards she would never linger in front of a mirror again...even if it told her beautiful lies.

"Estrellita Celeste Alphonso, my candied yam, my shining star, my moon bow, why do you torture me so?"

She turned around and watched a short portly man waddling towards her, the adoring look in his eyes chasing her sullen mood away. "Nano, where have you been? I expected you to propose to me at least half an hour ago."

The elderly man cackled at her comment, brushed some dirt from his faded denim shirt and displayed a mouthful of gleaming white dentures. "My sweet, I was unavoidably detained whilst in the courses of my duties. Only enunciate the word and we shall go tonight...elope as planned. And, on our honeymoon, I shall concoct a potent sancocho from the virile meat of a brave gallo, one slain in the heat of battle. I shall be like a tiger." He made a fist.

"Yes, and you could wash your stew down with half a gallon of Mamajuana," she said, referring to a local tonic that was rumoured to be an aphrodisiac. "Then I know for sure that you would be going to meet your god that night."

"Mmm, yes. Perhaps you are right, my wild orchid. Cooler heads should prevail. After all, how could I betray my safe familiar wife, my comfy slipper, for the painful temporary euphoria of a leather stiletto?" he said, and winked at her.

"A leather stiletto, am I?" she gasped in mock horror.

"A compliment, Estrellita, I assure you. And speaking of gods, did you know that the word *vulcanize* is derived from the name of the Roman god of fire and forge?" he said, raising his eyebrows inquisitively. "His name was Vulcan."

"No. I didn't know that. It's very interesting though."   "A n d that Charles Goodyear was the first man to ever use sulphur to vulcanize rubber?"

"Amazing. That rubber should be cured now," she said, raising her voice over the hum and tinker of the factory's machines and minions.

"Of course, yes, yes. Don't let me keep you from your tasks. Then it's off to the drying racks with them. And then to have shoe soles stamped from them," he said, nodding his head vigorously and speaking rapidly.

"Hey, do you know where the word *sole* comes from?" she asked him, knowing that he did.

"Coincidently enough, I do. It's a Latin word. Well, it's derived from the Latin word *solea*, which means soil or ground," he said, beaming with pride.

"Exactly. I think you're wasting your talents here, Nano. You should become a schoolteacher, with all the things you know."

The little man blushed for a moment before answering. "Well, thank you, my sun-kissed chinola, but I'm afraid that this is it for me. I do what I do. I know what I know. I have my encyclopedias, and I watch my *Jeopardy* on the television. It's enough for me. However, you, Estrellita, you are still so young and, as everyone knows, so talented. As much as it would break my heart not to see you anymore, I look forward to the day when I walk in here and find that you are gone. This is no place for a star."

"Thank you. It's nice to hear sometimes."

"And did you know that Charles Goodyear was the first man to ever use sulphur to vulcanize rubber?" he asked her again, his eyes drifting towards a memory he once had.

She smiled gently at him. "No. Tell me more—"

"Estrellita!" someone yelled.

The fury within the sound of her name caused her to flinch. She turned around and glared.

Don Camino stood akimbo on the catwalk, his black avian eyes trained on Estrellita and Nano as if they were field mice.

"Estrellita," he repeated, lowering his powerful voice and pointing an accusing finger at her. "I don't pay you to stand around and gossip with my broom boy. Besides, in five minutes, he won't even remember that you two had a conversation.

"Nano, I'm growing tired of inventing reasons as to why I should keep you on here. I could hire a monkey to do your job. Quit grinning, clamp your grill and go and clean something. Earn your wage this week for a change."

"Yessir," Nano mumbled. He avoided Estrellita's gaze and shuffled away in embarrassed silence.

"And, you," Don Camino said to Estrellita, "in my office. Ten minutes."

He turned on his heel and stomped off, the weight of his arrogance shaking the metal walkway in its frame.

Don Camino gargled with some peppermint mouthwash and awaited Estrellita's arrival. He was more nervous than he would care to admit.

His real name was Miguel Jose Ortiz. He was thirty-eight years old, tall, broad shouldered and powerful in every sense of the word. He was the only son of an affluent family from Santiago de los Caballeros. He had been educated in the United States, earning a degree in economics and business from Stanford University. He had returned home, founded Don Camino Shoes and had quickly become wealthy in his own right by exploiting the desperation of his country's rural poor. He had a vast labour pool from which to choose compliant and hardworking people, a workforce that had long ago had any uppity notions such as fair wages or benefits beaten out of them by one despotic government after another.

Estrellita entered Miguel's office and stopped just short of slamming the door. The spacious air-conditioned room had been expensively furnished in masculine heavy pieces. The smell of citrus and sandalwood greeted her as if she were family.

"I suppose late is marginally better than never," he said. He satin a thickly padded chair, his feet resting on top of a massive desk. "Well, don't just stand there pouting. My time is valuable. Come to me." He waved her over, enjoying the fact that she obeyed.

She sauntered towards his desk and stood defiantly before him. She noticed an inscription engraved into the vamp of a bronzed shoe that sat on the edge of his desk:

There are things in this world that people
either need or want; shoes are both.
—Don Camino

She rolled her eyes heavenward and smirked before allowing the full weight of her disdain to settle on the object of her revulsion. "You rang?"

Miguel ignored her comment, returned her stare and rapped a gold-plated pen against the palm of one huge hand. "Estrellita," he began, exposing his perfect white teeth, well aware that whenever he smiled, dimples appeared in his tanned cheeks, "you look tired. Your work is hot, dirty...and offensive." He wrinkled his nose in mild disgust. "Let me take you away this weekend. We could go to a five-star spa. You would be pampered and powdered, wined and dined. Just say yes, and I will change your drab existence for something...well, let's face it, something a bit classier."

What a face, she thought. It was a rare man who could actually benefit from a broken nose, a jagged scar, something, anything, to mar the banality of his prettiness—something that would help him look more like a man ought to. She giggled to herself, imagining her fist flattening his hawklike nose and her telling him that it was a favour, free of charge.

"Don Camino," she began, purposely ignoring his frequent requests to call him Miguel. "As I have told you in the past, relentlessly, in fact, I don't find you attractive in any way. I will not go out with you, no matter where, no matter when. Now, I don't know what it's going to take for you to accept that, but accept it you will."

Aside from a mild twitch in his left eye, Miguel showed no sign of the strain he was under from maintaining his facade of serenity. Like everything else in his life, sex had always come easy to him. He had bedded scores of gorgeous, intelligent, accomplished women, the type of women men made fools of themselves pursuing, and all he ever had to do to gain access was walk into the room.

Dirty peasant, he thought. Admittedly, a stunning one, but still just a peasant, and no muckraking uneducated shack dweller was going to refuse him a night inside her wetness.

"It's your boyfriend then, is it not?" he said. "That convict, that greasy punk? So is that your type then? The bad boy? What a cliché. You think that makes you deep or something? A suffering poet? Makes you a homegirl or some such shit, lusting after lowlifes and losers?" He wanted to reach out and smack her across the mouth. If she wanted a prick, he would accommodate her.

"You're pathetic. I'm with Jaragua because he's a man, a man who has the strength to show kindness and the strength to make you eat those words if you ever had the *cojones* to say them to his face."

"So is it tough guys who actually get you hot or do you suffer from a Florence Nightingale complex and it's only the irredeemable douchebags who get your juices flowing? Does it make you feel like an angel of mercy to pet a mangy street cur, lick his festering wounds for him… the ones his own tongue can't reach?"

She stared up at him in open-mouthed astonishment. What a phony, she thought. He had been coddled and catered to since birth, and the result of all that indulgence was an overgrown spoiled child who had never been told: "No, you can't have it."

"I'm finished with this conversation, with your foul mouth and with you," she said. "So unless you have something relevant to say to me, you know, regarding work, then I would like to return to mine." She would have quit right there if her family didn't need the money so badly.

He swished his hand through the air as if he were swatting at a fly. "So go. Back to the sulphur pits, Estrellita. Back to the noble grind. Back to eking out an inferior living as one of the sweaty class. I pity you."

She stopped before reaching the door and whirled around, her thick black hair cascading down around her shoulders and capturing the room's light. "You condescending bastard. Save your pity for the mirror, where I'm sure you spend half your day. It's you who will never know the pleasure and challenge of a real life, one that you actually earned instead of one you were handed. You know and I know that I mean nothing to you. So I have to wonder. Why is your ego so fragile? Maybe having big feet and big hands doesn't always equal…big everywhere else." She flung the door open and walked out his office before he could reply.

He smashed both his fists down on top of the desk, his body shaking with anger. "Putona," he cursed.

He had already paid a stupid amount of money to see her boyfriend thrown in jail. The police had promised Miguel that Jaragua would die inside. "Lead or silver," he had said.

Whatever it took, he would have her. It wasn't her pride that stood in his way, he thought. It was her *dreams*. She thought she was destined for more, and that kind of belief was an insurmountable obstacle for him. He had nothing to offer her if she was convinced that her talent would one day afford her a better life.

"Take away her dreams, and she will beg to warm my bed," he whispered.

AT THE FEET OF THE MASTER

WHEN IGNACIO WAS STILL a child, his father initiated him into the world of cockfighting. He was of an age when a boy tried to emulate his father, even one unworthy of such flattery.

He would never forget the excited look in his father's eyes on the eve of a big match. He would return from his work at the Monti Cristi salt flats, his crusty shirt cinched around his waist, salt etched into the creases of his face like war paint. "Hard day today," he would grumble.

His father would then take a plate of food from his mother without a smile or a thank you, his tone insinuating that the monotony and damage of his toil was somehow her fault. He always said that if someone dug him out of the earth a decade after the flats had put him there, they'd find a perfectly preserved corpse—no rot, no stink, no worms, just a timeless cadaver mummified from all the salt ground into his bones over the years.

His words had caused Ignacio countless nightmares.

"But tonight we go to the gallera," his father would say, as if betting on the gruesome death of some hapless fowl somehow made up for the tedium of his life.

Whenever they went to the pit, his father's personality would change. No longer the humble salt miner, his chest would swell with a sense of purpose, a pride that replaced his belligerent swagger with a gentler step, a step that no longer dared the world to look down upon him. A gallero kept his word. He honoured his wagers. He was part of a fraternity, privy to knowledge. He kept secrets, secrets that fathers passed on to sons.

Moreover, whenever his father spoke to him about the ways of the gallero, he spoke with an uncharacteristic patience, in a manner that sounded something like love to Ignacio. And because it made him feel closer to his father, Ignacio had tried to share his passion for the blood sport. The problem was he came to care about the birds, turning them into pets and giving them names.

"Go fetch numbers three and seven. We're pitting them today," his father would say. Ignacio would nod obediently and go and get Hector and Rafael. Number two he called Bullet, number five was KingKong, number one was Julio, number four was Ace, the list went on.

He attempted to hide his feelings whenever a stronger competitor was killing one of his roosters, whenever those who bet blue instead of white were cheering its death, but he was unable to. He would turn away from the gallera in tears, the weight of his father's disappointment constricting his breathing.

For many years, after leaving home, Ignacio had not even set foot inside a cockpit, rejecting the barbarity of his father's world for one of music and dance. However, he had found that life came at a person in waves of irony and déjà vu, forcing everyone, eventually, to feel like a hypocrite. It made a guy feel like throwing a stone into a pond and cursing the ripples it created.

<hr />

Ignacio shuffled between a double row of wood and wire coops. He clucked his tongue and wiggled his fingers at his gallos, four of which were training for an upcoming bout.

Galleros referred to a gamecock's pre-fight conditioning as a keep. Depending on the beliefs of the trainer, a keep could last between ten and thirty days. Ignacio had found a moderate amount of success using a three-week keep.

He squatted and peered in at one of his veterans. The grizzled rooster crowed loudly and cocked his head, displaying its myriad of battle scars.

"Yes, Vikintoro, I can see that you're irritated, but don't worry, I have a fresh young one for you to spar with. Soon you will be back in the spotlight again, back where you belong," he said, and winked at the bird.

Like all the roosters Ignacio chose to bring to point on fight day, Vikintoro was within an ounce or two of his ideal weight and had bright alert eyes and an aura of vitality that would sometimes translate into a victory at the gallera and sometimes not.

Ignacio stood up and walked over to the coop of his latest acquisition, a young bird he had been nurturing for the past six months.

"Hello, Mr. X," he said, unlocking the coop and gently picking up his protégé. He turned the bird this way and that, pleased that he displayed no aggression towards him. He had no time for training man-haters. In his opinion, they were undisciplined troublemakers, not the stuff of champions.

He was a beautiful rooster—curious, energetic, with a sharp yellow beak, intelligent pearl eyes, cinnamon and ivory plumage, a crimson comb and wattle and strong black legs. He was a graded bird, a Spanish Jerezano with one-sixteenth Shamo bred into him for shoulders and ruggedness.

Sugar Ray speed with Tyson power.

"A headhunter," Ignacio said, referring to the breed's predilection for head strikes.

"What shall your name be?" he asked, mimicking the way the rooster turned his head sideways to look at him. "Any ideas? No? All right, we will spar you first and then decide, because we can't call you Mr. X forever. You need to show me who you are...what you are. Then you get a proper name. What say you?"

The bird squirmed in his hands, turned his head in the direction of the other roosters and crowed mightily.

"Oh, is that how it is?" he said, chuckling as several unseen roosters crowed back, letting the newcomer know that they would enthusiastically meet his challenge. "Now I know for sure where the word *cocky* came from. I only hope that you can back up your boast, my friend, because today you will meet one of my proven fighters. He has six wins, and he doesn't care for braggarts."

Ignacio stroked the rooster and walked into a twisted stone and stick shack where he kept his birds' feed and equipment. The room smelled of leather and camphor oil.

He sat down on a short three-legged stool, flipped Mr. X over and fitted a pair of red leather muffs over the bird's spurs, his natural weapons. "Now look at you. Your gloves even match the colour of your comb, huh?" he said, and affectionately fingered the scrotum-like wrinkle of loose skin that crowned the rooster.

A few minutes later, Ignacio dropped Mr. X into the centre of a ring of rocks and began to thrust Vikintoro towards him. The roosters lunged and crowed at each other. When he was satisfied, Ignacio tossed his champion into the pit and watched closely as the two birds clashed. He was looking for any signs of cowardice in his newest warrior and monitoring his natural ability to defend himself.

Vikintoro attacked the inexperienced rooster with an intensity that temporarily overwhelmed the younger bird. He quickly drove Mr. X into the dirt with a flurry of kicks and beak strikes.

"Toro," Ignacio said, and jammed a fist into the air.

Mr. X rolled away from the onslaught and sprung back to his feet, his hackle feathers raised and his eyes blazing.

The two circled one another for a moment before simultaneously leaping off the ground and colliding in midair. They planted their landings, shoved up against one another, tested the other's strength and threw jabs.

Ignacio watched in amazement as Mr. X knocked his champion to the ground, leapt on top of him and began to deliver some payback. In seconds, he had his talons around Vikintoro's head, pinning the other bird to the ground and attempting to peck his eye out.

The older bird used his ring savvy to escape being blinded and then scrambled to his feet, shaken and wary.

Ignacio knew that sexually mature roosters in the wild would often fight to the death, unlike other birds that preferred to posture and pose their competitors into submission like fashionistas on a Madrid catwalk. However, nobody could teach heart or intelligence, and as he watched Mr. X easily avoid another desperate lunge from Vikintoro, he felt an excitement rise up inside him, one that made him feel young again.

"Mambo," he said, and swivelled his hips.

When it became apparent that his veteran was losing, he mercifully stepped into the ring and scooped him up, leaving him with enough confidence to fight another day.

"Okay, my beauty. Yes, I know," he cooed.

He ran a calming hand over the distraught bird's back, removed his muffs and placed him on a frayed rope that hung between two wooden posts.

"Hey, don't look so sad. Everyone needs to taste the bitterness of defeat, huh? If victory is all you've ever known...how do you know if you deserve it?"

He swung the rope back and forth a couple of times before releasing it, forcing the bird to work on his balance and tone his muscles.

"As for you my, pugnacious friend," he said, looking down at Mr. X, who continued to stare hard at his opponent. "You, as green as you are, have just bested my finest fighter. You are going to be a star." He picked the bird up off the ground and kissed the top of his head. "And you have shown me who and what you are today. You are a dancer, a dangerous one, with an instinct and grace that reminded me of someone very special. Your new name shall be Mr. Mestizo." He held him up to the sun and laughed.

He had named the bird in honour of the most talented dancer he had ever known. Mr. Mestizo was one of the original mambo dancers from the Palladium Ballroom in New York City, and he had performed at the famous club every Wednesday evening for over a decade.

Ignacio had named several of his roosters after legendary dancers. He had a Puerto Rican bird named Mr. Ramos, another called Mr. Garcia and one from Havana he had called Cuban Pete. However, Mr.

Mestizo possessed a superlative quality, and Ignacio had been waiting a long time for a bird to come along who deserved the moniker.

He walked behind a bamboo blind that he had fitted out with palm leaves. It was important that his birds couldn't see each other during their training, because if they did, they would become agitated and injure themselves attempting to get at one another. Ignacio had always enjoyed the table-work aspect of conditioning gamecocks. Even though it could be dull and repetitive work, he took great pride in watching his charges develop, seeing how their strength and endurance increased under a steadily mounting workload.

He picked the rooster up under the wings and pointed him towards a lightly padded waist-high board. "These are called flies, Mr. Mestizo, and today I shall only ask you for twenty; however, by the end of the week, I shall require one hundred."

He tossed him towards the fly board. The confused bird flew straight over the obstruction and landed awkwardly in a cloud of dust and feathers.

"No, no, no. You call that graceful? Don't embarrass your namesake again with that sort of clumsiness."

After a few more failed attempts, the rooster flew straight to the board every time.

"Yes. Good work. Again, my beauty. Make me proud." Ignacio released him into the air once more. The bird hit the fly board with both feet, rebounded effortlessly and stuck his landing in the dry soil. He looked like a Romanian gymnast seeking gold.

The bird strained against Ignacio's hands, eager to continue the new game, to exercise his growing muscles and vent his natural aggression.

"Okay, Mr. Mestizo. That will do for today."

Ignacio picked up a plastic bottle and sprayed the rooster with a mist of cool water. "Yes. You like that? Mmm, nice and fresh, huh?" he said, stroking his damp feathers and admiring the bird.

"Soon you will fight in the gallera, something that I believe you were born to do. You have a destiny, I can feel it," he said, and walked back to his coops.

Ignacio fought his roosters in the postiza, an exciting discipline where the final outcome depended as much on endurance, health and conditioning as skill and heart.

In the United States, the Philippines and many other countries, they attached razor-edged gaffs to their roosters' spurs, weapons that were more than double the length of the plastic spikes used in the postiza. As far as Ignacio was concerned, these matches were knife fights between drugged-out mutants. He had watched the big roosters battle, and he had found them boring. Gamecocks such as the Baltimore Topknots, Warhorses and Irish Gilders were plodding and methodical birds that required nothing more than one lucky haymaker to win a match. They reminded him of barroom brawlers with beer guts.

The smaller predominately Spanish or Cuban birds that fought in the postiza were avian gladiators, with fast feet and killer instincts. They struck at the head seventy-five percent of the time, and they were finishers not showboaters.

Ignacio believed that it was only in the latter stages of battle that a combatant's true character was revealed. It was only when exhaustion, injury and fear of death had stripped away all pretences, eroded any veneer of guts, that a warrior's true spirit could be glimpsed. To Ignacio, revelation was what cockfighting was all about.

"Are you hungry?" he asked, as he opened Mr. Mestizo's coop and placed him on top of a small mound of clean straw. "Strong boy like you, of course you are. Wait here for me."

He walked back into his feed shed and mixed up sixteen regular meals and four special ones. A couple of years earlier, he had questioned a local bodybuilder named Twoton Timmy on his nutritional beliefs. Twoton had told him about a form of diet manipulation known as carbohydrate loading. The technique was physiologically sound, and nutritionists had proven that if an athlete depleted their glycogen stores through a carbohydrate-restricted diet and intense exercise, their muscles would have the capacity to stockpile more glycogen once carbohydrates were reintroduced into their system. The amount of energy a muscle was capable of producing was in direct correlation with the amount of glycogen stored in that muscle. All that meant to Ignacio was that on fight day his birds would be able to hit harder and fight longer, and that was all he needed to hear.

His roosters' diet consisted of top quality corn, cracked wheat, laying pellets, hard-boiled eggs—for which he called them cannibals for eating—raw liver, cottage cheese, mangoes, bananas, honey and vitamin B12. The proportions of each ingredient varied from meal to meal and from bird to bird, depending on individual nutritional needs.

When the purple plastic bowls of feed were prepared, he cracked open small glistening vials of liquid ginseng and drizzled the elixir over the food destined for Mr. Mestizo and the other three roosters in his keep. He considered ginseng to be his secret weapon. He believed that the ancient tonic strengthened his birds' constitution, protected them from disease, gave them energy and contributed to their overall health.

"Five thousand years of Chinaman wisdom is good enough for me," he said, and emptied one of the vials into his mouth. "Disgusting."

He walked outside and distributed the food among his birds.

"Yours, I saved for the last," he said, getting down onto his knees and peering at Mr. Mestizo. "Here you are, my beauty. A more delicious and nutritious stew than many human beings will eat this day. I shall burn in hell for such deeds, and I don't think that Saint Francis of Assisi will be able to save me either."

Ignacio watched his newest fighter attack his food and smiled at him with affection.

"Destiny, Mr. Mestizo. Who says that roosters or dogs don't have one the same as humans do? Some say what I do is cruel, but I bet if you could choose, you would rather have a shot at the glory that lives inside you, would rather die in battle, than become a box of Chicken McNuggets."

SALTIES

THE STILLNESS PRIED MAXIMO from his purgatory, a disturbing realm as terrifying as the images that greeted his waking eyes. He stared at the heat-blistered expanse of still water before him, a vast primordial ooze that stretched towards infinity. He watched prehistoric beasts gliding just below the surface, their glassy eyes searching for easy prey.

"Baron Samedi's wading pool," he said.

He peeled himself from the sticky drum-tight abdomen of the dead cow he was relying on for a life raft and then gagged at the putrid stench that accompanied the effort. The animal's rigid legs stuck straight up into the air, and he could hear the gurgle and squeal of trapped gases within its cavity.

He felt sick to his stomach.

He swatted vainly at the legions of maggot-birthing flies that buzzed and crawled all around him.

After a minute, he gave up and looked over at his sister. "Lourdes, are you okay?"

"Shh. There are monsters here. Real ones," she whispered. Her lips were pale and trembling, and her gaze never left the water.

"Look at me. Look here, Palomita." Maximo reached over and pulled her by the arm. The second he touched her, she shrieked hysterically. The scream stretched and flexed its way across the lake. It was a terrifying sound, and it sent panicked flamingos leaping for the sky. They looked like ballerinas bound in pink silk and bloody feathers.

"I saw them, Maximo. I saw them eat her. They ate Mrs. Ramierez, and she was my friend, and she was nice, and she gave me treats, and they *ate* her, and they are going to eat us too." The words and tears tumbled out of her in a cathartic rush.

"No, they aren't going to get us."

His words sounded as useless as he felt. He craned his neck and looked around, searching for something, anything that might offer them some hope. He could see the hunched shoulders and scowling profile of the Sierra de Neiba mountain range, a moody giant with broken limbs and sweet breath.

Too far

He turned, shielded his eyes from the scorching sun and squinted at a thin slash of green in the distance. It looked like an algae bloom atop a lake of coffee.

"Isla de Cabritos."

His father had taken him there once to see the huge rhinoceros iguanas that stalked the island like mini dinosaurs. He was certain that it was the same island and that reaching it was their only chance of surviving another day.

Maximo leaned down and began the daunting task of paddling a dead cow across a crocodile-infested lake. He scooped and slapped at the water for the next hour, his aggravation and exhaustion growing by the second. Sweat streamed down his forehead and stung his eyes. His exertion caused the pain in his damaged leg to return, and he gritted his teeth against the shockwaves of agony that bolted through him with every stroke.

After a while, he stopped paddling. All he had done was force their morbid raft to complete a lazy futile circle. He slumped back into the greasy embrace of the animal's haunches and gasped for air. His throat constricted in rebellion, refusing to swallow the lump of welder's slag that each breath spiked down his airway. He looked longingly at the fetid lake and licked his parched lips.

The sun oozed out of a blue-skin sky. It throbbed like a malignant melanoma, a cancerous pustule spawned in a demon's forge, and it radiated ill will down upon them.

Maybe just a mouthful, he thought, just enough to moisten, to wet.

He would not actually drink it. As he leaned down and cupped some water into his hand, he thought about a Bible story his mother had read to him once.

"Just a sip," he mumbled.

Something about an apple and a snake

The moment his shaking hand pressed the foul water to his lips, a strong wind rippled over the lake and found him. It came from nowhere, fresh and invigorating—an invisible balm. It quieted his mind, cast the flies and heat from his body and nudged his boat of blood and milk towards dry land.

He raised his face towards the unexpected grace and closed his eyes, the forgotten water in his palm dribbling through his fingers.

Something about a parting of the sea

They were moving.

He spread his arms wide, smiled and tried to embrace the unseen pleasure. Somewhere, far away, he could hear the sound of his sister's laughter, an avian soprano searching for a sympathetic ear.

"Maximo, I'm not afraid anymore."

"You never were," he said.

He reached down and snagged a piece of driftwood out of the water. "This will make a good oar, if we should need one."

He struck the huge fleshy dome between them as if it were a giant tambora drum. The hollow sound reverberated comically throughout the animal's innards. The children stared at the preposterous bladder and then doubled over with laughter.

"Do it again. Do it again," Lourdes said.

He whacked the stretched skin repeatedly, flaying music from the animal's hide. It was a crazy sound in a crazy place. Maximo and Lourdes convulsed in laughter after each hammer blow. They laughed until tears streamed down their faces and he couldn't even lift his makeshift drumstick.

The wind continued to favour the unlikely sailors, gusting steadily and pushing them towards safety.

Maximo wiped tears from his face, took a deep ragged breath and pointed towards the Island of Goats. "Enough merengue," he said. "Look there. We're going to make it. I can paddle us in from here if I have to."

They could clearly make out the scrubby vegetation and squat cacti that covered the island, as well as the unexpected and disturbing sight of clothing. It was everywhere—pink, blue, green and yellow, underwear and bras, shirts and skirts, all of it strewn along the island's thin pebbly beach like discarded party favours after a New Year's Eve celebration.

It had a sobering effect on them.

"So many people," Lourdes said.

Maximo had just opened his mouth to answer her when the first crocodile struck. The massive reptile exploded out of the opaque water, clamped its jaws around the cow's neck and began to corkscrew its body. Before the children could react, another crocodile burst from the lake and attacked the waterlogged carcass. It tore off a wormy chunk of decaying meat, bolted it down and lunged for more.

Without thinking, Maximo swung his stick like a battle-axe, crashing it down on the head of the closest crocodile. The stunned beast blinked its displeasure and slid moodily back into the lake. He screamed and swung at the second one, his war cry eclipsing even Lourdes' high-pitched shriek.

Suddenly, a third and then a fourth crocodile burst from the lake, joining the feast. Maximo brought the club down repeatedly on any part of any crocodile he could see. He tried to kill them with every blow. He swung, screamed and kicked at them, his rage intensified by the injustice of it all. They had survived so much together, too much, to die within sight of land.

There were at least six crocodiles ripping into the carcass, and it was twitching and shaking as if it had returned to life. When he no longer had the strength to lift the wood, Maximo spat and cursed at the reptiles and waited for the end to come. His eyes met Lourdes', and he hoped that when the beasts took her, she would not suffer too much.

It was surreal when the first reptile sunk its teeth into him. It chomped down on his injured leg, instantly snapping the bone. There was little pain, just a sense of pressure. Maximo grunted in surprise but otherwise showed no emotion. It was over. His heart, his memories and his dreams would all temporarily sate a crocodile's hunger before it shat out the stubborn bits. That was all he was destined to become after all, just something's lunch and a bowel movement.

The cow's belly erupted like an organic volcano spewing its ropey entrails and gases into the air. Maximo plunged into a stew of stomach bile and slippery organs. He grabbed hold of the animal's thick ribs and kicked at a crocodile's snout with his good leg. It was all so surreal that he wasn't surprised to see a huge black bird hovering above him in the sky, blotting out the sun. He could feel the wind and power of its massive wings.

He would always remember the crocodile's head exploding as a sharpshooter sunk a hollow-point bullet into its tiny brain. The last thing he saw before passing out was the blurry sight of a soldier fast-roping down from the heavens like a combat angel, his semi-automatic weapon spitting vengeance and death at the fleeing monsters of Lago Enriquillo.

FREEDOM AND THE VIRGIN
OF ALTAGRACIA

A GUARD LEANED AGAINST the bars, impatiently rapping his baton against his thigh. "Jaragua Domingo Ventura, answer or you can stay here."

Jaragua's name careened through the cellblock's ranks like a steel pinball and bounced off his skull. He bullied his way through the press of bodies.

"That's me, Jaragua Ventura," he said, facing the very guard who had bashed his kidneys until he had pissed blood.

"Get yourself together. You're going home. One hour."

"I have nothing. I'm ready now."

"One hour, and if you're not waiting right here, then I will assume you're enjoying our hospitality and I'll leave you here for another week," the guard said, and marched off.

Jaragua walked around the place, touching fists with several men and wishing them luck.

"Have a beer for me, my friend," a familiar voice said.

"Hey, Manny, I was looking for you," Jaragua said, slapping palms with the man.

"So what are you going to do now?" Manny asked.

"Ahh, you know. Go straight. Get an honest job, maybe in the fields or construction work. Sort my life out."

Manny's eyes widened, and he stared at him for a second before wagging a finger at him. "Hey, that was good. You almost had me there. Maybe you should consider becoming an actor instead."

"Not pretty enough, my man." Jaragua grinned.

"When I get out of here, I'm going home to my island, back to Puerto Rico, where the people speak proper Spanish," Manny said. "You're welcome to drop by if you ever make it over. Here, take my number."

Jaragua accepted the scrap of paper from him and then impulsively peeled a 100-dollar bill from his roll. "It isn't often that I meet someone inside who isn't a complete hijoeputa. Treat yourself to some powder, on me. And maybe spend some of this on food as well, you scrawny junkie."

"Wow. Hey, man, thank you," Manny said, solemnly taking the money from him. "I won't forget this, and if you ever need something, and if I can help, I will."

"Take care, Manny."

"You too, brother."

A short time later, Jaragua walked out of the prison and into the searing heat of the midday sun. He had heard somewhere that *Higuey* was a Taino word—like *barbecue* and *hammock*—and that it meant "land where the sun shines." He smirked at the thought. Within the heartless walls of Higuey Prison, inside a cellblock known as the slaughterhouse, darkness ruled.

He quickly flagged down one of the numerous motorcycles that buzzed past him, a coughing sputtering swarm of asthmatic hornets that served as his country's taxis.

A teenager wearing a thick gold chain and no shirt braked hard in front of him. Jaragua got on.

The noisy motoconcho burned up and down the town's busy streets. The driver swerved around potholes, vendors, chickens, goats and other vehicles with unlikely success. The omnipresent strains of merengue and bachata splashed over Jaragua like cool rain, coaxing a smile onto his pallid face.

While the boy waited, Jaragua exchanged some dollars for pesos, bought new clothes and shoes and changed in the street. Ignoring the giggles of three girls, he ripped his stinking clothes off and hurled them into the gutter in disgust. He poured a plastic jug of water over his head and scoured as much filth from his nakedness as possible. The fresh water felt so good that he screamed in pleasure. He slipped on a pair of fresh clean chinos and a long-sleeved white cotton shirt.

"Don Caminos," he said, proudly holding his new shoes up for the approval of his chauffeur.

"Cool," the boy said, looking unimpressed.

Jaragua leapt back onto the bike and told the boy where he wanted to go. He gripped the bike's seat tighter than was necessary. He felt anxious about his next stop.

They pulled up in front of the Basílica de Nuestra Señora de la Altagracia, a destination that thousands of devotees made a pilgrimage to every year in search of miraculous cures and blessings.

"Wait for me," Jaragua said to the boy, and started up the steps towards the cathedral.

As he walked, he looked up at a pair of cone-shaped domes on top of the roof. They reminded him of praying hands. He blessed himself, took a deep breath and entered the church.

He walked slowly down the centre of the aisle. He felt small beneath the soaring concrete walls and reproachful eyes of the painted saints.

Warm sunshine filtered through a wall of stained glass and bathed the church in an iridescent light, the beauty of which struck a long-dormant chord of reverence deep inside Jaragua.

He knelt down in front of an opulently framed glass-encased image of Our Lady of Grace. He was only able to glance at the iconic figure for a second before bowing his head in humility.

He could smell candle wax and lemons.

"Sweet Virgin…" he began before stopping. "That didn't come out right…sorry." He coughed self-consciously. "Dear Virgin of Altagracia, hear my prayer."

He raised his eyes slightly until he could see the Baby Jesus in the painting's nativity scene.

"I ask nothing of you for myself. I am lost. A sinner, a thief…a killer," he whispered, half expecting someone to order him off his knees and out of the cathedral. "You are the queen of all hearts. There is nothing that I can conceal from you. My prayer comes from the only gentle place I have left inside me. Protect my family for me, if they are still alive. Protect them for me until I can. They have never had much and have asked for less. They deserve better... Amen."

Jaragua blessed himself and got up off his knees.

He looked away from the venerated portrait, turned around and walked quickly towards the exit. The hollow sound of his footsteps echoed throughout the cavernous space like the pounding of a judge's gavel.

Guilty, Guilty, Guilty

He pushed the heavy doors of the church open and broke into a light jog. He felt as if he had just committed a crime.

"How much for your motoconcho?" he asked the boy, pointing at his battered black and red Yamaha.

The kid pushed his Boston Red Sox baseball cap further back on his head before answering. "Not for sale. This is my living."

Jaragua pulled money from his pocket. "Three hundred cash. I take it now."

"Hah," the boy replied. The sound was closer to that of a cat expelling a hairball than one of human incredulity. "Give me five and it's yours." He rubbed his thumb and index finger together as if they were made of wood and he was trying to start a fire.

"Criminals, everywhere I look. Last offer." Jaragua held up four 100-dollar bills and fanned the air with them.

"Sold," the boy said, and snatched the money from his hand.

Jaragua leapt onto the bike, fired it up and sped away, leaving the smiling teenager in a cloud of steel-blue exhaust and a rooster tail of sangria-coloured earth.

He roared down Hermanos Trejo Avenue, ignoring the people who tried to flag him down for a ride home. He rocketed past rows of brightly painted cinder-block buildings. They had advertisements and political slogans plastered over their mauve, teal and chartreuse facades. He navigated around half-naked old men astride half-dead horses, and ancient trucks piled high with rickety loads of plantains, coffee, mangoes and pineapples. He sped past other motoconchos transporting people, livestock and explosive bottles of propane, past a beautiful young girl dancing in the middle of the road and an old woman with a load of laundry balanced on top of her head.

He followed the arthritic spine of the road out of Higuey and into the fertility of the encroaching countryside, merengue and the screams from Higuey Prison fading further and further with every twist of the throttle.

He headed south towards the sea.

After spending so much time in a cage, Jaragua felt intoxicated with his sudden freedom, with the vastness of the sugarcane fields that surrounded him, surging towards the horizon like a green tsunami.

AN ORISHA AT THE PALLADIUM

A STEAM TRAIN BURNED across the salt flats with apocalyptic speed, a soot-shrouded warhorse punishing the damned beneath its churning hooves and iron muscles. Ignacio was standing too close to the tracks. He wanted to back away from the danger, but he felt paralyzed. His chest constricted painfully, and his breath deserted him through his unhinged jaw. The train's wheels shrieked like shackled harpies clutching at the flutter and tease of his billowing shirttails, attempting to drag the old man to his death.

He felt defenceless against the mortal inertia of his weakening knees, his failing spirit. He was being drawn ever closer to his doom. He could see the gaunt faces and empty eye sockets of the train's passengers staring down at him in sightless accusation, a silent cavalcade of people he had once known, once loved—people he had called friend, lover… wife and daughter—all the people he had abandoned or failed in his life.

After losing his family, he had developed a profound fear of ever loving too deeply again, of ever suffering another loss capable of breaking the fragile truce he had tendered with his own conscience.

He reached out to the spectres of his past.

"Forgive me."

The shrillness of the train's whistle slapped the lamentation from his lips and sent him tumbling out of his nightmare. He awoke with a scream and thrust both his arms into the air.

"I'm not ready."

The cold sobriety of his surroundings came slowly into focus, and he sighed in relief. He rolled onto his side, wiped the perspiration from his forehead and swung his legs off the bed.

"Just a dream," he said, shaking the cobwebs and quiver from his mind.

Ignacio pushed himself off the bed, ignored the protest of his aging joints and shuffled over to a flimsy propane stove. He brewed himself a pot of thick black coffee, poured a cup and sat down at a rough-hewn wooden table. He spooned a mound of sugar into his cup, sipped at the syrupy liquid and ran a hand through his dishevelled hair.

The night pressed itself to him like an obese lover smothering him with wet needy kisses. He looked longingly towards a small open window but no breeze came. The trill and burp of hundreds of tree frogs knocked on his humble walls and crept in under his door, filling the small space with their irrepressible chorus. The frogs competed against the howling blizzard of voices that raged within his mind.

He reached over and switched on an old radio. It had a pair of tinfoil-wrapped antennas jutting from its back like robotic appendages.

After some squelch and squeal, Tito Puente's classic cha-cha-cha "Oye Como Va" smoothed its way into the room, settled into a chair across from Ignacio and banished the tree frog symphony back to the wilds.

A smile flirted with the corners of his mouth as he listened to the famous tune. He loved what Carlos Santana had done with the song, but for Ignacio, Tito would always be the man. He lazily scraped his bare feet over the earthen floor, performing an uninspired rendition of his once-lauded moves.

He avoided looking at the dusty heap of musical instruments lying abandoned in a corner of his stone cottage—a German accordion, two saxophones, a guiro, maracas, a tambora drum and, of course, his beloved brass: a trombone, a tuba and three trumpets. All of their sweet voices were smothered years ago beneath the weight of his guilt.

He poured himself another cup of coffee, knowing that there would be no more sleep for him that night. Besides, the older he got, the less sleep he required, one of the many surprises that Father Time had sprung on him.

"And now something a little bit special," the DJ said as Tito faded out. "For those of you who are in the know…enjoy. For those of you who are not, listen…learn. This is a classic hit, merengue cibaeño at its finest, from one of its most mysterious merengueros. I'm talking about that elusive MIA star of yesteryear Ignacio dos Santos and the Hacienda de Ritmo performing their nineteen-fifty-nine massive hit 'Estrellita Luminosa.'"

Ignacio lowered his cup and stared at the radio in disbelief. He willed himself to turn it off, smash it and hurl hot coffee on it, anything to stop what was coming. Instead, he blinked once, swallowed hard and prepared to go to hell.

Her song began to play, and her face emerged from behind his tissue-paper ramparts.

"Face the music," he mumbled, and frowned.

The melody bounded into the room like a puppy unaware that some people were immune to its charms, that some people hated dogs.

The song that Ignacio had written for his late wife within hours of meeting her reminded him of everything he once had and of everything he had lost.

His own voice coming over the radio sounded foreign to him, the vocal chords not yet damaged by the drink. His voice gyrated and strutted around the room with a racy confidence, slinging innuendo, cajoling and cajiving. It was a phantom preserved in vinyl, one capable of reaching out from the past, seizing Ignacio by the lapels and forcing him to acknowledge his crimes. He closed his eyes, rested his head on the table and, without any further protest, allowed the memories to flow.

It was the late fifties, Thanksgiving Eve, New York City. Ignacio and his band had built a simmering reputation as a hip-swinging, hot, young merengue band. They had performed all over Puerto Rico, Cuba, Miami and NYC, generating interest and amassing a fan base. However, it wasn't until a Jewish lawyer from Brooklyn caught their act that things really began to heat up.

His name was Mordechai Finkelster, but everyone called him 'the Funky Finkster' or 'the Funky Sphincter,' wholly dependent upon the mood of his spastic colon. He wore zoot suits, spoke like a beatnik, smoked French cigarettes and never missed temple.

Funky had believed in Ignacio and the Hacienda de Ritmo from the first time he heard them. He had flown them in from Florida to record their first album, all on speculation and all on his dime.

After a day of laying down tracks, they had all gone to the Palladium on 53rd and Broadway. The ballroom was electric pulsation and neon noise. Ignacio had seen Marlon Brando there that night, one arm around an exotic beauty and the other around Max Hyman, the club's owner.

Ignacio had squeezed into the place with his best friend, Anthony Dominguez, who was also the band's accordion player. They were sharp-suited, spit-shine-booted, and there for two reasons: to dance with pretty girls and to take in the premier American performance of charanga bandleader José Fajardo, non-stop from Havana.

The admission had been two dollars, a couple of bucks to see the legendary flutist do his thing.

Fat city

Ignacio and Anthony used to hang out on the right side of the club, hallowed ground at the Palladium, where only the best dancers dared to tread.

Ignacio pressed the back of his hand to one cheek and wiped away a single tear. He listened to the words he had written—his ode to the only woman he had ever loved—and remembered the first time he saw her.

Fajardo had been performing his smash hit "Ritmo de Pollos," and the crowd had been just melting, roaring their approval every time he hit another impossibly perfect high on his flute—the Pied Piper casting his spell over all but one.

She had been crying the first time Ignacio saw her, and perhaps it was for that very reason that she had appeared so exquisite to him. She had been an oasis of sorrow amid a sandstorm of swirling jubilation. She had been sharing her misery with another woman (who, as it turned out, was her younger sister), and he had been unable to stop staring. Her hands had been doing as much talking as her mouth—and what a mouth: soft swollen lips wet with tears and fierce emotion.

He would never forget the sudden rush of certainty he had felt as he approached her, a psychic-like premonition that he was looking at the woman he would marry. She was petite; had thick, shoulder-length, dark hair; light brown skin; and eyes that looked out at the world with a gentle condemnation.

He had eased his way through the crowd until there was nothing between them except glitter and illusion. He had been just about to blurt out something stupid when Estrellita's sister held a non-negotiable hand up to his face, halting his advance and causing his mouth to open and close in silent angst. He had felt like a dying fish laying in the oily bilge water of a rusty tanker christened *Rejection*.

"Por favor, señor," she had said, her voice telling him that she was Cuban and was in no mood for messing.

He had stood there for another couple of minutes, being ignored, inhaling Estrellita's perfume, his eyes tracing the arc and plunge of her cheekbones. He would have been content to stand there indefinitely had the situation not become so unexpectedly awkward.

The girls had then suddenly turned towards him in a synchronized display of sisterly solidarity.

"Que?" they had asked in unison, arching their eyebrows in aggravation.

He remembered stammering something about his concern for her and asking why she was crying, but the exact words he used were forever lost to him.

Exasperated, Estrellita had told him the problem, hoping that he would leave her alone. She'd had no time for hipsters with cute smiles and scores of other dollies.

When she had finished speaking, he knew that the gods above and the demons below had orchestrated their meeting that night.

"Did it look something like this?" he had asked her, pulling a necklace from the pocket of his maroon suit and dangling it in front of her damp eyes. "The clasp must have come lose. I found it over there," he had said, gesturing towards the stage with his free hand.

"But...how could you have known? You brought it to me, of all these people, my necklace."

"I didn't know it was yours. I just saw you crying, and...do you believe in destiny?" he had asked, handing her the necklace and smiling at her.

She had stared down at her heirloom for a long moment, wrapped her fingers protectively around it and looked back up at him. "My mother gave me this necklace, and my grandmother gave it to her, and I will pass it on to my daughter on her sixteenth birthday. This necklace is homage to destiny, and your returning it to me is no coincidence. We were supposed to meet, you and I. Have you ever heard of Santería?"

He had told the little he knew about Santería, that it was an Afro-Cuban religion and that it had profoundly influenced modern-day music and dance, that mambo, rhumba and conga had all evolved from the religious practices of West African slaves, from such tribes as the Yoruba, and Congo, who used drum rhythms and ritual dance to honour, summon and worship their deities. "The word *mambo* itself is the name given to a high priestess in voodoo," he had said.

Anthony had then handed everyone a drink, whispered "killer" into Ignacio's ear and took Estrellita's sister off to actually do the mambo instead of just talk about it.

Estrellita had then touched her glass to Ignacio's and smiled at him for the first time, and he had known then that he would do anything to remain within the affection of that smile for the rest of his life.

"My mother was a Santería priestess back in Cuba," she had said. "She gave me this necklace just before she died. It has eight gold and eight jade beads because yellow and green are the favourite colours of Orunmila, an Orisha whose number is sixteen and whose domain is wisdom and destiny." She had leaned towards him in an effort to be heard over the music.

"What's an Orisha?"

"Sort of like a guardian angel...like you," she had said, and giggled.

Like me, he had thought. She *likes* me.

He had sipped his drink but could hardly taste it. All his senses had been tuned towards a face painters coveted, a cocktail dress the colour of jealousy and a pair of pastel pink lips speaking words far too deep for a Wednesday night at the Palladium, words that had told him his love possessed an ancient soul and a heart that would require his patience to win.

Daddy Yankee's Reggaeton hit "Gasolina" slashed through the fog of his memories and forced his eyes reluctantly open.

Ignacio sighed heavily, and pushed himself to his feet.

He knew what was going to happen next, and he was powerless to stop it. Whenever remorse fell upon him like a fever, a part of him ached for the oblivion that only intoxication could bring.

He slouched his way over to the stove, the stiffness of his body recalling every second of every day he had suffered on Santo Domingo's stone streets, two decades in perdition, a place he had never intended on escaping.

He opened up a cupboard over the stove, rummaged about and pulled out an unopened bottle of rum. He returned to the table and sat down. He wrapped his hands around the bottle as if they were cold and the fire inside the alcohol might warm them. He stared at his reflection in the amber liquid. It had been almost four years since he was able to face what had happened to his family without the help of the drink. Forgiveness was another matter.

He had sat like that countless times, the same unopened bottle in front of him, tempting him, smirking at him, flirting with him like a whore past her prime. So far, his desire to continue living had managed to defeat his thirst for numbness, and that was what it came down to:

life and death. He could find other ways of dealing with the mistakes he had made in his life or he could return to the booze and die, and one was all it would take, just a measure, a shot, a dram, just a taste to send him screaming back into the abyss of alcoholism.

He pressed the bottle against his forehead and rolled it back and forth. He was never sure how his personal form of Russian roulette was going to end, and a part of him didn't care.

"I don't deserve this peace, this home, this chair—no bed, no birds, no trees. I deserve nothing. I am nothing," he whispered into the bottle's ear, allowing his tears to run down the glass surface. "I betrayed you, Estrellita. Your last words, I did not honour them. I killed our daughter as surely as if my own hand held that gun, and because of me she had no Orisha, no guardian angel to protect her that night. Because of me."

He dissolved into a wretched heap, his head resting on the rough wood surface of the table, his body shaking from the intensity of his weeping. When things got that bad, he felt as if he had only the most tentative of holds on his sanity, a frayed rope attached to the boom of a crash-jibing ship christened *Madness*.

Then the sensation came over him as it had done before, during the worst of it. He felt arms wrapping themselves around him, a deeply comforting embrace, loving warmth that encouraged his submission. He never questioned the feeling, never tried to make any sense of it, lest knowledge somehow stopped it from happening, nor would he ever open his eyes during the experience. He was too afraid of what he might see.

After a moment that may have lasted for a minute or an hour, the sensation faded, and he raised his head from the table.

"Thank you. Yes, I know. No, not tonight," he said, and slowly stood up. He walked back to the cupboard and shoved the bottle of rum behind some mottled plantains and dented cans of black-eyed peas.

"Not tonight," he repeated, picking a long stalk of sugarcane off the floor. He took a machete from a hook on the wall, lopped off a piece of cane the length of his forearm and proceeded to shave it.

As a boy, he remembered reading about thirteenth-century

Dominican monks. The mendicant order believed in poverty, obedience, chastity and the practice of self-flagellation. The monks proclaimed that *the discipline* was capable of saving the repentant, of expiating sins and turning aside divine retribution—all things that Ignacio felt he was in need of.

He walked over to his bed, reached under it and took out a cat o' nine tails. The menacing-looking whip was made of rawhide, and it had nine knotted thongs springing from the baton. They looked like a Rastafarian's dreadlocks.

He bit down on the cane, placed one hand on the back of a chair and leaned forward, allowing the chair to take his weight. He flicked the cat o' nine tails out with a practiced ease, recalling that seamen used to call the feared instrument "the Captain's daughter." He had always found that amusing.

He lashed the whip across his naked back with conviction, grunting in relief as the rawhide caressed his skin. He bit down harder on the cane between his teeth and continued to swing the cat. He felt calmer with each consecutive blow, the deep ache in his heart gradually being replaced by a pain he could bare.

As he chased his deliverance, saliva and sweet cane juice drooled from his mouth and pooled in the dirt at his feet.

Lash
In the name of the Father
Lash
And the Son
Lash
And the Holy Ghost
Lash
Kiss the Captain's daughter
Lash
Mercy
Lash
What's the matter?
Cat got your tongue?

No longer able to lift the whip, Ignacio spat the gnarled cane from his mouth, gasped for air and slowly slumped to his knees.

"Forgive me," he whispered, as a swarm of hungry mosquitoes descended on him like a plague.

PHANTOM PAIN

MAXIMO TWITCHED AND MOANED in his hospital bed, coiling the sheets around his clammy body like seaweed on an anchor chain. In his mind, he was walking along the edge of a sugarcane plantation on the outskirts of Barahona.

Years earlier, the dictator Rafael Trujillo had ordered huge swaths of land to be planted with the perennial cash crop. Long after the strongman's death, the fields were still exploiting Haitian backs. During harvest time, thousands of desperate men were trucked across the border to reap the cane. They lived on the peripheral of Dominican society in squalid shantytowns known as bateyes.

Maximo's father had been one of those men.

As he walked, Maximo could feel sweat trickling down the hollow of his back, a salty river within the rift of a fertile valley. He bit off another chunk of cane and chewed the woody grass. He extracted juicy mouthfuls of sweet water from the pulp, draining the vitality and nourishment from the plant until there was nothing left to spit back at the earth except a ruinous lump of spent bagasse.

The cane fields did the same thing to a man.

He watched the ponderous progression of a black steam-driven locomotive as it wheezed and huffed its way through the slaughtered fields, its battered carriages piled high with broken cane. It looked like a gigantic iron hedgehog sniffing its way towards the refinery.

He whacked the tall grass with his length of shaved cane, flushing white-throated crows from their hiding places. They flew into the air in pairs, cursing him with their song.

He stopped and raised a hand to his forehead, shielding his eyes from the sun's glare. A smile spread across his face when he recognized the floppy panama hat his father always wore, a faded blue bandana tied around its crown. However, he didn't require an old hat to pick him out from a distance. It was because of the way he worked that Maximo was always certain that it was he. His machete would rise and fall like an automated guillotine blade, a haze of glinting metal that decimated everything in its path, leaving the other men breathless and struggling to keep up.

"Papi," Maximo yelled, waving his hand through time and memory.

The machine-like repetition of Solomon's movements ceased, and he tilted his head towards his son, his middle child, and truth be told, his favourite.

"Maximo," he hailed. His voice was raspy from the dust and thirst of his work. He raised his machete high into the air, his chest still heaving with exertion, his face concealed within the solemn shadows of his straw hat.

The men around him immediately stopped working, grateful for any reprieve from the mindless whistle and thwack of their endless days. The men ambled towards him, smiling, calling his name, sucking their teeth and clucking their tongues.

Solomon reached an arm out, encircling Maximo's shoulders with it. "You will never see my son in these fields," he said. "This one is no Congo. You will see my son pitching for the Marlins one day."

"The Mets, Papi. I'm going to pitch for the New York Mets, not the Florida fishes," Maximo said.

The men howled their approval and jumped around like excited children, his father's laughter the loudest of all.

"That's right, Maximo," Solomon said. "Your dream, nobody else's, and remember, nobody can ever take that from you, nobody can ever crush that hope. Only you, if you ever stop dreaming, ever stop believing. Only then does it die."

"Maximo."

His name floated down to him from somewhere high above.

He looked to the sky, searching the towering banks of cumulus clouds for the source of the voice.

"Maximo."

The voice came again, only clearer this time and more forceful.

"Wake up. Please, wake up."

He groaned his displeasure. The voice was interfering with the warmth and happiness of his memories. The image of his father began to flicker and fade as if he were watching him on an old black and white television set with bad reception.

He wanted to stay where he was.

"Pleeease, wake up," the persistent voice said, finally dragging him back to the unwelcome world of the conscious.

He opened his eyes slightly, squinted at the harsh white light of reality and received needles of pain in the base of his skull. He clamped his eyes shut and acknowledged a host of other throbbing pains as they lined up and gleefully announced themselves, one after another. He had no idea where he was, but judging from the noise that boiled all around him, he was in an asylum. He pressed his hands over his ears, vainly attempting to block out the bedlam.

"Are you all right?"

He could feel Lourdes' warm breath against his hand. It was time to face the world once again. He opened his eyes and cleared his throat of phlegm before speaking. "Where am I?"

"In the hospital. Are you all right?"

"I think so. Everything hurts, especially my leg. What happened to me?"

"You don't remember?" she said quietly, her big eyes growing even larger.

"If I remembered, then I wouldn't be asking. Sometimes you can be a real pain, and I've got enough of them right now. So just tell me."

"I better go and get Dr. Sanchez," she said. "He's really nice. He's from Cuba, and he said that you got a fever and you're on drugs and if you wake up, I should go get him right away." She made a serious face and climbed down from her chair.

"Lourdes, what are you talking about?"

"Wait here," she said, and ran from the room.

Maximo sighed, let his head flop back onto his bed and had his first good look around the place. He was one of many patients crammed into a windowless dormitory. The place looked like a cross between a torture chamber and a war zone. A string of naked light bulbs stretched across the ceiling, unsympathetically illuminating the misery below. The mattresses on the antiquated beds were thin wedges of compressed material stuffed inside a cracked shell of seasick green vinyl, and they felt as horrid as they looked. The name of Jesus was simultaneously cursed and beseeched. Others cemented deals with the devil or issued ultimatums to distraught relatives.

He could smell antiseptic, bleach and shit.

"Good day, Maximo. I am so pleased that you have returned to us. How do you feel?"

Maximo looked up and saw a doctor standing at the end of his bed. He was short, thin and bearded, and he spoke a melodic form of Spanish that sounded strange to Maximo's ear.

"I am Dr. Sanchez. You have been in and out of consciousness for five days now. We have all been very worried about you, especially this little one here." He smiled down at Lourdes, who had attached herself to his hip.

"What happened to me?" Maximo asked.

"What happened to you?" the Doctor repeated.

Dr. Sanchez blew his breath out and ran a hand through his thick black hair. "First of all, let me tell you that you are very brave, and were it not for your sacrifice, both of you would not be here today. Do you remember anything at all? The flood in Jimaní, the crocodiles, the army helicopter that brought you here?"

And that was all it took, just the key words to unlock the door to Maximo's repressed memories. He closed his eyes and saw flashes of his ordeal, a stack of snapshots from someone else's adventure, a horror movie that starred a boy who resembled him and a stunt double who didn't. The images made him feel nostalgic for his previous ignorance.

"Yes, I remember…everything."

He looked over at Lourdes. She sat on a plastic chair by the side of his bed, happily swinging her legs back and forth and humming to herself.

"You all right?" he asked her.

"Uh-huh. I miss Mami and Papi. I hope that they're coming to get us soon," she said, her innocent eyes dulled by uncertainty.

"Yeah, me too, Palomita."

The Doctor nervously cleared his throat before speaking again. "You are correct to never give up hope. Many people are turning up alive, each with their own harrowing tale of survival. Your parents could well be two of them." He pulled a few coins from his pocket. "Lourdes, would you do me a favour? Go down the hall to the soda machine and buy a Coca-Cola for you and your brother?"

After Lourdes had skipped from the room, Dr. Sanchez sat down on the edge of the bed and frowned. "Is there anyone else, anyone other than your parents, someone who may be able to care for you and Lourdes until their whereabouts are determined?"

Maximo shook his head. "No. There's nobody. An older brother, but nobody knows where he is."

"Relatives?"

"No. My mother's family disowned her for marrying a Haitian, or maybe it was because he's a cane cutter. Anyway, I never knew them. My father's family was murdered when that crazy man was in power, that Papa Doc Duvalier. The Tonton Macoutes came in the middle of the night. He was twelve. They killed everyone. He hid under a bed. But my parents are alive. Lourdes and I survived, so why not them?"

"Yes, there is still a chance. But let's forget all that for the moment."

Dr. Sanchez placed a hand on Maximo's forehead. "It looks like your fever has finally broken. How do you feel? Are you in any pain?"

"I feel okay except for my leg; it really hurts."

"Maximo, what you're experiencing is a phenomenon known as

phantom pain. Your leg is not causing you any discomfort…it just feels like it is."

"Hah. I'm no doctor, but I know if my leg is hurting. Don't you think I'd know?"

"There is something I have to tell you." The Doctor sighed. "Your leg was damaged beyond repair. Even if you had received immediate treatment, the diseased water…the rot. I am sorry, but we had to amputate your leg above the knee within hours of your arrival here."

The words thudded into Maximo's gut like leaden downriggers, knocking the wind out of him and shattering his future. For the first time, he stared down at the flat spot beneath his sheets, the spot where his leg should have been.

There was nothing there

He clamped his teeth around a scream that had no end and tore the bedding to one side. He grasped at the short stump of swaddled meat; it looked like a trussed up ham hock. His hands scurried frantically over the discoloured bandages, needing to confirm by touch what his eyes told him to be true.

"But, I can feel my toes…" Maximo said quietly, wiggling his non-existent digits for the Doctor, trying to convince him that he had made a mistake.

"I'm very sorry. We did our best to save it."

Maximo turned his face away and felt the first of many tears begin to roll down his cheeks. Dr. Sanchez's voice faded away to a distant empathetic drone, a consoling cadence that rose and fell like pollen on a summer wind.

Maximo drifted away from it all.

He could see the massive JumboTron at Shea Stadium, could see its glittering brilliance through a curtain of game-ending rain. He watched as the Mets slogan "Ya Gotta Believe!" sparked and sputtered across the short-circuiting screen. It blinked once and went dark.

DREAMS, MERENGUE
AND CIGARS

ESTRELLITA ADJUSTED HER HEADPHONES and stared out the window of a bus. It was the beginning and end of a tedious day, an anesthetized life and a deafening implosion. She mouthed the words to "Enamorame" by Papi Sanchez. The pensive tune matched her mood.

She watched the countryside go by and tried to ignore the sour stench radiating from a work-weary man seated across from her. His glazed eyes were fixed somewhere to the left of zombie.

She thought about Jaragua, the only man who had ever made her feel vulnerable, the only man she had ever allowed inside her heart, inside her body. She whispered his name and closed her eyes.

She had still not gotten over the anguish she had suffered when she had tried to visit him in jail. After a long hot journey, she had arrived at Higuey Prison, clutching a bag of fresh fruit, medicines and chocolate, but the guards had turned her away. They gave her no explanation; they simply insulted her with their eyes and then dismissed her. Shortly after that, her whole world had caved in. Details of the prison riot permeated the headlines, and since the death toll became public knowledge, Estrellita had cried herself to sleep every night.

The bus lurched to a stuttering stop, shaking the weight of her burden from her shoulders. She exited into the heat and serenity of Tamboril. She turned up the volume on her MP3 player and began to sway her hips to one of her favourite songs, "Porque Me Amaste" by Milly Quezada. The Queen of Merengue inspired her, and her music had heavily influenced Estrellita's own compositions.

As she made her way home, she picked her way through an obstacle course of uprooted water mains, gurgling sinkholes and excavated mounds of stony muck—the Licey River had overflowed its banks again. She smiled at the familiar faces in her neighbourhood, creating fantasies for the young men who buzzed by on their motorbikes. She waved at a group of rowdy field workers, watching as they slam-dunked dominos and rejuvenated their parched bodies with frosty green bottles of El Presidente beer.

She pulled her headphones from her ears and enjoyed the omnipresent merengue and bachata tunes that vied for her attention as she walked on by. She adored many bachata songs. Merengue, however, was her soul. To her, it was more than a musical style or a popular dance, more than a national icon or cultural phenomena. Merengue was the essence of her people's spirit, a spirit that didn't respect self-pity, knowing that a smile was free. It was an attitude, and it demanded that you held your head higher and laughed louder when you were at your lowest. It was the life force of her nation, a blood oath. It was pulse and movement, the fortitude of an unbreakable back. Merengue was a Dominican birthright.

Estrellita was the lead singer and guiro player in a merengue band called Rocket and the Cinnamon Roosters. Her mother had given her the nickname Rocket because she used to sit for hours and stare up at the moon when she was a little girl, telling anyone who would listen that one day she was going to go there.

She stepped over a sleeping dog and opened the door to her family's two-bedroom apartment, a concrete and rebar structure that was as drab outside as it was colourful inside.

"Papa, Mama, I'm home. Where is my little Zorro hiding?"

"Shh. You will wake him," her stepfather said. He was sitting on a plastic-wrapped turquoise sofa, his sleeping son's head resting in his lap.

She tiptoed theatrically across the floor and smiled down at her little brother. "Sorry, Papa."

She fanned the air around her head with both hands. "How many of those today then?"

He held up a smouldering cigar. "Of what? These?"

"Yes, those gravediggers, those coffin spikes."

"Before I answer that, nurse, do you know what it is, exactly, that you are referring to with such disrespect?"

"Yes, I do," she replied, inflicting her voice with just the right amount of disapproval. "It is a big nasty tobacco torpedo, one aimed at your heart."

He smiled at her, a gesture that dropped years of arthritic pain from his handsome face. "This," he said, holding his cigar between swollen and gnarled fingers, "this is a robusto. Dominican olor binder, Dominican Piloto Cubano filler and a Colorado Maduro wrapper. Can you not smell the pepper, Estrellita? The cocoa? The earth itself?" He feigned indignation.

He had been a cigar roller for most of his life, a profession that many people in Tamboril aspired to. Estrellita's mother had met him while employed at one of the many cigar factories that had mushroomed up all over town during the cigar boom of the nineties. It was an era that saw the Dominican Republic supplying fully half of all the premium cigars smoked in North America.

"Yes, I know," Estrellita said. "A robusto or two now, a Churchill after dinner and, of course, the regal Cohiba before bedtime. I know, Papa. You love them all. But please try to cut down...for me?"

"Besides looking at your and your mother's beautiful faces, it is the only pleasure that remains for me."

"So which do you want to do for longer, smoke cigars or bathe in the light of the Alphonso girls' radiance?" She struck an exaggerated pose and sucked her cheeks in.

He laughed, moistened the end of his cigar and looked up at her with adoring eyes. "I'll try," he said, and meant it.

Before his crippling arthritis had ended his days as a cigar maker, he and Estrellita's mother had become a legendary team, she the buncher and he the roller. They had relied on the other's skills to produce between seven and eight hundred quality cigars a day, a symbiotic relationship that had evolved naturally into a romance.

During the gold rush days, foreigners had descended on the unsuspecting town of Tamboril like anemic locusts. They used cutthroat tactics and bribery in their efforts to lure the local talent away from the Dominican factories.

"Poachers" her mother had called them, and her stepfather had ridiculed them for using green tobacco in their cigars.

Inevitably, the neophytes' ventures had all failed due to their ignorance of the cultivation, curing and manufacturing of tobacco. That and their total lack of respect. Ruined and reeling, the gringos and their greed had fled the island. Bankrupt warehouses disfigured the town like fleshless skulls, their dark cavernous doorways drooling scraps of uncured tobacco onto the sun-baked streets.

Estrellita picked up a crumpled tube of analgesic cream from the table and squirted a blob of it into the palm of her hand. "Here," she said, gently taking hold of one of his deformed hands. "Let me help you."

He winced as she began to work the soothing ointment into his inflamed joints. It smelled like menthol and cayenne pepper.

Her mother had remarried almost eight years ago. She rarely spoke about the man who had abandoned her when she was pregnant. Moreover, whenever Estrellita had broached the subject of her real father, her mother's eyes filled with such sadness that she felt guilty for badgering her about him.

"Some men are not bad men… They are just weak," her mother had said, her words forever altering Estrellita's perception of masculinity.

Estrellita looked down at her stepfather as she applied the salve and smiled. He was pretending that her touch wasn't painful to him. He was a decent man, a man who did what he said and said what he meant. He was the only father she had ever known, and she knew how difficult his affliction had been for him to accept. He used to be a physically strong man—a worker—his identity so entwined with his need to work, with his ability to provide for his family, that the insidious disease had robbed him of much more than his once-firm handshake.

"Thank you," he said when she had finished, and then, not knowing what else to do, he lowered his eyes and watched his son sleep.

"I'm going to get ready," she said quietly.

"Of course, you're singing again tonight. I almost forgot."

"Yes, and we are getting better all the time. Just wait and see. One day, when I'm a rich and famous merengue star, I'm going to buy us a big house that we all can live in, all together…by the sea," she said, walking from the room.

"I dream of this day," her stepfather said.

Estrellita showered the stickiness of necessity from her smooth tanned skin, slipped on a pair of tight white slacks and covered her breasts with a white halter top. She posed in the mirror, casting a critical eye over her fit body. She was well aware that many of her male admirers followed her from show to show for reasons that had little to do with music. She didn't mind. Stardom was as much about sex appeal as it was about talent, and she was willing to use everything she had in order to become who she was born to be. She stroked a brush through her freshly washed hair until it glimmered.

Her band had an ongoing gig at a local car wash, an outdoor disco that typically saw more drinking and dancing than wet chrome and soapsuds. She couldn't wait for the rush of the limelight. She had just finished tying an emerald-green kerchief around her head when she heard her mother come in sounding excited about something.

"Estrellita, where are you? Look what I have for you."

"What is it, Mama?" She rushed from her bedroom.

Her mother held up a beautiful bouquet of flowers. "Look at these."

"They're gorgeous. Who gave them to you?"

"Yes, who? A secret admirer?" her stepfather asked, and smiled a bit too widely.

Her mother laughed at his expression. "They're not for me, silly goat. I'm not a young beautiful girl anymore. But I know someone who is."

"Yeeaah," Estrellita's brother suddenly squealed, his voice thick with sleep. He had no idea what was taking place, but he understood happy.

"They're for me?" Estrellita asked, certain that Jaragua had sent them.

"Yes, for you, Rocket." Her mother handed her the flowers.

Estrellita took them and pressed her nose to the nearest bloom. "Mmm, they smell like vanilla. What are they?" She tore open the white envelope that accompanied them.

"The orange ones are lilies, the pink ones are oleanders, but I don't know what the blue ones are. They look strange…kind of human-like," her mother said.

"They're monkshood," her stepfather said, "blue monkshood, and unless I've gone senile, I seem to remember that there is a negative meaning behind them, something to do with danger. They're a warning of some kind."

"Stop scaring her," her mother said, swatting his words out of the air. "Flowers mean this and that. Nobody really knows anyway, least of all men, and as long as they're not black roses, I think she's safe."

Estrellita removed a plain white card from the envelope and read the cryptic note:

These flowers represent the frailty of all beauty.
Enjoy yours, while you still can.
—Miguel: tongue kiss

She felt a cold anger bolt through her. She ran to an open window and hurled the flowers into the street.

"Cabron."

She watched with satisfaction as the colourful bouquet sank into the bubbling gravy of a monstrous sinkhole.

"Have you gone crazy?" her mother asked.

"You know who they're from, Mama," she said, her eyes narrowing.

"Yes. Yes, Rocket, I know who they're from, and I also know who they're not from." She placed her hands on her hips. "They're certainly not from that other one, the one whose name shall not foul these lips. They're certainly not from some mafioso with cunning eyes and hands that itch to do the devil's work."

"You know nothing about Jaragua and even less about Miguel. A pig dressed in a silk suit still acts like a pig." The volume of Estrellita's own voice rose to match her mother's.

"Oh, I know your thug, Estrellita. I know him better than you do. I know his *kind*. All he wants from you is one thing…and as much of it as he can get, and then when he has had his fill, he'll be gone. He will leave you behind, your swollen belly telling the whole world what a little fool you are," her mother said, aiming the same old words at the same old wounds.

"Just because Papa left you, doesn't mean Jaragua will do the same. Maybe Papa couldn't live up to your standards. Maybe none of us can." Estrellita turned and ran into her bedroom, slamming the door behind her.

She was breathing hard and fast. She felt ashamed for speaking to her mother in such a manner, but if she felt hurt, she hurt back. She sat down on a small padded stool and looked at herself in the mirror above her makeup table. She looked like a shock rocker. Black mascara ran down her cheeks like stress cracks in marble.

"Shit," she said, blotting at her face with a tissue.

There came a soft knock at her door that told her it was her stepfather even before he opened it and poked his head in. "Can I come in?"

She nodded her head.

He closed the door behind him and took a seat on the edge of her bed.

"Don't be angry with her," he said. "She only speaks this way because she wants the best for you, a better life, maybe the one she had hoped for but never got. She doesn't want you to ruin your life."

"Ruin my life? She would have me ruin it by throwing myself at a man I don't love, don't even like. Why? Because he can give me *things?* I'm not some puta."

"Estrellita," he said, his face tightening at the word, "what you say is beneath you. Your mother has sacrificed everything for you and your brother."

"I know, Papa." She looked away. "I'm sorry. I just don't know why she won't give Jaragua a chance, just meet him, share one meal. Then she would see."

Because he felt the same way as his wife—about their daughter being involved with a convict—he remained silent.

He then got up, went to Estrellita and rested one knotted hand on her shoulder. "Apologize to her," he said. "You have been born with the gift of music in you, but believe what I say. If you allow your heart to harden, you will never become the singer you could be. Bend with the storms, and like a coco palm, you will weather them. Rigid like a pine tree, and you will break."

"Okay, Papa," she said, and smiled up at him.

A few minutes later, she entered her mother's bedroom.

Her mother was kneeling before a shrine to the Virgin Mary, her fingers flying from one rosary bead to another as she performed her latest novena. Estrellita had little doubt as to the subject of her prayers.

"Mama."

Her mother held a finger towards her in stern warning. Estrellita sat down on the tiled floor, crossed her legs and waited.

The contrasting images that her mother had affixed to her walls bore mute witness to their drama. Crucifixes and pictures of saints were interspersed between fearsome papier-mâché masks known as lechones. People wore the masks during carnival time in the Cibao region, and oddly, their twisted and frightening features seemed at home among all the iconic imagery.

Estrellita looked up at a portrait of Saint Jude, his arms outstretched, his eyes limpid and beseeching. There was Saint Francis of Assisi, his stigmata graphically depicted, his body posture feminine, his lips an unnatural red. A reproduction of Guido Reni's portrait of the archangel

Michael hung above the bed—he had drawn his sword, and Satan was cowering at his feet.

"Angels and saints, demons and sin, blood and punishment—how about having a little fun some time?" she mumbled under her breath.

She sighed as she watched her mother's lips silently mouthing the Lord's Prayer for the umpteenth time. Things had been desperate for her mother in the past. She had known hunger perhaps a bit too intimately to ever forget it. However, her mother flaunted her suffering, wearing the hardship of her life with a pride Estrellita found difficult to understand. Her mother had told her that without Jesus she would not have survived. Although Estrellita respected her faith, she often wished that her mother would give herself a little more credit. Estrellita believed as much in the human spirit as the holy one.

She watched as her mother pressed her lips to the metallic feet of her crucified saviour, blessed herself and stood up.

Her mother placed her beads inside a small stone box, her actions slow and steeped in ritual. "I'm tired, Estrellita. What do you want?"

"I just wanted to apologize. I didn't mean to hurt you with what I said."

"I'm sorry too. Sometimes I forget how alike we are. How can a stubborn mule fault her babies for being stubborn?"

She took her daughter's hands into her own. "I worry for you and your brother. All I have ever wanted was an easier life for you than the one I have had. I don't know where you're going. I don't know why you turn your nose up at the opportunities that come your way."

"You know exactly where I'm going, or at least where I hope to be one day. It's just that my vision isn't the same as yours. Everything I do is for my music...for us, our family, for our future." Estrellita tried to gently squeeze her passion into her mother's rough hands.

A wistful smile spread across her mother's face as she listened. She reached out and stroked Estrellita's cheek with the back of her hand. "Your dreams," she said. "You don't want to give up on your dreams. Well, nobody does. Do you think that your father and I wanted to give up on ours? Or perhaps you think that we never even had any? Everyone dreams of a bigger life, a shinier one. My ambitions didn't include thirty years of toil in a tobacco factory. I've spent my life rolling a desiccated weed, one that robs people of their ability to breathe. Do you imagine that as a young girl I lay awake at night pining for such things?"

Estrellita shrugged her shoulders and lowered her eyes.

"I dreamed of becoming a doctor," her mother said, "and that must sound as naive to your ears as it does to mine, but that was *my* dream."

"You never told me that before. You never—"

"Shh. It doesn't matter now. Look here." She held her prematurely aged hands up to the light and splayed out her tobacco-yellowed fingers. "The stink and stain of my life's compromise has been tattooed into my very flesh. My own skin reminds me daily of the vast chasm between dreams and reality. I don't want the smell of sulphur to become your legacy. Why won't you give Miguel a chance?"

"Mama, please. We can speak of anything but him, or Jaragua— speaking of giving someone a chance."

"Fine. I don't want to argue anymore."

"I won't give up on myself. I won't settle for less. I'm going to sing my songs. I have a voice. Why can't you hear it?"

"I hear it, Rocket. I know. I see. But life is not a movie or a book. Life is much more insidious. It leeches your hope away one small failure at a time, patiently eroding your dreams until, like your youth, one day it's gone…and all you dream about is a reliable paycheque and eight hours of sleep each night. There comes a time when we must leave childish ways behind us, a time when we must step into the shoes of adulthood."

"Even if those shoes give us blisters and cause us to limp? Even then?"

"Keep a piece of yourself, as I do, locked away," her mother said, ignoring her response. "Take it out from time to time, when God's back is turned. Dust it off; remember it. Because all dreams ever amount to is just a private ache and the vague notion that you once wanted to be somebody else…somebody better."

Estrellita shook her head slowly from side to side and hoped that her mother couldn't see the pity in her eyes, as it would have enraged her. "The world will have to crush what I hold dear. It can stomp my dreams into the ground, but it won't do so without a fight. It won't do so with my blessing."

She didn't blame her mother for her views. Her mother had come from a different time, from an era of oppression and fear. The only thing Estrellita feared was the prospect of having reached the end of her life and realizing that she given up on herself.

Her mother took her by the shoulders and turned her around to face her reflection in a mirror. She cupped a hand under her daughter's chin and proudly displayed her profile. "*This*, Estrellita, this is the greatest dream of countless men. A woman's beauty is more precious to a man than all the pieces of paper in all the universities of the world. It's more treasured than her knowledge of dead painters, gay poets and five-syllable words. It eclipses her station in life. He covets it. It's a commodity, a bargaining chip. However, it's a fleeting one, one that will tarnish with age, and unlike silver, its lustre can never be reclaimed. Use what God has blessed you with. Marry well."

Estrellita frowned at her mother's words and wondered how such a strong woman could still harbour such weak views. "I'am going to use what God gave me...my voice," she said. "And let me tell you something I know about marrying well. Let me tell you something about Miguel Ortiz. The only reason why that narcissistic moron is even remotely interested in me is because I said something to him that no other female has ever said before. I said *no*. Once his ego was satisfied, I would be nothing more than another receptacle for his royal seed."

"Watch your mouth. I raised you better than that."

The sound of a car horn in the street abruptly ended their conversation. Estrellita ran to the open bedroom window and stuck her head out. "Manny, basta ya. I'm coming," she yelled down at her bandmates.

She kissed her mother on both cheeks. "Don't worry so much about me; everything is going to work out fine, for all of us."

"Go, Rocket...merengue tonight for your memories tomorrow."

"Try to stop me."

Estrellita turned away and quickly left the room before either one of them could say something that would ruin the moment. She took the stairs two at a time, anxious to embrace the heat of the night, the heat of her passion.

HOMECOMING

Jaragua sped through Sierra de Baoruco National Park, leaving a thick dust cloud in his wake. Since leaving Higuey, he had travelled along the coast. He had ridden through the sugarcane stronghold of La Romana, through San Pedro de Macorís—a seaside town that had given the world more Major League Baseball stars than any other place on earth—past expansive coconut groves, groomed beaches and the all-inclusive resorts of Boca Chica and Playa de Guayacanes.

He had stolen a few hours' sleep in Santo Domingo before pressing on through Bani, Azua and Barahona. He had pushed his protesting motorbike beyond its limitations, and the smoking exhaust pipe was burning his calf through his jeans.

He patted the bike's fuel tank as if he were encouraging an exhausted but loyal steed. "Not far now."

Squat plump cacti erupted out of the vast limestone plains like acne on a teenager's cheek. In the distance, the sun's rays scorched the pine forests of the Sierra de Neiba mountain range and spread across the surface of Lago Enriquillo like an oil slick.

A pack of emaciated dogs chased him from the last whitewashed settlement between him and his hometown. Their yelping sounded like a warning. He swerved around a gang of muscle-bound rhinoceros iguanas. They had planted themselves in the middle of the road, their ruby-red eyes scowling defiantly at him from beneath the fringe of their black mohawks.

Sick beasts

When Jimaní finally emerged from behind its shower curtain of heat and humidity, any hope Jaragua harboured dissolved like sugar beneath a tropical rain. He twisted the bike's throttle and bombed down into the destruction that the Soleil River had left behind. He grinded the bike to a gravel-spewing halt and dropped it on the bleached ground, where it wheezed like a flogged and lathered horse.

He staggered towards a bone-white slash of desolation, towards the barrios of La Quarto, Sector las 50, Batey Bomba and Sector Negro. He stared in horror and sank down to his knees.

"It's all gone...everything."

The floodwaters had eradicated so many lives—it had destroyed everything that the community had built together, their memories, the past, the future, all of it flushed away.

He felt guilty for having no tears to shed—he was numb. He ignored the sound of footsteps behind him and continued to gape at the bleak landscape with lidless eyes. Even when a shadow laid a gentle hand on his shoulder and spoke his name, he could not move. The voice was from another time, a naive time, one he could barely remember.

"Milka," he said, finally turning his head and looking up at the first girl he ever kissed. "You're alive."

He stood up, drew her to him and hugged her with an intensity that surprised them both. He felt her stiffen and then just as quickly relax into the comfort of his once-familiar embrace.

"And my family?" he asked, whispering the question into her ear.

"I'm sorry," she said, shaking her head and pulling away from him. "I don't know anything. There have been reports of survivors, but in all the chaos, victims were flown to different hospitals, some to Haiti. Nobody knows much except from the bodies that were recovered."

"And what of your family?" he asked.

"No, they did not survive...this." Her dark brown eyes searched his face for an answer he could not provide.

"I'm so sorry for you."

Two low-flying army helicopters passed over them and flew off in the direction of Haiti, where the destruction and death had been just as catastrophic.

Jaragua and Milka walked silently together. Jaragua struggled with the surreal morbidity that surrounded him. Clothes hung limply from the branches of naked trees—they looked like melted timepieces from a Dali painting. Houses that had weathered the storm unscathed peered down at him from atop mounds of eroded earth like smug bullfrogs squatting on magic toadstools. He could only imagine what it must have been like for the lucky ones, people clinging to the roofs of their houses and watching as their neighbours were swept away to their deaths.

The closer they got to the epicentre of destruction, the stronger the stench of decaying flesh became. Jaragua placed a hand over his mouth. They watched men in uniform digging shallow pits and lining them with rotting cadavers, mass graves that punctuated the obscurity of the villagers' lives. He looked over at the town's desecrated cemetery. Coffins stuck out of the ground like loose teeth in a busted jaw. Some of them were smashed open, allowing scavengers to dispute ownership of their gruesome contents. He stepped aside as a Red Cross truck lumbered past them, its sides emblazoned with the international symbol of goodwill.

"Such disrespect. Mother Nature is a sadistic bitch," he said. He wiped sweat from his forehead with the back of his hand and scowled at the carnage.

"You can see how high the water was there," Milka said.

He looked at the brown tidemark that encircled the area. It ran around everything he could see—dwellings, street signs, utility poles. It was like the dirty ring left inside a bathtub after a rough and tumble boy had finished bathing.

"This whole area must have been under water," he said.

"Some people drowned in their own beds. They put bars on their windows to keep themselves safe, and that's what killed them."

A bare-chested young boy approached them. He was pushing a wheelbarrow full of fruits, ice and milk.

He flashed an infectious entrepreneurial grin and pointed at his goods. "Morir soñando?"

"How would you like to die dreaming?" Jaragua asked her, referring to the drink's name.

"And who wouldn't?" she replied, offering him a weak smile.

"Two please, muchacho."

Jaragua and Milka sat together on the gritty stairs of an abandoned colmado and watched in silence as the boy prepared their refreshments with gusto and flair. He used a wooden spoon to mash up some lemons and oranges. He added sugar and ice to the pulpy juice and then chilled it by tossing the concoction back and forth between two wide-mouth mason jars.

"Bravo," Milka said.

Thus encouraged, the boy splashed milk and ice into another jar and sent the mixture flying through the air with a cavalier disregard for spillage. He combined the milk with the fruit juice and sugar, repeated his maraca mambo, strained the beverage into two plastic cups, speared a straw into each one as if he were trying to injure them and then handed them to his customers.

"Dreams die slowly, and that is how you must enjoy these," the boy said, and smiled.

"Dreams never die. They become much-loved songs that you have somehow forgotten the lyrics to," Milka said.

Jaragua accepted the cold drinks and handed the boy twenty dollars.

"Señor, this is American dollars. I cannot make change for this."

"It's a tip. For the entertainment," he said, taking a long pull on the straw, "and for the best morir soñando I've ever had."

Not having to be told twice, the boy jammed the bill into the front pocket of his jeans and grabbed his wheelbarrow by its handles, determined to make good on his escape before the loco stranger regained his senses.

"Thank you, señor and señora. Enjoy your batidas. My name is Horacio, and I have to go now. Adios!" he said, bouncing his rickety cart over the same ruts and stones that had brought him to his good fortune.

"See ya, Horacio." Milka giggled as she watched him go.

"That was nice of you," she said to Jaragua. "I know his family. He's a good kid."

Jaragua nodded and sipped at his drink.

"What will you do now? What are your plans?" she asked him.

"The hospitals, every one of them from here to Haiti and from Haiti to hell. If any of my family has survived, I will find them. And if they haven't, I will bury them. They deserve a cross in the dirt...having lived so long in it."

"And after that?"

He shrugged and thought about Estrellita.

"It was nice to see you again," he said, and kissed her cheek. "I have to go."

"I heard you were in prison again," she said as he walked away.

"I was."

"And now?"

"And now?" he repeated without turning around. "I'm not."

Milka watched him go, watched him until he was a smudge of brown on the rim of a porcelain coffee cup. She was thinking about how a boy became a man and all that was lost in the transition.

THE SPORT OF KINGS

IGNACIO WATCHED ONE OF his toughest roosters leap into the air and try to drive his spur through his rival's eye. The fight was a bloody one, and over a hundred men were crammed into Puerto Plata's premiere cockpit to witness mayhem and scream until they were hoarse. The place smelled of hangovers, fried cheese and cigar smoke.

"Come on, Cuban Pete," Ignacio said. He threw looping haymakers and sharp uppercuts into the smoky air, reacting to every lick that his bird absorbed or delivered.

The exhausted gamecocks circled each other warily, and despite their wounds, neither would surrender. When the birds clashed yet again, the crowd roared its approval. They pecked hard and deliberately at each other's head, each trying to snag some loose skin and yank his opponent off balance.

Ignacio dangled his arms over the low circular wall that ringed the cockpit, his bony fists clutching wads of sweaty pesos. "Now, Cuban Pete, sidestep and strike. Strike!" he screamed, his voice barely audible above the surge of emotion that swelled all around him.

Cuban Pete's left eye was swollen shut, and Ignacio knew that even if his fighter survived the match, his days in the pit were over. A blinker was good for nothing save the soup pot.

The other rooster lunged forward and drove his spur through Cuban Pete's back. The sharp point pierced his lung. A communal moan arose from those in the stands who had bet blue, while everyone else cheered the brutal blow. Ignacio's fighter went down, and his opponent wasted no time in mounting his adversary and using his sharp beak to perform the coup de grâce. The victorious rooster continued to peck at Cuban

103

Pete's head until there was nothing beneath his talons but a twitching mass of feathers and gore.

Ignacio closed his eyes and hung his head. He could hear his bird rattling and dying. It was moments like that when the money in his hands made him feel sick. It was moments like that, that made him feel as if he had betrayed himself as well as a friend.

The stands erupted in cheers and curses as the winning rooster crowed and strutted about the pit. A handler approached Ignacio and presented him with Cuban Pete's quivering remains.

The man placed a fist on his chest. "He was a brave one. Big heart."

"Thank you," Ignacio said.

He handed the man some money and pointed across the ring at a burly young Dominican wearing a white tank top and a winning grin. Ignacio could see the butt of a handgun sticking out of the man's waistband. By the end of the afternoon, many men would have gambled away their week's wages. Making eye contact with a stranger on the opposite side of the pit, and through a series of gestures, cement their barters. Only a desperado would renege on a bet. Breaching the palabra de gallero had serious consequences.

Ignacio cradled his dead rooster in the crook of his arm and headed towards the exit. He needed some air. He walked over to his sunburned truck and placed Cuban Pete inside a canvas sack.

"We all become our fathers in the end, eh, Pete? Tonight I will honour you by making a special sancocho," he said.

The adrenaline-rich meat of a rooster who had died in battle was famous for infusing Dominican stew with an especially hearty flavour, and all galleros agreed that the bittersweet meal fuelled their desire to be between their woman's legs—and perhaps that explained the clusters of crones who waited outside the gallera, hoping to purchase a dead rooster.

"Well, you will be the last one to fight for me this day," he said, peering through the wire mesh of Mr. Mestizo's coop.

Ignacio had trained him hard over the past three weeks, and he was anxious to see if the promise the bird had displayed during his conditioning would translate in the pit. He had given the bird a full three days' rest and had loaded his system with carbohydrates for the last forty-eight hours. He found that bringing a gamecock to point on a particular day was easy as long as the bird had been properly cared for. On fight day, all of his roosters were ready to go, many of them feeling so frustrated from the inactivity and enforced celibacy that they were positively spoiling for a scrap.

He poured a tablespoon of strong black coffee into Mr. Mestizo's water dish.

"Not long now, my dancer."

He took a bottle of warm water from the cab of his truck and walked towards a mature mammee apple tree. He plucked one of the large brown fruits from a low bough and sat cross-legged in the tree's shade. He unbuttoned his shirt, cut into the sweet fruit and watched a bleating goat shamble past him, dragging its frayed tether behind it as if it had escaped a hanging.

"Perdón, señor."

Ignacio turned his head and looked up into the smiling face of a woman large enough to have supplied himself and all of his birds with shade.

"Si, señora?" he said, considering how someone so big had managed to sneak up on him.

"Me llama Georgina, umm, me turista," she said, stabbing a finger into her own chest. "Que…umm, what I mean is—" she stammered, while kneading her hands together like pasty lumps of bread dough.

"Are you American? Because I speak English. My name is Ignacio."

"Oh yes," she said, sighing her relief. "I'm American, from Washington—not D.C, west coast. I teach, so…I'm a teacher." Her smile pushed her cheeks so far up her face that her eyes almost disappeared. "I was just wondering what exactly is going on in there. It all sounds so very exciting and curious."

"What we're doing here today, señora, is fighting our cocks."

She took a step backwards and clutched her handbag a little tighter. "Your what?"

"Our cocks. We are testing them to see whose is the strongest, the bravest. I'm resting my cock before the next battle." Ignacio smiled up at her without exposing his teeth.

The woman frowned in disgust and took another step backwards, her lips forming themselves around harsh words. She was certain that she had never met a cruder man in her entire life, and she was just about to say so when a shrill crowing arose from inside the cockpit.

"Oh…oh," she said, and smiled. "You mean chickens. You're fighting chickens, like the Mexicans do. Is that correct?"

"Por favor Dios," he said, raising his eyes heavenward and pressing the palms of his hands together. "No, señora. These are gamecocks, not chickens, and to call these valiant birds a name that is a synonym for cowardice is insulting."

"I meant no offence." She looked around for her husband and wondered if she were in danger.

"Have you ever seen a cockfight? You know they still hold them in your country and not just the Mexicans."

"Me? Oh no, no. Never. I mean, it's fine for you and, well, others. If it's your culture, I mean to say, then it's understandable. However, I just think that the whole thing is rather cruel." She nodded her head up and down and frowned at him in mild disapproval.

"Would you consider your famous Presidents George Washington, Thomas Jefferson or Andrew Jackson to be cruel men, señora?"

"Well no, of course I don't, but what does that have to do—"

"All of those men raised and fought game fowl. Cockfighting is the world's oldest spectator sport. It's the sport of kings, of emperors and sultans."

"Really? Is all that true?"

"Hand to God. It used to be called the royal pastime, and it was enthusiastically embraced by Queen Elizabeth, Charles the Second, earls, lords and ladies. Henry the Eighth even had a royal cockpit built at his palace in England. The Chinese and the Romans loved it. There are records dating as far back as the sixth century heralding the merits of the sport...of the birds."

"But why? They're just chick— roosters for God's sake. What's the big deal? Is it for the gambling?" She pressed her floppy sunhat down over a mass of springy red curls.

"Do you have time for a story?" he asked her.

She looked at her watch but didn't read the dial. "Yes, I think so."

"Once there was a powerful Greek general named Themistocles, and he was fighting a great war with Persia. One day, this mighty warlord witnessed two game fowl doing battle by the side of the road, and he saw in them the most desirable of attributes, traits that any warrior would be proud to possess. He saw courage, tenacity, a never-say-die instinct that transcended species and spoke to his heart. He instructed his troops to watch the birds, learn from them, to try to emulate their fearlessness. Afterwards, the Greeks went on to conquer the Persian army.

"Upon his return to Athens, the General had an amphitheatre built in order to pursue cockfighting, and he passed a law making attendance at such events mandatory for all young men. He hoped that the birds would teach future warriors about fortitude...about fighting on even when you know you are going to lose, when you know that you are going to die. And remember, señora, the General could have used any animals to teach these lessons—wolves, tigers, bears, they were all available. Do you think that he chose the humble rooster by accident?"

"Lions, tigers and bears, oh my," a voice said.

Ignacio looked up and saw a lanky man approaching. He wore a Hawaiian shirt and a sneer.

"Oh, Dan, I've been waiting for you," Georgina said. "This man's name is Ignacio, and he was just telling me the most fascinating story."

"Yeah, I caught the tail end of 'er. It sounded pretty wild, baby, but not half as wild as I'm gonna git if I miss my tee-off time." He mimed a golf swing and hitched a thumb over one shoulder. "Let's mosey."

"It was a pleasure meeting you, señor," Georgina said, reaching down and shaking hands with Ignacio. "I don't think that I will ever look at a box of Cornflakes the same way."

"Excuse me?" Ignacio said.

"Oh, it's cultural, I guess. It's a breakfast cereal with a rooster on the box. A rather iconic symbol, I would say."

"Fore!" Dan said, shading his eyes with one hand and watching the trajectory of an imaginary ball.

Georgina rolled her eyes and sighed like the long-suffering mother of a hyperactive child.

"Hasta luego, mi amigo," she said, and smiled at Ignacio.

"Hasta luego, bonita."

Ignacio checked his watch, got to his feet and walked back to his truck. It was time to heel his new bird for his first bout.

He dropped the tailgate of his truck and pulled the bird out of his coop. The rooster was vibrating with energy. He was as sharp as any bird he had ever trained, his alert eyes shifting menacingly towards the sounds of battle arising from the gallera.

"The waiting is over, Mr. Mestizo, and you are on point. You even scare me," he said, opening a plastic toolbox.

"You ready for me, Ignacio?" a short thin man said. He had a blue butcher's coat over his clothes and a Brugal rum cap pulled down low on his forehead.

Ignacio could smell peanuts and Old Spice cologne. "Right on time, Carlos. I was just about to heel him."

The man took a seat on the groaning tailgate and spoke. "Not like you to be missing the action. Many good matches in there today."

"Yeah, I just needed some air, think a little bit."

"Hey, I'm sorry for your loss today. He was a fine one, Pete was."

"Thank you. Anyway, I would like to introduce you to Mr. Mestizo." Ignacio held the rooster towards the other man.

"Ahh, he looks magnificent. Dubbed and trimmed," Carlos said, referring to the practice of shearing the bird's comb and wattle and plucking out the leg, abdomen and vent feathers.

"He'll make weight," Ignacio said.

He turned the bird over in his hand and used a penknife to whittle his natural spurs down to stubs. Carlos watched as he heated up a red glue stick and applied the hot adhesive to a pair of sharp spurs.

"Do you remember when postizas were made from turtle shell?" Carlos asked.

"Yeah, my father used them all the time, but with the infections and everything...I suppose plastic is better, and they still look like tortoise shell anyway." Ignacio pressed the postizas' cups firmly down over the bird's stumps.

"The rooster your boy here is fighting today," Carlos said, shaking his head slowly back and forth. "A tough bastard, my friend. Five straight victories now, and decisive ones at that."

"So I guess we are going to win a lot of money by betting on Mr. Mestizo," Ignacio said. He wrapped strips of medical tape around his bird's legs.

"Yes, if he wins. Mucho."

"This one is a deadly dancer, Carlos. Wait and see. Bet blue."

Ignacio twisted lengths of dental floss up, over and around the bird's new weapons. He wiggled the spikes, scowled and eyed them suspiciously from different angles.

"He is well heeled, señor," Carlos said, looking at the older man with respect.

"They'll do, I suppose." Ignacio handed the bird over to Carlos.

"Don't worry so much. This one is a knot of muscle and blood. I can feel it. He will do fine," Carlos said, trying to ease his friend's mind with words he didn't believe.

"One second." Ignacio bent down and kissed his bird on top of the head. "Mambo."

Ignacio took his ringside seat, twisted his fingers into pretzels and awaited the action.

The handlers entered the ring with the two birds encased in white cloth bags. Ignacio watched closely as they weighed each bird.

"Three and half pounds for both," Carlos called out.

A murmur of approval rippled through the boisterous crowd.

Ignacio could hear some talk of numbers; however, the heavy betting would not begin until after the men had gotten a look at the fighters. The handlers cleared the pit and took the roosters out of their bags. A third man entered the ring, carrying a mona, a pawn of a bird used solely to enrage and frustrate the fighters. In a form of ritualized teasing, the man beaked the mona with each bird, the cocks responded by straining against their captor's hands and crowing loudly.

The crowd erupted, placing their bets in the usual chaotic yet somehow eloquent language of the Dominican gallero. The odds heavily favoured Mr. Mestizo's death.

Ignacio only hesitated for a second before turning around in his seat, throwing up some fingers, nodding, pointing, yelling and putting every peso he had on the line.

The noise in the arena climbed several decibels as the birds hit the ground. The ferocity of Mr. Mestizo's attack stunned even Ignacio.

The young rooster charged his more experienced opponent. He leapt high into the air, pivoted and drove his spike into his challenger's back. The rooster absorbed the blow and lashed out with an intensity that demanded respect. This was going to be a war.

"*Venga azul!*"

"*Blanco, blanco!*"

As the fight raged on and both roosters began to drip blood, the veteran turned away from the battle and began to run.

"No. It's a trick," Ignacio said.

Everybody knew that the wounded bird was employing a crafty technique known as wheeling. A losing bird would sometimes bolt in the hope that his tormentor would give chase. If he did, the wheeler would stop short, spin around and drive his spur into the unsuspecting bird's head, killing him instantly.

Mr. Mestizo didn't attempt to pursue the wounded bird. He simply stood in the middle of the twenty-foot ring as if he owned it, his eyes focused on the wheeler, and it might have been Ignacio's imagination, but he was sure that he saw contempt in his rooster's eye.

Finally, the other bird, tired of the ruse, returned to the fight. He blinked, shook his head in an effort to clear the blood from his eyes and charged. It was a desperate and brave attack.

What Mr. Mestizo did next Ignacio never could have taught him. However, nobody would ever forget the speed with which his gallo avoided the attack or the grace with which he leapt into the air or the strength he used to drive his spur through his opponent's neck.

The crowd cheered the incredible maneuver as Mr. Mestizo sunk his talons into the dying bird's head, pinned it to the mat and crowed triumphantly.

"Mambo," Ignacio said.

He slid over the pit wall, picked up his bird and licked the blood from his face. He mumbled his gratitude as men pounded his back and congratulated him on his win.

"Yes, yes, I know you are," he cooed as the excited bird continued to roar and thump his chest. "And you did, and you will. Of course, yes, all of it, my mambo king."

He had wagered ten thousand pesos at eight-to-one odds. He had won over two thousand U.S. dollars in eleven minutes, in a country where the average person earned fifty dollars a week.

Ignacio left the gallera with his trouser pockets bulging with coin and his chest swelling with pride. He stroked Mr. Mestizo's back as he walked towards his truck, soothing and reassuring the stressed bird. He returned him to his coop, sprayed him with cool water and placed a thick sliver of fresh mango beside him.

"You're still trembling," he said, rubbing a finger under his beak. "Don't worry. That's normal. Remember, to deny your own fear is to forfeit the chance to conquer it."

He settled himself behind the wheel of his truck and patted the bag containing Cuban Pete's carcass.

He drove away, filtering his way through Puerto Plata's narrow streets. He turned up the volume on the radio and smiled when a bachata song oozed through the cab. Nothing could ruin his mood.

"At least it's Frank Reyes."

He mouthed some lyrics. *Today I am going to be happy, with or without you.*

He looked over at the bag beside him and smiled gently. "Vaya con Dios, Cuban Pete."

The late afternoon sun felt good to him as he made his way towards the coast. He passed a row of bunker-style shops, their concrete facades slathered in political slogans and adverts:

DRINK COKE

RE-ELECT HIPOLITO

VOTE FOR LEONEL

EL PRESIDENTE BEER

He waved at a mischievous horde of shoeshine boys and laughed at a pretty girl feigning indifference to the posturing of a local lothario astride a motochonco. The everyday scene suddenly appeared so idyllic to him...so luminous. He watched street vendors hawk their mountains of green coconuts and ripe pineapples and their sweet cane juice. He watched as others danced to merengue or sat in the shade, sipping cold drinks. He grinned at a man pushing a wheelbarrow; it contained the bottom half of an enormous yellowfin tuna.

Ignacio had a champion gallo whose heart was as big as his strut, and destiny had just unbuttoned her blouse and invited him to suckle on one of her milk-laden breasts...and who was he to deny her?

THE CHERRY HUNTER

MAXIMO SAT ON THE cracked vinyl of his hospital bed and surveyed the deck of playing cards spread out before him. "Go fish," he said.

With bored amusement, he watched his sister's inefficient attempts at cheating. It was even funnier to him that her stolen knowledge rarely helped her win. He looked away for a moment, giving her the opportunity to peek under some of the cards.

His stump had healed quickly over the last few weeks, and he had earned the hospital staff's respect with the quick mastery of his crutches and the eventual return of his grin.

He looked towards the doorway as Dr. Sanchez entered the dormitory. There was an overweight man hovering over him, mopping sweat from his flushed face and jabbering away.

"Children, I have amazing news. Do either of you remember Mr. Kirschjager?" the Doctor asked, a smile breaching the stubble and fatigue on his face.

Before either could answer, the big man was coming towards them. He looked like a myopic sumo wrestler at an eating contest.

"Mein Gott, kinder," he said in his native German before switching to Spanish. "Children, children, thanks be to God you both are alive, that you have been spared that which many were not." As he spoke, his thick lips sprayed them with a fine mist of spittle.

He embraced Lourdes, smothering her tiny frame with his huffing presence, his blood sausage fingers clutching and grasping at her with a stifling affection. He released Lourdes and peered down at Maximo from behind a pair of thick eyeglasses.

"And Maximo. My poor boy, my poor brave boy. Your parents

would have been so proud of you, of the way you sacrificed yourself to save your sister," he gushed, placing the back of his meaty hand against Maximo's cheek.

"I don't know you. I've never met you before," Maximo said.

"Me neither," Lourdes said. She crossed her thin arms and jutted out her bottom lip in support of her sibling.

"Well of course not, and it's not so surprising. You were both so young when I left. Why, Lourdes was barely out of her poo pants. However, I was very close friends with your parents. I am your Uncle Ollie, an honourary one…no relations." He folded his hands like a friar about to say grace. "At that time, before my own mother's illness called me home to Deutschland, I was active in the church, involved with charitable work on the island. This is how I came to know your family. And speaking of which, has anyone heard from your older brother Jaragua?"

Both children silently shook their heads back and forth.

Ollie looked sideways at the Doctor, and seeing that he still had the Cuban's trust, he continued his hammy performance.

"I'm only here to offer my support and assistance. It's a miracle that I found either of you in all the madness that has transpired since the flood, but find you I have. I can offer you both a better life, a future. Rehabilitation for you, Maximo, schooling for Lourdes. A home."

Dr. Sanchez smiled as he listened to Ollie speak.

Maximo stared at the blubbering man with suspicion. His parents had never mentioned an Uncle Ollie before, and he knew that his father would rather die than accept charity.

But he knows about Jaragua.

"Perhaps you don't remember this man, Maximo," the Doctor said. "However, his arrival must be viewed as a blessing. Many children live day-to-day on the streets. We have few options, and you need to consider Lourdes, consider how vulnerable such a young girl would be out there with no one to look after her."

"I will look after her. I always have," Maximo said, clenching his jaw.

Ollie held the flat of his hand towards the Doctor. "Oh Mein Gott. Nobody could ever question that, Maximo. It's just that now you may require a little help, that's all, just a little help. I'm only doing what I know your parents would have wanted, God rest their souls." He blessed himself as he spoke; the movement looked more like an affliction than a sign of respect.

"Our parents are still alive," Maximo said.

Ollie frowned gently at the boy, his face a perfect mask of empathy and fatherly concern. "Of course they are, Maximo. Nobody meant to imply anything to the contrary. I have no doubt that your parents have survived, that they shall be knocking on my door one day soon and asking to see their babies. But until that day comes, I feel it is my duty and my privilege to take care of you both. All I need is your permission."

"It's best for everyone," Dr. Sanchez said.

Maximo looked over at Lourdes and raised his eyebrows slightly. She smiled back at him and clapped her small hands together.

"Okay, we'll go, but it's only until my parents are found," Maximo said.

"Excellent, excellent. Don't worry. Everything is going to be splendid, you will see," Ollie said. "Doctor, thank you for all your assistance. I shall care for these two as if they were of my very own loin. Now, as the children are making ready, there are papers for which I am to sign, yes?"

"Yes, there are, and there is a long line for available beds around here. I don't see why we cannot all go together, right now."

"I approve, Doctor, yes, yes. I am in total agreement with this wisdom. Come, Maximo," Ollie said, handing him his crutches. "And you, sweet Lourdes." He bent down and placed a wet kiss on her forehead, a kiss that lingered a moment longer than was prudent. Ollie silently cursed his stupidity and smiled innocently at the Doctor.

An hour later, Ollie left the hospital with a handful of official forms and two children he had never seen before.

They crossed the parking lot and arrived at a Chevrolet Silverado with a crew cab. Maximo could see the sun's reflection in the truck's gleaming metallic paint. To him, it looked like it was capable of breathing fire, an iron-plated dragon with a grill full of sharp teeth and a voracious appetite.

Bleep, Bleep.

"What's that?" Lourdes asked.

"This? Oh, this is my little clicky," Ollie said. "It unlocks the doors on my truck. Do you like it? Would you like to try it?" He held his keychain out for her approval.

Lourdes took hold of Maximo's hand, pressed her face against his arm and shook her head.

"A bit shy, are we?" Ollie said, thinking her to be maddeningly coy.

He opened the truck's doors, helped the children into the back and then wedged himself behind the steering wheel.

"Comfy cozy?" he asked, and started the engine.

He slid the windows down and waved goodbye to Dr. Sanchez and a couple of nurses in front of the hospital. "Wave to them, children. Happy smiles too. That's it. Bye-bye to your old lives, never to return." He waved with panache, the gesture reminiscent of a great painter signing a masterpiece.

Ollie accelerated down the road with reckless abandon. He felt elated, untouchable. The trap had been set, sprung and two brand new bunnies snared. He couldn't help but feel pleased with himself. He was certain that he could have become a respected actor in another life—a character actor, of course; he had no illusions regarding his looks. After all, he thought, actors were nothing more than skilled liars, and he had spent a lifetime perfecting his lies, polishing the facade he presented to the outside world, an act that had saved him from ruin on more than one occasion and in more than one country.

He adjusted the rear-view mirror so that he could see Lourdes in it. A real little princess this one is, he thought. He ran a sluglike tongue over his horse teeth. She was so precocious, so flirtatious. He had caught her sly glances, her carnal smile.

She knows she's hot

He watched as she cupped a hand over her brother's ear and whispered something to him.

"Ollie, do you have something to drink? Some water?" Maximo asked, squeezing his sister's hand.

Ollie whirled in his seat with the agility of a startled rhinoceros. "Mr. Kirschjager!" he bellowed, his big voice filling the truck's cab with its hostility. "It's Mr. Kirschjager from now on. Don't try me, boy. Do you understand?" he snarled, his face turning a violent red.

Maximo was so shocked that he simply nodded his head in mute compliance.

"Here," Ollie said, passing over a plastic bottle of water. "But *you* may continue to call me Ollie—only you," he said to Lourdes, his voice becoming gentle and playful.

He turned onto the highway, got the vehicle up to speed and set the cruise control. It was a long way to Puerto Plata, and he wanted to arrive before dark. He rearranged his large frame and settled in for the long haul. His eyes quickly returned to the mirror and the children's reflection in it. He frowned as he watched Maximo hold the big bottle of water for Lourdes to drink.

The boy is so protective of her, he thought. He hoped that he wouldn't have to dispose of him. Crippled or not, the boy was capable of earning his keep, and as long as he learned his place and stayed in it, Ollie saw no need to kill him.

As for his little Palomita—as he had heard Maximo call her—he had special plans for her. All he needed to do was exercise a bit more self-restraint this time. He had damaged his last little pony beyond repair and was unable to realize a profit from it.

"Thank the saints for Third World countries and natural disasters, eh, children? Makes my life a lot easier. Did you know that in English my surname translates to 'the cherry hunter'?" he asked, and laughed loudly. The sound was terrifying. It was too high-pitched, too feminine, to have emitted from such a burly man.

Maximo put his arm around Lourdes and looked out the tinted

window. The landscape was a blurry undulating ribbon of cocoa foam and green patterns. Lourdes cried softly as the truck hurtled down the highway towards the Amber Coast and whatever fate awaited them there.

AT THE CARWASH, YEAH!

Estrellita lashed her head from side to side, her long black hair falling across her face like a widow's veil. She worked her guiro until her arms ached and her bronzed skin glistened with moisture. With every second she spent onstage, she felt as if she were bridging the chasm between her dreams and the reality of her mundane existence.

Her band's popularity had continued to grow with every performance, and the car wash was jammed with dancing couples. The men dressed in cotton slacks and loose colourful shirts. The women wore tight loud outfits and spiked heels. She finished her song and smiled down at the group of young men who followed her from gig to gig. Her bandmates called them her stable.

"Someone I know, someone special to me, loves bachata, and I love merengue," she said. "I think that this song is as close as the two can get without quarrelling. From the incredible Juan Luis Guerra and Four-Forty, I give you 'Bachata Rosa.'"

Jaragua leaned against a wall and watched her from the shadows. He sipped his third rum, marvelled at his girlfriend's performance and ignored the mild jealousy he was feeling.

She finished the song, bowed low and accepted the thunderous applause.

"Now, you know that there can be no Rocket without the Cinnamon Roosters," she said, directing the audience's appreciation towards her bandmates and winking at her sax player Manny.

"Our last song this evening is the most beautiful song ever written. It's about a man's love for his woman," she said, eliciting wolf whistles and cheers from the crowd. "It's an old song from an old merenguero, one who fell off the face of the earth before I was born. You may not remember the name Ignacio dos Santos, or even his band Hacienda de Ritmo; however, I'm certain that you will recall his greatest hit, 'Estrellita Luminosa.'"

The band launched into their final number.

At the mention of the song, Jaragua looked down at the exact words tattooed across the back of his hand and remembered when he had given her the nickname. It was on her birthday, and he would never forget the way she looked that night or the excitement in her voice as she leapt from his arms and turned up the volume on his stolen radio. She had told him how much the song meant to her, while swaying her hips in sympathy with the melody. She had danced naked in front of him, her raw sensuality bewitching him, the holy glow of seventeen papaya-scented candles flickering across her body like an aurora borealis worshiping a rising constellation.

"From now on, *you* are my Estrellita Luminosa," he had said that night, and despite her mild protests, the nickname had stuck.

He closed his eyes and listened to her sing the familiar lyrics. Her voice had the ability to simultaneously wound and heal. It could conjure dormant memories, prickle one's flesh and cause the listener to fall madly in love with her—if only for the duration of a song.

As he waited for her to leave the stage, he downed his drink, chewed on a chunk of ice and allowed his thoughts to return to his family. After a frustrating search of the hospitals and shelters, he had grieved his loss, dulling his pain with drugs, prostitutes and drunken brawls. He smiled ruefully at the memory of one administrative minion who had tried to help him. She had been staring at him in wide-eyed horror from behind a twisted wire cage like some terrified lionkeeper, towers of yellowed paper files threatening to devour her alive.

Hopeless

He pressed his lips to the wooden crucifix that dangled around his neck from a leather cord. "If it is your will," he whispered.

He had no explanation for the sudden emergence of his long-forgotten faith. Once the Virgin of Altagracia had ignored his prayers, he thought that he would have once again directed his wrath towards God. Instead, he had purchased a cheap necklace and slipped the talisman over his head with a sense of relief.

Shaking the thoughts from his mind, he looked up and saw Estrellita making her way through the fawning crowd. He moved to intercept her.

"Excuse me, señor," she said, avoiding eye contact.

As she began to brush past him, he reached out and took hold of her wrist.

She looked down at his hand. "Estrellita Luminosa," she said, reading his tattoo.

"Jaragua," she said sadly, and looked up into his face.

"Estrellita."

He pulled her into his strong arms, and their mouths met with all the urgency of uncertainty, their lips expressing the depth of their yearning. The power and silence of their kiss saying more than any words ever could. They embraced each other tightly and whispered the words they had dreamed of speaking for far too long.

"Come," he said, leading her to an empty table.

"I tried to visit you in Higuey," she said, "but they turned me away. Then the riot was all over the news, and, oh God, Jaragua, the flood, your family."

He told her all that had happened to him since they had last been together, leaving out the parts he figured she didn't need to know. She ran a finger across his new tattoo and looked into his eyes, eyes that stared back at the world with a violence and doom she would never see.

"I'm so sorry. Poor little Lourdes and Maximo...your parents. Maybe they survived. Maybe—" she said before swallowing the rest of her words. Thousands had perished in the flood, and she didn't want to offer him any false hope.

"You will always have me," she said. "No matter what happens in this life, I'll stand by you."

He kissed her hands.

She could have anyone she wanted, he thought. He felt humbled by her devotion to him. He had always believed in himself, always knew that he could be more, but nobody else ever had, not until her.

She wrapped her arms around his neck. "Now, what are your plans? Are you here to stay? Tell me that you're going to leave that life behind. Tell me what I need to hear."

She loved him despite his dangerous lifestyle, not because of it, and she had been waiting a long time for him to embrace the strength that she knew was inside him. Her greatest fear was that his perception of what it meant to be a man was unalterable and that it was as different from hers as the worlds they inhabited.

"We have tonight. We have here and now," he said, brushing a loose strand of hair from her face. "I will be going away soon, not far, and we can meet, whenever, wherever. I have a chance, a way for us to have the life we have always wanted, but I have to make some money first. Without it, nothing ever changes. I've never pretended to be something I'm not. The street and all it offers is all I know and, besides you, all I need."

She looked away from him. She had always seen the tragedy with which he led his life, even if she closed her eyes to it. There was an emptiness in the man she loved, a grasping voracious hunger that was simply beyond the power of her influence. It was the thirst of someone who had wallowed in the trough of poverty and never stopped to appreciate the view. The schemes that he whispered into her ear late at night kept her awake long after he had fallen asleep, plans for a future she knew would never arrive, but she admired the hope in his eyes. She would watch the rise and fall of his chest with a sadness born of the realization that a wolf would always answer the howl of other wolves.

"The night is calling, Estrellita," he said, playfully cupping a hand over one ear. "Can you hear it? Do you know what it's saying?"

"No, I can't hear it," she said, and stuck out her bottom lip.

"It's saying merengue...merengue and maybe even a little bachata."

She smiled, giving in to his charms. "Where are you taking me, then?"

"Only to every club in Santiago, where I can dance with the sexiest girl in all of Quisqueya, in all the world."

She jumped up, pulled him to his feet and kissed him.

"I don't care about tomorrow," she said. "You're here now, and we love each other. We're young. The rest of it will be as it will be. Now come on. I want to have some fun."

She took him by the hand and led him into the vibe and hustle of the busy street.

ACROSS THE DIVIDE

IGNACIO LIFTED THE LID off a pot of simmering rice and waved the escaping steam away with his hand. He poked at his concoction with a fork, hoping that his dinner guest would like it.

He had come to his enjoyment of cooking late in life, having been fed by his mother first, his wife second and a rum bottle third. Cooking allowed him to express his creativity, the way music used to. He found that the two arts had many similarities—both were instinctive, primal, and they brought happiness to others. He often thought that a good name for a cookbook would be *Listen to the Flavour*.

He peeled a large yellow and black plantain and then rubbed some crushed lime, chillies and salt into a thick slab of yellowfin tuna.

"A little butter and tarragon," he said aloud, placing a skillet on the stove. "Two minutes either side...perfect. Black pepper to finish."

He had just begun to wonder if his guest had fallen asleep when a timid knock sounded at the door.

Ignacio crossed the room, flung the wooden door open and pointed his chef's knife at Marco. "You're late."

"I had to get this for you." The kid extended a huge pineapple towards Ignacio, his face all but hidden behind its prickly mass.

"Welcome to my home." Ignacio took the offering from him and waved him in with the tip of his knife. "This will be our dessert. Thank you."

Marco took a seat and watched Ignacio toss handfuls of plantains into some hot oil and then slide some fish into a buttered pan.

"I hope you like tuna," Ignacio said.

"Any Caribbean man who doesn't has no right to be living in the islands," the boy said, grinning and inhaling the scent of the cooking fish.

Ignacio spread the food out between them and sat down across from Marco.

"Ting?" he said, offering Marco a Jamaican soft drink made from grapefruits.

"Please. I love them so."

"Now don't be shy, boy. I'm an old man, and you are a growing one. I expect you to eat most of this."

"I'll do my best."

The two men ate in silence.

"My mother used to say that anyone who talked too much at the dinner table was telling the cook that they didn't like the food," Ignacio said.

Marco dropped a fish bone onto his plate and mimed that he was zipping his lips closed.

"Like this," Ignacio said, and laughed.

After dinner, Ignacio chopped the pineapple up and handed Marco a dripping slab.

"Thank you so much for dinner," Marco said, accepting the pineapple. "I don't remember the last time I ate such a fish as him."

"It's nothing," Ignacio said, wondering why he had not invited the kid up sooner.

"Everyone, all the workers, they are saying that Mr. Mestizo is becoming famous, that he is a champion now," Marco said.

"That is all true, my young friend. He's the one all cockers dream about discovering. I love him so much that every time he fights, I feel sick in my stomach and I say this is his last one. But he keeps winning, and who am I to deny him his destiny?"

"How many challengers he has mashed up?"

"Nine. Five of them in the first minute or so. Nobody can believe his moves, his heart."

"Are you going to enter him in the world championships in Santo Domingo?"

Ignacio was well aware of the rapidly approaching competition. It was the biggest of the year, attracting the best cockers in the world. Army brass, famous baseball players, wealthy businessmen, drug lords, all of them would be there, as would their toughest birds—cocks with proven bloodlines and royal pedigrees. It was the World Series of cockfighting, and Ignacio could think of little else.

"One hundred thousand U.S dollars to the winner, Marco, and that's just the prize money. The gambling is legendary. I heard that last year an Arabian oil sheik lost ten million dollars to an American, some baby-faced computer billionaire. Ten million dollars gained and lost in a few minutes of blood and feathers. Of course Mr. Mestizo and I are going. Do you know much about cockfighting?"

Marco hissed air through his teeth. "Who me?" he said. "In Haiti, the fighting rooster is king. It's part of our life. Even our President Aristide, the one who ran away, his symbol is the gamecock. In Haiti, we call him Kok Kolite."

"Yes, I know. But the roosters in Haiti could never stand up to our Dominican ones. Ours are far too strong and ferocious," he said slyly, purposely baiting him.

Marco threw his head back and forced a laugh. "With respect, everyone knows that the bravest most skilled roosters live in Haiti. Everybody knows this." He grinned good-naturedly.

"Let's say that the birds of *this* island are the greatest on the planet," Ignacio said, and touched his pop bottle with Marco's.

Ignacio knew that their conversation was microcosmic, skirting the deeper tensions that existed between the two countries. He still remembered the shame that the dictator Rafael Trujillo had brought down upon his nation after he had come to power. In an irrational response to plummeting sugar prices, he had ordered the army to murder all Haitians living in the Dominican Republic. Over twenty thousand people were hunted down and killed, their bodies hurled into the aptly named Massacre River. The image of thousands of bloated flyblown corpses drifting lazily downstream was one of Ignacio's earliest childhood memories.

"What was your life like back in Haiti? Do you have family waiting on you?" Ignacio asked.

"No. Some cousins, up near Maniche, I think, but I never seen them before."

"What happened to your parents?"

"My father worked the Port-au-Prince docks, loading and unloading cargo ships. It was very hard work, and it broke his body long before was natural. I think I was about seven when he left."

"He left you and your mother?"

"Yes, but not how it sounds. He built a raft from old inner tubes and plywood. He said that he was going to go to Florida and that he would send for us once he was there, that we deserved a better life."

Marco thought about the last time he had seen him. His father had been standing on his leaky raft, waving goodbye, the gentle swell coaxing him away from shore. Marco had sat on the sand with his mother and watched his father's slowly diminishing silhouette until the sea swallowed him up.

"My mother always told me that Agwe would protect him and that one day he would return," he said.

"Who would protect him?"

"Agwe. In my religion, in voodoo, he is known as the master of the sea. He is an Iwa, a deity. We sacrificed a black rooster and offered some strong dark rum and fine Cuban cigars to Agwe. Maybe I will never see my father again, but a mambo once told me that she had seen him. She said that he was walking along the shoreline, in the moonlight. She said that he left a trail of seaweed and shells behind him and that he walked like a zombie," he said matter-of-factly.

Ignacio smiled at the boy's superstitious beliefs and remembered how closely Santería paralleled voodoo, many of their rituals being indistinguishable from each other. He often wondered why those who claimed to believe in gods and goddesses found it so difficult to tolerate different points of view. The ideologies and doctrines varied greatly, the dogmatic rhetoric ranged from repression to freedom, from karma to animal sacrifices; however, it seemed to him that all religions were saying the same thing.

Love thy neighbour

"And your mother?" Ignacio asked.

"Hurricane George took her from me, ripped her right out of my arms and up into the sky along with the roof of our shanty. She didn't even look afraid, just surprised. I been on my own since then."

"I'm sorry."

"No need for sorrow, sir. Baron Samedi beckons to us all. Just some he wants to visit with sooner than others. I offered him a young lamb and some small cakes in her name. I am sure he was pleased. I will see her one day, one happy day."

"Is there someone else, then? A girl?"

Marco grinned and looked down at the floor. "Yeah, she in Cité Soleil," he said. "One day soon, I must go back for her."

"She waits there for your return?"

"Yes, and she working. She only fifteen, but she work twelve, fourteen hours a day peeling them little arunges."

"Them little what?"

"*Ar-un-ges*. You know, tiny bitter ones, them grow up in the Nord Province there. Haitian labour is cheap, so the people are employed to peel them by hand. The skin is left to dry in the hot sun. A carpet of arunges as far as one can see. The smell is wonderful." Marco inhaled as if he were right there. "The work, unfortunately, is not, and the pay is insulting."

"Acres of orange peels? What do they use them for?"

"They make liqueurs from them. Expensive ones. French ones, you understand."

"Yes, I know," Ignacio said, nodding his head, and taking another bite of the pineapple. "So what do you want to do with your life when you return?"

"Return to Haiti? Oh no. I only meant to get my girl. I am doing now what I wish to do with my life. I want to make rubber. I want to learn from you how to make the best rubber I can and make a better life. There is nothing for me back home."

"Words I am happy to hear. You are doing very well here. All you are hoping for is possible."

Ignacio noticed that Marco derived pleasure from the mundane—eating lunch in the shade of a tree with the other men, running down a hill, having a lumpy cot in the corner of a humble shack, having a place to lay his head and read his books. The heart that craved the least in life seemed to be the most content. What was the use of achieving great things if they only left one feeling unfulfilled and yearning for more?

"Marco—"

The lights went out, plunging them into darkness.

"I'll get some candles," Ignacio said, and sighed.

The sheer frequency of blackouts rendered the event unworthy of comment. Ignacio set several half-melted candles on the table; their flickering flames cast eerie shadows around the stone cottage, giving the two men sinister appearances.

"Many workers come and go, Marco, and I cannot fault them for it…an extra peso is just that. However, I have always rewarded loyalty, and you have proven yourself worthy of such reward. I need a man who has an interest in his work, someone who won't be moving on so quickly. I was thinking—"

The sudden squawk and flutter of his roosters prevented Ignacio from finishing his thought. The two men tried to stare through the wall, each unaware that they were holding their breath.

Ignacio had just risen out of his chair when his birds erupted in alarmed crowing. The older man was across the room and out the door faster than Marco thought possible.

"Mr. Mestizo."

Ignacio hurtled down the steps and charged out into the velvet embrace of the night.

"No, cabron!"

He raced fearlessly towards the dark figure standing beside Mr. Mestizo's cage. The intruder ripped the rooster out of his coop, stuffed the struggling bird into a burlap sack and sprinted away. Ignacio could feel his old heart hammering mercilessly against his sternum.

The thief ducked into the shadows and leapt over the last row of coops that stood between him and a successful getaway. He had planned to run off through the field, laughing at the old man chasing his dust. Instead, he screamed in agony as his ankle snapped beneath his weight.

The injured thief had barely gotten back to his feet when Ignacio was on him. Ignacio lashed a fist across the back of the man's head. He seized the burlap sack and yanked it away from the silent figure.

Ignacio stuffed his hands into the sack and rummaged frantically about, oblivious to the weapon in the other man's hand. "Mr. Mestizo, I'm here."

A flash of silver was all he saw, like a small quick fish in the shallows of a coral reef, and then his head exploded in pain and stars. Ignacio crumpled beneath the vicious blow. He smelled dirt, tasted blood and then passed out.

A person often meets his destiny on the road he took to avoid it.
—Jean de La Fontaine

Nothing happens unless first a dream.
—Carl Sandburg

PART TWO

THE TANNERY

THE CHILDREN HAD NO idea where they were or where they were going. They watched the truck bulldoze its way deeper into the darkening folds of the sub-tropical forest.

Maximo squeezed his sister's hand and tried to ignore the pain in his amputated leg. For something that no longer belonged to his body, it ached horribly.

Eventually, the foliage thinned, and they drove out of the jungle and into a scrubby clearing.

Ollie pointed a finger at a group of low-lying structures. "That is where you will live now. Live and work. And there is much work to be done. Oh yes, my little cherries, very many chores indeed."

Maximo looked out at the stone and wood warehouses with a sense of dread. They huddled together like conspiring thugs, their ashen faces scarred and faded, their rust-streaked tin hats pulled down low over squinting eyes. He could smell smoke and chemicals and something else, a repulsive smell—like something dead.

Ollie veered away from the buildings and drove towards a small house. It sat on the edge of the clearing like a cruel overseer, its windows reflecting the last of the day's light. It looked as if it were wearing mirrored sunglasses.

He braked hard, blew out his breath and cut the engine. For the first time in many hours, the rumble and roar of the powerful truck ceased.

"Out, children. Everybody out. We have arrived." He threw his door open and slid out from behind the wheel.

Maximo and Lourdes shut the door behind them and watched as

a young Dominican girl came bounding down the front steps of the house. She was only twelve or thirteen years old, but her eyes held the wounds of someone much older.

"Welcome home, Mr. Kirschjager. I have been waiting for you. I have cooked something nice," the girl said, pulling down the hem of her short skirt.

"I'm not hungry," he said, "at least not for the burnt puke that comes from your pan. Feed it to the goats."

"Now attention, girl. This is Lourdes." Ollie placed his hands on Lourdes' shoulders. "Lourdes, this is Tika."

The two girls looked shyly at one another and mumbled their greetings.

He gently pushed Lourdes towards the other girl. "Take her inside. Show her around. No food. I will be along in time, and I shall prepare her a meal myself."

"Maximo?" Lourdes said as Tika began to lead her away.

"Boy, this way. Follow me," Ollie said.

Ignoring him, Maximo went to his sister. "It's all right, Palomita," he said, bending down and looking into her eyes. "You can go with this girl. I won't be far, and I will see you soon."

"Boy, to me. Now. Come," Ollie snapped. He already hated hearing someone else refer to Lourdes as Palomita. She was his now, and the sooner the boy realized it, the better.

Maximo kissed Lourdes on the cheek and then hobbled after the big German.

By the time they entered the first building, Maximo was breathing heavily, sweat drooling down his face. His first impression of the cavernous space was that it reeked like a slaughterhouse. He cupped a hand over his mouth and nose and gagged.

"You had best get accustomed to that because this is where you shall be spending your days from now on. This is the fleshing house, and it has no time for pansies," Ollie said, looking at him with disgust. "I run a tannery here. Do you know what that is?" he asked rhetorically.

He lumbered off in the direction of a series of huge stainless-steel vats. They looked like witch's cauldrons full of nasty simmering secrets. Maximo followed him over to the steaming kettles and peered down into the oily liquid. Inside, animal skins swirled lazily around. They looked like restless eels. Boys no older than him tended the vats with long wooden poles. They refused to make eye contact with him.

Close by, other boys fed skins into a noisy machine with quickly revolving helical blades. The machine stripped the fat and flesh from the hides with a mechanical efficiency that caused Maximo to recoil. Other workers scraped hair and tissue from skins they had stretched over smooth wooden beams or pounded at them with oddly shaped metal tools.

It was all a bit overwhelming to Maximo, and all he could think about was how tired he felt.

"Pay attention, whelp." Ollie said. "I make leather here, and this is where you will find yourself tomorrow morning and every morning after that—sun up to sundown. You will be slopped, watered, bedded down and expected to work off your debt to me. In return for my generosity, your muscle, such as it is, and your obedience is what I demand. I expect you to learn as well as sweat. After all, it's not as if I am asking you to learn how to read or something."

"I already know how to read," Maximo said.

"Oh, do you? A regular Rhodes scholar, are we? A half-Haitian Dumbminican who thinks he's educated because he can read a street sign. You are a donkey, and a crippled one at that. Your options in this life are few, so shut up and listen." He brushed past Maximo with such force that he almost fell into one of the vats.

"Here, we soak the salted hides. There, we immerse the clean skins in lime to loosen the hair and soften the membrane."

Maximo struggled to keep up with Ollie as he careened about the place with an escalating arrogance. He pointed at enigmatic machines and murky liquids. He instructed and cursed, berated and insulted, until finally he lead Maximo out of the fleshing house and into the relative freshness of the night air.

"And next door we have the beam house. To me, boy." Ollie snapped his fingers and walked towards the neighbouring building.

"It smells like shit in here," Maximo said, and coughed.

"For once, you are correct. You're smelling dung, dog and chicken feces, to be exact, and buckets of urine." He walked over to the bank of rotating drums.

There were two filthy boys in front of the machinery. They were trying to make a dent in the mountain of steaming animal excrement before them. They filled their shovels and sent their foul loads hurtling into the spinning drums, only to have the machinery spit half of it back at them.

"It's called bating," Ollie said. "The enzymes in the waste relax the pelts before the pickling and the tanning may proceed. However, I have no doubt that these words are lost on you. No matter. You will learn or you shall know my anger. And now to the far corner. Come. I'm tired of your weak eyes drooping like half-masted flags."

Maximo lurched reluctantly after him, the stoic set of his jaw masking the pain he was in. The closer they got to the far end of the building, the quieter it became. Maximo could see animal skins stretched tightly between sapling frames like drum skins. Other boys busily pulled fallow-coloured pelts back and forth over braided cables. Their faces flushed from the effort.

"This is called brain tanning, and you don't need to have one to do it," Ollie said, and then cackled loudly. It was a remark he repeated every time he entered the area. Nobody laughed with him.

"That vat there, the one that looks like tomato soup, do you see it?" Ollie asked, pointing at the largest of several containers.

"I see it."

"That's a solution of cow brains and water. Do you know why we soak deerskins in brains? And, ya, I say deerskins, not cow skins. Answer please." He stared hard at the newest addition to his labour camp.

Maximo simply shrugged his shoulders and wondered if he had enough strength to push Ollie into the vat of cow brains.

Ollie leaned down until their noses almost touched. "It's alchemy, boy. Brains contain lecithin oil, a substance well suited to breaking down hide glues. This is an ancient art form, one that produces the softest and most expensive buckskins the world has ever known, even in today's automated society." His rank breath engulfed Maximo with its damp foulness.

"Well, anything to say? Any questions so far?" Ollie asked.

Maximo looked up at the perspiring sunburned man and suppressed an urge to laugh. To him, Ollie's eyes peering down at him from behind the thick lenses of his glasses looked like two panic-stricken jellyfish trapped in an evaporating tidal pool. "Yeah, I got a couple of questions," he said. "When can I see my sister and how much will I be getting paid?"

The words had barely passed his lips when Ollie backhanded him. The vicious blow knocked him off his crutches and sent him sprawling. Ollie advanced on the helpless boy, bellowing like a threatened water buffalo. Just as he made ready to hoof his downed prey, a skinny Dominican boy named Jesus stepped between them and held up his hands.

"Please, Mr. Kirschjager. He is new here, and stupid. Let me teach him, show him how you like things done," he said.

Ollie's eyes darted between the two boys, and he clenched and unclenched his hands in a rare moment of indecision.

He pointed a finger at Maximo. "You will speak to me with respect, and you will earn your keep or else you will find yourself thrown onto the street, never to see your sister again. Understood?"

Maximo glared up at Ollie and wiped blood from his battered mouth.

"And you. Are you the big man now?" Ollie said, confronting Jesus. "You think you're his saviour, trying to live up to your holy name?"

"No, sir. I am only trying to help."

"And so you will then. I'm placing the gimp in your hands. He will work with you, and I shall hold you to answer for his learning, for his actions. Understood?"

"Yessir. Understood."

Ollie shifted his weight from one foot to the other, searching the boys' faces for any signs of guile. He always suspected that people imagined him to be unintelligent, that they thought themselves capable of taking advantage of him. By the time they realized their mistake, it was too late.

"All of you back to work." He turned and stomped away.

"Sperm whale," Jesus muttered.

His comment broke the tension, and everyone laughed.

"Here, let me help you up," he said, reaching out to Maximo. "My name is Jesus. That is Tomas, there is Flaco, and the ugly one is Javier."

"My name is Maximo Caesar Ventura, and my sister's name is Lourdes, and that bastard has her up at his house. Why are there no girls working here?" he asked, resting his weight on one crutch.

His question ushered in a sudden uncomfortable silence that did little to alleviate his fears.

"I think that Ollie prefers men to work his leathers because we are stronger and thicker-skinned, like leather," Jesus said. "Don't worry just now. There is nothing you or any of us can do tonight to change anything, but one day maybe we can. Now tell us, how did you lose your leg?"

The morbid curiosity that his amputation elicited came as a surprise to Maximo, and he knew that it would take some time to adjust to all the unwanted attention.

"A crocodile bit it off," he said, and shrugged his shoulders.

The ring of grimy boys burst into laughter.

"All right, if you don't want to tell us what happened, then just say so," Jesus said, placing a hand on Maximo's shoulder.

"It's the truth. My family and I got caught up in the flood in Jimaní, and we were washed down into Lago Enriquillo. It was there that the crocodile got me."

The tanners nodded their heads in solemn approval of his adventure, silently wondering if they had the strength to survive such an ordeal.

"Were you swimming when it bit you?" Jesus asked.

"No, I was floating on top of a cow."

"Aww, yeah."

"Good one."

"Phwsss, okay."

Maximo shook his head and said nothing.

"Anyway," Jesus said, "you look tired. Come on. I will give you a quick walk-through of the leach house next door and then show you where your bunk is. The roosters around here don't wait until sunrise before they start to sing."

Maximo said goodbye to the other boys and followed Jesus out of the building.

Jesus pushed open a heavy wooden door and ushered Maximo ahead of him.

"This is where the hides come after they leave the beam house," Jesus said. "Only the cowhides, of course. Our skins, the deer and elk, they go from us to the smokehouse and then back to us for more finishing. It takes a lot of hard work, many hours. That is why the Americans and Canadians ship their skins here—cheap labour."

They walked beside a long row of quivering stainless-steel vats.

"How long have you been here?" Maximo asked.

"Three years."

Jesus pointed at the triangular-shaped tubs. "These are the rockers."

Maximo watched the suspended hides as they shook back and forth in the black water. Their agitation had a desperate quality to it, like something drowning.

"And the rest of the big square pits here," Jesus said, waving a hand through the air, "they are handlers, and the massive pits at the back there are the layaway vats. About one hundred sides can be stuffed in each one. The cowhides will soak in them for months before they we hang them out to dry."

The two boys passed a couple of older men. The men nodded their heads, smiled and stole glances at Maximo's stump.

"They are two of the best tanners around," Jesus said. "They use ground-up chestnut bark from France."

"For what?"

"For tanning. What else? It is known as vegetable tanning."

Jesus felt proud of all the knowledge he had acquired over the years, and he was pleased that he finally had someone with whom he could share it.

"Oh," was all Maximo could manage before stifling a yawn and closing his eyes.

"Come on," Jesus said. "I'll show you where we bunk. The finishing house, the smokehouse and the drying loft can all wait for another time."

Maximo nodded and followed his new friend out of the tannery. The two boys walked slowly across a field of thorny grass and desiccated coconut husks. The landscape looked like a picture from a magazine, one enticing frozen westerners to thaw their moods and rejuvenate their souls with some Caribbean mojo.

"Do we receive any money for the work?" Maximo asked, already wondering when he might be able to leave.

Jesus kicked a coconut husk high into the air. "Yeah, we get paid, so to speak. You will earn two hundred pesos per day. The older guys get a little more."

A slow smile spread over Maximo's face as he calculated how much money he could save in one month. "Four thousand pesos? Lourdes and I will be leaving this place in a few months, maybe even sooner."

"My friend, you are forgetting about paying for your food and lodging, not to mention whatever you owe the company store. You know, for toothpaste, soap, tobacco, rum, beer, chocolate. It's all available, and it all costs extra. The sperm whale even trucks in girls once a month. There are over fifty men working here. We work fifteen hours a day, seven days a week, and most of us are actually in debt. There is no escape, Maximo. At least not that way."

"What about the police?"

"What about them? What he does isn't exactly illegal. We work for a wage, and we run up credit in excess of what we earn. If we run off, we are the criminals. Besides, the police come here to socialize. They have some free drinks; they get their grease. You know how it works. Same shit all over the world."

"So this is it?" Maximo asked as they arrived at the bunkhouse.

Jesus pushed open a squeaky wooden door. "This is it."

Inside, the accommodations were rudimentary but clean. Two long rows of bunk beds dominated the military-style barracks. The blue plastic footlockers at the base of each bed were the only splash of colour in the room. Maximo could smell laundry detergent and insect repellent.

"We are number eleven, there on the right," Jesus said. "You can have the bottom one, my old one. I'll move up above. Probably easier that way."

Maximo allowed his crutches to fall out from under him, and he collapsed onto the surprisingly soft bed. "Thank you, Jesus...for everything." He curled himself into a ball and pulled his pillow under his head.

"Nada. Toilets to the back, sinks and showers. Only cold water, of course, but the pressure is good. We take our meals out behind the building. Just get up early, make your bed, keep your shit in place. The beluga will dock you an entire day's wages for anything he can think of. Don't worry. You'll see how it all works here—" Jesus stopped midstream when he noticed that he was talking to himself.

Maximo was asleep and snoring lightly. His last thoughts before sleep took him like a mugger were of his sister. He hoped that the girl Ollie had called Tika was helping Lourdes the same way that Jesus was helping him.

EL GUAPO

Jaragua rode through the island's breadbasket, a verdant swath of land that supported coffee, cocoa and tobacco crops. His motorbike was leaking oil, and the exhaust sounded like a goose being garrotted. He swerved around a couple of produce-laden mules attended by a skinny kid flicking a switch of bamboo across their shredded flanks.

His head was throbbing from his recent bout of excessive partying. He managed a weak smile as images from the previous week flashed through his mind: he and Estrellita stumbling out of the clubs along El Colina, taking in live performances by merengueros such as Rosario and Anthony Santos and bachata artists such as Sex Appeal, Frank Reyes and, his favourite, Krisspy.

He and Estrellita had spent long hungover afternoons in bed together, abandoning their sanctuary when the moon appeared in the night sky like some fat mischievous god urging them to come out and play.

The hilly terrain flattened and stretched towards the prosperous town of San Francisco de Marcorís, a place ringed by rice paddies, seeded with fine examples of colonial architecture and home to some of the country's more notorious drug lords.

He rode another mile down the well-paved road before the residence he was looking for emerged from between the gently sloping grasslands. It looked like a luxury yacht adrift on an emerald-green sea. He stared at the opulent white mansion in disbelief. It was a sprawling structure with glass domes and huge terraces, all of it surrounded by a ten-foot-high brick wall.

He pulled over to the side of the road, dismounted the hissing bike and savagely kicked it into a drainage ditch. "Die," he cursed, and walked towards the mansion.

A moment later, he was standing in front of a pair of wrought iron gates and looking up into a security camera.

"Good day, Mr. Ventura," a voice crackled through the metal intercom box. "Come up to the house."

The gates parted and swung quietly inward.

Jaragua was disappointed that half a dozen Uzi-toting henchmen and their snarling attack dogs hadn't greeted him. He smirked at his own fantasy. "Not like the movies."

A freakishly tall Haitian was waiting at the front door for him, silently beckoning him forward with a hand that resembled a splayed Japanese fan. Jaragua nodded to him, walked into the home's vast foyer and gawked at the blatant display of wealth. He stared up at the glittering crystal chandelier above his head and then down at the marble and gold mosaic beneath his feet.

"You made it all the way on that shitty little hornet," a familiar voice said.

"Juan, good to see you," Jaragua said as the Colombian approached.

"How are you going to be a feared soldier with biceps I can feel the bones through?" He gripped Jaragua's upper arms.

"It doesn't take much strength to pull a trigger."

"Or to swing a machete, huh?" Juan said, and burst out laughing. "Come on. Lesson number one: never keep the boss waiting."

Jaragua and the Haitian followed him up the stairs, the click-clack of their combined footsteps sounded like the pathetic efforts of a rhythmless tap dancer. After a long and winding journey, the trio arrived at a pair of heavy oak doors.

Juan raised his fist to knock when his phone rang. "Yessir?" He turned away from the two men and spoke in hushed tones.

"That was him; you can go in," Juan said to Jaragua. "*Just* you."

Jaragua stepped through the doors and found himself inside one of the large glass domes he had seen from the outside. The circular room was an eagle's nest with panoramic views of the surrounding countryside—and kept so cold that his skin began to prickle.

A tall broad-shouldered man stood with his back to Jaragua. He was dressed in a white linen suit, and his posture seemed unnaturally rigid.

"Come in, Mr. Ventura," he said in a deep and somehow damaged voice. He pointed at a couple of plush white leather sofas. "Take a seat."

Jaragua crossed the floor quickly, conscious of his shoes on the pristine broadloom. He could detect a faintly medicinal odour in the air.

"Juan tells me good things about you...tells me that you're handy with tools?" the man said without turning around.

What is wrong with your voice?

"Tools?"

"Oh, come on now. Use your imagination. Make the leap, for Christ's sake. Knives, guns... Sinking in, is it?"

"Yes, sorry." Jaragua cleared his throat. "First of all, I just want to thank you for this opportunity—"

"I haven't offered you one yet."

"No, sir, you haven't."

The man turned around and gave Jaragua his first look at his horribly disfigured face. His skin was stretched painfully tight over misshapen facial bones. It looked shrink-wrapped, as if someone had taken a blowtorch to it. "Address me as El Guapo."

Jaragua looked away for a second and instinctively knew he had made a mistake.

"Look at me." El Guapo's twisted mouth denied him the ability to enunciate clearly. He spoke like an amateur ventriloquist afflicted with throat cancer. He rushed towards Jaragua and leaned down until their faces were only inches apart. "Yes, that's it. Get a good look. Satisfy your natural curiosity. Get it out of your system."

Jaragua stared back at him. He was startled by the man's surprisingly feminine eyes. They looked like two larimar jewels set into the scarred magma of his burned flesh, their beauty even more compelling for the ugliness in which they were imprisoned.

El Guapo straightened up and glared down at him. "Finished?"

"Yes," Jaragua said, not trusting himself to say anything more.

El Guapo seated himself opposite Jaragua. His suit blended chameleon-like into the white of the sofa. To Jaragua, he appeared to be nothing more than an animated head and a set of fluttering hands.

"Shortly after my...accident," El Guapo said, "when I heard that they were calling me *the handsome one*, I personally cut the tongues out of the mouths of five men and two women. Would you like to see them? I have preserved them in jelly jars. They look like rotting oysters."

"I don't mind if you want to show me."

El Guapo smiled for the first time, a tortured repulsive display that had Jaragua praying he never had to endure the man's laugh.

"Perhaps another time." El Guapo produced a green emery board and began filing his well-manicured nails.

"I am telling you this to illustrate a point," he continued. "When a man acts out of anger, out of emotion, he is like puppet, and the puppet master is whoever had the power to pull his strings. I robbed my enemies of their ability to control me by embracing the name El Guapo...much the same way American blacks embraced the term *nigger*, diluting the strength of its oppressiveness. I will still punish those who insult me. However, I shall do so with ice instead of fire. Do you understand?"

"Completely," he said, not at all sure what the man was trying to say.

El Guapo stared silently at Jaragua and continued to shape his nails. He seemed to be waiting for something.

Screech, screech, screech.

Jaragua tried desperately to think of something to say.

El Guapo beat him to it. "You're not much of a conversationalist, are you?" He blew powdered calcium from his nail file and slipped it into his pocket. "In fact, I find you to be a bit of a dullard—uneducated, slow-witted. Basically, you're little more than a street tough—a thief, a drug addict, an amoral reprobate. Ain't that so, Mr. Ventura?"

"You're half right," Jaragua said, his temper rising with every word. "I'm uneducated, but I'm not stupid. I'm a thief, but I'm trustworthy. I enjoy drugs, but I'm disciplined. As far as that last one…a repro*whatever*… you forgot I'm uneducated, so save the impressive words for someone who can appreciate them." He stood up and looked towards the door.

El Guapo lunged off the sofa and confronted Jaragua. "You're so desperate to escape the soul-sucking poverty of your birth that you'd be happy if I hired you as my personal whipping boy. Not only would you take the job," he said, craning his neck towards Jaragua like an irate tortoise, "but you'd probably blow me for it." He ejected the words from his mouth as if they were obstructing his airway.

"You know, you're kinda pretty when you're angry," Jaragua said.

The words had barely reached the air when El Guapo had the muzzle of a gold-plated .45 pressed between Jaragua's eyes. "Say it again, pencil dick." He pulled back the gun's hammer.

Jaragua had always figured that his life would end violently, but he never imagined it would be in such an asinine manner. "Blow me."

El Guapo's eyes widened, and he looked at Jaragua as if he were seeing him for the first time. "Welcome aboard, soldier," he said, lowering the weapon and grinning his hideous grin.

He walked away from Jaragua and snatched a manila envelope from the surface of a glass coffee table. "I don't pay my men. I reward them upon the accurate execution of my orders. You shall live here along with my other trusted employees, and you shall immediately cease all drug use. If these terms are agreeable to you, then consider yourself part of our little fraternity."

A test. Some kinda stupid test

"Absolutely, El Guapo, and thank you for the chance." He hoped that he would be capable of safely navigating the dangerous canals of the man's psychosis.

El Guapo handed him the large envelope he had in his hand. "I had only one reservation about hiring you, and that was your lack of family…that terrible flood in Jimaní," he said, shaking his head and frowning. "A man without loved ones is a liability to me because he has nothing to lose but his own life. He has nobody he cares for and therefore nobody for me to exact revenge upon should said halfwit ever decide to fuck me. Now look inside that envelope."

Jaragua pulled a handful of 8x10 photos from the envelope and flipped through them. They were pictures of him and Estrellita in Santiago. There were close-ups of her smiling, of them kissing, dancing. There was even one of them asleep in their hotel room, Estrellita's breasts exposed.

"Your woman is very beautiful and quite the little songbird as well, is she not?"

Jaragua stared back at him and crushed the photos in his hand.

"No need to fret. If you fuck me, I will only punish you. Kill you, is what I mean to say. However, if you fuck me and get away with it, I will have this little chicken gang-raped by sexual sadists before I personally slit her throat. Do we have an understanding?"

"I would never do that. Fuck you, I mean." Jaragua's voice quivered with impotent rage. He had to use more willpower than he knew he possessed to prevent himself from attacking the man.

"Well, excellent. Then I will never have to do that either…fuck her, I mean."

El Guapo flipped open his cell phone and whispered into it. A second later, the Haitian giant entered the room, his eyes as blank as the expression on his face.

El Guapo handed Jaragua a thick wad of money. "Five grand. Consider it a signing bonus. Get yourself some decent clothes. NCM here will outfit you with a reliable weapon."

Jaragua looked down at the money in his hand with mixed emotions. "What's his name?"

"*Non compos mentis*. It's a Latin term that means he's completely insane," El Guapo said.

Jaragua nodded. He wondered if being crazy was a prerequisite for acceptance to the crew and, if so, what that said about him.

"We're done here for now, Mr. Ventura. NCM, show him to his quarters. He's going to be apprenticing with us."

Jaragua and NCM nodded in unison, turned and walked towards the door.

"I will send someone to collect you around midnight, Jaragua," El Guapo said. "I have something rather special planned for this evening. Something I believe you will enjoy. Please be ready."

HAVANA AND THE WHEEL

MARCO PRESSED A WET cloth against Ignacio's forehead and wished that the electricity would come back on. He gently propped the old man's head up on a pillow and watched candlelight flicker across the bed, caressing Ignacio's sallow skin with compassionate fingers.

Ignacio moaned and stirred, his hands rising into the air to ward off or embrace whatever images were haunting him. To Marco, it looked like he was in hell. However, if Ignacio could speak, he would have told his sentinel not to worry because he was actually in heaven.

There are perhaps a handful of times in anyone's life when they feel absolute happiness, moments when the cosmos bestow upon an individual all that they require in order to experience utter bliss, a gift as fleeting as the perfect snowflake on a warm tongue. The problem with such a blessing is that people rarely recognize their good fortune until long after it's gone and they look back—with the laser clarity of hindsight—and whisper…"*shit*."

Ignacio was as guilty as anyone else was when it came to not appreciating Lady Luck, even when she kissed him full on the mouth and then slapped him for being so blasé about it. However, *that* night, he was in heaven, and he knew it.

He glided along Havana's streets in his spanking candy-apple-red 1958 Caddy. The ragtop was down, and the chariot was loaded with his bandmates and a few dollies, the creamiest of which was cuddled up next to him. He drove along the coast, inhaling ocean breezes and new leather.

They passed some of the swanky pleasure domes that Batista and the Mob had so successfully developed—legendary hotels and casinos such as Montmartre, Comodoro, Capri and the fantasy world of Sans Souci. They were places where the likes of Meyer Lansky, Santo Trafficante and Fat the Butch plied their shady trade.

Everyone was as young and beautiful as the night, and Ignacio leaned over and kissed his girl, his Estrellita. She was wearing a custom couture gown fashioned by the exclusive New York designer Mainboucher. He looked at her swaddled in the dress' shimmering opulence, its ivory satin reflecting the Cuban moonlight, and knew he couldn't live without her.

The cats in the backseat were getting rowdy, mugging and waving at anybody who happened to look their way. Ignacio revved the audacious car's V8 engine and marvelled at its ferocious growl. He could just feel the beast's frustration as he cruised slowly through the town, could sense the restrained energy of the 335 horses he had corralled under the shiny hood.

It was then that Ignacio's song came on the radio.

"Estrellita Luminosa" was a huge hit in Miami, NYC, Puerto Rico and parts of Central America, but that was the first time any of them had heard it played in Cuba, and everyone just went nuts. Merengue leapt into the car like a feral animal, rubbed itself affectionately against its creators and then escaped into the street in search of new admirers.

"That's you, Estrellita," Juanita said, leaning over the seat and throwing her arms around her sister, both of them falling away in bits. Everyone sang along with Ignacio's voice, and Estrellita feigned embarrassment at some of the song's more risqué lyrics.

It saddened Ignacio that his song received no airplay in his own country. While campaigning for the presidency, Rafael Trujillo had draped himself in the flag of merengue, something that had sickened true merengueros. Not content with stomping all over the country's constitution or abusing the citizens' human rights, the dictator had corrupted the last pure thing the people held close to their hearts. He had taken their music, their dance, and he had prostituted it, used it to promote nationalism, further his own political agenda and fuel his megalomania.

The strongman had even toured with various merengue bands, terrorizing and repressing artists who wrote and performed songs of tribute to the brutal regime. Trujillo's own brother operated La Voz Dominicana, a major radio station that broadcast live merengue, or more accurately, live propaganda. The oppressive state of affairs was the reason why Ignacio and Estrellita had not returned to the Dominican Republic, choosing instead to split their time between Cuba and the United States.

Ignacio brought his car to a smooth stop as his song faded out. Bodies spilled from the big boat, and they all swaggered into one of Havana's exclusive Casino Deportivos.

The joint smelled like hair spray, shoe polish and cologne, and it was a crucible of heat and sexual tension.

They had gone there to participate in an intoxicating new dance that was steamrolling through the nation. The dance was called rueda de casino, and it had originated among Cubans of African descent.

They invaded the dance floor en masse. The orchestra had just finished warming up, and the first rueda was about to be formed. Fifteen couples jockeyed for position, and as the band began to play, all eyes turned expectantly towards the caller. The casino wheel was as close to a Latin square dance as one was apt to get, and it was imperative to understand the caller's commands.

"Te amo," Ignacio had said, leaning into Estrellita.

She silently echoed his words, smiling with her eyes as much as with her lips.

The caller belted out some commands, wasting no time in getting the wheel spinning. His signals instructed the dancers to perform intricate steps before changing partners. Ignacio's attention was so fixed on the caller that he had no idea where Estrellita was in relation to himself. He continued to switch partners, his vision a dizzying blur of colourful gowns, smiling faces and spinning bodies. He waited for his girl to be returned to him.

"Enchufa," the moustachioed caller said, his remark causing the dancers to smirk as they performed the move. The term meant "to fit together," and like so many of the commands in the rueda, it was a double entendre.

"Dame una. Dame dos," the caller said, demanding that hands be offered and partners switched.

Ignacio knew it was Estrellita the moment he felt her delicate hand slip into his own. Maybe it was the smoothness of her skin, or perhaps it was the way her fingers curled inside his palm like a nesting bird, but it was more than that. He felt as if he had known her touch before, had always known it, and would know it long after their bodies had returned to the wind and sand.

"Exhmbela," the caller said as Ignacio turned towards Estrellita. The command meant to show her off, and this he did easily, feeling a surge of pride as his arm encircled her slender waist. The couples paraded around in a spirit reminiscent of the pomp and ceremony so evident in French court dances of the eighteenth century. The ladies stepped lightly, an exaggerated air of refinement and simulated aloofness accompanying their every gesture.

Ignacio only had her for a moment before the heartless caller demanded that the dancers switch partners yet again. As he reluctantly let go of her hand, she looked back at him over her shoulder, pouted, blew him a kiss and smiled. It was at that exact moment—that magical forever moment—that Ignacio understood the true meaning of happiness. He understood that it had nothing at all to do with a new car or some song on the radio. Happiness lived within the depths of his woman's dark Spanish eyes and within a smile that promised nothing but offered the world.

Heaven

"Ignacio," the caller suddenly called, causing the entire wheel to come to a rubber-screeching halt. "Please, wake up."

Ignacio mumbled incoherently, stumbled into the fractured spokes of the wheel and wondered why he could smell pineapple.

"It's me. Marco. Tell me you're all right."

"Marco?" Ignacio said, his eyelids flickering rapidly. His mind was trapped somewhere between the past and the present, between his youth and old age, between happiness and what had become of him.

"Yes it is I."

As the painful throbbing in his head grew, Ignacio's bittersweet memories fled back to the secret corners of his mind, and he regained his senses.

"My head," he said, touching two fingers to his wound and opening his eyes. "Marco…we ate dinner and—"

"Yessir," the boy said, relieved that Ignacio was not going to die after all. "You remember? We in your home, we had your beautiful fish, and the pineapple, and then that thief come to us like a pox on the wind."

"Mr. Mestizo?" The sadness of his loss caused his body to sag in defeat.

Marco pointed towards the bottom of the bed. "Look there."

Ignacio raised himself up onto his elbows and squinted. He could see nothing but grey shadows and despair.

"Marco, I'm so tired—" he began, when he heard a familiar clucking and the sound of rustling feathers. "Mr. Mestizo? Is that you?" He struggled to sit up.

Marco placed a hand Ignacio's chest. "Please, lie back down. Rest. It is dark, but he is there. He is perched on the rail of your bed. He been like that all into the night. He been watching over you, and he is safe."

Relief surged through Ignacio's system like a blood transfusion. "But how? What happened?"

"I was right behind you and shocked at your speed. I saw everything. That swine hit you with a piece of pipe. Him lucky not to be killing you, an older gentleman and such." Anger darkened the tone of his voice. "I beat him like a yellow dog. I beat him with fist and foot and stick and stone." He clenched his fists and looked down at his skinned knuckles.

"Are you all right?" Ignacio asked him.

"Oh yes, I am fine. I left him with enough skin to crawl away into the brush like a snake on him belly. I do not think he will return."

Ignacio laughed at the boy's account and placed a hand on his arm. "Thank you, Marco. I cannot tell you what you have done for me. That rooster has given me hope. He has allowed me to dream again…and at my age, these things are priceless."

"I am happy to be able to help you and your champion."

"I want you to be the rubber house foreman from now on. You're up to the job, and, of course, there is more money with the position."

"No. No, sir. Antonio is the foreman. I couldn't—"

"Antonio is leaving us. He is going to serve ridiculously garnished drinks to sunburned tourists down in Punta Cana—him, a man of tools, a man of woods and metals. Can you imagine his chunky paws trying to waiter? He'll shatter those fancy cocktail glasses like they were made out of spun sugar." He laughed. "So you won't be taking anyone's job, and this isn't about what you have done for me. It's not charity or reward. You are the best man I have here now, and you have earned the position. So what say you?"

Marco was still for a moment before answering. "This is the biggest honour of my life. I love to make the rubber. Thank you. I accept your kind offer, and I am going to make the best rubber for you. The best in the whole world." He was glad that the room was dark and Ignacio couldn't see the tears in his eyes.

THE PIGMIESTER PERFORMS

LOURDES PUSHED AND SLAPPED at the only window in her bedroom, but it wouldn't open—just like the door. She could see her brother hobbling across a field. He was with another boy, a skinny boy who sent coconut husks sailing into the air with powerful kicks.

"Maximo!" she wailed.

She hammered her hands against the window and willed him to look her way. She watched his shadow lengthen. It stretched towards her as if it had heard her cries. She turned away from the window, threw herself on her bed and punched and scratched at the menagerie of stuffed animals that littered it. Finally, she collapsed into a quivering knot of fear and loneliness.

She hated the house, and she hated her new room—with all its toys and glitter and locked doors and strange smells. But most of all, she hated the older girl Tika, who had pushed her down and accused her of stealing her room. Tika had pulled her hair and said that all the pretty things used to be hers, and then she had slapped Lourdes and called her names. Lourdes didn't know what the words meant, but she knew from the look in the other girl's eyes and from the ugly twist of her mouth that she never wanted to be called them again.

When no more tears would come, she rolled over, sat on the edge of her bed and waited for something to happen. Ollie had told her that he was going to look after her. He had said that he loved her and that he would be her new papa. She didn't want a new one. She smoothed her tiny hands over the expensive fabric of the dress Ollie had given her to wear. It was purple with white lace, and it fit her perfectly. She looked down at her black patent leather shoes and, despite her mood, grinned at her reflection in them. Ollie had also presented her with a pair of white knee-high socks and a purple ribbon for her hair. He said that pretty girls deserved pretty things.

She felt afraid of him at first, but now she found herself staring at her bedroom door and wishing that it would open, that he would return and keep her company. He was nice to her.

She jumped down from the bed and returned to the window, hoping that Maximo would still be in the field. She stared out into the darkness. All she could see were the orange glow of some distant lights and the haggard silhouette of a few coconut palms. She froze when she heard the jangle of keys on the other side of her bedroom door. There was a momentary scrap and fidget of metal on metal before the door swung open and a smiling Ollie entered her room.

"Hello, my cherry. Look what I brought to you." He was balancing a shaking tray of food and drink on one hand like an inept waiter. "Treats. Delicious treats just for you. Oh…and look at how sweet you look in your new clothes—like a living doll." His eyes probed and molested her.

He kicked the door closed behind him and placed the tray on a yellow plastic children's table with four green chairs stationed around it.

"Sit. Please, sit down. You must be famished. Poor little thing," he said, spreading his arms wide and pulling a chair out for her.

Lourdes took the offered seat and stared hungrily at the feast before her. It was a child's wish list of edibles: cupcakes with colourful icings, macaroni and cheese, hotdogs on squishy buns and chocolate brownies topped with crushed walnuts. Wasting no time, she bolted down a cupcake, half a hotdog and several heaping forkfuls of pasta.

"Easy, Palomita. It's all yours. You don't want to make yourself sick, now do you?" he said gently, parental concern creasing his brow.

"Uh-huh," she said while stuffing the other half of the hotdog into her mouth.

He poured some orange soda into a tall glass. "Here. Drink some of this."

He watched the child closely as she noisily gulped down the fizzy pop. He had always had trouble with the drugs, sometimes administering too much and having to deal with a vomiting and nearly comatose liability or using too little and having his victim wake up at the most unfortunate of times. He suspected that whatever nightmares the drugged girls may experience, they were preferable to the grotesque reality that awaited their fluttering eyelashes. He figured that five milligrams of Valium was a reasonable dose for someone as small as Lourdes; however, it was far from an exact science.

"Drink it all up before the bubbles go away. There's a good girl."

He eased his ample behind onto one of the little chairs. He looked like a sinister clown balancing on a ridiculously tiny bicycle.

When she had stopped eating, he chatted amiably with her. He reassured her that all was well, that she and her brother would be safe with him. He answered all her exasperating questions and calmed all of her bothersome fears until finally her eyes became glassy, her speech became slurred and her motor skills regressed to that of an infant.

She slipped from her chair and collapsed to the floor.   "S l e e p well," he whispered hoarsely.

He sighed deeply and moistened his thick lips with his tongue. The anticipation was delicious to him, and he took his time getting up from his seat. He felt like a child himself, a naughty one who had secretly crept down the staircase on Christmas Eve to unwrap the shiniest of all his gifts.

He sauntered from the room, whistling the tune from Maurice Chevalier's song "Thank Heaven for Little Girls." A few minutes later, he returned with an armful of electronic equipment. He threw the deadbolt on the door, drew the blinds on the window and began setting up his makeshift studio.

He placed a digital camcorder on a tripod, swivelled its callous eye towards the bed and connected it to a laptop. Next, he secured a couple of powerful lights to tall stands, their merciless glare also aimed at the bed. Ollie made decent money operating the tannery; however, it was all just a front for the child pornography ring he headed. It was a multibillion-dollar industry worldwide, and it accounted for approximately one quarter of all pornography traded over the Internet.

The fact that Ollie was getting rich from the exploitation of children was secondary to him. It was like paying a crackhead to smoke some rock.

He disrobed with exaggerated movements, flinging the clothes from his body as if they represented the moral restraints of society, a civilization that would never understand the beauty of the thing they had labelled repugnant. He giggled to himself as he bent down and scooped Lourdes up into his arms. She was such a treasure to him, so petite, so fresh and clean—untainted by the corrupting influence that knowledge would eventually bring.

A cherry girl for the cherry hunter

He gingerly laid her down on the bed, enjoying the warmth of the lights on his bare ass. He picked up his trademark rubber pig mask and slipped it over his head. The grotesque mask had the word *PIGMIESTER* scrawled across its forehead in scarlet lipstick. He inhaled deeply and noisily, loving the oddly erotic smell of the rubber.

He turned on the camera and began to adjust the image. He wanted so badly to keep this one for himself. Tika had been about Lourdes' age when he bought her and begun training her up. However, Tika had begun to develop as of late, her breasts becoming puffier and more swollen by the day—and the pubic hair. He suddenly stopped focusing the camera and held a hand over his mouth. The thought of hair—down there—had always made him feel ill.

He had toyed with the idea of allowing Tika to toil in the workers' kitchen, or perhaps wash the camp's linens, but he knew that one day the accusations would fly and the fingers would point, so he had arranged to sell her to a local brothel instead. It would be better for everyone if she were a doped-up whore when she decided to open her mouth. And besides, he thought, she should be grateful that he didn't just put her down like an old dog who had outlived its usefulness. He had done it before.

He looked directly into the camera and squealed loudly. He had his fans, like-minded individuals who pay exceedingly high premiums to watch his live streaming video. Peer-to-peer file sharing, encryption, data destruction software—the tools and techniques for avoiding Interpol were numerous. The Internet had united the world's pedophiles like nothing before ever had, and Ollie was one of the community's rising stars.

He crawled onto the bed and snuffled around the unconscious girl like a wild boar searching for truffles. He moved his quivering rubber snout closer to her body and snorted, squealed and mimed for the camera. The blotchy pink and white folds of his obese body undulated and shook with the effort of his monstrous parody.

As he began to undress her, he reminded himself that he must use restraint. A man whom Ollie would never dream of crossing had already laid claim to his newest baby flesh, and he would only pay top dollar for virgin meat.

No matter, he thought as he slid one long white sock down Lourdes' tan leg, there were plenty of games he could play, plenty of room for improvisation, while still leaving the girl...cherry.

THE COSSACK AND KOPI LUWAK

JARAGUA FOLLOWED THE COLOMBIAN down a winding staircase. Jaragua had been asleep when the man knocked on his door, midnight having come and gone two hours earlier. Whatever special event El Guapo had planned, it was running late.

The two men silently descended into the mansion's subterranean labyrinth and filtered their way to a set of fortified iron doors. Jaragua felt that he was about to finally taste the marrow of the syndicate's bones.

"La Gallera," Jaragua said, reading the engraving on a solid gold plate above the double doors. "This is some weird spot for a cockpit."

The Colombian swiped an electronic passkey through a black box on the wall. There came the sound of heavy tumblers and cogs before he pushed the doors open and sneered at Jaragua.

"So much to learn. Around here, knowledge is dangerous," he said, and waved him into the noisy room. "No turning back now."

Jaragua stepped through the doors and looked down into the shadows of a deep circular pit in the floor, its walls streaked with rusty slashes. It was enormous, far bigger than any gallera he had ever seen before. He could smell hashish and sawdust.

"Voyeurs, kinkoids and fellow freakinstiens, may I present to you the latest addition to our sordid little club, my newest apprentice, Jaragua of Jimaní," a familiar voice said, its tortured rhythm floating down from the smoky ceiling.

The room filled with nervous laughter and condescending applause. Jaragua looked up at the cascading tiers of plush sectionals, sofas and ottomans that ringed the mutant cockpit and the bizarre crowd that occupied them. El Guapo sat ringside on an oversized red leather chair and glared down at him. He was dressed in an indigo cotton suit and was stroking the head of a huge muzzled Rottweiler.

"Shyness is not a trait I value. So if you please, Jaragua, join me here," he said, waving a jewel-encrusted hand over an empty seat.

As he made his way towards El Guapo, Jaragua noticed that the room was virtually humming with a perverse energy. It pulsed through the oddly intimate atmosphere like an electrical current. Men and women lounged about the amphitheatre in various stages of undress. They drank champagne from crystal flutes, groped each other, snorted fat lines of powder from glass tables and leered at him in a unified display of unrepentant hedonism.

A bare-breasted Japanese girl wearing a studded dog collar handed him a glass of champagne and ushered him to his seat. "It is a Krug— Clos du Mesnil, nineteen ninety-five. I hope it is acceptable," she said, and walked away.

He felt disappointed that she had not bowed. He sniffed suspiciously at his champagne and wished he had a beer.

El Guapo looked at him, his yellowish tongue darting from his wound of a mouth like the head of a venomous snake. "Ever bang a geisha?"

"I don't know what a gaysha is," Jaragua said.

"Why am I not surprised?"

El Guapo stood up. "Attention one and all. It is time to satisfy our most primitive of urges, to hearken to the bloodlust that dwells in all mankind. It is time for a cockfight."

The crowd whistled and cheered El Guapo's grandstanding, their dilated pupils reflecting the room's light like a hundred tiny black mirrors. Jaragua couldn't understand why everyone was so aroused. The excitement was visceral, and it transcended any ordinary cockfight. He was missing something.

"I am pleased to announce that we have acquired a very ferocious and talented challenger for tonight's bout. All the way from Brazil, from the slums of Rio, I give you the Harvester." El Guapo pointed down into the pit just as a bank of lights flooded the arena.

A blue door inside the pit shot straight up into the air like the blade of a guillotine, and a heavily tattooed man stepped into the pit to the strains of "T.N.T." by AC/DC. The Harvester stood well over six feet tall, wore nothing but a pair of blue shorts and had the freakishly muscled body of a steroid abuser. He stared defiantly at the people who had paid to witness a death that evening, spat on the concrete floor and jammed his fists into the air.

The fighter's posturing elicited as many cheers as boos from the amped-up spectators. Jaragua could see two curved blades tied to the man's elbows with blue leather straps, the honed edge of their stainless-steel brilliance sparkled beneath the glare of the overhead lights. He couldn't believe that he hadn't figured it out sooner. Rumours of human cockfighting had circulated throughout the Dominican Republic for years, but he had never really believed the stories.

"Blue pays ten to one," El Guapo continued. "Place your wagers, people, and you all know the punishment for disrespecting the word of the gallero. This warrior has dispatched three opponents to date, and since he is still alive, you may safely assume that he has never lost."

The Harvester stalked around the ring, performing impromptu demonstrations of the Brazilian fighting art Capoeira. He twirled in place sending roundhouse kicks whistling through the air. He jumped, landed, spun around and then drove his blades into the throat of an imaginary adversary.

El Guapo applauded the man's efforts. "Excellent skills. Very scary.

"And now, without any further ado, I give you the most feared mortal combat warrior our clandestine competition has ever produced. Hailing from the gulags of Siberia, with eleven kills to his credit, coming through the red door now, fear him, respect him, for he is… the Cossack."

The red door slid smoothly upwards, and the champion stepped quietly into the pit. A song from the album *Snow Lion* by Aquarium began to play. He had a lean muscular physique and was smaller than Jaragua would have imagined. He wore red shorts and had the same evil-looking knives as the Harvester, only his were fastened to his arms with red leather straps. The two warriors turned to face one another. They crossed their blades in front of their chests and bowed their heads.

"My valiant gallos," El Guapo said. He seemed reluctant to surrender the limelight, a fact that amused Jaragua. He thought that someone as facially challenged as his new boss would have naturally shunned the bright light of attention.

"As you are both well aware, this is a death match," El Guapo continued. "There are no rules, no rounds and no time limit. There will be no quarter given, and I shall personally shoot any fucker who refuses to deliver the coup de grâce." He noisily cleared the phlegm from his throat before finishing. "Warriors, let blood be spilled."

The men in the pit immediately crouched and began circling one another. Their survival instincts narrowed their field of vision and drowned out all ambient sound. They tested each other's reflexes with feigned attacks and half lunges. They threw devastating elbows, their blades cleaving the air with deadly intent.

The Harvester threw a strong kick and connected with the Cossack's knee, causing him to stumble forward. The Brazilian drove his blades forward in an upward arc, slashing the other man's cheek open.

The crowd cheered wildly as a splotch of blood landed on the wall behind the Russian. The Harvester charged in, slashing his knives at the smaller man, hoping for a quick finish. The Cossack looked stunned, unable to regain his equilibrium as the vicious onslaught continued.

The Harvester's confidence grew with every kick and thrust, with every second that the other fighter avoided his power. He connected with another kick to the body. The Cossack grunted in pain. The men's weapons clashed together, the sound of metal on metal screeched throughout the amphitheatre. As they pushed against one another, the Harvester saw something in the Cossack's eyes that emboldened him like nothing else could have—he saw fear.

The huge Brazilian pursued his elusive foe around the pit, his waning energy evident in the way he was gulping air, struggling for an elusive breath. He swung wildly at the Russian, but the man was too quick. Giving up the chase, the Harvester stood in the middle of the pit, heaving, dripping sweat and waiting until the other man decided to come to him.

The Cossack moved towards his exhausted foe with a confidence that exposed his previous deception. The Harvester felt his limbs turn to rubber as he realized his mistake. He looked into the advancing Russian's eyes and saw that there was no longer any fear there—it had never been there at all.

The Harvester lifted his heavy arms and attempted to block the Cossack's attack, but he was too slow. The Russian ducked under the man's sluggish defence and sank one of his knives deep into his abdomen. He let out a war cry and spun back out of range.

The crowd erupted as the wounded man clasped his hands over the puncture. He collapsed against the pit wall, blood spurting from between his fingers and bubbling from his mouth. The Cossack advanced on his wounded prey, not willing to win the battle by hanging back and allowing the other man to bleed out. The Harvester pushed himself away from the wall and prepared to take his executioner to the grave with him.

The Cossack lunged forward, blocked his opponent's desperate strike and severed the man's bicep muscles with two slashing movements. The Brazilian stumbled away, his arms dangling uselessly by his side. The Cossack paced in front of the doomed man, his eyes locked on his throat.

"Kill him! Kill him! Kill him!" the mob chanted, their faces shining with homicidal glee.

Jaragua turned around in his seat and looked around the room. He was shocked to see several couples engaged in vigorous sex, their glazed eyes fixated on the gruesome scene below.

The crowd began to stomp their feet and clap their hands in time with their macabre chant, eagerly soliciting the loser's death.

The Harvester swayed unsteadily on his feet, his breath wheezing in and out of him with diminishing urgency. He was waiting for the end to come. He didn't have to wait long.

The Cossack saluted him by crossing his blades and then nearly decapitating him with a stunning roundhouse blow.

The Russian drove both of his fists into the air as the lifeless body of the Harvester crashed to the concrete floor. "Twelve!" he roared, his body drenched in blood.

The shrieks of pleasure that accompanied the brutal climax were nothing short of orgasmic. The crowd clapped and stomped as the Cossack turned and disappeared through a hole in the wall, the red door slamming down behind him.

"Holy shit," El Guapo said, once again standing up and addressing his followers. "Who can beat that animal? I trust everyone got their money's worth tonight?

"I apologize for having to leave so abruptly...but I must get my beauty rest," he said, silently daring anyone to laugh. Nobody did. "Thank you all for coming this evening. Feel free to stay as long as you like. Snort, drink, smoke, fuck, whatever cranks your shaft. Until our next encounter, I bid you all au revoir."

He took hold of his Rottweiler's chain and yanked the cringing beast to its feet. "Jaragua, please accompany me to my sanctum. We have business to discuss." He whispered something into the ear of the topless Japanese girl, something that made her giggle.

After a long silent walk, the two men settled into the buttery softness of El Guapo's twin white leather sofas once again. Jaragua looked up through the glass-domed ceiling and smiled at the starlit night sky above him. It reminded him of the bioluminescent trails that fishing boats left in their wake. He thought about Estrellita.

"Do you drink coffee?" El Guapo asked him.

"Of course."

El Guapo pressed a phone to his ear. "Sugar?"

"Two."

"KL, one with two," he said into the phone before tossing it on the table. "I trust that this evening's shenanigans were not too off-putting."

Jaragua frowned at the man's choice of words. He wished that he would speak plainly. "I'm sorry, but what do you mean by that?"

El Guapo looked at him as if he had just vomited on his expensive broadloom. He sighed heavily. "Did you have fun tonight, Jaragua? The event wasn't too repellent, too repulsive? It didn't offend your delicate nature?"

"I enjoyed the fight if that's what you're asking. Who are those men, and how did they come to be what they are?"

"They are gallos," El Guapo said as he stroked the head of his dog. "They are warriors who have had the misfortune of being born in the wrong century, being born into a world that no longer values such attributes as bloodlust and ferocity. The world of today reserves its respect for the spineless, for the preening artist and the pretty poseurs, chickenshits who have paper-shuffled and canoodled their slippery way into positions of power while real men sweep the streets."

"Why do they do it? Money?"

"The reasons why they do it are as individual as the man. However, money is a universal motivator."

"Is it making them rich?"

"Depends on the fighter's infamy, on his mystique and popularity. Anywhere from ten thousand dollars to over a million."

"I think the risk is too high."

"Hypocrite. You work for El Guapo. You risk death every day that you are in my employ, and I doubt if you will earn as much in a lifetime as the winner of tonight's match made in nine minutes." He sneered at Jaragua, oblivious to the silvery string of saliva that spiralled from his mouth like a spider's dragline.

Jaragua shrugged and hoped that such conversations would not become part of his regular duties.

"Beside the point anyway," El Guapo said. "It's a fascinating diversion for me and a handful of wealthy aficionados. The bouts are held here, in Cuba, South America and occasionally New York. I also fight real cocks. You know, ones with talons and beaks." He finally treated Jaragua to the horror of his twisted laugh, a spectacle that left him squirming for an exit.

A pretty young black girl entered the room. She wore a sheer wrap of white cloth around her nakedness. "Your coffee, señor," she said, looking at the floor. The cup rattled on its saucer.

El Guapo pointed at Jaragua. "For him."

The girl left the coffee on the table and scurried from the room.

"You are about to savour the most expensive coffee in the world—two hundred U.S. a pound," he said as Jaragua reached for the cup. "It's called kopi luwak. In savage tongue, *kopi* means coffee and *luwak* means weasel. More accurately, it's an Asian palm civet, a catlike creature related to the mongoose. It's an arboreal nocturnal marsupial that inhabits the islands of Java, Sumatra and Sulawesi, gorging itself on the ripest and reddest coffee cherries that its greedy little nose can sniff out."

Jaragua sipped at the hot liquid. "Sounds like you really know your weasels."

"After feeding, the luwak excretes the undigested coffee beans. A unique fermentation takes place in its gut and bowel, an alchemy of digestive enzymes and flora that mysteriously produces the most prized beans in the universe."

Jaragua stopped tasting the coffee and stared at El Guapo over the rim of his cup. "What, exactly, are you saying?"

"Exactly that."

"What?"

"What you are thinking," he said, smiling and enjoying his guest's discomfort. "The locals pick through the luwaks' feces, harvesting the beans for sale."

"That's not true."

"Oh, but it is. The humble luwak shits gold." El Guapo giggled. "Taste it again. Do you like it?"

Jaragua shrugged and then gulped back half the cup's contents, swishing it around in his mouth as if it were fine wine. "Honestly, the best and strangest coffee I've ever tasted. Delicious."

El Guapo leaned forward and stared at Jaragua. "Okay, but *what* does it taste like? Describe it."

"I can't really. Like syrup maybe, or caramel-like but not quite. It's something strange. Something I have no words for."

El Guapo slumped back onto the sofa and scowled. "Yes. That's what they all say. Fucking delicious, fucking ambiguous and no fucking help."

"Well, what do you think it tastes like?" Jaragua asked him, feeling confused by the man's sudden petulance.

He looked at Jaragua with disgust. "Huh? I would never consume something that some beast had shat upon a jungle floor somewhere. Do I look like a filthy barbarian to you?"

"No."

Just fucking crazy

"So forget that," El Guapo said. "I should have known better than to think that you would have the imagination or the vocabulary to paint a picture of it for me.

"Down to business. Tomorrow you shall accompany a couple of my most loyal soldiers on a little mission. Your father was a bloody Haitian. Yes?"

"Yes. He was Haitian."

"Good. Then I assume that you can speak that bastardized Haitian patois that passes for a language?"

"I can speak Creole if that is what you're asking me," Jaragua said through his tightening lips.

"Excellent, because you shall be venturing into that plagued vacuous shithole of a country come the morrow. Occasionally, being born a half-breed has its advantages."

Jaragua stared at El Guapo and hoped that the hate he was feeling didn't show in his eyes.

El Guapo leaned forward and attempted to pout his plasticine face. "Oh, did I touch a raw nerve? Well get over it because you're in good company. Where do you think I got these from?" He stabbed two fingers towards his own blue eyes. "My father was a white prick from the Netherlands...or so my mother tells me, but in all honesty, she's entertained so many pricks in her life that I no longer trust her judgement. Now any more questions before you fuck off?"

"Yes," Jaragua said, and stood up. "I was just wondering why you have a muzzle on your dog. He seems so docile."

"Aha! Signs of life on planet Jaragua. I muzzle Abel here because he is weak, and that quality perpetuates his own victimization. He deserves no mercy. As a pup, I whipped him until he pissed at the sight of me. His brother Cain, however, has an entirely different personality, one which I have also taken full advantage of, and if you fail me in Haiti, you shall see what I mean by that."

MARKET DAY

IGNACIO FINISHED SHAVING AND splashed some Calvin Klein Obsession onto his razor-burned cheeks. Years ago, when he was still living on the street, some clown had thrown a bottle of it at him, told him that he smelled like shit and had a good laugh. He had kept the cologne to remind himself of the insult he had allowed his life to become.

He put on a clean faded denim work shirt, wincing as the material made contact with the fresh lacerations on his back. He ran two fingers over the raised scar on the side of his head, a souvenir from the rooster thief. The wound had required stitches, but after what had happened to his wife while she was in hospital, he no longer trusted doctors.

Charlatans, bloodletters, purveyors of snake oil

He squatted down and peered at Mr. Mestizo, who now resided in a coop beside his bed. He looked at the rooster with the pride of a father whose son had become a stronger man than he ever was. Mr. Mestizo had taught him that life itself was less valuable than the way it was lived. The bird was a seasoned fighter now, and his cockiness had been replaced by something else, something that didn't strut or bluff, something quieter—the calmness of belief.

"I am going to market my rubber today, going to reap what I have sown."

He placed some food and water in the cage, scratched the bird beneath his beak and said goodbye.

He left his stone cottage and squinted at the rising sun. He watched the morning rays surge across the distant green fields like a riptide, its vermillion rays lapping against his sandalled feet.

Solar surf

As Ignacio walked through the tall grass, he could see Marco and a few other men standing beside his delivery truck, their white T-shirts billowing in the wind like flogging sails. He smiled and raised a hand in the air. He could see a mountain of smoke-cured rubber lashed onto the truck's aging back.

"Morning, boss. See you got the boys going early," he said, beaming at Marco.

Marco rubbed the truck's hood as if it could feel his touch, his dirt-streaked face shining with pride. "She all set for Puerto Plata."

"Let's go see Don Camino, then. Marco, you're up front with me. The other men can ride the rubber."

Ignacio and Marco climbed into the cab. The springs of the bench seat sagged and moaned beneath their weight. Ignacio rolled down his window and repositioned the mirror. He could smell spearmint chewing gum and motor oil. The truck trundled its way down the uneven track towards the highway. The men riding on top of the swaying payload held on tightly and laughed like children at an amusement park.

Ignacio switched on the radio. "How about some merengue?"

"How about some bachata? Or better yet, some rara or racines?" Marco said.

"Bachata is the music of bitterness."

"But some you like. You changing, I know."

"Some, yes, as long as it lifts your soul. Perhaps it's not I who is changing but the music."

To Ignacio, bachata was little more than Latino blues marinated in the misogyny of rap. The originally romantic lyrics had given way to a preoccupation with drunken nights, brawling, brothels, poverty and incarceration.

"Music should be about escaping one's sorrows, not wallowing in them," Ignacio said. "It should make you smile and move your feet. It should liberate. It should strengthen. Life is hard enough without singing about it."

"Respectfully, sir, music is rebellion. Music is change, and more often than not, music is pain."

"Wise beyond your years." Ignacio smiled at him.

He found some racines on a Haitian radio station (an unlikely copulation between voodoo rhythms and American jazz). He turned up the volume and looked out the window at some cane farmers torching their fields. He watched the fire incinerate the beige chaff, leaving dark smouldering soil and grey ash in its wake. The smell of the burning fields always reminded him of his mother, a woman who had spent her life in front of an open fire, adding wood, poking coals, simmering oils and frying fish. She always smelled of smoke and soot, the perfume of a peasant's love.

He backed the truck up to the loading bays at Don Camino's shoe factory and cut the engine. He and Marco laughed as the truck wheezed and rattled its way towards silence like a ham actor dragging out his big death scene.

The rubber was unloaded and weighed, and Ignacio went inside the factory to receive his money. The noise greeted him like an old friend whose company he had never actually enjoyed. The factory smelled of sulphur, pine oil and glue.

Santa's sweatshop

He walked along a catwalk and looked down in sympathy at the workers below him. They tinkered and tapped with their shoemakers' tools. They stitched leather, bonded rubber and bit their tongues until they bled. Hulking machines squatted among the toiling masses like alien dictators, electrical cables jutting from their industrial arms— whips about to be cracked.

Kiss the Captain's daughter

"Good day, Consuela," he said, greeting Don Camino's secretary.

"Good day, Ignacio," she said, and smiled warmly. "Go on in. He's expecting you."

He thanked her and walked into Miguel's office.

"Good day, Don Camino. I have brought you your rubber, and I am here to be paid."

"Ignacio, come in…ah, on second thought, I'll come to you. I just had the rugs shampooed." Miguel crossed the room in three or four great strides, the expensive fabric of his tailored suit whispering rude things into Ignacio's ear.

Swish, swish, you smell like shit

Swish, swish, here's some cologne…ha, ha, ha

He pointed at the paper Ignacio had crunched up in his hand. "I assume that's for me."

"Oh, yes. It is." Ignacio smoothed out the invoice and handed it over.

As Miguel looked over the numbers, Ignacio cursed himself for feeling so humble, for feeling so grateful to be receiving that which he was owed.

Miguel produced a thick wad of pesos out of nowhere. "I think you're taking advantage of my generous nature, but I'm going to pay you anyway."

He counted a stack of notes onto Ignacio's flattened palm and then opened his office door. "See you next month."

Ignacio slowly formed the money into a roll, looked Miguel squarely in the eye and offered him his hand. "Best hevea rubber on the island."

Miguel squeezed Ignacio's hand harder than he needed to and ushered him out the door.

He worked a handkerchief over his hands. "Price of doing business, I suppose."

Ignacio left the factory, took a deep breath and watched a boy with a wooden leg struggle to unload a flatbed of tanned leather. Sweat streamed down the boy's face as he wrestled rawhide onto the loading bay. He seemed determined to keep up with his friend. Ignacio smiled to himself. There was a determination in the boy that reminded him of someone so many years ago.

The appearance of a heavyset man shattered his nostalgia. He couldn't hear what the man was saying to the two boys, but his displeasure was obvious. Ignacio was about to turn away when the man suddenly shoved the crippled boy, sending him tumbling off the loading bay.

"Hey, cabron! He is just a boy. Let him be." Ignacio picked up a piece of wood from the ground and walked quickly towards them. "Maybe you want to try your luck with an old man as well as a child with half a leg."

"And after he finished with you, then I take over," Marco said, falling in behind Ignacio.

Without a word, Ollie walked quickly back into the factory, slamming the metal door behind him.

"Here, take my hand," Ignacio said to Maximo.

"Thank you, but I don't need no help."

"Yeah, he don't need no help, buddy," Jesus said. "He's tougher than he looks."

Ignacio picked a baseball cap off the ground, whacked the dust from it and handed to the kid. "New York Mets, huh?"

"Yeah, I'm gonna pitch for them one day. I'm gonna go to New York and become a great baseball player. One day soon," Maximo said, suddenly feeling the need to tell the stranger that he was destined for more so he could save the pity in his eyes for someone who needed it.

"Ahh, dreams, and what would life be without them? My name is Ignacio, and this is my friend Marco."

"My name is Maximo, and this is my friend Jesus."

They grinned at each other and shook hands.

"I think you will like New York, but it's a long way away," Ignacio said.

"You ever been there?" Maximo asked.

"Once or twice."

"Well, I'm going soon, me and my sister, Lourdes."

"Well, my young friend, I hope that one day this island doesn't seem like a place you need to escape from. May I see your cap for a moment?" He pulled a pen from his shirt pocket and engraved a phone number under the bill of the cap. It was a number he himself had been meaning to dial ever since he had returned from the grave.

"I wish you Godspeed, Maximo," Ignacio said. "Call this number when you arrive. My old friend there will help you…if you need some, I mean, tough as you are." He winked at the boy.

"Okay."

"And can you give him a message for me?" Ignacio asked.

"Sure."

Ignacio bent over and whispered something into Maximo's ear. "Will you tell him that?" he asked aloud.

"No problem," Maximo said, and shrugged.

Jesus eyed the loading dock and licked his dry lips. "We had better get back to work."

"Nice to meet you boys," Ignacio said. "And if that tub of guts hurts you again, you come back here and ask for me or Marco. He cannot treat you that way."

"Thank you. We will," Maximo said, and returned to his work.

Ignacio walked away. He was thinking about how he had once been a part of the mass exodus towards that mythical city of glass and steel, of fame and famine—a diaspora that connected the two nations through blood and dreams. He wondered if the hemorrhaging would ever stop.

He cocked his head to one side. He could hear music, a song he had never heard before. He looked towards the far end of the parking lot at a group of picnic tables and people.

He handed Marco some money. "Good job today. Go get yourself and the men some chicken and cold beers. I'll be back soon."

He glided across the hot sticky asphalt, instinctively following the tempo like a honeybee chasing lavender on the wind.

Merengue

Ignacio could see a woman punishing a tambora drum, a handsome kid with a vertical cowlick of dark hair bending his bones to a tortured saxophone, another man stretching and collapsing the lung on a German accordion and a slender girl working her guiro as if she were grating cinnamon.

He walked closer, the smile on his face disintegrating as the girl with the guiro began to sing. In a trance, he walked towards her siren song. He felt like a spellbound sailor soon to be shipwrecked upon the rocks of his concealed past.

That voice…but you died in my arms

It was a voice he never thought he would hear again, a voice that could drive a pacifist to murder and a violent man to prayer. It was the voice of a ghost.

He stood just outside the circle of friends and watched as Estrellita turned to face him. He gasped loudly and stared into the shock of her reincarnated features.

Smoke and mirrors, shadows and shade, guilt and memories

"Sophia," he whispered, knowing that it was not his daughter, could not be his daughter. He had buried her. He had killed her.

Estrellita sang and danced and gazed compassionately at the old man who stood awkwardly off to one side, his eyes beginning to water. He looked…damaged.

Ignacio turned and stumbled away. He had to get away from her before he prostrated himself at her feet and begged for an absolution she could never grant. He had heard that everyone in the world had a twin, but what he had seen in the girl's eyes, what he had heard in her voice, transcended flesh and bone. It was more than a random blending of chromosomes, more than a heartless genetic conspiracy to replicate his deepest pain and his purest love. He was being given a second chance.

He quickly distanced himself from her voice and its echoes.

He was thinking about serendipity and how he could right an unforgivable wrong.

THE BOYS OF SUMMER

Jesus pounded a fist into his homemade catcher's mitt, forcing straw between the scraps of rawhide he had stitched together. He squatted down behind a sun-bleached cow skull that represented home plate and called out to Maximo. "Just like that. Keep them guessing."

Maximo slammed the baseball into his own lumpy rendition of a glove and fought to control his balance. The prosthetic leg Ollie had gifted him as if he were throwing a dog a bone was rudimentary and shock white, but he had learned to master it over the last few weeks. He squinted needlessly as another of his coworkers picked up the thick piece of shaved pine they used for a bat. Word of his pitching skills had spread rapidly through the tannery, and everyone wanted to see the one-legged wonder doing the impossible. After work, the men gathered behind their barracks to drink, smoke, take some batting practice and dream of a better tomorrow.

Maximo sized up his latest challenger. He decided to throw a four-seam fastball. He coiled his arm, braced himself on his good leg and released fire from his brimstone mound. The pitch was his validation, and it bulleted through the strike zone. The batter swung so hard that he lost his balance and landed face down in the dirt.

"Strike one!" their umpire yelled.

The rabble of onlookers cheered and jeered with equal enthusiasm, the pleasure of the moment chasing the hardship from their faces. Maximo looked over at them and waved. Even though he had become close with many of the men, he prayed he would never wear the mask of resignation as comfortably as most of them did. For someone with his ambition, contentment was a curse.

He stalked the mound like a wounded panther, imagining that he was Pedro Martinez, number 45 of the New York Mets. He looked towards his catcher, the batter morphing before his eyes from a wiry Dominican kid in a ripped T-shirt to the hulking form of infamous slugger Mark McGwire.

Jesus signalled him to throw another fireball, to which he shook his head. His catcher pointed some more fingers down towards the dirt. Maximo nodded.

He positioned himself, snapped his neck and released a perfect curveball, its 12-to-6 trajectory forcing the hapless batter to connect with nothing but air.

"Strike two!"

Jesus threw the ball back to Maximo and indicated that he should unleash his knuckleball. He agreed.

He positioned his fingers on the ball, spat an imaginary wad of tobacco juice into the dirt and virtually lobbed his next pitch. The ball danced through the air with abnormal buoyancy, careening and weaving like a drunken butterfly. The batter licked his lips hungrily as the enticingly slow ball wafted into range. He swung hard, grunting from the exertion.

"Three strikes! That's seven up and seven down!" the umpire hollered.

Jesus looked over at the men lounging on the picnic tables. "Who's next? We got time for one or two more victims before we lose the light."

"Not today. No more today," Maximo said, massaging his shoulder, even though it was his stump that was aching. "Besides, how many fastballs do you have to catch with your face before you realize that the light has already gone?"

Everyone laughed at his comment and agreed that tomorrow was another day, another chance for someone to get some wood on one of his pitches. Maximo removed his damp shirt and used it to wipe the sweat and dust from his face.

"I'll see you inside," he said to Jesus.

He walked a short distance and stared across the field, towards the amber glow of Ollie's house. Since their arrival, he had only seen his sister a few times. He now viewed their having been brought to the tannery as a kidnapping, as a crime.

Whenever he saw Lourdes, he felt sickened by the changes in her appearance. Her once sparkling eyes had taken on a glazed and lifeless look, ringed with the discoloured puffiness of stress and disrupted sleep. Then there was the way in which she had reacted to his presence. At first, she had been withdrawn and moody; however, the last time he saw her, she had been openly hostile towards him, the glint of accusation in her eyes causing Maximo great pain.

"Be brave, Lourdes," he whispered into the darkness. "I'm coming."

Ollie raged from Tika's bedroom, slamming the door closed behind him. The girl had failed to arouse him for the second time in as many nights, forcing him to hurt and humiliate her.

"Useless," he bawled as he thumped down the hall.

He entered his study, swatted a stack of books off his desk, flopped down into his recliner and reached for his bottle of bourbon. He splashed some liquor into a water tumbler and pouted his displeasure. "Tawdry fumblings in the dark. So distasteful."

The problem, he thought, was that he had abused all the girlishness out of her years ago.

"Define ironic."

As soon as I get them properly trained up, he thought, the very things I desired about them in the first place are gone. Their innocence, their fear, their shyness—all of it gone, replaced by a manipulative little guttersnipe who knows more tricks than a Reeperbahn window-sitter.

She really had to go

He lit a cigar, chewed on a mouthful of thick smoke and began to calm down. Her budding maturity sickened him. However, it was also the tears, the tantrums and her jealousy towards his precious Palomita. All of it had become too much lately, and the thousand dollars he had paid for her no longer seemed like a bargain.

In spite of everything, he had been putting off delivering her to a brothel in Santo Domingo.

"I am not a monster, not like some," he whispered hoarsely.

He pushed Tika from his mind, refilled his glass and considered visiting Lourdes. He had planned to let her sleep undisturbed for a few nights, as she had been a bit unresponsive lately, an unfortunate side effect of all the drugs he had been putting in her food.

He supposed that he could initiate the girl into some conscious acts sooner than planned. Although, the last thing he wanted was a repeat of the previous summer, when he had become obsessed with a little pony he didn't own, riding it too hard and ruining it for its owner. The loss of revenue aside, he had dealt his reputation a massive blow, and in the clandestine world of human trafficking, serious indiscretions tended to have fatal consequences.

"I can be careful," he said, wiping the tips of his sticky fingers on his trousers. He felt like a mischievous boy telling himself that he would just *taste* the chocolate cake.

No sooner had he convinced himself that it would do no harm to simply sit and chat with Lourdes when the phone on his desk rang. He reached for the receiver.

"This is Ollie. Speak please," he said, his rubbery lips almost engulfing the receiver.

"How is my package?" the caller asked.

At sound of the voice on the other end of the line, Ollie bolted upright and hurled the stub of his cigar into an ashtray as if he had just discovered that he had been smoking a giant Madagascar cockroach.

"Oh, yes, yes. The package is fine. Pristine. Not to worry," he stammered, his eyes widening in alarm.

"It had better be, you fucking pervert, because if it's not, I shall feed your infantile gonads to my Rottweiler."

"Umm, yes…ah, no. I mean that I have been a good boy. I haven't unwrapped it."

"Don't lie to me!" the voice exploded. "Of course you have. Do you think I'm an idiot…pigmiester?"

Ollie stood up and danced from toe to toe. He was sure that he was going to piss himself. "No wait. I can explain—"

"Save it, piggy. If I cared, you would be speaking falsetto right now, if you'd be speaking at all. What matters to me, and to my client, is that it's *cherry*. So, cherry hunter, is it?"

"Absolutely. You will see. Unsoiled, intact, pure cherry. I promise you."

"You embarrassed me once, Kirschjager. Do not imagine that you would survive an encore, even as good an actor as you are. *Squeeeal*," the voice said, and laughed. It was a wet suffocating sound, one that never failed to terrify Ollie.

"Never, never again. I am a good boy now."

"Our client will be flying in on a private jet, very soon now, and he will expect his package to be ready. I'm watching you."

Before Ollie could answer, the line went dead in his hand. He stood still for a moment and listened to the burring sound radiating from the handset, his mind racing. He hung up the phone, poured himself another drink and downed it in two gulps, ignoring how much his hands were shaking.

"I am too tired to play harmless games with it anyway. So fuck you, you…you…face like toilet vomit. Fuck you."

He looked around the room, hoping that it didn't contain any electronic listening devices.

DOMINICAN MULES IN HAITI

AN OLIVE-DRAB ARMY TRUCK rattled its way through the dusty Dominican border town of Elias Pina. The truck's lights disturbed the sleeping vendors who were waiting the day's trading beneath their tarp-covered stalls, their wares scattered about them in organized chaos.

The dawn would see hundreds of Haitians and Dominicans arrive at the ramshackle marketplace, haggling and fretting, eating and drinking. It was the closest thing to an African bazaar outside of the Dark Continent.

Jaragua waved smoke away from his face and silently cursed his driver, who puffed away on his umpteenth cigar and grinded the truck's toothless gears. He was sitting between two brothers who were so different from each other that he found it hard to believe that they had been squirted from the same womb. The driver was stocky and reticent, while his brother was skinny and never stopped talking.

"Uh-huh," Jaragua said, nodding his head automatically. He was thankful that the self-absorbed thug beside him required little input from his captive audience.

The sound of laughter suddenly vibrated through the thin steel partition that separated the truck's cab from its covered bed.

The driver banged a fist against the metal. "Shut up back there."

"Hey, Pedro, relax. They're young guys. They're excited. Don't you remember when we first started out? We were—"

"Enough, Pascal. You're melting the wax in my ears. We're almost there, so shut up," Pedro said to his brother.

"Why do you got to talk to me like that?" He slammed his fist against the dusty dashboard. "Especially in front of the new guy. How many times we done this run? And every time you say the same shit, like I ever get to talk anyway, and you said that I could drive this time. Another lie, you stinking donkey," he said, before staring out the window and falling into a moody sulk.

Jaragua silently thanked Pedro.

The truck belched and trembled its way out of town and steadily made its way down the highway towards the Haitian border.

"You can drive on the way back," Pedro said, lighting another cigar with the smouldering butt of his last one.

"Really?" Pascal said, a broad grin spreading over his unshaven face. "I didn't mean to call you a donkey. What I meant was—"

"Okay, shut the fuck up. We're there."

The border crossing consisted of a jeep, three Haitian soldiers and a frayed rope stretched across a desolate stretch of road. One of the soldiers walked into the middle of the road and levelled an AK-47 at the approaching truck.

As Pedro geared down, Jaragua gripped the Colt .45 he had tucked in his waistband. He almost wished he would get to use it. The vehicle came to a shuddering stop mere inches from the muzzle of the soldier's gun.

Pedro reached under his seat and took out a black plastic bag. He passed the bag to the smiling soldier. "Back in a few hours."

"We'll be waiting," the man said in Creole and then waved to his companions. The other soldiers dropped the rope and stepped aside.

As they progressed deeper into the Haitian countryside, Jaragua wondered if they were even on the same island. It was as if a swarm of locusts had selectively ravaged Hispaniola, their voracious mandibles chewing a ragged swath along the border between the two nations, leaving one side lush and defoliating the other.

"There," Pedro said.

They were approaching another roadblock, only this one looked far more intimidating than an old rope and some old friends. There were at least thirty heavily armed soldiers on the road ahead. Their vehicles were parked on the dirt shoulder. Jaragua could see a line of men working their way down the highway with brooms, clearing the tarmac of debris.

Following the excited hand gestures of the soldiers, Pedro parked the truck on the side of the road and killed the engine.

Jaragua stepped from the vehicle and was surprised to see bales of tobacco flying out of the back of the truck and thumping down into the dirt. There was choreography to the men's movements that disturbed him. He didn't like feeling like the odd man out.

An officer approached them. The man swatted a leather riding crop across the buttocks of any soldier within range and squawked like an irate parrot. He was very short and had a feminine quality to his face.

"I speak passable French, but keep your ears open for something I might miss," Pedro said to Jaragua.

"No problem."

The officer strutted up to Jaragua and the brothers. "I am Lt. Poincy. You and you I know," he said, whacking Pedro and Pascal each on the thigh. "*You* are new. Lieutenant Poincy does not like new." He thrust the handle of his riding crop into Jaragua's stomach with considerable force.

"El Guapo himself has sent him, Lieutenant, and after today, he is the man you will be dealing with," Pedro said.

"I do not like change. El Guapo knows this."

"Nothing has changed, sir. Only the driver."

The Lieutenant narrowed his eyes and studied Jaragua's face. "Why?"

"My brother and I will be overseeing operations in Florida from now on. But you have no need to worry. This man is most reliable."

"Worry? Lt. Poincy does not worry; he makes the worries," the diminutive man said, stamping one booted foot on the ground for emphasis and eyeballing the men.

He squared off in front of Jaragua. "In Haiti, we have a saying. We say that the leaky house can fool the sun, but it cannot fool the rain." He raised his eyebrows as if he had just presented Jaragua with a riddle that demanded an answer.

Jaragua remembered a proverb his father had been fond of quoting. "The cat scalded by hot water is afraid when he sees cold water," he said in perfect Creole.

Lt. Poincy's eyes widened in surprise for a second and then he threw back his head and roared laughing. For such a small person, he had an oddly baritone laugh.

"Exactly," he said, and tapped Jaragua's chest with his riding crop, only this time very lightly. "Exactly. You have brought me a sage, Pedro, a sage and a rogue, and one who can speak proper French instead of Spanish, the language of white swine. Yes. I think he shall suit my disposition."

The sound of an approaching airplane halted any further conversation, and all eyes turned to the sky. The Lieutenant ripped a radio off his utility belt, barked into it and ordered his men around with violent hand gestures.

Within seconds, a line of soldiers had formed on opposite sides of the highway. They ignited handheld flares that sent volcanic eruptions into the early morning air. Jaragua crouched and scanned the sky. The sound of the turboprop grew louder, but he couldn't see the aircraft.

"It's running dark," Pedro said. "There."

A Cessna Cargomaster dropped from the overcast sky like a metallic stone skipping over a slate grey pond. It thundered along the pyrotechnic salute and touched down on the makeshift runway, its tires screeching in alarm.

Jaragua piled into one of the jeeps alongside the other men and held on as the driver roared down the blacktop. By the time the jeep came to a stop, there were four armed men standing by the back of the idling airplane, and they didn't look friendly.

Jaragua watched in amazement as the soldiers swarmed over the plane and began unloading its cargo. They humped the stash of plastic-wrapped bales towards the truck. They looked like a procession of leafcutter ants.

"One thousand bricks of pure Bogotá bitch, non-stop from Colombia to our hands. Insane profit margins," Pedro said.

"I will be commanding this run from now on?" Jaragua asked, looking at Pedro for confirmation.

"Every two weeks, barring any political upheaval, any coups. You know how it is here. Even then, it's only a matter of restructuring. The march northward will never end. Just pray they never legalize the shit. El Guapo asked me to make the introductions etcetera. He'll make it official when the mood strikes him."

The two men watched as Pascal helped the soldiers cover the load of cocaine with bundles of yellowing tobacco leaf.

"You talk a lot more when your brother's not around," Jaragua said.

"Everybody talks more when he's not around, but I love him anyway."

The Lieutenant continued to rant and rave as a group of soldiers finished refuelling the Cessna and scrambled to clear the runway. The aircraft roared back into the sky. It banked and headed south. In another couple of seconds, it was gone.

Jaragua was speechless. It had all happened so quickly, so efficiently. He had always dreamed of being part of such a professional crew, and it looked like his dreams were finally coming true.

He jumped back into the truck, only this time Pedro was wedged in the middle and Pascal was happily gripping the truck's steering wheel.

Pedro passed another black plastic bag out the window. "Your bonus, Lt. Poincy."

The Haitian officer wrinkled his nose in mild disgust as one of his men accepted the bag for him. He stood on his tiptoes and peered inside the cab. "Sage," he said.

"Me?" Jaragua said, pointing a finger at his chest.

"Yeeess, you. If you are half as discreet as Pedro has been over the years, we will have a fruitful and symbiotic relationship. But never forget, you are in my country now, and here in Haiti we say that it's only when the snake dies that you see its true length."

He smacked the side of the truck as if it were a horse's flank. Strangely enough, it had the same effect. Pascal slammed the vibrating gearshift into first, stomped on the gas pedal and accelerated towards the border.

FLIGHT #587

IGNACIO CURSED SOFTLY AS a carload of rowdy teenagers swerved in front of him. He gently tapped the brakes and exited the fast lane. The kids threw obscene gestures and grins behind them and blazed down the highway with the horn wailing.

"Young and bulletproof, just like you, Mr. Mestizo," he said, patting the covered coop beside him.

He could smell the damp earth radiating off the coffee can he had clamped between his thighs. His life savings were inside the can—tightly bound rolls of damp American dollars.

He was driving to Santo Domingo to compete in the world cockfighting championships, where he would bet everything he owned on the warrior he had raised. He passed a gauntlet of roadside stalls, vendors selling river fish, ocean fish, crackling pork, fried cheese, plantain fritters, shrimp with half limes in paper cups, cane juice, empanadas, fresh fruit and Ignacio's favourite treat.

"Yams," he said.

He patted his grumbling belly and steered the truck onto the soft shoulder. He bought two fat ones from a man in a straw hat. The yams' roasted blackened skins had split open, revealing the turmeric-coloured sweetness within.

He sat in his truck with the doors open and devoured one of the yams. It smelled like charcoal and baked bread. To drown out the noise of the passing traffic, he turned on the radio and ratcheted up the volume.

"Eschucha me, muchachas y muchachos," the female DJ said, telling everyone to listen up. "This is a song that has gone from joy to sorrow,

189

from clapping hands to praying ones. Here is Kinito Méndez singing his nineteen-ninety-six hit, 'El Avion.' Where were you when you heard the news?"

Ignacio stared at the radio and allowed his second yam to roll from his limp hand. He would never forget where he was when he heard the news, when he heard that an American Airlines Airbus had plunged from the sky shortly after departing JFK Airport. The plane had crashed to the ground in Queens, having fallen through the weeping clouds like a metal crematorium and incinerating everyone onboard.

The song played on. The merenguero sang about the joy and happiness of boarding festive Flight #587, an early-morning departure that would transport its mostly Dominican passengers from the hustle and stress of New York City to the vibe and rhythm of their island. They would be home in less than four hours, bearing gifts of clothing, food, jewellery and kisses for the families they had left behind.

Flight #587

Two hundred sixty dead

Ignacio would never forget the song "El Avion" because the tragedy had also been the catalyst that gave him the courage to quit drinking and escape the streets. His eyes glazed over as he relived that morning in Santo Domingo.

When his tremors and hallucinations had become too strong, he had crawled out from beneath Duarte Bridge like a mummy from a sarcophagus. He had shuffled along the Ozama River, eventually wandering into the tourist stronghold of Zona Colonial, a perfect location to beg enough foreign sympathy to buy a bottle of cheap rum. He had stumbled past the Catedral Primada de América, the oldest church in the New World, where, in 1514, Columbus' son Diego had set the first stone.

It was just as he had entered Parque Colon when he heard the song. It had boomed across the square from a ghetto blaster sitting beside a shirtless youth lying beneath the shade of an attentive tree.

"El Avion! El Avion!" Ignacio had shouted, spreading his arms wide and dive-bombing the boy like a Kamikaze pilot in a rickety crop duster.

Amused by the drunk's antics, the boy had been the first to contribute to Ignacio's quest for liquid oblivion. He had tossed a few pesos on the ground and laughed as Ignacio scrambled to pick them up.

Ignacio had continued up El Conde, the street of choice for buskers and bums, hawkers and gawkers, tourists and locals. He had jingled the coins in the pocket of his grime-shiny trousers and hummed "El Avion." The song would be stuck in his head until another came along and booted it out. He had a constant merengue soundtrack looping through his pickled brain. On any given day, it could cause him to shake and shimmy, serenade a passing couple or throttle his ghosts with the chains they dragged behind them.

He had begged pesos and pitched and listed along the street. He had been a rudderless skiff in a storm of memories and indifference. He had sailed past souvenir shops, cafes, hotels and restaurants until he had noticed crowds forming in front of bars, the people staring up at huge projection screens, the blood draining from their faces.

He had squirmed his way through a group of punters who had gathered in front of an electronics store. He had pressed his face against the window, between two orange fluorescent banners proclaiming a bankruptcy sale.

He had watched the catastrophe of Flight #587 unfold on a wall of televisions granting him the mosaic vision of a blowfly. He had listened to a reporter with ridiculously coiffed hair describe the mayhem. There had been an inappropriate excitement in his voice that had angered Ignacio.

When it was over, the televisions had gone dark, and he had caught a glimpse of his own reflection in the window. It had been the first time he had seen himself in years. He had stared at the wasted stranger before him, at the dishevelled wreck he had allowed himself to become, and he had begun to weep. He had wept for those who had died so violently in puddles of burning jet fuel. He had wept for his daughter, for his wife, and finally, he had wept for himself.

He had slid down the window and left a saline smudge of dirty tears and regrets on the glass. He had left it there for the cleaners, for the tourists, for the consideration of saints he had stopped believing in. He had lain where he had fallen long after the last stiletto click and echo of boozy laughter had faded from the stone streets. He had stared up at an old moon with newborn eyes and, for the first time since his daughter's death, he had asked God for his help.

He had thought about the victims of the plane crash and how they had no way of knowing as they boarded the flight that they were about to alter the emotion and meaning behind a beloved merengue song. Nobody would ever listen to "El Avion" again and not think of them, not think about how they had died chasing life, their spirits forever entwined within the cadence and poetry of a nation's music and their united grief.

Two hundred sixty dead
One resurrected

Ignacio had arisen with the sun and ignored the charity that fell from his clothes and rolled into the gutter. It had giggled at his audacity and awaited humbler hands.

ARRESTED DEVELOPMENT

Tika stood naked in the middle of her sparsely furnished room and stared at her reflection in the mirror. She had taped her developing breasts against her chest in an effort to flatten them. She lowered her gaze, looked at her shaved vagina and frowned. He was right, she thought. She was ugly and useless.

She despised her body for betraying her, for maturing and driving away the only person who had ever shown her any affection in her short life. Hot tears stung her battered lip and dripped from her trembling chin.

"Stupid."

She slapped herself across the face—the way Ollie had—and because it felt good, she did it again. She sat down on the coarse wooden floor and remembered how nice the plush carpet used to feel beneath her bare skin, when she had lived in the pink room, before the other girl had shown up. She didn't hate the other girl anymore. She had none to spare.

She picked up a box of matches, lit one and touched the flame to the soft skin on her forearm. It was strange, she thought. She could smell her searing flesh, but she felt no pain. When the match burned out, she lit another and touched it to the same spot.

If Ollie no longer loved her, she thought. Nobody ever would. After all, her own parents had abandoned her by the side of a dirt road near Boca Chica.

She was five.

Tika could still remember the huge multicoloured curlers that her mother often wore in her hair, as if they themselves were a fashion statement instead of the curls they created. Selling fruit by the roadside had been her family's livelihood, and her mother had sat her down behind a wooden crate heaped with rosy mangoes. Sometimes they sold pineapples, sometimes plantains. But on that day—on that horrible lonely day that had changed her life forever—it had been mangoes.

She lit another match.

She had waited for her parents to return, peering shyly around the corner of the crate every time she heard the rattle and scrape of some old car passing by. She had even sold some of the fruit—all by herself—and she remembered how happy that had made her feel. She had been looking forward to giving the money to her mother when she returned…but she never did. Eventually, she had begun to feel afraid and had slunk down behind the fruit stand and tried not to make any noise.

Another match.

She could still hear the sound of softly squealing brakes as a car had come to a stop on the road beside her, and then she had heard the crunch of shoes on gravel. She had looked up, her wet brown eyes full of hope, the word *Mama* forming on her lips, but it hadn't been her mother. A gringo had stood there, his sweaty hair matted to his sunburned forehead, his magnified eyes staring down at her from behind the thick lenses of his glasses. She had felt like an insect under a microscope.

He had squatted down beside her and said her name, pronouncing it carefully, tasting the word. She had asked him if he knew when her mother was coming back, and she would never forget the stranger's reply. He had smiled gently, looked calmly into her eyes and said that her mother and father didn't love her anymore and that they were never coming back. His words had driven their way straight through her thin chest like daggers made of ice piercing her bleeding heart and flash freezing it.

She hadn't screamed. She hadn't cried. There was no explanation for her immediate acceptance and belief of his words except that all children—perhaps intuitively—understood exactly how much they were loved…or were not.

She had wrapped her tiny arms around Ollie's neck as he picked her up. He had bundled her into his car, kissed her cheek and told her that he was going to take care of her, that he would be her new papa—that he loved her. She remembered feeling relieved.

Tika watched the dying flame dance beneath her hissing and blistered flesh until it went out. She dropped the charred wood onto a blackened pile of withered matchsticks and frowned when she discovered that the box was empty. She stood up and moved catatonically towards the bathroom, her ruined arm twitching spasmodically by her side. She flicked on the light, flooding the room with a cruel brilliance that exposed things, secret things.

She ran a scalding hot bath, quickly clouding the room in a muggy haze. As the tub continued to fill, she removed the lid from the toilet tank, retrieved a plastic pill bottle from its hiding place and emptied its contents into her mouth. She chewed the diazepam with robotic efficiency, crushing the blue pills into a chalky powder. She filled a small porcelain cup with some water and washed the sedatives down her throat.

She thought that she would feel different when her special day arrived—frightened, elated, something. However, as she eased her bruised body into the water, she realized that she felt nothing at all—no rage, no sadness. She simply felt…done. And had she believed in God, she would have thanked him for it.

She felt so peaceful lying there cocooned within the seductive warmth of the water, so safe in the protective arms of her surrender. Nobody would ever hurt her again.

The pills leeched the anxiety and will from her muscles, and her head slipped slowly beneath the water. Her vision blurred, and she released her bladder.

She was so tired.

She blinked a couple of times and opened her mouth, allowing the water to flood gratefully into her accepting lungs. Her last thoughts before the silence and darkness blessed her with the calm she was seeking were of her mother. Tika thought about how proud her mother was going to be when she saw how many mangoes she had sold…all by herself.

JUDAS AND CAIN

TWENTY-FIVE THOUSAND DOLLARS, JARAGUA thought as he slipped on a pair of new leather shoes. He knew El Guapo would make millions from the cocaine shipment, but he couldn't care less; he felt rich.

He picked up his new gun. "Walther PPK, Polizei Pistole Kriminal," he said, admiring the weapon's lightweight construction.

He threaded his belt through the loops of his S.O.B. holster, slid the gun into its pocket and settled it in the small of his back. He threw on a loose white cotton shirt and viewed himself from different angles in the mirror.

"Invincible," he whispered.

It was strange, he thought, how money could increase a man's confidence so dramatically. He felt cooler, tougher—hell, he was semi-erect.

He left his room, took the stairs two at a time and moved towards the back of the mansion. As he walked, he remembered the warehouse in Santo Domingo where he had dropped off the coke—the legitimate face of El Guapo's distribution network.

Jaragua was stunned when he had entered the soundproofed dungeon below the warehouse. There had been over fifty people cutting and packaging their way through a mountain of cocaine. Except for their blue surgical masks and gloves, they had been completely naked. They looked like a group of swinging pharmacists. The presence of half a dozen soldiers brandishing Heckler & Koch MP5 submachine guns reminded everybody of the consequences of stealing.

El Guapo owned an import/export business. It supplied his chain of stores across North America. The shops were called Dr. Goodstuff, and they sold products exclusively from the Dominican Republic: sugarcane, coffee, cocoa, cigars, leather masks, wood and stone artwork, larimar and amber jewellery, freeze-dried tarantulas, monstrous centipedes encased in glass…and Bogotá Bitch.

Jaragua saw the Colombian standing in the hallway.

"Where's *El Guapo*?" Jaragua asked.

"The *boss* is out back by the pens, and I wouldn't keep him waiting if I was you."

Jaragua smirked openly. He was rising quickly in the organization, and he had already felt the heat of envy in some of the other men's stares…especially the Colombian's. Jaragua was starting to regret saving the man's life.

Fuck 'em

Jaragua walked out of the mansion and into a fenced compound. There were perhaps two hundred birds scattered about the yard—some in pens, some doing flys or rope work, others sparred, others crowed and strutted. It was a gladiator school for roosters.

"You've almost missed it, Mr. Ventura," El Guapo said. "Come and join us. The contest is just getting interesting."

A knot of men were watching a sparring session between two fierce battlecocks wearing red muffs that seemed frustrated at their inability to do any real damage.

"Gentlemen, I employ the most knowledgeable trainers. I have purchased birds from pugnacious and proven bloodlines. These animals want for nothing. Is it unreasonable of me to expect a champion to arise like a phoenix from the chickenshit?" El Guapo said, watching the birds fight. "These birds are called Aseels. The name is Arabic and means 'of long pedigree.' They are highly aggressive unpredictable troublemakers that many cockers refuse to train. However, within that rebellion dwells a valiant nature, one that refuses to be dominated. Sammy, remove their boxing gloves."

The men displayed a renewed interest in the match as the two gamecocks went to war. They lunged and pecked at each other, leapt into the air and laid in some wicked punishment with their natural spurs. The men in the yard joined the circle and began cheering on their favourite. The excitement grew as the battle deteriorated into a bloodbath. The Aseels lived up to their reputation.

Eventually, one of them began to stagger and avoid the other's attacks. It was something that galleros hated to see in their charges. The behaviour was known as ducking, and once learned, the habit could ruin a potentially great fighter.

El Guapo reached down, picked up the winning bird and stroked it gently. "Attila. That is your new name. Soon you shall be competing in the world championships in Santo Domingo, and if you embarrass me, I will kill your whole family."

He handed the agitated rooster to his trainer. "See to its wounds."

He then leaned down and spoke to the losing bird as if it were a naughty child. "And what should I do with you?"

"Excuse me, sir," Sammy said, "but he is also a very talented and expensive bird, and I think that with some training and some more time, I could forge a decent warrior out of him."

El Guapo seized the wounded bird around the neck and lifted it into the air. "This bird here, Sammy? This little fucker right here?" He shook the gurgling rooster. "He's a loser, and I am a firm believer in culling my flock to keep it strong. Weakness, like disloyalty, has a way of spreading through the ranks. This chicken pot pie right here is nothing but a cancer looking to metastasize."

He wrung the bird's neck and tossed its twitching carcass to the ground. "Don't feed its meat even to Cain. He cannot afford a more feeble spirit than he already has.

"Speaking of Cain, who here would like to go and say hello to my *other* Rotti?" he asked the small group of men around him.

Jaragua followed El Guapo and NCM onto the expansive terrace that ringed the huge house. He had no idea who the other men were, but he could tell from their demeanour that they were important to El Guapo.

They arrived at a concrete enclosure. Its rough high walls looked out of place beside the custom work the stonemasons had crafted onto the house's exterior.

Jaragua peered down into what appeared to be a lion's den. There were gnawed bones bleaching out in the sun, and deep claw marks scoured the earth around the perimeter of the pen as if whatever lived there had tried to escape.

"What's that sled of scrap iron for?" Jaragua asked.

"In due time, Curious George. In due time," El Guapo said. "You see, what I have done here, probably out of sheer boredom, was attempt to create something that would have given Dr. Frankenstein himself a chubby."

He pulled an Israeli .50 Desert Eagle handgun from a hip holster and fired two deafening rounds into the pen's far wall. Instantly, a massive Rottweiler erupted from the shadows and charged into the middle of the enclosure. It was a freakishly muscled salivating brute. It looked more like a silverback gorilla than a dog. The group of men gasped in horror and stared down at the terrifying animal.

"There he is. His name is Abel," El Guapo said. His tone was that of a proud father. "He has never, since being forced from his mother's saggy teat, been shown any affection. He has had his balls shocked with a cattle prod on a regular basis, been fed truckloads of anabolic steroids and been forced to pull that sled of iron around the yard. He eats nothing but raw meat. That is to say, I feed him live animals. The strange thing is nobody has ever heard him bark—not once, not ever. He growls, he gnashes his fangs, he drools and pants, but no barking. Odd."

He stared down at the dog for an uncomfortable length of time before continuing. "Jaragua, I have been rather rude. Allow me to introduce you to my lieutenants. This is Mr. Toronto. Beside him Mr. Puerto Rico, Mr. New York, Mr. LA, Mr. Chicago, Mr. Vancouver and finally Mr. Miami." He pointed lastly to a perfectly groomed man who smelled better than most women did.

"Oh, and Mr. Miami has another name, an AKA if you will," El

Guapo said. "He is also known as Judas motherfucking Iscariot." He then lashed the startled man across the head with his gun.

The man cried out and stumbled backwards into the barrel of the shotgun NCM had trained on him.

"Did you think that I wouldn't find out, Judas?" El Guapo asked, his voice calm and devoid of emotion.

"Please, El Guapo, I don't know what you've heard, but—"

El Guapo brought the butt of his gun down on top of the man's head. "Shut it, liar. Not only do you arrange to sell me out, but you also have the nerve to try and weasel out of your well-deserved punishment. I have friends everywhere, you fuckin' imbecile, and that includes inside the American DEA.

"Strip him."

Using a knife, NCM slashed and ripped at the man's clothes until he stood before the group, clad in nothing but a pair of black silk stockings and a red leather G-string.

It was Mr. Toronto who snickered first, then Mr. Chicago and then everyone just dissolved into laughter.

"Gentlemen. Gentlemen, please," El Guapo said. "All secrets shall come to light, eh, Judas? You look so utterly pathetic right now that I can hardly remember the man you used to be...if you were ever really him at all."

Mr. Miami took a deep steadying breath and wiped tears from his eyes. "Please, let me go. I'll disappear. I never would have testified. I was confused," he pleaded.

El Guapo put an end to his grovelling with a casual wave of his hand. NCM wrapped his huge hands around the man's ankles, flipped him over the wall and dangled him above Abel.

"Oh stop your whining and take it like a man, you ass-fucking little queer," El Guapo said.

The dog lunged at his meal, his jaws snapping just short of the man's head.

"I wonder, Judas, if, in all the ways you ever imagined you might die, did you ever consider that the Grim Reaper would one day come for you in the guise of a Rottweiler suffering roid rage?" El Guapo asked and then nodded to NCM.

Abel caught Mr. Miami in midair. The dog's powerful teeth clamped around the man's face, muffling the screams. The creature dragged his kicking prey the length of the kennel and back into the shadows from whence he came. Eventually, the man stopped screaming, and the only sound coming from the darkened corner was that of snapping bones and tearing flesh.

"Thank you all for coming on such short notice. NCM will see you out. He has a nice fat envelope for each of you." El Guapo dismissed the men by turning his back on them.

"Jaragua, a moment of your time."

"What can I do for you, sir?"

"As you know, Pedro and Pascal have been sent to Miami to replace the dog food over there. I only wanted to send one really, but as you know, they kinda come as a pair. One don't say shit and the other spews it. I assume Pedro told you that you're going to be in charge of our Haiti thing from now on."

"Yes. He mentioned it when we were there. I won't let you down."

"No, you won't. That goes without saying. I would also like you to take care of a special project for me, a rather sensitive matter that will test your commitment like nothing before ever has. Impress me and your stock rises exponentially... Oh right. You're not a fan of multisyllabic words, are you? Do good and me likey very much. I will inform you of the details when the time is nigh."

El Guapo pointed his handgun down into Abel's pen, closed one eye and sighted along the barrel. "Now leave me alone. I want to spend some time with my puppy."

TONTON MACOUTE

OLLIE SPUN AROUND IN his chair, stared up at the ceiling and wondered how much longer he would have to endure the charade that his life had become. He was weary of kissing the ass of mutant coke kings and corrupt officials, sick of sweating his balls off beneath a cruel sun, tired of the stench of shit, decaying flesh and body odour.

"I miss my home."

He thought about his native Bavaria and sighed. He missed the seasons, the cool air—and as stereotypical as it was, he missed the beer and the bratwurst. The only thing that kept him from going crazy was the knowledge that with every child he sent plunging down the pipeline, with every hit his website generated, his fantasy life edged closer to reality.

He dreamed of the day when he could escape the tannery. He would build a huge traditional home on the edge of the Black Forest, and there he would unleash his latest and most special of characters, a persona he would call the Strudelmiester.

He envisioned a website like no other, one where he would re-enact famous fairytales such as "Little Red Riding Hood," "Rumpelstiltskin" and, of course, "Hansel and Gretel." He would give new meaning to the concept of babes in the woods.

The Internet had permanently altered life on planet pedophile, its tentacles reaching out and connecting individuals who would have otherwise remained isolated. Pedophiles no longer needed to satisfy their depraved urges in murky basements beneath soiled sheets in fear of discovery, confining the damage they were capable of inflicting to those unfortunate enough to call them father, uncle, pastor or coach. It was the Wild West, a bold new world that exposed the universal depths of evil like never before.

"I have used enough restraint for a while," he said, and got to his feet.

He lumbered down the hall and unlocked Lourdes' bedroom door. He was about to enter when he looked towards Tika's room. He felt bad for being so mean to the girl the other night. After all, he thought, it wasn't her fault that she had outlived her usefulness, and besides, she would be gone in a couple of days anyway.

He went to Tika's door, pushed it open and entered her room.

"Tika, little squirrel, answer me now. I am no longer angry with you," he said, his voice probing the gloom for her hiding place.

"No hide-and-seeky tonight. Come out, come out, wherever you are," he said, pulling the blankets off her bed.

"My patience wears thin, Tika. Show yourself."

He could hear water dripping. "You are taking some cleansing?"

He walked towards the bathroom and pushed the door open.

"Mein Gott."

Tika stared at him from beneath the water, her accusing eyes locked on the monster that destroyed her.

"No, little squirrel. No."

He reached a hand into the cold water and pulled the plug, watching as the tub drained. Tika's hair reminded him of a nest of vipers as it swirled through the water. "Medusa," he whispered. "Perhaps it is for the better."

He took her by the arms and pulled her out of the bathtub. Her pale legs thumped loudly onto the tiled floor. He dragged her into the bedroom and spread a white sheet over the wooden floor.

"Poor Tika," he said, as he rolled her body up in the sheet. "Nobody ever loved this one. Only me."

He looked down at his handiwork and smiled. He had been dreading having to dump her at the brothel, having to endure the inevitable histrionics that would have followed.

Pain in the ass

He threw his bundle over his shoulder, grunted and headed for the door. He slapped a hand across her buttocks. "Now I know the meaning of dead weight. Ooomm-pah."

He walked out into the stillness and gloom of the hallway and heard a whimpering sound, one that was familiar to him. He turned around and saw Lourdes standing there. She wore a bright yellow sundress. Her eyes were wide, and her bottom lip was trembling.

She pressed herself against the wall. "Tonton Macoute," she said.

Ollie immediately recognized the term. It meant Uncle Gunnysack, a mythical Haitian bogeyman that bagged children up and carried them off into the night.

"Yes, Palomita," he said, gently lowering the body to the floor. "Uncle Knapsack sent me to collect this one. Come here. That's it. Don't be afraid." He fumbled with the damp sheet.

Lourdes looked down at Tika's bloated and purple face.

"You remember her, don't you? Well, she was a very *bad* girl. This is why Uncle Knapsack sent me for her. *You* don't want Tonton Macoute to come for you...do you?" he asked, giving her time to engrave the macabre image in her mind. "Tika told about the piggy—about the piggy and the games he likes to play, his secret games—and this is what happens to little girls who tell."

He took her hand and forced her to touch the dead girl's face. Lourdes made a choking sound, yanked her hand away and stumbled backwards.

"Go back to your room now, Palomita. Close the door and never tell anyone about the piggy, or about Tika, or Tonton Macoute will come for you and bury you in the ground so that the worms may eat you. Do you want worms to eat you?"

Lourdes turned and ran into her room.

Ollie giggled as he carried the body down into the root cellar. The girl was his now, he thought. He couldn't have planned it better if he had tried. She would give him no more trouble.

He dug a hole in the earth, kicked the corpse into it and filled it back in.

"There," he said, stamping the loose dirt down. He placed a burlap sack of potatoes at the head of Tika's grave like an irreverent tombstone. "Like you never happened."

THE STONING OF CALIGULA

THE RAIN DROVE AGAINST Maximo, and the mucky ground sucked at his wooden leg. He felt as if he were uprooting a sapling with every step. He could feel the rusty buckles and leather straps digging into his thigh. He lurched up the front steps of Ollie's house and banged on the heavy door with all his strength.

The door swung inward, and Ollie stood in the doorway. A white sheet draped loosely around his nakedness, his overfed body filling the void with its menacing bulk. Maximo could see his bare feet sticking out from beneath the hem of his makeshift toga. They looked like two dead monkfish, pale, puffy and scaly.

"You have ten minutes. Don't upset her." Ollie scowled and then turned away and thumped back up the staircase.

Maximo wrinkled his nose in disgust. The place smelled like boiled cabbage and alcohol. He walked into the living room, leaving a defiant trail of slurry behind him.

Lourdes was sitting on the edge of a floral sofa and staring out the window. She was dressed in an overtly feminine outfit. It was all lace and bows, satin and sickness—it wasn't what his tomboy sister would have ever chosen to wear.

He knelt down beside her and looked up into her face. "Palomita."

She stopped worrying a loose strand of her hair but otherwise gave no indication that she was even aware of his presence. She sat like a poised and fragile prima ballerina, a real-life Medora from the tragic ballet *The Corsair*. His heart broke at the utter transformation of the only person left in the world that meant anything to him.

"It's me. Maximo."

Slowly, she turned and faced him. "I want Mami and Papi to come and get me." Her voice had an unnatural monotone quality to it.

He took one of her limp hands into his own, hating her robotic compliance, the vacancy in her eyes.

"Why have you left me here all alone?" she asked.

He didn't know what to say to her. He wanted to tell her that it wasn't his fault, that he was just a boy, that he missed their parents too… that he was afraid. "I'm going to get us out of here. You have to trust me. I'm making a plan. Is that pig Ollie hurting you?"

Lourdes flinched at his words and withdrew her hand from his.

"What is happening to you, Lourdes? Please tell me. I want to help you."

She looked away from him, her tiny hand returning to a loose strand of hair. She began to hum the song "Thank Heaven for Little Girls." He reached out and embraced her, carefully drawing her in until he felt the tremble and tension of her secrets begin to bleed out of her. Lourdes sagged gratefully into the only safety and purity available to her.

"Where is that other girl Tika? Is she kind to you?" Maximo asked.

At the mention of Tika's name, Lourdes went rigid against him, and a thin hissing sound escaped her clamped lips. "No," she said, and pushed him away.

Her eyes darted frantically around the room, searching for a way out, a way to escape her brother's questions, the house and Uncle Knapsack. But most of all, she wanted to escape from the piggy, who looked nothing at all like the animals her father used to raise and who made terrifying noises and crept into her room at night on all fours like a shivering split-hoofed abomination.

"Palomita, what is it? Tell me."

She lashed out at him, scratching and kicking. Maximo fell away from her hysterical attack, tears welling up in his eyes as she landed blow after undefended blow.

Then she ran.

"Lourdes," Maximo said, limping up the staircase behind her.

He had just made it to the first landing when Ollie came clomping down the stairs like a hobbled Clydesdale. In a flash, he seized Maximo by the throat, lifted him off his feet and threw him into the air. He crashed down the stairs and landed in a dazed heap at the bottom, his prosthesis skidding across the floor behind him.

Before Maximo could even catch his breath, Ollie was on him, kicking him towards the door.

Ollie's face shined with glee. "Finally, you are getting a proper lesson." His foot connected with Maximo's head, then his stomach, then one to the kidneys.

Maximo vomited, rolled and covered his head with his arms.

"You foul, dirty, little heathen," Ollie said.

He picked Maximo up by the seat of his pants and carried him towards the door like a sack of flour. He opened the door, swung him like a pendulum and launched him off the veranda. Maximo collided with the wet ground, furrowing into the mud as if he were stealing a base. There was no pain, just a seething anger that spoke of insanity.

"Your visitation rights have just been revoked," Ollie said from the shelter of the porch. The sheet he wore billowed out behind him, exposing his ruddy genitals. "You no longer have a sister."

Maximo smashed his fists into the ground and crawled towards the house, rainwater streaming over his contorted face. "I'm going to kill you! My name is Maximo Caesar Ventura, and I'm going to kill you!" He felt something hard beneath his hands, and he dug frantically at the squelching earth.

Ollie laughed as he watched him clawing at the ground. To him, Maximo looked like a terrified mole that was desperately trying to return to the safety of its subterranean world.

Maximo's hands curled around two apple-sized stones, and he tore them from the mud. He threw a rock at Ollie's head. "Fastball."

The rock clipped the top of Ollie's ear and smashed through the window behind him. Ollie yelped in surprise and clamped a hand over his head. His eyes filled with rage until he saw Maximo reloading his throwing arm. He turned and lunged for the door.

The second rock nailed Ollie between the shoulder blades, knocking the wind out of him. He screamed, fell into the foyer and kicked the door closed behind him. He sprawled on the floor, groaned helplessly and flinched every time another rock struck the house. He could hear Maximo outside, ranting and cursing.

Ollie wheezed some oxygen into his lungs and cringed behind the oak door. "That's it. Bawl and tantrum like a piss-diapered baby. Kill me? No boy. The only one being killed around here is you...and I shall take my time with it."

THE SAVIOUR OF PUERTO PLATA

IGNACIO SAT IN HIS truck, looked at the arena and chewed his bottom lip. It was the sparkling jewel of Dominican cockfighting pits, a circular orange and beige building trimmed with blue neon lights and guarded by magnificent royal palms.

"The big show, eh, Mr. Mestizo?"

He felt like an impostor. He watched a steady procession of expensive automobiles pull up under the coliseum's carport. He frowned as well-dressed men swaggered into the building through doors that were held open for them.

You smell like shit

He rested his head against the steering wheel and considered not going in at all. He felt welcomed at other arenas, in places like Manoguayabo, a brooding pit that squatted on the roughest edge of Santo Domingo's fringe cloaked in diesel smoke and notoriety. There Ignacio had found respect. There Mr. Mestizo had become a rock star.

He stared into the hard glint of his champion's eye and felt immediately ashamed of himself. His rooster knew nothing about castes and pedigrees and couldn't care less about stacked odds and snivelling self-doubt. He was vital and strapping. He had crowed triumphantly over the carcasses of twelve challengers. He was ready to embrace his fate, be it fame or failure, and he had no time for the indecision in an old man's eyes.

Mr. Mestizo crowed loudly and rustled his feathers.

"Yes. You are right, of course. I apologize for that. You will be world champion whether I like it or not," he said, stroking him through the

211

cage's wire mesh. "After this tournament, what do you say about retiring? I will buy you a harem of pretty hens and build you a comfortable roost with clean straw. We can grow old together, sitting beneath the shade of a cashew tree, eating sweet mangoes and swapping war stories. Mine half-truths and fantasies; yours the stuff of legend."

The rooster pushed up against Ignacio's fingers and clucked softly.

"Sounds good to you? Yeah, I know, especially the part about the harem." He chuckled.

"Come on. Let's go introduce you to high society."

Ignacio carried his bird into the coliseum. Once inside, he was confronted by a wiry man with the temperament of a terrier on taurine.

"Name?"

"Ignacio dos Santos."

The man blinked rapidly, violently chewing a wad of gum that had surrendered its flavour hours earlier. "Your rooster's name, not yours."

"Oh. It's Mr. Mestizo."

The man stopped chewing, stopped writing and stared hard at Ignacio. "Say again?"

"Mr. Mestizo. That's his name."

"Where the hell have you been? Hey, chicos, over here. It's Mr. fucking Mestizo, or at least this old guy says it is."

"Go to hell," a big man said, dropping a bird of lesser fame on the floor and walking over.

"Where? Bullshit. Show me," another man said, pushing his way through the crowded room.

"Right here. The brown and white one," the wiry man said.

"Actually, if you look closer, you will see that he is cinnamon and ivory coloured," Ignacio said.

"Yeah, sure, buddy. Whatever shade you want. The only thing I want to know is if this is the rooster that every dirt farmer, cane cutter and shack dweller from here to Neptune has been gibbering about."

A group of men clustered around Ignacio, judged Mr. Mestizo with their eyes and voiced their cynicism.

"He's a dunghill."

"A mongrel."

"Half-caste."

Ignacio swallowed the insults before replying. "Mixed blood is strong blood. As Dominicans, you should all be aware of that fact," he said, while stroking his bird's feathers.

"We will know soon enough if this is the saviour of Puerto Plata. Now weigh him," the wiry man said.

"I have heard that name, but call him Mr. Mestizo," Ignacio said.

"No problem, amigo. Several well-known galleros have expressed an interest in pitting their champions against your local bully here, Aseels, Jerezanos, purebred gamecocks that many here believe will make short work of your back-alley scrapper."

"Three point five pounds exactly. At least he knows how to make weight."

"Good. We're done, Eduvigis—"

"Ignacio."

"Sure. Whatever, buddy. When I find an appropriate opponent for your chicken, I'll call you to come heel 'em. Meanwhile, I suggest you go and check out the calibre of fighters the world has assembled here for this tournament, and don't wager your pocketful of change too quickly."

"Gracias, señor," Ignacio said, and bowed slightly. "And I hope you have the huevos to bet against my...what did you call him...my chicken? Please, wager every peso you have against Mr. Mestizo, and the only bird in your soup pot tonight will be crow," he said, and walked away.

He followed the sound of cheering until he was inside the amphitheatre. In all his days, he had never seen such a cockpit. The two roosters in the ring strutted across a green felt floor that resembled the groomed perfection of a billiard table. The ascending tiers of seats were filled with animated clean-shaven men who drank their beer from a glass and wore gold around their necks.

He found a place to stand and looked down at the double row of plush chairs that ringed the cockpit. The wealthy and the ruthless, Dominican plantation owners, Haitian sweatshop proprietors, famous baseball players, Filipino crime bosses, army brass, Texans in Stetsons and the odd coke king occupied them.

Over the next few hours, he watched intense matches between Toppies, Hennies, Bankivas, Cuban canelos, Malays, Aseels, Shamos and Kelsos. There were high-stationed beauties and squirrel-tailed grunts, birds of mottled plumage and others of solid colouring. He studied the different fighting styles of the world's best. He witnessed examples of cutters, shufflers, duckers, wheelers, ground-and-pounders, peckers and strikers, headhunters and leg-breakers. The exhilaration and tension in the air was palpable, and money changed hands as quickly as the competitors fell.

Ignacio wrapped his fingers around the seven grand in his pocket and thought about Mr. Mestizo. He felt like fleeing back to the refuge of his rubber trees.

IN A NEW YORK STATE OF MIND

MAXIMO FOLLOWED JESUS THROUGH the smokehouse. They brushed against hanging elk and deer, animals they had never seen alive. The place was a mausoleum, a desecration, a burial ground for souls from a green glen and a blue planet.

Jesus pushed a loose plank to one side. "Through here."

Maximo squeezed through the narrow opening and stepped into the shaded covertness of a grove of pine trees. The fresh air washed over him like a cool rain. He sat on a rock and hung his head between his knees and coughed.

"I think we can steal ten minutes or so before anybody curses our laziness," Jesus said.

Maximo shrugged his shoulders and laced his fingers.

"How's your face?" Jesus asked.

"Fine. My ribs still hurt, but nothing is broken. I don't care anyway. I stole a knife from the kitchen. After work today, I'm going to knock on the door, and when that bastard opens it, I'm going to gut him like a pregnant sow and get Lourdes out of there...she and I are leaving. Tonight."

"Maybe there is a better way—"

"No. Tonight. And if you want to continue calling yourself my friend, don't try to stop me."

Jesus remained silent for a while before speaking again. "There's a boat. In a few days, it's heading to Puerto Rico."

"A yola?"

"Yes. I know when and where. If we can get Lourdes out of that house—without you going to jail, I mean—then you're half way to New York."

"I don't have any money."

Jesus looked at the purple and black bruise on his friend's face. It crept over his cheekbone like an unfortunate birthmark. "I have some money. Not a lot, but probably enough for the captain of a yola. It's yours if you promise me you won't kill Ollie."

Maximo looked over at him and forced himself to smile. "I didn't mean what I said about you not being my friend anymore. I can send you the money back once we reach New York."

"So you won't harpoon the ballena?"

Maximo laughed and placed a hand over his ribs. "Not if I don't have to. When does the yola leave?"

"A few nights from now. Moon will be full."

"From where?"

"Nagua."

"I won't forget this," Maximo said.

"Hey, when you become the first stumpy-legged pitcher in the majors, I won't let you forget it. Now we need to figure out how we can sneak into Ollie's house and get Lourdes."

"I have a plan," Maximo said. "I got the idea from a story my mother told me once. I don't remember it all, but it was about a bunch of Greek dudes who built a wooden horse. They used it to get into some castle."

"A wooden horse?"

"Yeah, they called it a Trojan horse."

"Hah. Trojan. Like the condoms," Jesus said, and laughed. "But where are we going to get a wooden horse?"

"Never mind. You will understand soon enough. You're going to love it." Maximo touched knuckles with his friend. "Now come on. Let's go back and pretend like nothing is different."

SHORT EYES

A SLEEK GULFSTREAM G350 banked smoothly and descended on the Caribbean island of Hispaniola. The private jet had departed from JFK Airport a few hours earlier, and its owner was determined to be standing on the terrace of his Fifth Avenue penthouse apartment in time to watch the sunrise over Manhattan.

Keegan Sherbet stretched out a pallid emaciated arm and listlessly scooped a handful of gummy bears from a crystal bowl. He had a small heart tattooed on his forearm. A larger one surrounded it. The bleeding organs were bound together with barbed wire.

His name was Irish, and it meant "little fiery one," an ironic moniker considering he was as tepid as the neglected bathwater of an octogenarian suffering from dementia.

"Bring me another cream soda," he said, knowing that the drink would arrive before he was finished swallowing his wad of jellies.

He was thirty-five but looked ten years younger and he had the mannerisms of a spoiled moody teenager. He was diminutive and bloodless and had made his money by creating websites. He had gotten in, gotten rich and gotten out.

"Flying is soooo boring," he whined, looking to his bodyguards for sympathy.

The two men were as tough as they appeared. There were ex soldiers who had believed all the lies the military had force-fed them. One was British, the other American, and the atrocities they had committed for flag and country had so eroded their morality that they could no longer distinguish good from evil, murderer from patriot, henchman from protector. Keegan was making his attack dogs wealthy men. He adhered

217

to the philosophy that you got what you paid for, and the price of a once honourable man's soul was never going to come cheap.

"Hope you guys like Thai food," he said.

"Dog's bollocks, sir," the Brit said.

"Yeah, and that's just the appetizer," the American said without smiling.

"Ha ha. Well, I hope you do because that's where we are all going to be as of next week. Bangkok for a month or so and then on to that sinful little smuthole Cambodia. I gots me a hankering for some sweet young sushi…gonna eat me some Asian."

"Sushi is Jap food, sir," the Brit said.

"I know that, knobgobbler, mudshark. It was a play on words. Do ya think I made a couple a hundred millys by not knowing where the *fuck* sushi comes from?"

"Sorry, cur."

"Yeah, whatever." Keegan slumped deeper into his chair and stared out the window at the twinkling lights far below. He was waiting for one of them to speak.

"Got any new jokes?" the American asked.

Keegan crossed his arms over his sunken chest. "Maybe."

"Go on, then. Let's hear it," the Brit said.

"Fine. What's the best thing about twenty-five-year-olds?"

"Got me."

"Dunno."

"The best thing about twenty-*five*-year-olds is that there are *twenty* of them. Ta-da," Keegan said, spreading his arms wide.

"Good one."

"Yep. Very funny."

"I realize that I didn't buy you two for your engaging personalities, but the occasional shit-eating grin every now and then wouldn't go astray either," Keegan said, and glared at them through the petulance of his sulk.

He looked out the window again and thought about the Pigmeister and his amusing online antics. The German had become a reliable source of baby flesh, and the moment Keegan had laid eyes on the new girl, he knew he would own her.

There was no time to waste, he thought. There would be plenty of distractions in Asia. He would fly the girl back to New York, destroy her and then have his men dump her body in the Hudson River. He shifted his weight, relieving the pressure on his erection.

"How long till we land?"

CHIMERA

Maximo felt as if he were suffocating. The weight of the potatoes pressed against his chest and constricted his breathing. He could smell the earthiness of the tubers and the burlap of the sack that imprisoned him.

"You don't look anything like a condom," Jesus whispered through the cloth, his coffee-scented breath filling the claustrophobic space around Maximo's head.

"We have to stop talking now," Maximo said.

"I know. Good luck, my friend."

"Thank you, Jesus. When I have a place in New York, you can come and live with me and Lourdes."

"I would love it, and maybe I can see snow, even if it's only the grey kind that I've seen in pictures. You know, like on the streets."

"Yeah, and we can have a grey snowball fight. See ya soon."

"Goodbye," Jesus said.

He stood up and faced Kazi, the huge man who carried Ollie's supplies down into his root cellar every month.

Kazi pointed at the bulging sack of potatoes on his trolley. "He in there?"

"Yes, so be gentle. I will give you your rum and smoke tonight."

"I will share a drink with you as a friend, but everyone knows what goes on up there and everyone knows that it has to stop. I'm happy to help."

Kazi wrapped his powerful hands around the cart's handle and pushed the load towards Ollie's house.

"They're potatoes, not fine china, damn you. Throw it down and get the rest of my things," Ollie said.

Kazi released his grip on the burlap sack. The hard landing knocked the wind out of Maximo.

Ollie's eyes narrowed, and he looked around the tiny room. "What was that?"

Kazi doubled over, placed a hand over his ribcage and tried to imitate the sound. "Sorry, Mr. Ollie. I felt something bad, inside. Give me a minute."

"You're almost ready for the pasture, huh? I remember when you used to throw sack-a-spud around like popcorn bags, and the size a you, like an ape," Ollie said, shaking his head and frowning.

"I'll get the rest of your stuff."

"And quickly, ya?"

Maximo gripped his butcher knife so hard that his fingers ached as much as his spine. It took all his willpower not to squirm and moan from the throbbing in his back. He needed air.

Kazi stacked commercial-sized jars of dill pickles, sauerkraut, hot mustards, Greek olives, marinated artichokes and banana peppers on the cool ground beside Maximo and then left the cellar. Maximo heard steel doors slamming, bolts sliding, locks snapping and Ollie muttering under his breath.

Ollie surveyed his horde of food. "Bush monkeys, prostitutes and thieves. Good, ya, and my spuds, and my tasty things. Yes, all are accounted for."

Maximo froze. Ollie was so close he could smell his bitter sweat.

"Sleep well, Tika. Always I loved you." Ollie turned off the light and walked from the room.

Maximo listened to Ollie's footsteps as he climbed the stairs and listened to the chirp and fidget of insects as they came to inspect their new food. He lay there in the dark, eating the hammer of his own heart and tasting the bile of his own stomach.

Sleep well, Tika? Always I loved you?

He would wait until he heard the cocks' crowing, then he would do whatever he had to.

The blade of a knife thrust out of the burlap sack and carved a jagged slit down its abdomen. Maximo spilled from its dusty uterus and rolled onto the floor in a puddle of potato placenta and numb limbs. He spat dirt and curses and crawled from the afterbirth towards a revenge that made him tremble.

The fresh air in his lungs made him feel light-headed. He gripped his knife, crept up the cellar stairs and pushed the door open.

He slipped into the kitchen. He then grabbed a dishtowel, tied it around the base of his wooden leg and hobbled silently through the hall. The closer he got, the more the butterflies in his stomach came. He had never felt so simultaneously alert and paralyzed in his life. The darkness and threat of the second floor beckoned to him, dared him, mocked him. He listened intensely, but the only sound he could hear was that of his own breathing, and it was deafening. He wrapped his sweaty fingers around the hilt of his knife. It suddenly seemed puny and dull.

Sleep well, Maximo. Always I loved you

He thought about his sister. The image shot brass through his nerve. He swallowed hard and made his way up the staircase. The house betrayed his presence with every creaking footstep. He stood in the shadow and silence of the upper floor and listened. The laboured sound of air being swallowed and expelled escaped from one of the rooms. Somebody was snoring.

What's that?

He stared at a crouching figure at the far end of the hall. He was sure that it was Ollie, his obscenity swaddled in a piss-streaked sheet, his torso tensing, about to charge down the hall like a wounded buffalo. Maximo blinked a few times and saw nothing more threatening than a settee and a vase of plastic flowers.

He followed the sound of the snoring and peeked into an open room. Ollie was passed out in his office chair. His gaping mouth and protruding belly was cloaked in moonlight. Maximo felt exhilarated as he inched his way towards him. He stood over Ollie and watched him battle for each putrid breath. There was an open jar of Vaseline in his lap.

Maximo raised his knife into the stale air and murder of his decision. He aimed his strike at Ollie's fleshy throat, thought better of it and lowered the blade to the man's hairless chest instead. He was about to strike when something on the desk caught his eye. The object glinted and spoke to him of free will. The bundle of brass keys passed no judgement. They simply winked at him, suggested another way and waited while he decided. He slowly lowered the knife and picked up the key ring.

"I could have killed you," he mouthed, not knowing that very soon he would wish that he had.

Leaving Ollie sleeping in the chair, Maximo made his way to the last door on the landing and rattled the knob. It was locked.

He pressed his lips against the door jamb and felt cool air rush into his mouth. "Lourdes," he hissed, not knowing if she was even in the room. He stared down the hall and strained to hear Ollie snoring. He could hear nothing.

"Maximo?"

The sound of his name coming from behind the door was so soft, so fleeting, that he was sure he must have imagined it.

"Lourdes? It's me. Maximo."

"Maximo, you came," Lourdes said. The relief in her voice broke his heart right through the thick wood.

He fitted different keys into the lock and tested them. "Hold on. I'm going to get you out of there."

"Hurry, Maximo, before the piggy hears you."

The urgency in her voice sent jolts of panic through his hands and into the fumbling keys.

The piggy?

Click!

The sound of the lock opening flew through the house like a mockingbird with a tale to tattle. The door fell open, and Lourdes stood before him. She wore a pair of pink pyjamas with purple squirrels stencilled all over them.

"Lourdes." He squatted down and embraced her. She felt thinner than he remembered.

"You came," she sniffed, and hugged him back.

"We have to go. Right now," he whispered. "We have to be very quiet but fast."

"Okay," she said as he took her hand. "Oh, but I can't go without yellow teddy." Her eyes grew wide with alarm.

"Who?"

She pointed towards her bed. "Yellow teddy. My bear."

Maximo saw a stuffed teddy bear lying on the clean white linens, its glass eyes sparkling and beseeching. "No, Palomita. There's no time."

Lourdes looked back and forth between Maximo and her stuffed toy, her bottom lip quivering slightly. "But she's my friend. She made me feel better…after…after…" she said, leaving out the words that no child should ever have to speak.

"Hurry. Quickly. Get your bear."

Lourdes ran to her bed, snatched up the toy and started back across the room.

"That's it, Palomita. Quietly now."

She stopped suddenly and hugged the bear to her chest, the blood draining from her face. She took a step backwards. "Piggy's here," she whispered.

Maximo whirled around just in time to catch a glimpse of something lunging at him. It was something unholy, something with the body of a man and the head of a swine. The creature squealed and pummelled him to the floor. It bit and scratched at him and smashed his head until he stopped fighting back.

Maximo cried out and fell into the abyss, a black hole filled with bug-eyed chimeras and shrieking purple squirrels.

Don't hurt her

THE COLISEUM

Ignacio watched a tall Plexiglas tower descend from the rafters. The odds were three to one against Mr. Mestizo, and Ignacio had bet his life's savings on the upcoming bout. If he lost, he would have just enough money left over to buy a couple of yams for the long drive home—or a bottle of rum.

An official placed the fighters in cloth bags and weighed them from scales attached to the trophy-laden tower.

"Three point five for both," a handler barked at the crowd.

Murmurs of approval rippled through the stands, and outrageous wagers were cemented.

Ignacio wrung his hands and watched as Mr. Mestizo was beaked against his competition and then teased with a precocious mona. The tower shot upwards, the ring was cleared and the gallos were released. The fight was on.

The Puerto Rican rooster bobbed and weaved his way towards Mr. Mestizo. They called him El Matador, and he had killed two top birds since the tournament began and another seven in his homeland.

Mr. Mestizo patiently circled his latest foe, feigning lunges and testing his opponent's reflexes, his muscles vibrating with coiled violence. The Puerto Rican rooster mistook his adversary's caution for something tamer. He crowed loudly and rushed forward. Mr. Mestizo leapt into the air like a hypnotic danseur and then pivoted and snapped a roundhouse blow at his attacker's head. His postiza pierced the bird's neck and severed his brain stem. El Matador was dead before he hit the ground.

Mr. Mestizo landed lightly, his talons twisting themselves into the green mat. He didn't even turn around to make sure that his rival wasn't getting back up; he simply cocked his head to one side and rustled his feathers as if he were slapping some dust from his favourite shirt.

It was the quickest kill of the tournament, and it took a moment for the full impact of what had happened to resonate throughout the stunned audience.

"Limpio!" someone yelled, and that was all it took—pandemonium.

Ignacio jumped over the low wall, scooped Mr. Mestizo up and raised him into the air. He kissed his bird repeatedly on top of his head. "My mambo king."

"Congratulations, señor," the dead rooster's owner said, his eyes riveted on Mr. Mestizo. "Never has one of my gallos gone down like that. A lucky hit, I think."

"Perhaps you are correct. El Matador was a fine warrior. I'm sorry for your loss."

The man frowned and handed over a brown paper bag. "Twenty one thousand. It's all there. I am well known here."

He took the bag and peeked inside at the stack of bills. He would count it later. "Thank you. I trust your word."

Twenty-one thousand dollars

Ignacio pushed his way through the throng of well-wishers and back-slappers, the paper bag clasped securely in his fist.

A swarm of hands reached out to his beloved rooster, desperate to make contact with his feathers. They reminded Ignacio of the way the faithful and afflicted had snatched at the hem of the robe of Jesus.

THE PRICE OF FAME

A RAVEN-BLACK CADILLAC ESCALADE crouched on the edge of the tarmac at Luperon Airport like a predator awaiting its next kill. Jaragua sat inside the expensive SUV and watched a jet touch down on the runway. He was to escort the owner of the plane to a secret location in the hills above Puerto Plata, make sure he got what he came for and then see him safely off the island.

He pressed a button on his two-way radio and spoke into it. "Everything cool there?"

"We're right where you left us. All is good," a static-choked voice answered.

"Stay put. I won't be long."

"We'll be waiting."

Jaragua had left his crew and their army truck full of tobacco bales hidden in a cane field near Sosúa. El Guapo had sprung the airport errand on him as he was leaving for Haiti. He had presented Jaragua with the new vehicle and told him that if he passed tonight's test, he was the right-hand man he was looking for.

Left hand, right hand, he thought. It didn't matter. Nothing was going to stop him from achieving his goals, from becoming who he always knew he could be, from becoming the next Dominican coke king.

He drove onto the landing strip, got out of his vehicle and stood in front of it. The headlights cast his elongated shadow across the deserted stretch of blacktop.

Two men exited the plane and approached him. One was tall, one was short, and they walked in a manner that told Jaragua all he needed to know about them.

"You are a friend of whose?" the shorter one asked in perfect Spanish.

"I work for El Guapo. I am here to assist you."

The taller man brought a radio up to his lips and spoke. "Green."

Jaragua watched a scrawny man slouch across the runway, his fists jammed into his baggy jeans, his white sneakers gleaming under the headlights' glare.

"If you *must* refer to me directly, call me Big Dog. This one here is Buddy, this one is Dude and I shall call you Chico," Keegan said and then climbed into the backseat of the SUV.

"We'll give you directions," Buddy said.

"Easy peasy, mate," Dude said.

The powerful Escalade raced down the highway and exited at a barely discernible dirt road. Jaragua shifted to all-wheel drive and smiled as the SUV leapt like a cat through the foliage.

Keegan studied Jaragua as he drove. Another hard one, he thought with amusement. Like his two tigers, only less disciplined—a maverick, a rebel, a fucking loser. Keegan suffered bullying throughout most of his life, especially at school. He had been knocked about and humiliated by the bigger boys and ignored or ridiculed by the girls. He never tired of wielding the power that money had given him. The things he could get away with, the manner in which he could speak to people and still have them smile at him, kiss his ass—it was simply intoxicating.

He liked to taunt tough guys, guys like his new driver, guys who used to stick his head in urinals and make him say he was a faggot. He enjoyed witnessing the collapse of their bogus pride, the corruption of their personal codes. He would expose himself—warts and all—and watch as they struggled between their desire to kick his teeth in and their lust for money.

It was for this myriad of complex reasons that Keegan—the little fiery one—made the fateful decision to yank on his new tiger's tail.

"Tell me, Chico, have you seen my package? Is it fresh?" he asked in an innocent voice.

"No, Big Dog, I haven't. But I'm sure that your package is…whatever it is…fresh, yes."

"Reeeaallly? Hear that, Dude? Catch that one, Buddy? Chico here has no idea what we are here to pick up. Who here thinks that I should tell him exactly what he has gotten himself mucked up in?"

He raised his own hand into the air. "Oooh, oooh. I do. I do. Hu-mon-tra-fi-kin. Children to be exact. Does that bother you?"

Jaragua stared straight ahead and tried to concentrate on the road. He felt as if he had just switched to autopilot. "No. None of my business."

"No? Is that right? So allow me to clarify. You have no problem, as long as you are well compensated, with the sale and consumption of baby flesh. By baby flesh I refer specifically to our package, a six-year-old girl with the most unruly mass of dark curls, hair I shall be pulling as I violate her."

Jaragua gasped at the man's words. They hammered his solar plexus and contracted his entrails. He turned his eyes on Keegan, a demon who had just sprouted horns and a tail. He was aware of movement in the backseat and then he heard a gun being cocked.

"Yeah, that's right. So what up now, muthafucka?" Keegan said, his vivid green eyes dancing with mischief and malice.

"I work for El Guapo. I am here to assist you and see you back to your plane." Jaragua's own voice sounded foreign to him.

Greed

Keegan flexed his fingertips together and smirked. "Excellent, Smithers."

Tough guy, Keegan thought with satisfaction. Fucking pussy. He had his confirmation yet again. Money trumped morality. There were no heroes, and nobody gave a shit about orphans in Third World countries.

Let the games begin

The vehicle lumbered from the cover of the forest like a black bear seeking garbage bins. They drove past a huddled mass of structures that belched smoke and stench into the air and glowered at the newcomers in morose silence.

"That house there. Park in front of it," Buddy said.

Keegan pinched his nostrils closed. "God, this place reeks. Fuck-a-mia."

Jaragua continued driving, but his mind was shrieking at him to splatter the three men's brains all over the interior of his suddenly way-too-expensive vehicle. He thought the package would be something normal like drugs or money. He wanted nothing to do with hurting children. He parked in front of the house and forced a mask of calm over his seething emotions.

Keegan turned to his bodyguards. "Wait here. I got my radio."

"Are you sure, Big Dog?" Dude asked him.

"I'm not helpless, am I? I know the Pigmeister, and my nigga here ain't gonna do shit."

Jaragua silently followed Keegan up to the front door of the house. He could feel the comforting weight of his handgun pressing against the small of his back. He just wasn't sure if he was going to use it or not.

Keegan rang Ollie's doorbell, and the two men waited. They could hear somebody thumping around inside like a Minotaur in a nursery.

REUNION

Ollie entered Lourdes' room. "So there you are, and look how pretty you look, all ready for your exciting journey."

Lourdes sat on the edge of a green chair, her legs clamped tightly together and her gaze rooted to the floor. She wore a baby blue dress made of Egyptian cotton.

Ollie brushed a strand of hair from her face. He was pleased that she no longer flinched whenever he touched her. "I will miss you terribly," he said, and thought about the man he was about to sell her to.

Over the last couple of years, he had supplied Keegan Sherbet with six girls, but never before had he felt so sad to see one go. Even in the twisted world of diaper monsters and playschool freaks, Keegan had earned himself a reputation for being deviant in the extreme. Ollie's Palomita would suffer greatly.

"If you were mine, never would I hurt you. I love you."

Lourdes finally turned her eyes on Ollie and spoke. "Where is Maximo? What did you do to him?"

Ollie regarded the child with awe. Perhaps it was her unbreakable spirit that made her such a treasure, he thought. Whatever the case, it was the first time she had accused *him* of bad behaviour instead of the piggy. "Me? Why not a thing, little squirrel. I would never hurt Maximo. It was the piggy, remember? The piggy hates Maximo."

Lourdes stared directly into Ollie's eyes and screamed at him. "I hate the piggy, and I hate you!"

Ollie's face flushed red. "The piggy gave Maximo to Uncle Knapsack!" he screamed back at her. "The worms are eating him the way they ate Tika."

Lourdes' muscles went slack, and her eyes deadened. The weight of his words crushed any rebellion she had left in her.

"I have sold you to a most disagreeable man for a most agreeable sum of money," Ollie said. "I don't think that you will enjoy your new handler. No, not at all. And I think there comes a time when you will pine for this room, for the piggy and all his gentle games. Yes. Yes, I think that day will come, and also—"

The sound of the doorbell interrupted his tirade. He looked out the window and saw a black Escalade idling in front of the house. The doorbell sounded again, and he hurried from the room, thumping noisily down the stairs.

Ollie flung the door open. "Good evening— Oh...two? I don't know you," he said to Jaragua. "What is all this, Mr. Sherb—"

"Big Dog," Keegan said.

"Huh?"

"Just call me Big Dog tonight."

Keegan pushed past Ollie and entered the house. "This is Chico. El Guapo sent him to wipe my nose and powder my ass. Don't get your panties in a twist, Herr Swinehunt. Chico's a lapdog."

"This is good. However, I remain nervous of new faces. You understand," Ollie said, and turned towards Jaragua. "Would you be terribly insulted if I required you to provide some proof?"

"What do you want to know?" Jaragua asked.

"Tell me, please. Who won the last battle in El Guapo's most special gallera?"

"Red won."

"And the champion's name?"

"The Cossack."

"Just so. Good. You understand the...umm...private nature of our dealings here tonight, then."

"Jumping Jiminy Cricket, Herr Paranoia, self destroya. He's bought and paid for, just like my package. Now enough jitterbugging. I *want* to see my baby flesh, and she had better be cherry. No screwups like the last time, I trust?"

"Oh no, no. Virgin meat. I swear it. I have been a good boy. Nothing except piggy playfulness. You have downloaded my work, yes?"

"Occasionally. For shits and giggles. So off we go. Maidenhead revisited."

"What does this mean?"

Keegan opened his eyes wide and spoke to Ollie as if he were autistic. "Maidenhead. You know, the hymen? It's a play on words. Look, whatever. Where is she? I've got a plane to catch."

"Yes. Up the stairs, then," Ollie said, leading the way. "Palomita is waiting."

Palomita?

The name hit Jaragua like a fond memory and a bitter taste.

Lourdes died in the flood

In a trance, he followed the other men up the stairs. He felt as if he were floating and looking down upon himself—at a man he no longer recognized.

He watched as Ollie fitted an iron key into a lock and twisted it. The German said something that made the smaller man laugh, but Jaragua didn't hear his words—there was a screeching inside his head, a maelstrom, a hurricane, a banshee.

The door swung inward under its own weight, and a golden light pierced the corridor's darkness. The light shone like vengeance and glowed like holy death on the edge of an archangel's sword.

Jaragua stepped into the room and felt hot tears well up and blur his eyes. "Palomita," he said hoarsely.

He smashed his handgun against Ollie's temple, knocking him to the floor. Keegan squawked and raised his radio to his lips. Jaragua whirled around and lashed metal across his face. The little man yelped, dropped his radio and fell back against the wall, blood streaming from his shattered nose.

Jaragua holstered his weapon, wrapped his hands around Keegan's throat and lifted him into the air. "Die," he hissed, crushing his airway with maniacal strength.

Keegan's face went from red to violent purple. He scratched weakly at Jaragua's hands. His eyes bulged, his legs twitched and spittle gurgled from his mouth. Jaragua could feel every sweet second of the man's death, and it felt like the most blessed moment of his entire life. He continued to choke the man long after it was necessary, until he heard a soft whimpering coming from behind him. He dropped Keegan's lifeless body on the floor and turned around.

He stepped over Ollie's motionless form and squatted down in front of Lourdes. He felt guilty for not having found her sooner, for not having tried harder. "Palomita, you don't have to be afraid anymore. It's me. Jaragua. Do you remember me? I'm your brother."

Lourdes pressed her face into the warmth and comfort of her yellow stuffed bear and backed away from him. "Where's Maximo?"

"I don't know. After the flood came…you remember the flood? Was Maximo here with you?"

She nodded. "Mami and Papi are in heaven. Me and Maximo rode on a cow, and then the monsters in the lake came, and the piggy hurt Maximo…and me." She pointed at Ollie.

He had no idea what she was talking about; however, the distress in her eyes told him more than he needed to know. "It's over now," he said, ignoring the painful constriction in his chest. "Do you know where Maximo is?"

Lourdes leaned into him, cupped a hand over his ear and whispered, "Piggy gave Maximo to Uncle Knapsack, and the worms are eating him like they ate Tika."

Jaragua brushed a tear from her cheek and kissed her on the forehead. "Can you be brave for a little while longer? Can you wait here in the closest until I come back?"

"Uh-huh," she said. Her small hands clutched at his sleeve. "I remember you, Jaragua. Don't let the piggy sneak up on you too, okay?"

"I won't."

What had they done to her?

"Hide in the closet," Jaragua said. "I'm going to see if I can find Maximo, and then I'll come back."

"Promise?"

"I promise, sweetie. I'll be right back."

"No. Promise you'll find Maximo."

"Yes. I will find him."

He hoped he did not have to break a vow to a child who had very little faith left to lose. He walked up to Ollie and kicked him in the ribs, breaking three of them. Ollie grunted and rolled over.

"Up, piggy," Jaragua demanded. "Is that you? The Pigmeister?"

Kick

"You hurt children."

Kick

"Where's Maximo, you pedophile piece of shit?"

Kick

"Okay. Just...please," Ollie said between gasping breaths. "A moment to think—"

Jaragua rammed the muzzle of his gun into Ollie's ear. "Get up."

Ollie struggled to his feet. His broken glasses were mashed into his face, and blood was running down the side of his head.

"Maximo?" Jaragua asked again.

"Umm, yes. He's in the cellar, but he is—"

Jaragua punched him in the face and sent him reeling into the hallway. "Downstairs. Make one sound and I'll spill your brains."

The two men walked down into the dimly lit cellar.

Jaragua looked around for his younger brother. "Where is he?"

"The boy was so wilful," Ollie stammered, his brain and tongue dancing at the end of their noose. "If anything, I provided for him, such a spirited one—"

"There's no way out, filth. You're already dead, so stop trying. Tell me where he is or I'll cut your dick off and make you swallow it before you die."

Ollie licked blood from his lips. He sighed and pointed. "He's there...hanging."

Jaragua saw that something had been suspended from a thick ceiling beam and that the something was squirming. He turned and kicked

Ollie between the legs, a solid connection that rattled both men's spines. Ollie fell to the ground, puked and writhed in a pain he never knew existed.

Jaragua pulled out his knife and cut his brother down. "Maximo, are you all right?" He ripped duct tape from Maximo's mouth and sliced through the rope on his wrists.

Maximo hyperventilated for a moment and looked at Jaragua as if he were a hallucination. "Lourdes?"

"She's upstairs, but we're not safe yet. There's two men outside, dangerous ones."

Maximo pointed at a pale stick of pine. "Pass me my leg."

Jaragua glanced at his brother's stump for the first time. "What the fuck did he do to you?"

"No, not him. Before, in Lago Enriquillo…crocodiles." He strapped on his leg and stood up.

"You're taller than I remember," Jaragua said, looking at him with a respect that had nothing to do with height.

"And you're meaner looking than I remember," Maximo said, and smiled.

"We can talk soon. I'll put him in the ground. Lourdes is hiding in her closet. Go to her. I'll be right behind you."

Maximo stepped forward and swung his wooden leg with all his strength into Ollie's face. The doomed man's front teeth clattered into his mouth like yellowed dominos. "Give me the gun, Jaragua," he said, holding out his hand. "I want to be the one who pulls the trigger."

Jaragua looked at the flat blackness in his brother's eyes and saw all that he had survived, saw that he was no longer dealing with a boy. His gaze rested on Maximo's palm, on the crease that fortune-tellers referred to as the fate line.

"Bro, my soul is lost. I won't help you lose yours." He took Maximo's hand and held it up to the light. "See? No blood. I promise you, if you do this thing, these hands will never throw a baseball again…not ever."

Maximo nodded slowly. He was ashamed at how relieved he felt.

"I'll get Lourdes," he said, and turned to go. "And, Jaragua, thank you for not forgetting about us."

Jaragua winked at him and waited until he was gone.

He yanked Ollie onto his knees, aimed the gun at his face and then thought better of it. He picked a piece of pipe off the ground and hefted it in his hands. It was heavy with rust.

"Time to go tell your story to the devil. See if he has any sympathy for ya." Jaragua gripped the pipe with both hands and raised it over his head.

Ollie squinted up at his executioner. A faint smile shuddered across his bloody lips. "Thank you," he whispered.

Jaragua smashed the pipe down with all the anger and muscle he had in him, splitting Ollie's head in two. "My pleasure."

He dropped the weapon and left the cellar.

When Jaragua entered the kitchen, he saw Maximo and Lourdes huddled together by the back door. "Have you seen anybody else?" he said, crouching down.

"No. Nobody. Lourdes and I have to go now," Maximo said. "There's a yola in Nagua. It leaves tonight for Puerto Rico, and we have to be on it. We're going to New York."

"A yola? Are you crazy? Hundreds have died trying to cross the Mona Channel. There's got to be a better way. And what about Lourdes? Has she not been through enough already?"

"I will take care of her. I always have." Maximo's eyes narrowed. "Tell me another way, Jaragua. Can you stay with us? Help us?"

Jaragua lowered his eyes and gently rapped his gun against his forehead. "Soon. It's complicated. I have to go to Haiti first, and my girl is in danger. But wait—"

"No. We're going, and when we get there, I'm going to pitch for the Mets, and all of us will have a better life."

"That's just a dream. You don't know anybody there."

And you've only got one leg

Maximo showed him the phone number Ignacio carved into the brim of his cap. "I got this…from a friend. I trust him."

238

Jaragua turned and looked over his shoulder. He was sure he heard whispering. He had no choice but to let his family go. He took the ball cap and scratched another phone number into the beak.

"His name is Manny. Call him when you reach Puerto Rico. He will help you. Tell him that Estrellita Luminosa sent you," he said, knowing that even if his tattoo artist forgot him, he wouldn't forget his work.

Jaragua pulled a fat roll of bills from his pocket. "Here. Take this. There's a couple of thousand dollars here. I will meet you two weeks from today in New York. Go to Rockefeller Center. There's a bronze statue there called Atlas. Wait beneath it all day for me. Can you remember all that?"

Maximo nodded and screwed his cap down onto his head. "Estrellita Luminosa, like your hand says."

"Exactly."

Maximo hugged his brother. "I love you, Jaragua."

"And me to," Lourdes said.

Jaragua hugged them and kissed their cheeks. "Palomita, stay close to Maximo. Now go." He opened the back door, checked for assassins and waved his brother and sister away.

He watched as they jogged across a scrubby clearing and disappeared into the midnight brush. It was the last time he would ever see them.

Jaragua cursed under his breath and crept towards the front of the house. He had no illusions that the two bodyguards were still waiting patiently in his truck. He slid along a wall in the foyer, his gun searching for a target. He stared into the dark parlour. He could see nothing, hear nothing...but he knew.

He threw himself on the floor just as gunfire erupted from the room. Bullets tore chunks from the wall behind him. He fired back, aiming at the muzzle flashes.

Buddy stumbled from the room, his weapon dangling by his side. "Cunt," he said, and fell face down.

Dude pressed a gun to the back of Jaragua's head. "Drop it and stand up."

Jaragua pushed his gun away and stood up.

"I taught him to use that word," Dude said. "Yanks don't use that word so much, do they? And it's a cracking good one too, isn't it?

"Well, you certainly made a right Eliot Ness of this, haven't ya? Killing the proverbial goose who laid the golden egg and all, yeah?"

Jaragua slowly slid his knife from its sheaf.

"Silly wanka," Dude said, lightly rapping his Glock on the back of Jaragua's head.

Jaragua whirled around and sank his blade straight through the man's left eye and into his brain. The Brit stumbled backwards, sent two rounds into the wooden floor, shivered and collapsed.

"Dude, kill first, talk later," Jaragua said.

He ran from the house, jumped into his vehicle and sped off into the night.

There were two things on his mind.

Cocaine and Estrellita

*…but don't go by yola, don't be filled with illusions,
because in the Mona Passage the sharks will eat you.*
—Wilfrido Vargas

Alas for those that never sing, but die with all their music in them.
—Oliver Wendell Holmes

PART THREE

MIDNIGHT RUNNER

Nagua is a hard-working secretive town located on the island's northeast coast. Coconuts, cacao and rice are all major contributors to the local economy, as is the illegal transportation of desperate souls across the Mona Passage, a two-hundred-mile voyage through unpredictable shark-infested waters.

Maximo and Lourdes squatted in the darkness with the other paying customers, awaiting their chance to add their names to the growing list of missing at sea. They were about to launch a yola from Death's Head, a beach that had seen more corpses than fish wash up on its shores over the years.

The woman beside Lourdes suddenly yelped and leapt to her feet. "Tarantula," she hissed.

Lourdes giggled and used a stick to nudge the spider away. "Don't be afraid," she said.

Before the woman could reply, the captain of the fishing boat barked some orders, and the launch was underway.

Maximo and others lifted the boat off the sand, shuffled towards the water and waded up to their waists in the warm Atlantic. They looked like a monstrous hermit crab returning to the sea.

Maximo steadied the bobbing craft while Lourdes and the others climbed over the gunwales, flopping into the boat like gaffed fish.

The Captain swatted at the girls' behinds as they struggled out of the water. "The rest a ya now, in ya git. Come on. Load 'er up." He had broad African features, a frightful mass of salt and sun-bleached hair, faded blue tattoos and an American accent.

In minutes, the boat was dangerously overloaded, and still people wiggled and fought their way onboard. The boat groaned and pleaded as it sank deeper into the water. His greed satisfied, the Captain twisted the throttle of a cranky outboard engine. The motor retched and choked and spewed black smoke.

"If ya gotsta puke, try an' make it to da rail, an' unless ya wanna eat your own vomit, don't puke inta da wind," the Captain said. Several passengers translated his words into Spanish.

The yola ran low and dark out to sea. It carried ninety-four people, no navigational equipment, no lights and only seven lifejackets, one of which Maximo had secured around Lourdes' neck. He had paid an extra hundred dollars for it.

Maximo and Lourdes rested their heads together and allowed the gentle ebb and flow of the boat's inertia to lull them to sleep. He hoped that they would be able to see Puerto Rico when they awoke.

Lourdes shook Maximo awake.

He opened his eyes and peered over the weathered rail. He could see nothing but water.

"Look. It's so pretty," she said, staring into her first sunrise at sea.

The morning sun had just breached the horizon. It shot flaming spears across the surface of the water, igniting wave crests and illuminating a school of flying fish. The fish sparkled in midair like diamond-feathered birds.

Maximo looked at his sister. Her long-dormant smile had finally returned, and the lucid glow in her eyes cut through the black memories of her abuse like burning tungsten. "The prettiest thing I ever saw," he said.

As the day stretched towards Hades, the sea flattened and sulked, its gentle tranquility casting a net of deluded optimism over the vessel's forlorn silhouette.

Lourdes fanned stench and vapour over her flushed face. "I'm so thirsty."

"Captain, can we have some more water please?" Maximo's voice struggled to the surface, temporarily escaping the stifling atmosphere of the wooden kiln.

The Captain's eyes continued scanning the distant horizon in that ambiguous manner that seamen often affected. "No more ta give ya."

"But you said you would supply drinking water and that we should bring nothing because of the weight."

"An' I brung ya wada aplenty. Ain't my fault ifinya drunk 'er all down so quicklike. Now conserve yer energies by clamping yer yap. Ya won't espire 'fore we make da coast."

A woman handed Maximo a plastic jug with a couple of inches of warm swill left in it. "For the little one."

"Gracias, señora," he said, taking the jug and holding it while Lourdes gulped some down.

"And a sip for you as well," the woman said.

Maximo filled his cheeks and allowed the water to slowly trickle down his throat. It tasted like pomelo and cane juice.

The sun rose higher into the clear sky, hammering silver coins from brown hides. A brine of bodily fluids churned around the boat's bilge and simmered in the Caribbean heat. The people prayed for a breeze, but the wind was too lethargic to raise its voice above a whisper.

Maximo rested his head against Lourdes' shoulder and thought about all that had happened to them since the flood had swept them away. He wished they were back beneath the leaky protection of their family's shack, back when his only concern had been baseball, his only complaint the bickering hogs his father kept.

It had only been a few months since the disaster, but to Maximo, the carefree days of his childhood seemed like a story he had been told once, a vague memory of a lanky boy who ran bases and knew that his mother would always have a pot of rice on the boil and a smile with which to serve it.

He examined his fellow refugees through burning eyes. The yola carried a predominately female cargo, a destitute group of women and children whom fate had tossed into the salt and chafe of a wooden coffin that mocked their dreams of a better life.

His gaze met that of a teenage girl's. The hardship of her journey had failed to imprint its scar upon her. She smiled weakly at him. There, on the precarious edge of a flat world, she had found the strength to offer a stranger the warmth and beauty of her smile. Maximo loved her for it.

After the girl closed her eyes, Maximo thought about how he would return one day to his island, to his country, to his home. He thought about how he would return in triumph the way that Sammy Sosa had—like a hero, like a legend. He would do what he could to help ease the burden of poverty that had forced so many of his people into the wilds, leaving them at the mercy of a capricious sea god, one whose eyes blazed with the righteousness and bloodlust of a born-again zealot, his trident poised to smite down the frail and the foolhardy.

He watched the sharks that shadowed the wheezing boat. Their grey dorsal fins resembled the tips of knives as they cleaved the placid water. They were patient hunters that tracked the scent of desperation and disaster as readily as blood and urine.

"El Jeffrey," a woman said in a singsong voice. "In my land once again."

People smiled and giggled at the words, grateful for any diversion from the tedious rise and fall of their tribulation. The woman was quoting lyrics from a much-loved song called "Mi Tierra." It was from the album *El Jeffrey*, recorded by a popular merenguero of the same name.

"My land has palm trees," a different voice offered.

"My land is hot," yet another person sang.

"My land has mountains."

Somebody began hammering on the side of the boat, turning it into an improvised tambora drum. Its deep voice vibrated through the hull and rolled down into the deep.

A man turned a metal comb and a pocket knife into a guiro. "Tell me you are a good friend."

"Should I stay or should I go away?" a new voice ventured.

Maximo sat upright and sang, "My land has three seas which kiss it."

More people joined in. They laughed and clapped hands. They made music from tin cans and plastic jugs, from seasoned wood and liberated spirits.

"My land is a flower."

"More mambo. Lotsa mambo," a woman sang, her horrible singing voice making everyone laugh harder.

Maximo whispered into Lourdes' ear, and she immediately jumped to her feet, stood as tall as she could and delivered the final line of the song: "And merengue lives, El Jeffery."

The boatload of castaways responded to her sweet voice with applause and cheers. Lourdes blushed, dropped back down and hid her face behind her brother's arm.

BLOOD ON THE CANE

JARAGUA HIT THE REDIAL button on his cell and pressed the phone to his ear. "Shit." He snapped the clamshell closed and tossed it on the seat.

"No connection?" the Colombian asked.

"No," Jaragua mumbled under his breath.

He had hoped that he would be able to rip off the truckload of cocaine without having to kill anyone; however, the Colombian's suspicious demeanor was putting an end to that fantasy.

El Guapo had sent a spy.

"Who ya calling?"

"Your sister. She owes me change," Jaragua said, growing tired of the Colombian's prying eyes and sour face.

"Are ya calling El Guapo?"

"Hey, cabron, who's in charge here?" Jaragua said. "You? No... Fuck no. So shut your mouth or I'll make an ashtray out of your tongue and give it to El Guapo as a present. He likes tongues."

The man sucked his teeth and narrowed his eyes. "Unlike the boss, I see a snake before me and maybe it's you who will be facing the mongoose and not I. Now pull the fuck over. I gotta take a piss."

Finally, Jaragua thought, the words he had been waiting to hear. "Yeah, sure. Maybe we both could use a break."

He left the main road and drove into a sugarcane field. He followed a jagged slash of torched grass until he discovered a small clearing, a secret hollow that welcomed only moonlight and murders.

"Ten minutes. Let the men stretch," Jaragua said. He set the handbrake and wrapped his fingers around the hilt of his knife.

The moment the Colombian's hands left his AK-47, Jaragua struck.

He swung hard, burying his blade into the man's throat, ending his inquisition. He could feel the slick heat of the man's blood as it jetted over his hand and splashed onto the dash.

"Yo, boss," somebody yelled from the back of the truck, "why we stopped here?"

"Piss break," Jaragua called back. He took the dead man's weapon, flicked the safety off and jumped from the cab.

"Hey, Colombian, whatcha doing? Taking a shit?" one of the men said.

"Yeah, you taking a shit or something? Come and get a puff on this," someone else said, sucking noisily on a joint.

Jaragua approached the laughing group of men and levelled the AK-47 at them. "The Colombian's dead, and unless I see guns hitting the dirt, you're all going to join him."

Three of the four men thought that Jaragua was joking. The fourth man immediately dropped his shotgun.

"The rest of you can die laughing if you want. Not a bad exit." Jaragua said, raising his firearm and sighting down the barrel. "Or you can drop your fucking guns and get down on the ground."

More guns fell from their owner's sweaty hands, and men dropped to their knees in surrender—all except one.

"I always knew you wuz a crazy horse, but stealing from El Guapo? You respect nothing," the man said, his hand hovering over his slung Uzi. He felt like a movie star.

"You're not fast enough, Tito… Nobody is. I won't kill you. Drop it, and I will tie you up. All of you will live. I swear on my mother's soul."

"You swear on the soul of a godless whore. You will spare us the same way you spared the Colombian."

Jaragua recognized the look in Tito's eyes. He knew that the man's ego was about to get him killed, and there was no avoiding it.

Tito went for his Uzi, and Jaragua pulled his trigger. Hot rounds hammered reality into the man's torso, convincing him that he was *not* Tony Montana after all.

The men scattered like stray dogs chasing each other's tails. The AK-47 spoke harshly to the fleeing men. It didn't speak to them in Russian or Spanish, not in Chinese or Arabic—it spoke to them in a language that all men understood, in a language that required no translation and knew no tender words.

Jaragua stared dumbly at the bodies all around him. Their blood looked black beneath the moon's sallow influence. It bubbled from their wounds like untapped crude, forming pools of oily plasma in the scorched earth. His ears rang from the sudden silence, and his nostrils flared from the scent of gunpowder, a smell he loved. He blessed himself and kissed the wooden cross that hung around his neck. He was surprised that his lips weren't charred from the contact.

He dropped the AK-47, climbed back in the truck, kicked the Colombian's corpse out the door and tore through the cane fields.

He raced down the highway towards the town of Tamboril, frantically dialling Estrellita's number. Her line rang twice and then went dead. He cursed and floored the gas pedal.

LAST DANCE IN TAMBORIL

Estrellita closed her bedroom door and peeled a damp yellow towel from her naked body. The Caribbean night lapped refreshment from her moist skin, slipping its humid tongue into the firm hollows of her youth—places it had no right exploring.

She sat on the edge of her bed, pushed her wet hair behind her ears and picked a colourful piece of paper off the floor. It was an advert for an upcoming merengue festival.

"Rocket and the Cinnamon Roosters," she said, reading her band's name for the hundredth time. Even though it was alongside a dozen other hopeful unknown artists, the words leapt out at her like a neon sign in the blue sky of her future. The weeklong festival in Puerto Plata would attract a huge audience, giving her band the exposure they were seeking. She was determined to make an impression.

Sighing, she flopped back on her bed and allowed her favourite daydream to seduce her yet again. In her mind, she could see herself under the hot lights and lasers of Santo Domingo's Olympic Stadium, an undulating mass of people before her, writhing in an orgy of adulation and merengue fervour. She was performing one of her megahits from one of her many multiplatinum albums, headlining the most important Latin music festival in the world, and everybody loved her.

Jaragua was there standing in the wings, his strong arms wrapped protectively around their first child. He was clear-eyed and clear-headed. He had given up the streets but had retained his edge, becoming dependable, not boring. They would grow old together, laughing about the narrow escapes, about the madness and the peril. A crazy life, which at the time had seemed so tragic, had ultimately provided lessons for their son to learn, hardships he would be spared.

As she thought about Jaragua, her hand moved down between her legs, she moaned and whispered his name.

"Estrellita."

Her eyes flew open, and she sat up.

Jaragua?

She listened intensely. All she could hear was the blood-seeking drone of a starving mosquito targeting her heat. She sighed and told herself that elaborate fantasies and hearing voices weren't a healthy way to pass an evening.

A small white stone sailed through her open window and skittered across her bedroom floor.

"Jaragua," she said, and leapt to the window, one hand covering her breasts.

Jaragua stepped out from the cover of a passion-fruit tree and smiled up at her. "Estrellita Luminosa, let down your hair."

"Oh my God, like magic. I dream you, and you are here."

"I dreamed the same dream. Come to me."

"Wait. I'm naked... I'm coming."

"That was fast," he said, and winked at her.

"Animal. Wait right there, mister."

She threw on a pair of white cotton shorts and a pink camisole and flew from the house straight into his arms.

Their mouths found each other, reassured each other. Their bodies entwined in an erotic fantasy that had never known fulfilment.

"I've missed you so much," she whispered, hugging him tightly.

He kissed her neck, tasting her skin. "I've ruined everything. We don't have very long. I don't know where to begin—"

She placed her hand over his mouth, stilling whatever fresh dilemma he was about to visit upon her. "Shh. I don't want to hear it, not now. It's just you and me. I want to be alone with you. I want you inside me. Where can we go?"

The urgency—in her voice and eyes—struck him in the heart and travelled rapidly southward. Without another word, he took her by the hand and led her through the orchard behind her house and across a clearing. They walked until they reached the burned-out shell of an abandoned rectory.

"That's my truck," he said.

The vehicle looked at home among the rubble and desolation of the crumbling ruins. He helped Estrellita climb inside, and then he tied the heavy canvas closed behind them. The truck smelled of tobacco, hemp and tar, but all Jaragua could smell was the citrus in her hair and the power of her need.

He eased her down onto the bales of tobacco and removed his shirt. Estrellita wrapped her arms around his tanned waist and ran her lips over his hard stomach muscles. Together, they ripped her shirt off. Jaragua encircled her dark erect nipples with his tongue, one and then the other, back and forth, again and again. He pulled her shorts from her and they groaned in unison as his fingers dove into her wetness, as his lips parted hers.

"No matter what this life takes from us, Estrellita Luminosa, nobody can steal this moment. Here, tonight…it's ours forever."

"Forever," she said, moaning as he entered her.

She kissed his shoulder as he thrust himself deeper and deeper into her, losing himself in the only warmth and acceptance he had ever known in his life. Tears rolled silently down her cheeks as they rocked each other towards the calm, rediscovering what had never really been lost. They made love until dawn, their sweat and juices dripping from their slick skin and seeping into their makeshift bed of tobacco and rope, canvas and cocaine.

They lay motionless in the heat and humidity of their breathless space, their limbs entwined, their eyes alert, their bodies far from the sleep they craved.

Jaragua traced his fingers over her back and kissed the top of her head. He couldn't understand how he could have endangered her life the way he had. As long as she remained on the island—and El Guapo remained alive—she was in jeopardy.

"I found my brother and sister," he said.

"What? Maximo and Lourdes?"

"Yes. I found them. They were living in the hills above Sosua, at a tannery of some kind."

"Thank God. Where are they now?"

"Trying to make it to New York."

"How?"

"They went to Nagua. There's a yola—"

"A yola?" she said, sitting up and looking at him. "Why would you allow that? They're only children. You know what happens to people on yolas in the middle of the sea."

"It's complicated. You have no idea. And believe me, Maximo is no longer a boy."

"Well, maybe not, but Lourdes—"

"Trust me. I had no choice. I'm going to meet them in New York. I will take care of them, and I want you to come with me. We can start a new life there."

She yanked her shirt from under him. "Unlike you, I have no need to escape my old one. I love my life, my family. I love *Quisqueya*, and I have no desire to become another Dominican York living in the glass canyons in the frozen grey."

"I can't stay on the island. Things have changed. We're in danger, but in New York, I can become a Latin king and you will be my queen."

"No," she said, tears falling from her blazing eyes. "I always knew this day would come. When your life caught up with you...with us. So go. Go to New York. Run away to the same place you are now. Because do you know what's waiting for you there? Yourself, Jaragua. That's what. Waiting to ruin your *new* life the way you've ruined your old one. Your old one, the one I used to be a part of." She buried her head in her hands.

"I'm sorry, Estrellita. I tried to be the man you wanted me to be. If your love wasn't so blind, if you could see me as I really am, you could never love that man. You don't know what I am, the things I've done. I have crossed a man who would use you to hurt me. Please, come with me, just until I know it's safe to return."

She wiped her cheeks and looked at him, her lips tight and set. "I am performing with my band in Puerto Plata next week, and none of your creepy friends are going to stop that."

"No. You don't understand how dangerous—"

"I don't care. My music is my life, and I won't be chased from my home. I've done nothing to deserve this."

Jaragua clenched his fists in frustration. "At least think about it. I can make you happy…everything will be great once we're in New York. Go to Puerto Plata. Take some time. Tell me where you'll be, and I will come to you."

She sighed and looked away. "I will be staying at that little hotel we once stayed in. You know, with the green doors?" She avoided his eyes, knowing that if she looked into them, she would do whatever he asked of her.

"Yes, I remember."

"I have a lot to think about, and I'm not making any promises. Come and see me when you can, and I will have an answer for you."

He wrapped his arms around her. "Just stay away from here for a while, and be careful. Trust nobody."

The atmosphere felt suddenly oppressive to her. She broke away from him and climbed out of the truck.

Jaragua jumped to the ground and came up behind her. "I love you," he said.

"I know. I just wish that love was enough for you." She took his hand and pressed her lips against his tattoo. "The way it was for the man who wrote the words to our song."

She kissed him goodbye and left him standing there.

He watched her go, watched her walk away slowly through a field of Quisqueya orchids, her fingertips brushing against the lavender and gold of their petals, her hair blowing out behind her, black as her mood.

CHARON'S CROSSING

THE REFUGEES SCREAMED THROUGH their gritted teeth as the yola slammed its way across the Mona Passage.

The open vessel pitched down the face of a rolling whitecap and buried its bow into the trough. A torrent of black water surged into the boat and swept a dozen people into the darkness.

Lourdes and Maximo clung to each other and fought the sea.

"Don't let go, not for nothing!" he yelled, his voice barely audible above the howling wind.

The pounding and shrieking continued throughout the night, and by early morning, the squall was gone along with half of the people who had set out from Death's Head Beach. The battered boat limped like a crippled animal through the stillness of a deep fog. The morning sun drilled wispy holes through the steamy seascape, casting grey shadows over the shivering survivors.

Maximo lay against the vessel's broken ribs and listened to the soft weeping of those around him. He looked over at Lourdes and was amazed at her courage. She had become, somehow, fearless.

He looked at the others in the boat, his eyes scanning the twisted jumble of limbs and misery for a single face, one with a special smile. He couldn't see her. He asked the gods of his mother to protect the girl for him, and he asked the gods of his father to help him find a place in the world. Just a patch of earth somewhere and a bed that didn't stink of someone else's nightmares and a door—a solid one—that no amount of trouble could ever break down, one he could retreat behind and lock whenever the world disappointed him. Just a place to rest, a place to dream.

BWWAAHHH!

The warning issued from a sixty-five-thousand-ton Panamax freighter. It released its foghorns and steamed through the passage at criminal speed. The fog distorted the sound, bouncing it off blinding walls of white and spiking its echoless voice towards a seabed of treasure and pirate skulls.

Cries of renewed terror arose from the survivors, and the Captain twisted the throttle of his resilient outboard.

"Every eye on da wada," the Captain yelled, fear stealing the bluster from his voice. "Where? All eyes now. Where is she?" Maximo couldn't see it, but he could feel it. He sensed a change in the atmosphere, a sudden increase in pressure, a rush of cool air. The yola was being sucked towards the ship. He peered into the shifting treachery of the fogbank and held his breath. He could hear a rushing gurgling sound, a robotic thumping that charged the air with kinetic power.

"There it is!" Lourdes yelled.

Maximo pointed at a looming black silhouette and screamed at the Captain. The vessel swallowed his warning and emerged from behind a veil of shredded gauze.

BWWAAHHH!

The noise was paralyzing.

The colossal freighter burst through the mist like a white whale seeking literary fame. The ship's bulbous bow raced towards them like a torpedo, water spewing from its iron ram. There was no escape.

A WOLF IN SHEEP'S CLOTHING

ESTRELLITA BLEW KISSES TO the crowd with both hands. "Good night, Puerto Plata. We are Rocket and the Cinnamon Roosters, and we are going to be performing here all week long. Besitos."

She and her band left the stage and waded into the deep end of the street party. It was only the second night of the festival and already Estrellita had received praise from artists whom she had admired for years. She just wished that she were able to enjoy the moment a bit more.

"You were incredible tonight," her sax player Manny said. "And you looked beaut— ah, so professional," he said, and frowned. He was painfully aware that his handsome face did nothing for her.

"Me? You were the hot one up there, Manny, sexing up your sax."

"I appreciate that, but everyone knows who the star is, and, man, you were shining. Straight to the moon, eh, Rocket? And speaking of rockets, don't they require some kinda rocket fuel to soar? You know, some gasolina?"

"Not tonight. No gasolina for this gata."

Manny ground her reply between his teeth. "Goddammit. This should be the happiest night, the craziest week of your life, and all you can do is mope around and think about your hoodlum."

She looked at him out of the corner of her eye. "Because it's you, because you are the older brother I never had, I will ignore that... once."

An older brother, Manny thought. He forced himself to swallow the unintentional insult. "Sorry. I just want to see you really living this.

We've worked so hard to get this far. You should love the reward as much as the struggle."

Before she could answer, the rest of the band came running over, leaping about like an excited group of children on a school outing.

"Did you see the audience?" Amelia said. "And Juan Luis Guerra is here—JLG, for Chrissakes. I can hardly breathe." She was the band's tambora player, and she had muscles in her arms that most teenage boys would kill for. "Come on, let's go party. I need some *fuel*."

"That's what I say, but Rocket here isn't in the mood. Again," Manny said.

"You go. All of you. I don't feel so good," Estrellita said, and rubbed her temples.

"You're a better singer than an actress. Please, come with us," Amelia pleaded.

"I'm sorry," she said, kissing her friends on the cheek one after the other. "Tomorrow night. I swear. You won't be able to stop me."

After some additional moaning, the band reluctantly agreed to Estrellita's compromise and said good night. She watched them go, bouncing and cajoling their way through the swell of glowing faces.

Estrellita turned away and headed for her hotel. She cut an aggressive path through the crowd, ignoring the prowling young men who flexed their chest muscles at her and drooled their drunken sexuality at her sandalled feet. The chaos and clamour of the malecón fell rapidly away, and she weaved her way through a maze of narrow streets. She passed rows of Victorian era homes, their pastel gingerbread motifs lending the deserted laneways an air of fantasy and innocence they didn't deserve.

She moved quickly and thought about Jaragua. She wondered if she would be able to leave her beloved homeland to be with him, wondered if he would be at the hotel when she got there. *She wondered if he was alive*

Estrellita kicked a soda can out of her way and cursed softly. She was so angry with him for so many reasons—for putting their lives in danger, for giving his detractors the nails and thorns they needed to crucify him—but most of all, she was angry with him for not becoming the man she knew he could be, for continuing down a road that could never lead to their happiness together.

As she was filtering various scenarios and ultimatums through her mind, the streets were suddenly plunged into darkness.

She stopped cold, giving her eyes time to adjust. "Perfect. I wonder if this happens in New York."

Someone coughed in the darkness.

Estrellita squinted into the night. She saw movement. She could see somebody pressed up against the wall, watching her. She turned and walked away, her heart thudding thickly in her chest. She told herself that it was nothing, just somebody staggering home lost in the blackout, the same as her.

Then why were they hiding?

She quickened her pace. She could hear footsteps behind her. They sounded solid and sure. They had purpose, and they weren't the footsteps of an inebriated music lover. She turned left and then right, skipping from one corner to the next until she had no idea where she was.

You're in danger

Jaragua's words came back to her.

At the next junction, Estrellita glanced over her shoulder, bolted to the next corner and pressed herself into a recessed doorway. Her hiding place smelled of rotting food and piss. She watched the stranger from her vantage point. He stopped at the junction. He looked left and then right but didn't move. Perspiration trickled slowly down her spine; it felt like ice water. The man turned and walked away from her. He paused, cocked his head and then moved deeper into the shadows. She watched him go, relief flooding her suddenly liquefied limbs.

Just as her nightmare was vanishing, she heard a throaty growl. She looked down and saw a dog glaring up at her, its upper lip curling back over yellowed teeth. The little dog began barking. Its high-pitched neurotic yapping echoed through the empty corridors.

The man whirled and ran towards her.

"Stupido," she hissed at the dog, and sprinted away.

Her pursuer was so close that she could hear his breathing. She looked over her shoulder. He was gaining on her, his jacket flowing out behind him like a cape, his arms pumping like pistons, his black shoes clanging down like iron horseshoes. A jolt of adrenaline sent her feet flying over the cracked pavement. Her muscles quivered and burned from the effort, and she chewed her silent scream into metal shavings.

She rounded another corner and stopped cold. She was trapped in a decaying cul-de-sac. Having nowhere else to run, she tightened her fists and prepared to fight for her life. She could sense his presence behind her, could hear his ragged breathing. She spun around, avoided his lunging attack and drove her knee into his groin. He grunted in surprise, scratched at her face and landed on the ground in a rolling heap. She sunk a hard kick into the man's guts.

"Bastard!" she screamed, and kicked him again.

He curled into a protective ball and groaned. The third time she lashed out, he was ready. He caught her leg and yanked her off her feet. The impact knocked the wind out of her, and her elbow exploded in pain. She flipped onto her stomach and clawed at the asphalt, her hands searching for something she could use as a weapon.

The man's full weight landed on her, crushing her into the street. He pawed and ripped at her with grunting determination, his thick hands seeking purchase around her neck.

Something, please God

Estrellita's fingers curled around the edge of a pothole, and she tore at the crumbling road until a solid piece came away in her hand. She twisted beneath his weight and smashed the jagged asphalt against the side of his head. He screamed and fell off her. She was almost on her feet when he grabbed her by the ankle and pulled her back down. She screamed in rage, straddled him and raised the concrete into the air.

The man threw a protective arm across his face. "Don't. It's me," he whined.

Just as he spoke, the streetlights came back on. "Don Camino?"

"Yes, it's me. Jesus Christ. Are you trying to kill me?"

"Kill you? Why the *hell* are you following me? You attacked me."

"Attacked you? Following you? Are you insane? I wasn't even sure that it *was* you. Didn't you hear me calling your name?" His eyes were wide and bloodshot.

"No. I didn't hear my name," she said, her voice softening as her gaze swept over the damage she had inflicted. "I think I've hurt you. You're bleeding."

He touched his fingers to his wound and gasped when he saw the blood. "Mother of God, yeah you have. Please get off me. Let me up."

"Of course, sorry." She suddenly felt confused about what had happened.

Miguel sat up but remained on the ground. He blotted his scalp with a white handkerchief. "I wasn't following you. I apologize if I scared you. I watched you perform and then I tried to talk to you, but you walked away so fast…and then the crowd and the blackout."

He looked at his discoloured handkerchief. "Wow. You really nailed me."

Estrellita couldn't remember hearing her name, but she told herself that she must have been wrapped up in her own thoughts, that she had panicked. "Here. Let me help you up." She secretly felt proud of the way she had defended herself.

Miguel swayed unsteadily on his feet and grinned sheepishly at her. He looked so different from the man she had come to despise that she wondered if she might have judged him too harshly.

"You know, humility suits you," she said, and smiled. "So now that you have my attention, what was so important that you had to stalk me?"

He shrugged and handed her a white envelope. "I just wanted to give you your last week's pay and to ask you why you quit working for me. If it was because of my interest in you, I promise I won't—"

"No. That had nothing to do with it." She stuffed the money into her faded jeans. "It's just personal stuff. I'm sorry for hurting you, but I have to go. Somebody is waiting for me."

"Oh. Can I give you a lift somewhere?"

"No thanks. I'm staying close by."

"What? At a hotel or something?"

"Yes," she said, moving away from him.

Miguel groaned loudly, doubled over and held his head in his hands.

"Are you okay?" she asked, taking hold of his arm.

He slumped against her. "I think so. Just a little dizzy. You hit me pretty hard."

The last thing she needed was to nurse Don Camino, she thought. However, she had injured him, and he seemed so harmless all of a sudden. "Come with me. You can freshen up and rest a moment at my hotel, but then you have to go."

"Thank you. I won't stay long. I'll be fine to drive in no time."

They exited a side street, and Estrellita was amazed to see how close she was to her hotel. The evening's strange events had left her feeling completely disorientated. Miguel purchased a couple of mixed fruit drinks, and they walked towards a hotel with lime-green doors.

"Here we are," she said, turning her key in the lock.

She pointed at the bathroom. "You can clean yourself up in there." She hoped that he didn't overstay his welcome. After all, he was still Don Camino.

"Won't be a minute," he said.

He shut and locked the bathroom door, stood in front of the mirror and looked at the purplish welt on the side of his head. "Bitch," he whispered.

He splashed some water over his face, slicked his wet hands through his black hair and extracted a small vial of colourless liquid from the pocket of his trousers.

"And the lamb invites the wolf into its manger," he said, and grinned at his reflection. "Say goodbye to the person you used to be." He emptied the vial into his drink and walked out of the bathroom.

Miguel set his drink down beside Estrellita's and blew out his breath. "The flesh heals faster than the ego."

"Don't worry, Miguel. I won't tell anyone that a girl half your size kicked your ass," she said, and grinned.

He laughed at her remark and handed her one of the plastic cups.

"Here's to forgiving the past, appreciating the present and creating the future." He raised his cup.

"Poetic." Estrellita chugged the drink down, hoping that it would hasten his departure.

After enduring another fifteen minutes of Miguel's droning monologue, she began to feel ill. She blinked rapidly and wondered why his voice was bombarding her with waves of nausea. She stood up and stumbled into the wall.

Miguel was on her, his hands going everywhere.

"No—" She pushed him away and fell backwards onto the bed.

"Looks like the hellcat is nothing but a wet purring pussy after all? Try and kick my ass now," he said, and laughed.

He watched her struggle against the power of the drug, watched her struggle to comprehend what was happening to her. "GHB. Ever heard of it? Gamma-hydroxybutyrate, Grievous Bodily Harm, Liquid X, Easy Lay, the date rape drug, etcetera, etcetera."

She listened to his horrifying words and tried to stop the room from spinning. She felt as if her bones had turned to jelly. Her vision blurred, and she began to hyperventilate.

Jaragua, I need you

"What have you done to me, you coward?" she slurred.

"Wrong question, peasant. You should have asked, 'What *are* you going to do to me?'"

The last thing Estrellita saw, before oblivion found and bound her, was Miguel's lupine eyes and gnashing white fangs as he crawled onto the bed and stared hungrily down at her.

A FULL BELLY

THE MAN SEATED OPPOSITE Jaragua raised his glass and grinned around a mouthful of teeth that would have evoked envy in a mako shark. "'Ears to success," he said.

"Or something that can pass for it anyway," Jaragua said.

The men clanged their beer steins together, sloshing more ale onto an already drenched wooden table. A creaking ceiling fan drove cigar smoke and humid salty air over them.

They were drinking in the coastal town of Luperon, sequestered in the corner of a sailor's bar that attracted a menagerie of vagabonds, sea gypsies, off-key minstrels, escapees and drug runners.

Jaragua's companion banged his empty mug on the tabletop and waggled two fingers at an attractive barmaid. His name was Ziggy Magnusson, but everyone called him "the Greasy Belly" after his neglected sloop. He was a heavyset Icelander with unkempt sand-and-sweat blonde hair, a goatee of copper, jade eyes and tattoos that revealed a pride in his Viking heritage.

"Who da taught dat stowing up a bilge fulla yayo warr such tirsty wark?"

Jaragua scowled and looked over his shoulder. "Don't let the drink wag your tongue too loudly, and I still say we run straight to Florida. No fucking around. Drop anchor by one of the deserted outer keys."

"Nay. Might be yar allota tings, my frund, but a sailor yer no. We'll be captured un trown ina Yankee pen fer twenty yar, nay. We set off up da east coast as far as Canader, down da St. Lawrence Seaway un across Lake Ontario. We dock 'er up in Rawchester, New Yark."

"Raw where? I never heard of the place."

"No single soul as ever erd a dis place, and thar's da genius," he said, hunching over and whispering. "We truck da devils dandruff up ta da city, back door sweetlike, den we is da new cocaine kings a New Yark."

Jaragua drained his glass and considered his new partner's plan. "All right, because I'm not a sailor, and it's your boat, we'll go your route. But don't forget who's calling the shots once we're back on dry land."

Ziggy slammed his big-boned fist into the palm of his other hand. "Sealed!"

A tanned British barmaid placed two frothy cold pints in front of the men. "Take it easy there, luv. It's not your day off."

"Every day is Ziggy's day off now," he bellowed, his booming voice turning every glare and scowl in the tavern his way.

"Sweet Lamb of God, if that's true, then the Apocalypse has arrived early," she said, and winked at Jaragua. "Ave you heard about your mate's infamous day off and all?"

"No I haven't."

"Nay, nay, kitten," Ziggy said, while feigning embarrassment.

"Well, it goes like this," the barmaid said. "The Greasy Belly here used to be the head bottle washer and dogcatcher round these parts, didn't ya? Until one inglorious evening, when he was deep in his cups, mind ya, and doesn't he set fire to a goat, beat up a Frenchman and shag the boss' seventeen-year-old daughter in the toilets loud enough for the rest of the patrons to hear his porn star performance...which they enthusiastically applauded, mind ya."

Ziggy's barrel chest swelled with pride. "Yow, yow. She speaks true, dat's fer sure."

"And so the next morning the boss confronts the nasty Viking here, and what does Ziggy say? He looks down at the floor, all contrite-like, and he says...'But it was me day off.'"

Jaragua laughed at the story but not as hard as Ziggy.

"Can ya believe that bollocks? It was me day off. Fuckin' nuttah." She smiled at Jaragua and walked away.

"Thar's wut life is about. Conquest, drink and legend," Ziggy said, raising his beer up.

Jaragua frowned and realized for the first time that for Ziggy, smuggling a boatload of cocaine into the States was more about the adventure and bragging rights than the money.

"I'll go to Puerto Plata in the morning," Jaragua explained, "get my girl and then we set sail. Agreed?"

"If da weather agrees, den so do Ziggy."

Jaragua slugged back half his tankard as his cellular vibrated and buzzed in his pocket.

He flipped his phone open. "Estrellita?"

"Remember me, Judas?" The voice slithered into Jaragua's ear, dropped down into his bowels and constricted his prostate.

"El Guapo."

"Yes…it is. I was just calling to see if you were enjoying your last days on this earth, you immoral cretin, because I can assure you that your songbird won't be as fortunate."

Jaragua gripped the phone so hard he heard it crack. "Have you hurt her?"

"Do you recall what I said I would do to her if you ever fucked me over and got away with it?"

"Yes I do."

"Bright boy. Stupid fucking moron but bright. If by noon tomorrow you haven't returned to me that which you have stolen, I shall vent my insanity upon your woman, and then I shall locate you, at whatever safe haven you think you've found, and I'll make you watch a video of how horribly she died."

"El Gua—"

"Buckle your pukehole! You know, Judas, in spite of all the grief you've caused me, I'm morbidly curious to see if love can save the day or if your fear of death is stronger than your fear of living as a chickenshit pariah. You know where I live."

The line went dead.

Jaragua dropped the phone onto the table and stared out over the water towards the mangrove swamps where a cocaine-laden wooden sloop—christened *The Greasy Belly*—hunkered in the shadows, her nose pointing eagerly towards the open sea.

<hr />

"Love is such a liability, gentlemen. Remind me never to feel it," El Guapo said.

He pointed at the lime-green door of a Puerto Plata hotel, looked up at NCM'S impassive face and sighed deeply. "Kick 'er in."

CASTAWAYS

THE YOLA SURFED UP the wake of the freighter's bow and smashed violently into the side of the iron ship. Its freeboard splintered, and the little vessel was driven down into a deep trough of boiling white water. Wooden planks and bodies shot into the air, and the sea surged through the disintegrating boat.

Maximo was upside down and underwater. The black ship surged by him, grating his skin against the barnacles and rivets that stitched its swollen abdomen together.

Something about a whale and a boy named Jonah

The sound of the leviathan's heartbeat reverberated through his twisted limbs. He could feel the relentless bite of its bronze teeth, could sense its churning hunger.

The behemoth belched black smoke from its blowhole, defecated waste from its iron rectum and continued on its mindless way. The wreckage swirled behind the oblivious ship. The injured and dying floated in its wake like bleeding chum.

Maximo vomited saltwater and clung to the boat's fractured skeleton. He gulped air and scanned the debris for Lourdes. Other people hung from the driftwood with Maximo. They were wide-eyed and silent, shock having drained all the blood and emotion from their ashen faces.

"Lourdes!" he yelled.

"Maximo."

The sound of her weak voice skated across the surface of the water like a pond strider. He turned and saw a flash of orange amongst the

271

undulating debris. Lourdes was lying across a piece of timber and kicking her legs furiously.

"That's it. Kick. Come to me," he said.

He reached out, snagged his sister and reeled her in.

"Hold on here, tightly," he said. "Are you hurt?"

"No," she said, her huge brown eyes peering out at him from within the folds of her ill-fitting lifejacket.

They continued to cling to the flotsam for the remainder of the day. The cries and prayers of the other survivors gradually sank away until there was no sound at all save for the shriek of gulls that followed them like water vultures. Eight shipwrecked migrants drifted hopelessly in the deep waters of the Mona Passage, waiting for death to realize that he had missed them.

"Smoke," somebody said.

After hours of silent hallucinations, the voice was surreal and unconvincing. Maximo sniffed the air and slowly pried his head from the salt-lathered wood.

"Land. I can smell it."

A murmur of consent rippled through the castaways as a gentle breeze gifted them with the scent of soil, greenery, cooking fires and salvation. They turned their faces into the wind and inhaled greedily, their nostrils eating the fertility of the earth. They drew the essence of the terra firma into their lungs and refused to relinquish it.

The sun burned the last of the fog away, and broken things limped through the wispy swirls of melting condensate and into the clear Caribbean day.

"Look. It's Puerto Rico," Maximo said, pointing at the island's western shore. "And it's not a mirage."

In the distance, a frosting of sangria and lime crowned the rocky cliffs above Aguadilla's sugared beaches. The landmass marred the endless expanse of blue like an accidental streak of paint on an artist's otherwise pristine sky. The promise of deliverance had so completely captivated everyone that they failed to notice the sharks closing in.

Oceanic whitetips—the scavengers of human misfortune at sea—

raced towards their free meal, their glistening dorsal fins zigzagging through the placid water with silent efficiency.

"Jesus, no," a woman said.

Maximo turned his head and stared in disbelief. An enormous shark had a woman's legs in its jaws.

She looked right at Maximo and spoke calmly. "But it's my birthday tomorrow."

The fish shook her violently and sunk back into the water, leaving a geyser of red foam and a straw hat behind. The remaining victims screamed and flailed about, their frantic movements triggering a feeding frenzy. Another was taken below, and then an arm was bitten off. The sharks circled, and the sun shone.

Lourdes tapped Maximo on his arm and spoke quietly. "Let's go over there," she said, pointing at Puerto Rico. "Let's go now."

Maximo nodded. He waited until he saw no fins before shoving the both of them out into open water.

"Don't kick, Lourdes," he whispered to her. "Don't move. Don't speak."

He pressed his face against the rough fabric of her lifejacket, his body rigid. He stared at the shimmering land—so far away—and waited to be eaten.

The splashing and shrieking slowly faded away, and they drifted with the current. Maximo wanted to look over his shoulder, but he was too afraid of what he might see. Lourdes floated on her back, her eyes following the swoop and freedom of a pair of ospreys high in the sky above them. She had a thin smile on her lips.

Piggies can't swim

Maximo watched the coastline running parallel to them. The current was strong, and it wasn't on their side. He was so tired. He barely had enough strength to hold on to Lourdes' lifejacket, to keep from slipping away and drifting peacefully beneath the surface where he would be weightless and unburdened.

He felt Lourdes' small hands gripping his neck tightly. She pulled hard and said something. It sounded important. He couldn't even open his eyes; the salt had sealed them shut. He felt sorry for her. She never had the chance to become anything in her young life, anything except loved. He thought about his parents, and about Jaragua, about how much he missed them. He thought about his idol Pedro Martinez. He could see him standing up on the mound at Shea Stadium, smiling down at him like a saint. He imagined how good the hotdogs and dry-roasted peanuts must smell at such a stadium, at the church of baseball.

He breathed deeply and succumbed to the rocking motion of the sea. It felt like his mother's arms to him. He tried to visualize himself up on the mound, pitching for the New York Mets, but the image refused to come.

Ya Gotta Believe!

Maybe it was the water splashing over his face that was distracting him, or maybe such dreams were simply unattainable. Maybe all dreams were, and crushing them was a bit of a laugh for jaded gods who scorned humans and their pathetic delusions of grandeur.

Sleep
Peaceful and deep
And dream

EYES, EARS AND TONGUES

Estrellita arched her back and snuggled her head into the downy comfort of her pillow. She had been having a disturbing nightmare, but she couldn't remember the details.

"Jaragua?" she said, her voice thick from sleep.

She tried to stretch her arms over her head and found that she couldn't. Her eyes snapped open, and she pulled violently against her restraints, her panic mounting. She was tied spread-eagle on a bed in a room she didn't recognize.

"Finally. I thought you'd overdosed or something," Miguel said. He got up from his seat, sauntered to the end of the bed and looked down at her.

"Don Camino…what…how did I get here? Untie me," she said. Her mind was racing, trying to make some sense of what was happening to her.

"Do you honestly not remember how you got here? Nothing?" he asked, his voice an amalgamation of scepticism and awe.

"No. Untie me. Now."

"Amazing. No wonder so many sickos use GBH. Long story short: you're a fly in a web. I drugged you. You've been out for a few hours. I could have raped you. Didn't. Not my style. Bitches line up for what I got," he said, and grabbed his crotch. "However, I *am* going to do something to you that will make sexual assault seem kind."

He climbed onto the bed and straddled her chest.

She squirmed and bucked against him. "Get off me!"

"Whoa. You're a wild ride, aintcha?" he said, and laughed.

"Why are you doing this? I've done nothing to you. Let me go."

"Nothing," Miguel said, his voice darkening along with his features. "If you call publicly humiliating me nothing, if you call belittling me, rejecting me, making me feel worthless…nothing…then I guess what you are about to experience could also be called nothing."

He took a long case out of his pocket, opened it and gingerly extracted a loaded syringe. The clear liquid inside glistened its infamy at her.

"This is oil of vitriol," he said, "although it also goes by less mysterious names, such as sulphuric acid or, better yet, battery acid. It's the evil of choice for villains, fictional and real. The practice of disfiguring someone with it is known as vitriol throwing. It's huge fun in India."

She felt nauseated as she stared at the needle in Miguel's hand, at the revenge in his black eyes. "You're not going to put that on my face. Please don't."

Miguel laughed without smiling. "No, I'm not. Nothing as uninspired as that. I'm going to take from you something more precious than beauty. I'm going to take away your dreams, your hope. I'm going to take your music."

Despite the circumstances, Estrellita felt an uncontrollable rage boil up inside of her at his words. "Nobody can take that from me. Let me up and I'll blacken your other eye for ya…huh, stud, stallion? More like a castrated donkey."

Miguel backhanded her, grabbed her by her hair and shoved the tip of the needle close to her eye. "I'm going to stick this into your ears, one at a time. The needle will perforate your tympanic membrane, cross the Eustachian tube and bury itself in your cochlea. I will then squirt some vitriol…no, some fucking battery acid…into your ears, where it will devour your auditory nerve. The only music you'll hear after that is Simon and Garfunkel's 'Sound of Silence,' you bruja."

His threat drove fear so deep into her heart that she could hardly catch her breath. "You do this to me," she said, "and the only thing I will live for is to see you die."

Miguel smirked, pinned her head to the bed and brought the needle towards her ear. "Poor Estrellita. She used to sing, but, alas, she can sing no more, for instead of using H_2O, Miguel used H_2SO_4," he sang softly.

Please God help me

The second she felt the cold spike touch her inner ear, the door of the hotel room imploded, pelting the bed with splintered wood and brass hardware.

"What the fuck—"

The curse died on Miguel's lips when he saw NCM stroll into the room, a machete dangling from his huge hand. El Guapo and a short pit-bull of a man strolled in behind the Haitian giant.

"Oh, excuse me. It seems we have interrupted a rather intimate affair," El Guapo said.

Miguel jumped off the bed and backed away from the men, the forgotten syringe twitching in his hand. "Who are you guys? What the fuck do you want?"

"Tsk, tsk, tsk. I find profanity so distasteful, don't you, Estrellita?" El Guapo said.

He walked straight up to Miguel. "Give me the needle."

"Wait. Let me expla—"

"Now or I'll have my boys chop your hand off. Your choice."

Miguel gently laid the syringe in El Guapo's open palm. "Be careful with that."

"Why? What is it?"

"It's sulphuric acid," Estrellita said. "He was going to inject it into my ears, make me deaf so I couldn't sing, because I wouldn't have sex with him."

El Guapo looked at Miguel with something akin to admiration and grinned. "Is that true? You devious fucking turd."

"She's a liar and a cockteaser. She—"

El Guapo depressed the plunger on the syringe and sent a thin stream of acid jetting into Miguel's eyes.

Miguel sputtered, fell against the wall, screamed once and clawed at his face. "My eyes! You fucking freak! My eyes!" he screeched, and crumpled to his knees. His eyeballs melted beneath the corrosive liquid like two plump Riesling grapes being attacked by grey rot.

El Guapo squatted down and flicked open a buck knife. "You wanted Estrellita to hear no evil, and now you can see no evil." In one swift movement, he jammed his hand into Miguel's mouth, seized his tongue and stretched it over his bottom teeth. "Now you shall speak no evil."

He severed the organ at its root and tossed it over his shoulder. "Add that to my collection."

Miguel coughed up great gouts of blood, curled into a ball and continued to make wet choking sounds.

El Guapo cupped a hand to his ear. "What's that? Hmm... No. Can't make out a word. Perhaps there are bushmen in the Kalahari who speak gurgle, but I'm afraid nobody here does. So sorry."

He walked over to Estrellita and cut the ropes from her wrists and ankles.

"Thank you," she said, feeling more afraid of the man sitting beside her than she ever did of Miguel. "How do you know my name?"

"I know many things about you other than your name."

She rubbed some blood back into her tingling hands. "Are you friends of Jaragua's?"

"I don't like to throw the word *friend* around so lightly." He removed a long thin emery board from his pocket and began shaping the nail on his ring finger.

"Where is he?" she asked, trying not to stare at El Guapo's face.

He gently stroked Estrellita's cheek with the back of his hand. "Ah, the multi-million-dollar question. Where is Jaragua? Your boyfriend has something that doesn't belong to him, and now I have something that does."

"We broke up. I don't expect to ever see him again."

"It's too late for lies, as valiant as yours are. Now, I regret that— Oh, for pity's sake, would somebody please shut that blind beggar up?"

NCM crossed the room in two great strides, knelt down beside Miguel and silenced him.

"Thank you. A mercy killing, really," El Guapo said.

He turned his attention back to Estrellita. "As I was saying, it's a shame that you have to go from the frying pan into the proverbial fire, but go you must."

He sighed wearily, picked up one of her hands and patted it. "In a way, you're a very, very lucky girl. By noon tomorrow, you shall know, with certainty, whether your man loves you enough to die for you… and ya can't *buy* that shit, sista."

A LAMB TO THE SLAUGHTER

JARAGUA WALKED UP A long driveway and stopped at the front door of El Guapo's house of skeletons.

He kicked the door. "Open it!"

Before he could kick it again, NCM's coffin-sized body filled the doorway. He aimed a Mossberg pump-action shotgun at Jaragua's chest and waved him inside.

Three other men were waiting for him in the foyer. They pointed scatterguns in his direction and smirked.

"Shirt and shoes off," one of them said.

Jaragua kicked his shoes at the man who spoke and threw his shirt at the man beside him. "Take me to him, burriqueros."

The third man slapped his hands up and down Jaragua's legs and ran his fingers around the waistband of his jeans. "No weapons," he said.

"So anxious to die, huh? So let's go see the boss," one of them said.

NCM jammed the muzzle of his shotgun between Jaragua's shoulder blades and shoved him down the hall. They passed through a set of double doors and entered a smoky cavernous ballroom. The same group of people that Jaragua had seen at the human cockfight were lounging around the perimeter of the room on opulent furniture. The room had a sickly sweet chemical stench to it, like acetone-iced donuts. The chatter and chime came to a stuttering halt as he strode across the Italian marble floor. Mouths gaped, giggles froze in constricted throats and El Guapo's cult awaited permission to exhale.

El Guapo leapt from his throne. "I don't believe it."

Taking their cue, his disciples laughed, hurled insults and began to settle their wagers with drugs, money and sex.

"The odds were fifty to one against your showing up," El Guapo said. He walked unsteadily towards Jaragua. "You just cost me some *more* money, you filthy philistine."

"Where's Estrellita?"

"Whoa, back that shit right the fuck up, hero—stanking dead hero."

El Guapo turned to his audience. "Did you all hear that? My concubines and courtesans, Romans and reprobates, do you *see* the cojones on this ferret?"

The room erupted in boos, hisses and intoxicated squeals.

El Guapo pressed his mask of a face against Jaragua's and glared into his eyes. "I've got a better question. Where is my truckload of powder? Howzabout that one?"

"Close by. Now let me tell you how this is going to happen. I will—"

El Guapo lashed his handgun across Jaragua's head with blinding speed, dropping him to his knees. "You arrogant shit stain!" he screamed, his face flushing mauve with fury.

He cocked his weapon and aimed it between Jaragua's eyes. "Guess what, Judas? I'm rich enough to forfeit the load. You're going to tell *me*, you parasite? Fuck it. I don't want the coke. All I want is your bleached skull on a flagpole."

"El Guapo, sir," a chunky older man said as he bustled across the room, "you will have your revenge tonight. That's why we're all here. Nobody can afford to lose that much product. It's about reputation."

El Guapo hesitated, his damaged facial muscles twitching with indecision. "No, I suppose you're right Uncle Ramos." He lowered his .50 cal and licked sweat from his transparent upper lip. "If not for the rational genes I inherited from your side of the family, I would have self-destructed eons ago. Thank you."

He stepped back, breathed deeply and spoke calmly to Jaragua. "Arise, sower of lies, stabber of backs, king of treason, prince of sedition.

Arise. Your soapbox awaits thee. How, pray tell us, exactly is this going to…happen?"

Jaragua stood up, ignored the blood that trickled down the side of his face and stared at El Guapo. "I have a friend—"

"Bullshit! Nobody on this island would be dumb enough to be *your* friend," El Guapo said to the amusement of his audience.

"When I call him, he will drive up to the house. Once Estrellita is safely away, I will tell you where I've stashed your blow."

"Good, fine. I agree to your boring terms. Now call your lackey, and let's get this done."

"Where's Estrellita?"

"Why, right there," he said, waving his arm behind him. "Don't you recognize your own widow?"

A woman stood up and walked towards them. She was dressed all in black, a lacy veil concealing her features.

"Come hither, Estrellita," El Guapo said, "martyr of Tamboril, widow of Cibao, she who wears a veil of tears. Your knight has arrived, and love has, if not conquered all, at the very least saved your pretty little ass from a royal pudding pounding."

Estrellita ripped the veil from her face, threw it on the floor and flung herself into Jaragua's arms.

A smattering of applause and wolf whistles rippled through the spectator's ranks.

"Bravo," a female voice said.

"You shouldn't have come," Estrellita whispered into Jaragua's ear, her hot tears rolling down his neck. "He's going to kill you."

He kissed her cheek and hugged her fiercely. "Of our two lives, yours will always be more precious to me."

"Caligulites and hermaphrodites," El Guapo said, spreading his arms wide and turning towards his fans, "what we have been privy to here today is a testament to Hallmark cards and diamonds, poetry and roses. We have proof that a human being is capable of loving another more than life itself. It's something we read about in books, see on the silver screen but never actually believe, not until today that is."

Jaragua pulled his cell phone from his pocket and spoke. "If you're finished being a show pony, can we do this?"

"Ha. No shirt, no shoes, no service, fuckface. Now, have you ever heard of NGF? It's an acronym. It stands for nerve growth factor. Italian scientists in Pravia have determined that this oh so romantically named molecule is the culprit behind passionate love. It's responsible for the euphoria, increased heart rate, butterflies and mood swings that accompany infatuation. Can anyone believe that? And *eye-tal-ee-anos* at that. Pasta-munching pricks."

The room dutifully bemoaned the disheartening news, poured more champagne and waited for the show to continue.

"And what's more," El Guapo continued, "they gave this molecule a shelf life of eleven months. How long you two been together?"

"Longer than your pretty face has been repulsing the mirror," Jaragua said.

El Guapo grinned coldly at him. "Careful, pretty boy. Your songbird is still in a cage."

He turned his attention back to his guests. "Eleven months. Greasy imbeciles. What we have seen here today should slap the scepticism from the cynical mugs of scientists from Prague to Pravia. It would appear that love transcends biology, physiology, psychology—all of the overhyped ologies. It cannot be dissected, studied, interpreted or pigeonholed. Love is irrational, it is selfless, it is incomprehensible, and apparently love is something worth dying for."

El Guapo bowed low, accepting his thunderous applause. He waved his handgun at Jaragua and nodded his head towards the doors. "There's no encore, so start walking. Call your bitch."

Jaragua punched in some digits and pressed his cell phone to his ear. Half a dozen armed men watched his every move.

"How does it feel, Estrellita," El Guapo said, "to know that by the time your man has proved himself willing to die for you…he has to do just that?"

"What does it feel like? It feels like something you'll never know, like something you can never steal, buy or threaten, and it feels *nothing* like the emptiness that you wrap your arms around at night."

El Guapo rubbed his eyes theatrically. "Yes, you're right. I am sooooo lonely. I'd give up all my money, all my power, my stable of eager young fuck toys all for the nagging, tedious, clinging affections of one woman."

They exited the mansion.

Ziggy sat behind the wheel of an idling Land Rover. His green eyes bugged out of their sockets with fear and chemically induced insomnia.

"Your chariot awaits," El Guapo said.

"I'm not going without you," Estrellita said, pressing herself against Jaragua's chest. "They're going to kill you."

"No, they're not. It's complicated, but things can be worked out," he lied. "My friend will drop you in Puerto Plata. You'll be safe now. Go and perform, finish the festival. Wait for me each morning in the square on the steps of San Felipe Cathedral."

"Yes. Anything you say. But how can you expect me to sing? None of that matters anymore, not without you."

"Merengue, Estrellita, for me. Because I will know that at least for a time, there will be a smile on these lips," he said, tracing a finger across her mouth. "If I'm not there on the morning after the festival ends, then I won't be coming, and you will know that the only noble thing I ever did in my life was because of you."

Her tears spilled over his fingers and dripped to the ground. "I'm going to go to New York with you. Anywhere you want. Just come back to me…please," she said, her voice cracking with emotion.

"Okay, doves, my patience and curiosity have reached their limit. Wrap it the fuck up," El Guapo said.

Jaragua reached out and plucked a red rose from the manicured gardens that framed the mansion's entrance. He broke the thorns off the stem and tucked the flower behind her ear. "Promise me that you'll never give up on your dreams, that you'll never quit on yourself."

"I promise," she said, touching the rose. "And I'll wait forever."

"Not forever. Three sunrises and then forget about me," he said, and kissed her deeply. "Go."

She turned away from him and climbed into the Land Rover. As soon as she shut the door, Ziggy accelerated down the driveway.

She looked back at Jaragua for the last time and was shattered by what she saw in his eyes. It was an emotion she had never seen there before, and it was one she would remember for the rest of her life, replaying that haunted image throughout the serenity and alarm of her old age: her wolf, watching her leave, his dark eyes full of fear.

LIMBO

Estrellita stood on the stage and looked out over the throbbing street party. Her metallic silver dress radiated a heated sheen that resembled blowtorched tin. She felt a sudden rush of compassion for her countrymen. She bathed in the warmth of their happiness and turned her gaze towards the sea, towards the gently rocking fishing boats, towards the water that stretched all the way to foreign shores, the moonlight it coveted and the lament of separated lovers yearning for their homeland and the familiar kiss of moreno lips.

"I would like to sing a song for you, one of my own," she said. "This song is about dreams and passions, the impossible kind that make you want to quit before the fruit has ripened. It's called 'Sunshine and Green Mangoes.'"

She tapped a wire fork against a guira and launched into the number. Her song told the story of her love for Jaragua and his for her, and her heartache, exposed beneath the bright lights of her emerging stardom, had nowhere to hide.

Estrellita left the stage, avoiding her growing legion of fans by slipping through the narrow passage between the stage and a trailer full of sound equipment. She made her way to Parque Independencia and walked slowly across the square. A breeze that erased the age and withers from any soul it encountered ran its fingers through her hair, kissed her neck and wished it could take human form.

The twin white towers of Iglesia de San Felipe rose into the lavender sky like pale sentinels, two monolithic disciples, stoic pillars of salt and bleached coral. They announced to the faithful and the fallen that Jesus was home and not going anywhere soon.

Estrellita sat down on the church steps, stones worn smooth from bent knees and bloody prayers, from soldiers boots and barefoot children, from the saliva of hungry dogs and the slaughter of fatted calves.

She watched a group of rowdy locals stumbling down the street—Heineken-drinking Cabarete kiteboarding stars with golden-fleece hair, copper skin, ripped board shorts and stoned smiles. She took a rose from behind her ear and brought it to her nose. The flower had lost all its fragrance.

ATONEMENT

JARAGUA STOOD IN THE middle of a barren concrete bunker and stared blankly at a half-sized blue door. His body glistened with sweat, and the blades tied to his elbows glimmered in the dim light. A floor drain burped its foul breath into the room, and a rusty chain lay coiled in one corner like a copperhead pit viper cautiously eyeing its next victim.

He went down on one knee, bowed his head and blessed himself.

The blue door began to rise and then stopped. The stench of the amphitheatre slithered its way under the door. The place smelled like a breeding farm: wet leather, musk, straw and ammonia. "Estrellita Luminosa" by Hacienda de Ritmo began to play, and the door completed its ascent.

Jaragua ducked his head, stepped into the gallera and was crucified by the hostile crowd—a Christian being fed to the lions. He blinked up at the sparkle of lights above him, pawed at the sawdust beneath his bare feet and prepared to do battle.

El Guapo stood up and raised his arms into the air. He looked like a psychotic emperor presiding over the fall of Rome. "Bitches, witches, warlocks and defilers…a moment of your time."

The arena went silent.

"Thank you. What you see here before you is a broken man, a conniver and a contriver, a verminite and a turncoat. However, tonight, he is also a warrior, and he has a chance to redeem himself, a chance to erase the stain of his treachery. He can become in death that which he never was in life…respected."

Jaragua looked up at El Guapo and was surprised to see that the man was looking at him with something akin to affection.

"As the challenger refused to choose an appropriate nickname, one has been assigned," El Guapo said. "Tonight, he is to be called Skeleton One Eighty-Seven."

"Skeleton! Skeleton! Skeleton!" the excited crowd chanted.

"The odds are one hundred to one against the challenger, something that should humiliate him, I would hope. And now, coming through the red door, the most feared Russian on this or any other planet. I give you your champion, with twelve kills to his credit, the god of mortal combat...the Cossack."

The red door slid up, and the familiar figure stepped easily into the pit and crossed his blades above his head. The deafening ovation drowned out the music that the man had chosen for his entrance.

The two men faced each other in the pit.

The Cossack crossed his blades again and bowed to his opponent. Jaragua mirrored the man's actions.

"Let blood be spilled," El Guapo said.

Jaragua circled to his left, his heart was pounding so loudly that he could no longer hear the people above him. His vision tunnelled, and he shook the nerves from his quivering arms. The Cossack cut off his escape route, expertly working the pit's angles. There was stillness in his eyes and fluidness in his movement, things that struck fear into Jaragua's belly.

Jaragua lunged at his adversary and swung wildly. His attack was desperate and awkward, and he connected with nothing harder than stale air.

The Russian retaliated immediately. He stepped under his attacker's slashing elbows and sliced his chest open. Jaragua fell against the wall and was surprised to see blood bubbling out of the wound in his chest. He had felt nothing.

The Russian closed in, looking for a quick finish.

Use what you know

The thought flashed through Jaragua's mind as he backed away from his advancing foe. He was going to die unless he changed the rules of engagement. Forgetting all about his enforced weaponry, he clenched his fists.

The Cossack attacked.

Jaragua jabbed with his left and connected with the Cossack's face a couple of times. The stunned Russian stumbled sideways, blood trickling from his nose.

Before the Cossack could recover, Jaragua drove forward, ducking under a haymaker that would have decapitated him and sinking his fist into the other man's liver, doubling him over. Jaragua smashed his knee into his face, dislocating his jaw and dropping him. Instinctively, he delivered a vicious left hook. The punch reverberated up his arm, down his back and into his toes.

The Russian collapsed unconscious on the pit floor, a thin cloud of sawdust rising around his prone form. Jaragua jumped on him, seized him by the hair and yanked his head back. He could see the rapid beat of the man's pulse through his carotid artery. He aimed his blade and prepared to end it.

"Kill! Kill! Kill!" the voyeurs demanded, their eyes shining with bloodlust.

Mercy

The voice in his head wasn't his own. It was something else, and it sent shivers into the depths of his past and echoed across the violence of his young life. In a trancelike state, Jaragua released the man and got to his feet. He sliced the leather straps on his arms, allowing his knives to drop on the ground.

El Guapo bolted out of his chair and pointed a long bony finger at the defeated Cossack. "Kill him, you pig!" he screamed.

"Pig! Pig! Pig!" the mob chanted, their faces contorted in perverse exhilaration.

El Guapo whipped out his Desert Eagle and aimed into the pit. "You dare dishonour this gallera? After all you've done? Kill him or die like a streak of yellow rat shite."

Jaragua felt outside himself, as if he were floating. He knew no fear. He felt euphoric. "Diablo, these hands will kill no more," he said.

With a howl of rage, El Guapo shot Jaragua through both his thighs. "On your knees, fucker."

Jaragua buckled to the ground. One of the bullets had severed his femoral artery, and a jet of bright red blood sprayed across the dusty floor. He felt liquid warmth spreading through his body. He looked up at the ceiling and smiled. "I see you," he said, a look of rapture on his face.

"Who?" El Guapo asked, looking up and then back down. "Estrellita? Well, you can take this to hell with you, hero. I will hear your woman curse your mother's womb before I send her to join you. Do you hear me? She will die screaming!"

"Protect her," Jaragua whispered.

El Guapo shot him in the head.

He blew smoke from the muzzle of his cannon. "What a disappointment."

He hung his head for a long moment, his eyes focused on Jaragua's body. An oppressive hush fell over the spectators as they awaited his permission to enjoy the moment.

"NCM, you know what to do with his remains. Now, if you all will excuse me, I'm late for another cockfight."

DREAMCATCHER

AFTER FOUR DAYS OF war, three roosters had emerged as contenders for the title: a Bankiva from the Philippines, Mr. Mestizo and an Aseel. It was with a sense of dread that Ignacio watched the Aseel—known as Attila—dispatch his sixth victim. The bird possessed an unnatural ferocity. He attacked fearlessly, mindlessly, overpowering his opponents with the sheer strength of his thick muscularity and psychotic energy.

Ignacio was well aware that unscrupulous owners regularly injected their birds with toxic cocktails of steroids, methamphetamines, strychnine and cocaine. As the chemical experiment in the gallera pecked at his dead adversary and crowed hoarsely, Ignacio feared greatly for the life of his beloved rooster.

A tall man wearing a periwinkle suit and a cadaveric smile sauntered into the pit, scooped up the winning roster and held it aloft. He stared up at Ignacio and licked the blood from his bird's dubbed comb.

"Who can deny Attila his crown?" El Guapo said. "The winner of the next match fights this one for the championship. Expect no quarter."

⸻

"When we are at our strongest, God severs our Achilles tendon and judges us on our ability to limp," Ignacio said as he wound the final wrap of blue tape around his gallo's spurs. "Don't be too eager. This challenger is very dangerous, more of a threat than the ugly one's mutant will ever be."

Mr. Mestizo lay quietly in Ignacio's hands and voiced his contentment with soft clucks.

"First, you shall merengue to set the mood, then rhumba to confuse, cha-cha-cha to dazzle and then…as only you can…mambo. Then come back to me."

Ignacio was so fixated on heeling his bird that he didn't notice the man squatting by his feet until he spoke.

"Something special for you, señor?"

Ignacio looked down at the dishevelled wild-eyed man and instinctively pulled his bird closer. "Excuse me?"

The man looked over his shoulder, pretended to tie his shoe and flashed a small glass vial at Ignacio. "Something special," he said, his words leaking out from between his meth-ravaged teeth.

"No, cabron. My gallo and me are not interested in your drugs."

"Drugs? Ha. That is for the losers. If you dip your rooster's points in this poison, I guarantee he wins. One strike and you watch the Chinaman's bird drop dead from a heart attack."

Ignacio stood up and began to gather his belongings.

The addict clamped his skeletal hand around Ignacio's wrist and dug his dirty nails into his skin. "One hundred dollars."

"Release me, cucaracha."

The words had barley left Ignacio's mouth when Mr. Mestizo flew at the stranger, attacking his face. The man squealed, fell to the ground and turtled his head between his arms.

Mr. Mestizo beat his wings, crowed and stabbed at the cowering man until Ignacio pulled him off.

Ignacio hugged his bird to his chest and faced a silent wall of stunned cockers. "This leech tried to sell me poison, to put on the postizas, to cheat victory, to dishonour this gallera."

The room exploded in curses and scowls as a group of men set upon the criminal. They slapped and kicked him across the room and out the door.

Ignacio sat back down, smoothed Mr. Mestizo's feathers and spoke soothingly to him. Something on the floor glistened at him. Without thinking about why he was doing it, he leaned down and picked up the vial of venom the man had dropped.

"Ignacio dos Santos?"

Ignacio looked up quickly, an explanation for pocketing the poison already forming on his lips.

A short muscular Asian man stood before him. He had as much gold in his teeth as around his neck. "I am called Isko, and my champion is called Bituin, which means star in my language. I am honoured for my best fighter to face such a pride as your Mr. Mestizo," he said, extending his hand.

Ignacio shook his hand.

"Thank you. Yours is a Bankiva?"

"Yes, and yours?"

"Jerazano and Shamo."

"Oh, mister, mister, we going to have a good fight. I am so happy to see you are a principled man, no potions or trickery."

"No. My bird is real. And I trust that your Bankiva is of clean blood and spur?"

"Of course. In my country—"

"China?"

"China? Do I look Chinese to you?"

Ignacio shrugged and smiled.

The man forced a laugh. It sounded like a sea lion's bark. "I am Filipino. You have knowledge of the Philippines?"

"I have never been there, but yes I do. I apologize if I offended you."

"No. I take no insult."

"I have heard that cockfighting is popular in Asia."

Isko's eyebrows shot so far up his forehead that they almost disappeared into his hairline. "In my country, I am known as a sabungero, and we call cockfighting sabong. It is a way of life for us. I have fought Mitra Blues and Zamboanga Whites in Manila and Quezon City. I have conquered at the World Slasher Cup and inside the Dragon Pit. My best have been cheered by fifteen thousand people at Araneta Coliseum," he said, flashing his 24-karat smile once again.

"That's alota people," Ignacio said, and whistled through his teeth. "Mr. Mestizo has never known such fame. However, on this island, some call him the saviour of Puerto Plata, and I have twenty-eight thousand dollars that believes in miracles."

"Three to one against your bird, my friend. Twenty-eight pays eighty-four, and I accept your wager."

As match time crept closer, Ignacio struggled with his guilt. He rubbed a finger along Mr. Mestizo's beak and winked at him.

Have I become my father after all?

"Do you believe in reincarnation?" he asked the rooster. "No? Well I didn't either, not until I heard an angel sing behind a shoe factory. This apparition had the voice, the aura, of someone I loved even more than you."

Mr. Mestizo cocked his head to one side and patiently waited to hear the rest of the story.

"Rarely do the gods grant us the opportunity to redeem ourselves, to right our wrongs. I have been given a second chance to seek the forgiveness of a heart I had no right in breaking. My daughter has been returned to me, and the star she would have become is the star that a girl who makes leather shoes in Puerto Plata is destined to be. But she needs our help, señor, and help often begins with American dollars."

A man in a blue smock walked up to Ignacio. "Is he heeled and ready to pit?"

"Yes. One second," Ignacio said, and stood up.

"How you must scorn us humans," he whispered to his bird. "How you must laugh at our folly and madness, at our grasping and clutching. It's your fate and your burden to have so many dreams resting on your shoulders. I hope they are broad enough to bear a weight you never asked for."

MESSENGER

Estrellita chewed her bottom lip and watched some fishermen moving silently through the streets, walking towards the water and their lonesome boats. Sensing her apprehension, the rising sun peeked cautiously over the edge of the world and tiptoed into town unnoticed. It pocketed emerging yawns and encouraged hangovers. It petted sleeping dogs and caged parrots, ripened fruit, nuzzled lovers wrapped in cool sheets and sat beside a downhearted girl on the steps of a church.

Three sunrises

Growing bolder, the sun rose higher into the clear sky, a guiding light for the faithful who filed past Estrellita into the cathedral on their way to beg forgiveness, light their candles, worry their beads and pray for miracles. They ignored the pretty girl who sat each morning on God's stoop, staring at the horizon with condemned eyes, at a beautiful gallows of shimmering pastel hues.

And then wait no more

She rested her head on her arms and remembered when things had been different, simpler, when she and Jaragua had just met and everything was still possible, before reality had intruded upon the privacy and delusion of their dreams.

She felt a hand on her shoulder.

"Jaragua—" she said, looking up into the face of an elderly woman.

"Are you in need, child?" the woman asked her. Her face was the colour and texture of polished mahogany, and her eyes shone like two wet stones.

"No. I'm fine. Thank you," she said, her features collapsing in disappointment.

The woman reached down and pressed one of Estrellita's hands between her own hands, like a single leaf of parchment bound by the leather cover of a wise tome.

She pressed some money into Estrellita's palm. "This was for the church, but I think that you may need it more than they."

Estrellita stammered her embarrassment and tried to refuse the gift.

"Child, you cannot eat pride. I have seen you sitting here for three mornings now. I don't know what is troubling you, but I can see that you have your faith, and he sees it too," she said, pointing to the sky. "Nothing is forever—no joy, no sadness. Everything passes and so shall this."

The woman walked through the doors without waiting for a reply.

Estrellita gave the money to a barefoot shoeshine boy.

"Please, God, I need to know," she whispered.

When the winds came, she was watching a man sitting on a park bench, reading a newspaper. The sudden gust ripped the newspaper from the man's hands and scattered the pages across the square. They fluttered into the air and crashed back down along the street like graceless chicks on their fledgling flight.

The wind was a shifting oracle, and it sent a maelstrom of words and sand hurtling towards an unsuspecting Estrellita. The pages surged over the cathedral's steps and swirled around her.

She shielded her eyes as the newsprint soared into the air like grey bearded ghosts heralding doom and advertising El Presidente beer. A lone sheet of print pressed itself against her leg like a cat in need of stroking. She flinched at the contact and looked down at it with a sense of foreboding. The moment she touched the paper, the wind ceased to blow. She opened it up and read the headline: "More bodyparts found in Lago Enriquillo."

The photo accompanying the article leapt out at her. It was a vivid shot of a man's arm, severed at the elbow. It lay on the stony shore like a dead fish. However, there was something else about the photo, something more horrific than the image itself, something about the hand, something unimaginable.

"No."

Her watering eyes focused on the photo, on the hand, on some markings there—a tattoo. She leaned closer, already knowing the tattoo, the words it spelled and the hurt they would bring.

ESTRELLITA LUMINOSA

She stared at the hand for a long time, her mind searching for a way out, a way to deny what she knew to be true. Maybe it was a mistake, she thought. A similar tattoo, the same words but a different girl, a different song, a different life, one that didn't end like this. This pallid waterlogged lump of meat could never have belonged to the man she loved. She knew that hand, knew of its tenderness and of its strength, had felt its caress, had pressed her lips to the heat and ink of her own name. This lifeless thing lying amongst the arrowheads and teeth of a prehistoric lake could never have evoked such passions.

She let the page fall from her hand and watched it roll away from her. It tumbled like dice towards a graveyard, twisted like a belted kingfisher in a hurricane and spilled its guts along the street—a story in black and white and red.

Estrellita stood up and walked into the church, her dry eyes and calm facade belying her true emotions. Control was her only option because she knew that if she fell into her grief, she might never stand again.

She lit a candle. The solitary flame burned bright and hot, casting shadows over all it touched, over all it loved.

"Our Lady of Altagracia," she whispered, closing her eyes and raising her hands into the breathless air, "hear my prayer."

LOVE IS BLIND

BITUIN WAS A HIGH-STATIONED snow-white rooster with black legs and a battle-scarred beak. He was also a headhunter. He circled Mr. Mestizo warily, bobbing his head from side to side, his eyes searching for a chink in his opponent's armour.

The crowd cheered the two semi-finalists. The combatants were a kill away from a title shot, and the arena was going mental. The two roosters raised their hackle feathers, giving them the bizarre look of a bearded dragon in full flare. They raced at one another, left the floor, collided in midair and delivered punishment. They executed the manoeuvre repeatedly, leaping and lashing, each attempting to finish the other with every thrust of their sword, every stab of their beak.

Millions of dollars had been wagered on the match, and the stress of that gamble had cracked the voice and tightened the face of every man in the coliseum.

The Bankiva's plumage slowly turned a dirty pink from the blood of battle. He strutted across the centre of the pit, watching Mr. Mestizo back away.

Ignacio gripped the top of the pit wall and ground his teeth down to calcified stumps. He had never seen his rooster look so confused, so hesitant. He wanted to launch himself into the ring and save his friend. At that moment, he would gladly forfeit the money, his reputation, everything, if it were only possible.

Sensing another victory, Bituin—the star of Manila—pecked cruelly at his retreating foe, bullying him into submission.

Mr. Mestizo sucked air and looked around the ring for a way to escape. He crouched low and pressed his head up against the stained pit wall.

In a final effort to save his life, Mr. Mestizo charged. He looked like a wounded bull seeking revenge on a smug matador. The Bankiva sidestepped the ungainly attack and planted one leg and swung the other. The postiza punctured Mr. Mestizo's eye, blinding him.

"No. Stop it!" Ignacio yelled.

His misery was swallowed up by the glee and damnation that accompanied the career-ending injury. Mr. Mestizo rolled and fluttered across the green matting. The mob grimly called for his death and cursed his failing.

But did you know that I love him?

Ignacio looked away as the Bankiva flexed and gloated, primping its superiority for the entire world to worship.

Mr. Mestizo struggled to his feet and stumbled through the confusion of his end. The crowd lauded his valour with mixed emotions. The bird was finished, good for nothing save the cooking pot.

A blinker

Ignacio prayed for a swift end.

Bituin crowed in triumph. Any trepidation he had felt during the match had vanished, and he pecked casually at his rival's head, enjoying Mr. Mestizo's wheezing swan song.

What happened next is the reason why so many men around the world call themselves galleros, sabungeros or cockers, the reason they believe that the pit has more to teach them about life and death, courage and character, than all the long-winded lectures and poetic tomes ever spewed. Mr. Mestizo seized Bituin's cropped wattles in his beak, yanked him to the ground and pounded his spur through the bird's heart.

Once

Twice

Mambo

The Bankiva was dead.

There was a moment of astonishment, a bewildered silence that underscored the improbability of the surreal victory, and then there was bedlam.

Ignacio collapsed into the gallera, crawled over to Mr. Mestizo and hugged him, shielding the wounded bird with the hunched and knotted torque of his remorse. In a daze, he stood up and ran from the ring towards the refuge of the heeling room.

Madness boiled all around him, but it was muted and fractured. All he was conscious of was the vibration and wilt of the life he had risked. Men shoved disinfectant, gauze and advice into his fumbling hands as he pawed at his waning champion.

"Mister, mister," Isko said, holding a syringe in his open palm. "Medicine, magical stuff. Please, for the special one."

Ignacio looked at Isko and his needle and scowled.

"On my honour as a sabungero, it will help him."

Ignacio grabbed the needle. "How much? Where?"

Isko jabbed himself under his own arm. "Here. All of it."

Ignacio injected the enigmatic elixir into Mr. Mestizo's quivering body and was relieved to see how quickly it eased the bird's distress.

He swaddled Mr. Mestizo in the comfort of a dry towel and the safety of his embrace. "It's all right, my friend. You will dance no more. It's over now."

He pressed a sterile pad over the bird's sightless eye and cursed his own soul.

DELIVERANCE

THE CHILDREN DRIFTED ACROSS the black surface of the ocean at the mercy of ancient tides and indifferent currents. Maximo could feel small fish all around him nibbling at his saturated skin. He prayed that nothing hungrier would show up.

He looked at the distant lights of Puerto Rico dancing in the dark like fireflies in a Chinese lantern, oblivious to their own allure. Maximo watched Lourdes sleeping, watched her purple lips shivering beneath the full moon, and wondered how much longer they could hold on.

He wove his hands through the straps on her lifejacket, rested his head on the rough orange fabric and began to kick. He had no idea of time, no sense of distance, only the constant slap and drain of seawater over his face, the weak movement of his trembling leg and the vast starry sky above him. He tracked the steady progress of a faraway red light, followed it as it rolled and dipped with the undulating horizon, riding the gentle swell. Whatever it was, it was getting closer.

The sound of an outboard motor drilled a tiny hole through the cocoon of despair that encased the children, and they both looked up at the same time.

"What's that?" Lourdes asked. Her voice sounded parched and small.

"I don't know. An engine, I think."

The children stared at the approaching lights with mounting hope.

"One red and one green," Lourdes said.

Maximo raised his arms in the air. He waved frantically and yelled for help.

The silhouette of a small boat emerged from the dark sea. It wallowed in an inky valley and chugged up the proceeding rise like a mindless beetle.

The children yelled and waved as the boat continued towards Puerto Rico, the sound of its engine drowning out their voices.

"He doesn't see us," Lourdes said.

"Help us!" Maximo screamed, the effort ripping meat from his salt-cured vocal cords.

The engine's high-pitched whine receded, and the boat hesitated.

"It's turning around," Lourdes said.

The boat made a slow wide circle and motored towards the children. A flashlight beam swept over the surface of the water like a searchlight seeking convicts. It came to rest on two shipwrecked survivors.

"Lamb of God," a voice said.

Strong hands hauled the children out of the sea.

"Peter the fisherman," Maximo mumbled.

He was vaguely aware that he was lying on top of a great sea beast of some sort. Lourdes lay beside him, her eyes closed, her breathing shallow and raspy.

The fisherman twisted the throttle, and the boat surged forward. Whatever he had to say about finding two children adrift in the middle of the Mona Channel, he was keeping it to himself.

Something about a crowing cock and renouncing Jesus

"Are we headed to Puerto Rico or back to Hispaniola?" Maximo asked.

"Puerto Rico."

That was all he needed to hear.

He pulled his baseball cap from the waistband of his shorts and ran his finger over the numbers that had been carved into its bill. He couldn't remember the name of the man Jaragua had said to call, but he did remember that he was a tattoo artist. In his mind's eye, he saw Jaragua's hand stroking Lourdes' cheek. He saw the tattoo there—the one Jaragua had said his friend would remember doing.

"Estrellita Luminosa," he whispered.

He had heard it before. It was a song, an older one, and he remembered his parents dancing to it once on a special night.

The wooden boat—full of tuna and refugees—laboured towards the distant shore, and Maximo drifted into a beautiful memory from his childhood and towards a closer tomorrow.

LEGEND

EL GUAPO SLITHERED THROUGH the crowded heeling room, sat down beside Ignacio and cleared his throat.

Ignacio stopped packing his things and looked at the man beside him, looked at his hideous face without blinking and spoke. "Can I help you, señor?"

"I was just curious as to where the fuck you think you're going."

"What did you say to me?"

El Guapo crossed his legs and slid a thin peppermint candy into his ruined orifice of a mouth. "Your mongrel, your yellow dunghill of a scheming chicken, has a championship bout scheduled against my purebred Aseel."

Ignacio's eyes widened, and he placed a hand on Mr. Mestizo's coop. "You are either a fool or a madman, señor. My gallo has lost an eye. His days in the pit are over. He will never fight again."

"Most unfortunate...that eye thing. I would have preferred to see your imposter exposed under more just conditions, but I shall console myself with its death."

Ignacio stood up and glared down at El Guapo. "I was right the first time. You are a fool. Nothing and nobody can make me pit this bird again."

"Not even the welfare of your trusty houseboy Marco?"

"What—"

"If you don't fight for the championship, then not only will I turn your rubber trees into charcoal and your house into rubble, I will also punt that Haitian leech of yours back across the frontier, landing him squarely in the squalor and maggots of Cité Soliel, the slums he dreamed he'd escaped."

Ignacio's face darkened, and he clenched his fists. "As old as I am, I will punch your filthy words back down your throat, señor."

El Guapo cocked his head to one side and laughed, a spectacle that repulsed Ignacio. "No need to give yourself a stroke there, geezer. The choice is yours but believe what I'm telling you. I will see Marco washing himself in a puddle of malaria-laden mosquitoes. He will sleep in an open sewer and die with festering sores… Is your chicken's life worth more than his? Hmm, a dilemma."

Ignacio opened his mouth but no words would come out. He had no idea who the man threatening him was or how he knew about Marco, but he had no doubt that he would do as he said.

"You have a couple of hours to say goodbye to Cyclops here. I shall see you ringside," El Guapo said, and then walked away.

The upcoming match was as improbable as the odds that accompanied it. The galleros who crammed the coliseum had been reduced to a sewing circle of gossiping pensioners. Nobody had even heard a lie about a blinker fighting a healthy gamecock, not even in a backyard dispute, let alone a world title. The match reeked of corruption and payoffs. It was going to be a shameful display.

A bag containing eighty-four thousand dollars rested at Ignacio's feet. He had bet it all on Mr. Mestizo. He stood to win almost 1.8 million dollars.

Good luck

A well-dressed man walked into the middle of the pit and raised a microphone to his lips. "Galleros one and all, I welcome you to Quisqueya's premiere cockfighting arena," he said, and smiled like a screen idol. "After many hot-blooded battles, only two birds remain standing. This bout shall determine Santo Domingo's world champion, the most skilled and courageous gallo in the universe, of the ones who fight the true fight, of the ones who fight in the postiza."

The man left the pit, the crowd's disdain barking at his heels. The birds were weighed, pulled from their bags, beaked and released.

El Guapo's Aseel immediately rushed forward, shoved Mr. Mestizo to the ground and pecked at his good eye with sadistic intent. Ignacio looked at the floor.

The men in attendance began to boo. They had come to see a fair fight for the championship, not the slow torture of an already grievously wounded animal, especially one that had earned their respect.

Mr. Mestizo struggled to his feet and made a half-hearted attempt to defend himself. He even managed to land a few kicks, but they were weak and did no damage. Attila slapped and punished his helpless opponent around the pit, knocking him down and stepping back, allowing Mr. Mestizo to regain his footing before he knocked him down again.

The hyped-up Aseel seemed unwilling to finish the fight. He flexed and swaggered, crowed and scratched erratically at the green mating with his talons. His glazed eyes rolled and bulged from the drugs that pulsated through his system.

The coliseum had fallen unnaturally quiet. There was no more jeering or cheering, no betting, only the hissing of wind through teeth and the muttered anger of men who knew when their house was being disrespected. Someone patted Ignacio's back in sympathy, and another man spat tobacco-brown saliva into the pit, his eyes locked on El Guapo, the only man with a smile on his face.

The crazed Aseel chipped away at Mr. Mestizo's weakening spirit. He wanted to see his rival turn tail before he killed him.

Men began to clap their hands as a slow chant made its way around the arena. Mr. Mestizo's name had become a mantra, a holy word capable of shielding one from malevolence.

Mestizo, clap, Mestizo, clap, Mestizo, clap

Ignacio chanted his rooster's name, wiped tears from his eyes and stared hatefully over at the man who had forced him to sacrifice—to fail yet again—something he loved.

Mr. Mestizo, battered and desperate, turned and ran for his life. It was a sad moment, one that undermined the bird's previous displays of heart. People stopped clapping and looked away. They studied their hands, they looked at their feet, anywhere but at the gallera, where the final moments of a warrior's life were ending in disgrace.

Adaptation

The word flashed through Ignacio's mind as he watched Attila chase Mr. Mestizo around the perimeter of the cockpit. This is tactical, something his bird had remembered from a previous battle. Without warning, Mr. Mestizo whirled around and launched himself into the air. His feathers flared and soared, and he swung his leg like the dancer he was. He impaled his pursuer's head on his postiza and pinned the mortally wounded rooster to the mat. Using his sharp beak, he stabbed his revenge into the Aseel's head. Blood and feathers flew, the crowd roared and Mr. Mestizo became a god.

For the last time in his life, Ignacio jumped into the pit and picked up his bird. Mr. Mestizo sagged gratefully into the safety of his hands and shook from exhaustion.

The pit dissolved into pandemonium.

The MC called for order as men in blue smocks swept the pit of anyone who didn't belong there. Somebody handed Ignacio a clean white towel and a spray bottle full of water. He misted Mr. Mestizo and dabbed at his superficial wounds with the towel.   Ignacio accepted the winner's trophy and a cheque for one hundred thousand dollars. He smiled robotically and thanked everyone he knew and others he didn't. None of it seemed real, or even possible.

Dreamer

"And now," the MC said, "I'm certain that one of our trusted galleros here tonight would like to make good on one of the largest wagers this pit has ever seen."

All eyes fell upon the sulking figure in the front row, the man's expensive suit cheapened beneath the weight of their contempt.

El Guapo stood up, spat into the ring and glared back. "Who would have imagined that a dirty dunghill could have bested my top bird? Not I, obviously," he said, hefting a black canvas bag and grimacing. His antics earned him a few sympathetic chuckles.

"This bout was unusual," he continued, "as everyone knows, but the outcome was never guaranteed. This match had the drama and angst that makes our sport so intriguing. Everyone loves an underdog story, and tonight one such yellow chicken has managed to, by employing a rather deceitful tactic, eke out a victory over a vastly superior animal. Such is the fascination and flaw of the cockpit."

El Guapo tossed the bag of money into the air. It landed at Ignacio's feet with a heavy thump. "One point seven mil. Ridiculous odds they were anyway."

Ignacio ignored the bag and blazed holes into El Guapo's face. "Gracias, señor. By honouring your debt, you have erased from our memories *none* of your previous treachery," he said, stroking Mr. Mestizo's back. "You have called my rooster a yellow chicken, a dunghill, an imposter, but you forgot some other names. You forgot to call him a blinker and, as of late, a wheeler for utilizing a tactic you described as deceitful, but one, I'm sure, he would call survival."

As the grinning crowd clapped and whistled their approval, Ignacio slowly raised Mr. Mestizo above his head and turned in a slow circle. "And there is one other name that you forgot to mention, señor, the most important one of all. You forgot to call him champion of the world. Do you hear me? Champion of the world."

El Guapo scowled and turned his back on Ignacio. The capacity crowd stood and applauded.

The victory would become an island myth, a lie told by those who claimed to have been there, a fable whispered while rocking children to sleep, filling their dreams with the power of legend.

A MOMENT IN THE SUN

Ignacio left the coliseum. He had his trophy tucked under one arm, Mr. Mestizo in the crook of the other and his bag of money slung across his back. He breathed in the scent of West Indian Jasmine and silently thanked Lady Luck for all her blessings. His fortunes had changed. He had been given the power to alter destinies and rediscover his true path.

El Guapo walked out of the shadow of a cedar tree, spread his arms wide and sneered at Ignacio. "Look at you, flush and flash. No longer a humble rubber maker, no longer a drunk, no longer a gallero or a merenguero. So what the fuck are you now...except smug?"

Ignacio straightened his shoulders. "What I am, señor, is a very good question. One I have failed to answer, despite a lifetime of effort. Tonight, however, I am something that I never thought I would be again, something that has nothing to do with a bag full of money. Tonight, señor, I am respected. And you are feared, something that I'm sure feels like respect to you."

Before El Guapo could reply, Isko and three other Filipino men approached them.

"Mister, mister, you have trouble?" Isko said, placing a hand on Ignacio's shoulder.

"You're not in Manila anymore, you Filipino monkey," El Guapo said, "so I suggest that you and your heathen followers refrain from sticking your little dicks into places that will get them cut off."

NCM and another man stepped into the light.

Isko smiled coldly and spoke. "No, we are not in my city, that much is true, but the street is the street, and shit smells the same on the bottom of any sandal."

El Guapo's fingers tightened around the push knife he had palmed. As he moved towards Isko, the doors of the coliseum banged open. A handful of army officers spilled out into the night, their voices loud with rum and power.

El Guapo looked at them and pocketed his weapon. "Sometimes the sun shines out of a skinny dog's ass...eh, Chinaman?"

He turned on his heel and walked away. His two henchmen followed him like a couple of pilot fish on a great white shark.

"Thank you, my friends," Ignacio said.

"Come on, man, we walk you to your car," Isko said.

The group of men escorted Ignacio to his truck.

"Well, I guess you can afford a new one now," Isko said, pointing at the vehicle and laughing.

"I guess so, but it doesn't even seem real to me yet. It's more money than I ever dreamed of having...even wanting to have."   "Okay. I understand you, but you must watch out. Many men would harm you badly for such riches."

"I know, but don't worry for me. I wouldn't die for what's in this bag."

"I say goodbye then. I wish you extra special lucky life for you and your champion."

The men shook hands and smiled at each other.

"I'm sorry that your star, your Bituin had to go. I'm sorry for that," Ignacio said.

"I know you are, and for this reason, Buddha smiles on you tonight. Him say, 'Look, a true sabongero, one who calls himself a gallero.'"

Both men laughed at the remark, both wishing that they had the time to become better friends.

"I see you in Manila one day. I know that. At Araneta Stadium," Isko said. "But please do not bring your one-eyed pirate bird. He going to break my bank."

Isko and his men walked away.

Ignacio waved goodbye. "Don't worry. He's retired."

And so am I

Ignacio stuffed his winnings behind the driver's seat and fired up the vehicle. He looked over at Mr. Mestizo and stroked him affectionately. "What say you to some music? Any requests? No? Then how about some, oh, I don't know…some merengue?"

The moment he switched on the radio, Ignacio broke out laughing. He shook his head and turned up the volume. "If I never believed in signs before, I do now."

The song he was listening to was "La Gallera" by Juan Luis Guerra, an amusing composition about how an unlucky gallero had lost everything at the pit one day.

"Mi gallo candela," Ignacio sang to his bird.

"I lost my land, I lost my house, my dog today in the cockpit," he sang in Spanish. "I lost my double-breasted suit," he continued, laughing so hard that he began to cry, the full impact of what had happened finally dawning on him. "I lost my glasses, my clothes, my watch. Damn cockpit. I have nothing left now."

He used the collar of his shirt to blot the moisture from his eyes and breathed deeply. "No, Mr. Guerra. Tonight, the cockpit has been good to me."

He held his bird in front of him and marvelled at the gift he had received. "And it's all because of you, my cinnamon rooster," he said, and kissed the bird.

"But listen, my friend. My music is calling me once again, and after so many years of silence, the danger of her song sounds sweet and healing to my ears. She will suffer my excuses no longer. She turns up her nose, steps light and quick and demands that I follow. I shall start a new merengue band with a Puerto Plata angel…one who is oblivious to the wheels of destiny spinning towards her. Everybody knows that a star cannot hide its light forever."

He touched a sympathetic finger to Mr. Mestizo's bandaged eye, frowned and nested him within the folds of a warm blanket. "Sleep now, and when you awake, I promise you that we'll be back home."

Ignacio drove through Santo Domingo's narrow backstreets, filtering his way down litter-strewn alleyways and across vacant lots. He was so lost in the golden image of his future that he failed to notice that someone was following him.

ABSOLUTION

IGNACIO DROVE PAST A cluster of derelict railway cars. They huddled together like hobos sharing body heat, their hollow eyes staring sightlessly back at him. Taking a shortcut had turned out to be a bad idea.

Those look familiar

He was almost sure that he had spent a delirious night or three shaking within the sooty confines of their steel walls, hurling meteorites at neon cobras and watching them slither through the amber skulls of Taino chieftains.

The truck's single working headlight groped its way along the edge of a poorly defined road, cautiously probing the gloom with its needle of faint illumination. Ignacio hunched over the steering wheel, screwed his face up and squinted through the cracked windshield.

The headlights of another vehicle twinkled in the rear-view mirror. He could hear the growl of a powerful diesel engine as it barrelled down the steep incline behind him. Ignacio tapped his brakes a couple of times and watched in horror as the vehicle swerved across the road and bore down on him.

Light filled the cab of Ignacio's truck, ricocheting off metal and glass and slashing at his eyes. There was a surreal moment just before the impact, a weightlessness, an implosion that forced the air from his lungs and murmured its shockwave into his ringing ears. The sound of the collision shattered the nightmares of stray cats and vagrants, curling their limbs and claws into defensive postures and dilating the pupils of their rheumy eyes.

Ignacio's truck crumpled like a beer can beneath a construction boot. Glass fragments seeded the weeds and screeching metal hurtled down the embankment and skidded into the slick foulness of an open storm drain.

The red truck glared down at the smoking devastation, its throaty idling sounded like a callous snicker. The doors swung open in unison, and three men stepped out and surveyed the carnage.

"Go get my rooster," El Guapo said.

Before anybody could carry out the order, a bloodied Ignacio stumbled from the wreckage, took a few steps and collapsed in the culvert.

"Tough old bird," El Guapo said, and laughed.

NCM and another man searched the ruined truck for Mr. Mestizo.

"Is he there?" El Guapo asked.

NCM shook his head, looked at his employer and crunched his fists into raw-boned contempt.

El Guapo strode down the hill, kicking bottles and rusty cans out of his way. He jumped into the ditch, ignoring the squelch and stink that oozed out from under the soles of his expensive Don Camino shoes, rubber soles that contained the labour and love of the man lying at his feet.

He leaned down and peered at the jagged gash on Ignacio's face. He thought that the cut looked worse than it was. "What a bleeder."

Ignacio rolled his head to one side and groaned.

"Oh, come on now. Don't be such a lesbian," El Guapo said. "Sorry, I mean thespian. Just give me what I want, and I'll leave you to your misery."

"Behind the seat," Ignacio slurred, his gaze settling on the gloating face above him. He thought that Satan had absurdly radiant blue eyes, pretty ones that cultivated conceit and got your ass tossed out of heaven.

"Don't lie to me, old man."

"Behind the seat. My money. Take it and go," he said, and spat a mouthful of blood.

El Guapo grinned and clucked his tongue in disapproval. "You insult me, sir. Do you think I'm devoid of morality? I may be guilty of alota things, but welching on a bet isn't one of them. I will not dishonour the pallabra de gallero. The money is yours. However, I am curious as to how sweet a million-dollar chicken tastes. Must be like a buttery orgasmatron, ambrosia with a beak. Now where is that little blinker?"

"You're too late. He died."

El Guapo's face hardened at the prospect of being denied the revenge of his choice. "Bullshit. If he's dead, then where's his carcass?"

"I stopped side of the road. Gave it to an old woman."

El Guapo's smile returned. "Now I know your shittin' me. You forget. I saw you with that chicken. If it died, you'd spend ten grand on its tomb. So before I get angry, where is he?"

Ignacio opened his mouth to reply when a muffled clucking sounded from beneath his jacket.

El Guapo tilted his head to one side and smirked. "Looks like Mr. Mestizo takes to cockpits better than armpits," he said, and yanked Ignacio's coat open. "Ahh, there's my dinner."

El Guapo reached for the bird. Ignacio seized his arm and sunk his teeth into the drug lord's wrist. He was an old dog who suddenly remembered that he still had fangs.

El Guapo grunted in surprise and then smashed his fist into Ignacio's face a couple of times. "Good. Very good. Anything worth loving is worth bleeding for. I have new respect for you. But really, who fucking bites? That's an animal's defence." He seized the rooster by the neck and stood up.

Ignacio mumbled incoherently and raised his arms into the air, his hands clutching at the memory of a happier time.

"Console yourself with the money," El Guapo said, "and I will think of you as I pick Mr. Mestizo's meat from between my molars with one of his spurs."

"Wait," Ignacio pleaded, the anguish in his voice coming from a place most people had never been. "Please, just let me say goodbye… one minute."

El Guapo hesitated for a second before relenting. "When you tell this story, and I know you will, don't forget to mention that I was kind," he said, and tossed Mr. Mestizo into the air.

The bird tumbled onto Ignacio, squawking its indignation and resetting its ruffled feathers. Ignacio cuddled the bird and rolled onto his side, his back a battle shield, scarred and crested, storied and splintered. He whispered reassuringly to his traumatized rooster and surreptitiously slipped a hand into his pocket and extracted a vial of amber liquid. He unscrewed the cap and dipped Mr. Mestizo's spurs deep into the odourless fluid.

"Okay, freak, time's up," El Guapo said. "Your man/bird love scene is starting to sour my stomach. It's just a stinking chicken... Fuck."

"Mambo. One last time," Ignacio whispered to Mr. Mestizo.

El Guapo tried to grab the rooster, but Ignacio hugged the bird to his chest and turned away.

"Go to hell!" Ignacio screamed.

El Guapo kicked him in the kidney. Ignacio gasped in shock as a nauseating pain spiked its way through his body. His hands fell away from his bird. The second kick bounced his head off the cement and sent him spiralling into the void. He landed in a place where the past and present humped the sanity out of each other, siring ying-and-yang offspring with suicidal tendancies whose futures glowed like nirvana and smelled like green stomach bile.

"Mr. Mestizo," Ignacio muttered into the dawn of unconsciousness, his lips caked with blood and remorse. "I failed you. Mr. Mesti...my angel, my daughter...Sophia."

Somewhere within the hidden chambers of his mind, beneath secret catacombs, hollow bones, cobwebs and escape tunnels, Ignacio stood trembling before a padlocked door and listened to the tragedy trapped within. He listened to it kick and wail behind its barricade of injustice, a dangerous prisoner who would no longer play by the rules, no longer be ignored. His daughter's face undulated within the guilty twilight of his subconscious, laughing, crying, bleeding, dying.

Her eyes, he thought, so much like her mother's.

Her eyes, pleading for an absolution in death that she never received in life—exiled for the crime of being born.

"Papa, please...see me," she had said that night, that horrific unforgivable night that had ruined so many lives.

In his mind, Ignacio was back inside a small apartment in Santo Domingo, the one he had shared with his daughter. He floated in the limbo of his memories and looked down on himself and his Sophia, watching in quiet agony as the events that took her away from him unfolded like a tragic play.

It happened on her sixteenth birthday.

Ignacio watched himself fingering the small gold and jade beads of the necklace he had in his pocket. It was the very necklace that had brought him and his wife together. It was the same one he had promised to pass on to their daughter on her sixteenth birthday to provide her with the protection of an Orisha, the one who had watched over the Mendoza girls since Spanish boots had first tasted Cuban soil.

Give her the necklace

She held out her hand towards him. "I am here, Papa. Flesh and blood, and unlike Mama, I am still alive, and I need you."

Take her hand

"Help me, teach me, the way you do for your students, strangers who you encourage more than me," she said, fresh tears joining the cascade of years past.

"Enough, Sophia," he said. "I only coach those I think have a voice, have a chance. I don't encourage you because you're not a singer, never will be, so forget merengue. I won't help you to fail."

Ignacio hovered high above the scene and watched himself lying to his only child. He was slowly crushing her dreams, exacting revenge upon the creature who had taken his wife from him, having split her cervix and drained her life onto the operating table, greedily snatching existence from the nutrient- and oxygen-rich placenta of her dying mother.

And then he saw something, something he had never seen before all those years ago. As Sophia listened to his deceit, a wounded shame flickered across her eyes. She knew he was lying. She knew she had a voice and that he simply refused to hear it.

"Papa, I'm a good girl. Can't you see that? I want to be part of your world. I want to sing. I see you with your music, when you play merengue, and I see the man who my mother must have fallen in love with. Not this fraud, this empty shell who Mama must weep for in heaven."

Ignacio didn't want to see what was about to happen, didn't want to hear the last words he had ever spoken to her, but he was powerless to turn away. He watched himself—as a younger man, an angrier man—as his hand lashed out and slapped his daughter's face for the first and the last time.

"You spit on your own mother's grave, a mother you never knew!" he screamed, his words hurting her deeper than the flat of his calloused hand ever could. "Weeps for me? If it weren't for you, she would still be alive. You killed her," he raged, finally speaking his irrational beliefs and sealing both their fates.

Sophia turned away and flung the door open. With an anguished cry, she was gone into the night, into the heat and hustle of Santo Domingo's mean streets.

And she ran.

She ran until her dark hair stuck to her damp skin, until the sound of her tennis shoes slapping against sun-warmed asphalt matched the cadence of her pounding heart, until her lungs burned and her legs quivered and the words her father had spoken fell far behind her and she was in the arms of someone who loved her.

"I'm never going back there," she said, allowing the boy to kiss her pain away.

"You don't have to," he said. "You can stay with us."

The boy was three years older than Sophia, and he was an active member of the Dominican Liberation Party.

"Together we can change things. Topple this corrupt dictatorship that kicks us when we are down, that feeds off our repression like a parasite," he said, the idealistic fire in his eyes redefining her love for him. "It's time for you to join us. There's a demonstration tonight. We are going to shake El Presidente out of his ivory tower."

Sophia wrapped her face in a blue bandana and giggled at the image of herself as an outlaw. She marched through one of Santo Domingo's more notorious slums, parroting the political rhetoric that her new friends shouted into the fretting night.

The small group of activists failed to notice that a black van was monitoring their mini rebellion. The men inside the van were members of a paramilitary death squad know as La Banda. They maintained the status quo by executing anyone who opposed the rule of strongman Joaquin Balaguer, as well as street children, drunks, squatters, homosexuals and sympathizers.

Five men burst from the van, their automatic rifles adding unwanted heat to the tropical night. Sophia saw half her friends cut down by the barrage before her boyfriend grabbed her by the wrist and screamed at her to run.

And she ran.

Sophia could hear the shouts and gunfire of the killers behind her. She pumped her arms and flew across the cringing pavement. She looked over at her lover just as two bullets ripped through his back and exited out his chest.

Sophia threw herself on the ground, cradled his head in her lap and swallowed the dying embers of his wildfire eyes. The sound of heavy jackboots pounded towards her, an apocalyptic sound that thundered in the ears of the righteous and the damned, the hunted and the hidden, around the block, around the world and throughout the ages.

When she looked up again, she was staring into the barrel of a gun. Her assassin was no older than the boy he had just murdered.

"Wait—"

The gun silenced her.

Ignacio cried out. The sound traversed time and space, his torment suffered by stray cats and vagrants and young poets who wrote sonnets with bullets and pressed blood roses between the dog-eared pages of their Pablo Neruda books.

He watched himself running through the streets, towards the sound of gunfire, towards the sound of his daughter's waning sigh and the slamming iron doors.

"Sophia," he cried, falling to his knees and embracing the last heartbeat she would ever offer him. He looked into her lifeless eyes, eyes that would never see how much her father had loved her.

Ignacio blinked the horror away and saw himself standing beside his daughter's coffin, a necklace of jade and gold dangling from his numb fingers. He slipped the heirloom around Sophia's neck and fastened it. It was the same one that her mother had worn, and her mother's mother, and the one before that. It was the same one that was responsible for bringing Sophia into the world and then taking her from it.

"You had no Orisha to protect you that night. Now your mother can watch over you. You whom I never deserved and always loved," he whispered.

He saw himself in his sombre black suit, the wind buffeting the small congregation of friends and fellow musicians that surrounded him from afar. Saying nothing to anybody, he turned and went to get a drink, one that would last for the next twenty years.

The sound of his own despair dragged him back to reality.
Ignacio rolled in wet grime and struggled to sit up. In his confusion, he was certain that he had gotten drunk again and was back where he belonged.

Just one—a shot, a measure, a taste, a lake of burning rum

He rested his head in the crook of his arm and decided to die right there no matter how long it took. It was then that he felt familiar arms enfolding him in their strength. He sagged into the consoling warmth and cried on a shoulder he couldn't see.

"Forgive me, my angel. Forgive me," he said.

He felt lips pressing themselves to his cheek, and then for the first time in all the visitations, he heard a voice.

Forgive yourself

The words washed over him like a salve, vinegar and wine, body and blood, like the dawn, a holy comet and a falling star searing the scabs of self-loathing that hid within the creases of his wrinkled skin. It left him pink and scalded, reborn and squalling.

He turned his face towards the maroon sky and laughed. He opened his mouth and captured her tears, drank them, allowed them to course through the desert of his forsaken soul like milk and honey.

MAGIC BUS

"ANGEL'S TEARS HAVE NO salt," Ignacio mumbled.

Many hands grabbed him and lifted him up.

"Wait. I'm not ready." He opened his eyes and looked into the face of a bearded man.

"Take it easy, brother. We've gotcha. You were in a car accident," the man said.

Ignacio watched rainwater running off the brim of the stranger's panama hat and stopped struggling. The good Samaritans carried him up the embankment and into the comfort of their purple paisley hippie bus. They laid him down on one of the bunks, and a woman with a crew cut and a gap between her front teeth worked a cool cloth over his face.

"Are you an angel?" Ignacio asked.

His question made her friends smile and rib the girl about her altruistic nature.

"We're a family," she said. "We travel, we experience, we party. That's about it."

"Mr. Mestizo," he mumbled as the grim weight of gravity brought him fully back down to earth. "They ate my friend. Cannibals and cutthroats." He looked out the window and wondered if they stole his trophy and his money as well.

Ignoring his rescuers' protests, he stumbled out into the rain, made his way down to his wrecked truck and rooted through the destruction.

"It's still here."

323

He placed the trophy on the ground, pulled the duffel bag from behind the busted driver's seat and tore the zipper down.

The money was still there.

"I'd forfeit it all to have you back again, Mr. Mestizo."

He looked up the embankment at the rogues' gallery shivering in the rain above him. He looked at their unkempt clothes, tattoos and facial piercings, looked at their crazy purple bus and thought that the vehicle would be perfect for a touring merengue band.

"My friends, I'm about to change your fortunes. I want to buy your bus, and I'm a very generous man," he said, starting back up the hill.

The woman with the crew cut crossed her arms like a nightclub bouncer. "It's not for sale."

Ignacio grinned at her. "Yes, my dear, it is. It's the reason why our paths crossed tonight. Do you believe in destiny?"

KARMA DOES THE MAMBO

THE GOLDEN DART FROG of Colombia is the most poisonous amphibian on the planet. The indigenous tribes of the Amazon Basin routinely harvest its noxious secretions to create powerful weapons. One milligram of the lethal neurotoxin will drop three black rhinos in their charging tracks. One gram is enough to kill more than twelve thousand humans. One dipped postiza is more than enough to send a Dominican drug lord to hell.

El Guapo barged into his industrial-sized kitchen and tossed a squirming cloth bag onto a wooden butcher's block.

"Wakey, wakey, eggs and bakey, Mr. Mestizo," he said in a singsong voice.

He filled a large copper pot with hot water, slammed the pot down onto a burner and fired the gas beneath it. He dug around in a cupboard beside the range. He then tossed whole Spanish onions into the pot as if he were sinking baskets from the foul line. "Bit a onion."

He violently spiked a bunch of carrots into the pot, sloshing water onto the floor. "Bit a carrot."

He chopped the knotted top off the cloth bag with a cleaver made of gleaming Japanese steel.

"Come on, you. Chicken soup just ain't the same without a chook." He dumped Mr. Mestizo onto the butcher's block and flicked his finger across the bird's beak.

He leaned down and sneered at the bird. "Oh, sorry. Did that hurt? Did I hurt your feelings, you one-eyed mongrel turd? I'm going to make a delectable sancocho out a you, and you had better taste like one point seven million dollars. You had better taste like the sticky cream

325

between Aphrodite's Greek thighs, like Venus' vagina dripping with sex nectar."

He picked up a pepper mill and ground the spice over Mr. Mestizo's head. He laughed as the coarse shower distressed the bird. "That's it. Snort and snuffle. And how about a little proverbial salt in the old wound?"

He shook some rock salt into the palm of his hand and pelted it at Mr. Mestizo's ruined eye. The bird crowed and shook with frustration, his one good eye fixated on his latest adversary, on the soft throbbing vulnerability of El Guapo's throat.

El Guapo hammered another fistful of salt at the bird. "Too many cooks spoil the broth...eh, butterball?"

Mr. Mestizo scratched at the wooden surface beneath his feet and waited for a shot. He didn't have to wait long.

El Guapo rested his elbows on the butcher's block, eased his weight onto them and looked at the bird. "Tomorrow morning, as I'm evacuating what's left of you into the chunderbox, I shall reminisce on your victory in Santo Domingo, and then I shall flush that memory away."

Growing tired of the insults, Mr. Mestizo cocked his head to one side, planted his left leg, leapt into the air and drove his spur into El Guapo's neck, piercing his carotid artery. The bird landed gracefully and retreated.

El Guapo slapped at the side of his neck. He felt as if he had just been stung by a wasp. His eyes bulged in terror, and he stumbled backwards until he collided with the wall.

Mr. Mestizo crowed and strutted across the table and awaited his enemy's counterattack.

There wasn't going to be one.

The poison kicked El Guapo's legs out from under him, and he fell to the floor, gagging and convulsing. His tongue swelled, and his limbs went rigid with paralysis. His body quivered and quaked, and milky saliva spilled from his mouth in frothy globs. He looked like a malfunctioning cappuccino machine.

Within seconds, El Guapo went into cardiac arrest. He died choking on his own vomit and thinking one thought.

Well played, fuckface. Well played

Mr. Mestizo looked down on El Guapo's shivering corpse, flapped his wings and crowed mightily, a sound that would be heard all over Hispaniola.

Mambo

VAMPIRES AND CHARITY

IGNACIO'S WORKERS SHADED THEIR eyes with the palms of their hands, mopped soiled white rags over the backs of their necks and watched a dust cloud chase the tail of a purple dragon.

The psychedelic beast hissed and squealed and brought itself to a shuddering stop in front of the grinning men. The door of the bus caved inwards, and Ignacio emerged from within, a crooked smile peeking out from between the folds of his bruised face.

"Amigos," he said, throwing his arms into the air.

The men rushed towards him, laughing and whooping.

"World champion."

"And a blinker."

"All of Quisqueya has heard."

"Where did you get that bus?"

Ignacio embraced the men and told them the story of his success, about the bouts and the subterfuge, about Mr. Mestizo's bravery and skill, about wagers that rubber makers and farmhands had no right in making, no right in winning.

"So let us see him…this saviour of Puerto Plata."

Ignacio kept his smile in place and waved the question away. "We'll speak more later. Now tell me. Where is my foreman? Where is Marco?"

"He's down in the grove," one of them said, and frowned. "He got some bad news, we think. You know, more of the same in Haiti. This time it's the blue helmets and Préval supporters. The killing goes on. He was very angry."

Ignacio nodded and thought about the news report he had

listened to on his drive in from Santo Domingo. After President Jean-Bertrand Aristide fled the island, the United Nations had appointed an international force, the United Nations Stabilization Mission in Haiti (MINUSTAH), to police the country and bring some stability to a nation torn apart by escalating criminal and political violence. It never ended.

Ignacio handed each of his men a thick packet of money. "Take some time off and be good to your families, because in the end, that's all that will matter." He smiled at their shocked expressions, revelling in his newfound ability to change peoples' lives.

He walked through a meadow of prickly grass and scanned the woods for Marco. He could smell something delicious in the air. He had come to realize that Caribbean breezes communicated on a primal level. They connected people, they blabbed secrets, they broke bread and clinked glasses, they shared hardships and evoked dormant memories of sensuality, of nights wrapped in the tanned arms of someone you would never forget.

He stood still and embraced the silence and tranquility that his strand of Castilla rubber trees had always granted him.

Thud...thud

He saw Marco driving his fists into a tree.

Thud...thud

He walked over and seized the boy's bloody hands. "Enough, Marco... Stop."

Ignacio looked at Marco and gasped at the hostility stamped into his face. It was a side of the boy he had never seen before, a side of him that had survived the degradation of Cité Soleil. It was the fierce face of rag-and-bone poverty, one that had been there all along, waiting just beneath the surface until it was needed.

"What's wrong with you? Look at your hands," Ignacio said.

Marco held his hands up in front of his face, watching as rivulets of blood dripped from them and fell to the thirsty soil. He shrugged and stared off into nothingness, at a repressed memory, at a scar and a disgrace, at an injustice that never ended and at lives that would never begin.

When Marco spoke, his voice was calm and flat. "Have you ever heard of a man called Luckner Cambronne?"

"No. I don't know this name."

"Maybe you know him as the rest of the world knew him...as the Vampire of the Caribbean."

Ignacio nodded solemnly in recognition of the infamous nickname. The man had been the head of the merciless Tonton Macoutes during the reign of Papa Doc Duvalier, and his barbaric acts where well documented. "Yes. I know of him. He wore suits made of sharkskin, and before AIDS, he made a fortune selling Haitian blood to pharmaceutical companies."

Five tons of plasma a month, siphoned from the malnourished black arms of the Western Hemisphere's poorest country, destined for the ailing blue veins of the rich and the white

"It was the antibodies in our blood that made it so prized," Marco continued. "To survive the slums of Port-au-Prince, to fight against the diseases that killed so many, our blood mutated. It became stronger than more sterile societies...like America."

Marco squeezed his fists together and watched his blood drip. "Can you tell me why, then? Can you tell me why, if my people's blood is so expensive, so treasured, why it has always been spilled so cheaply?"

Ignacio placed his hand on the boy's back and said nothing.

"There's been more riots, more murdering, raping and lynching," Marco said. "My girl is back there. She not safe. Nobody ever is in my country. I can't work the rubber no more. She needs me, and I'm going to return to Cité Soleil."

"Come up to the house with me," Ignacio said.

The two men entered the stone cottage, and Ignacio rooted around in a trunk at the foot of his bed.

"Please, sit down," Ignacio said.

He unfolded a satchel of yellowed papers and traced his finger over the documents. He took a pen from his pocket and signed his name in several spots before sliding the papers across the table to Marco. "Take the pen and sign here," he said, pointing to a dotted line. "And here… and here."

Marco signed the papers without question.

"Keep these safe. They are proof of your ownership of this land, of the trees, this house. All of it is yours now," Ignacio said.

He pushed another envelope across the table. "There's one hundred thousand dollars in there. Go back to Haiti, get your woman, come back here and work the rubber. Have babies. Let them run in the fields and play in the sun. If this is your dream, then you've found it, and whatever happiness this life has to offer, it has found you."

Marco stared at the table for a long time before speaking. "I won't offend you with any false protest. I accept your gifts with a gratitude that has no words, and I tell you from my heart, my good friend, that I will make the best rubber in all the world, me and my girl, and that our first born will bear your name, and when these eyes close for the final time, this land is the last thing they will see."

"That's all I need to hear. Now go. Don't waste time. Take the truck and begin your new life, because all too often, tomorrow never comes."

Marco took the money and the papers and opened the door of the cottage. "And what will you do? Where will you go?"

"Back where I belong. Back to the dangerous arms of a demanding mistress. Back to my merengue."

Marco reached out and took Ignacio's hands into his own. "And whatever happiness there is in life, it waits there for you. Of this I am sure."

"Good luck, Marco, and listen to the radio. When you hear about a hot new band called Rocket and the Cinnamon Roosters, you will know where to find me."

The men smiled at each other and waved goodbye, both knowing that they would meet again, share a meal and listen to the sound of the wind through the rubber trees.

After watching Marco drive away, Ignacio walked over to his

neglected jumble of musical instruments. He squatted down, picked up his old trumpet and blew the dust from its brass body. "I'm sorry," he said, and polished grime from its mouth. "Your song shall be heard again. Remember, a voice is never new…only those who listen to it."

He laid the trumpet down and walked over to his stove. He took some items from a cupboard, placed them inside a plastic bag and left the cottage.

Ignacio walked up the hill and entered his smokehouse. He inhaled the scent of strangulation and considered the smouldering fire. Its molten heart pulsated within a ring of rocks. Grey ash tumbled through the air like weightless snakeskin.

He took an unopened bottle of rum out of his bag and smashed it on the rocks. The gesture was casual, free of anger or uncertainty—the redundant prop of a method actor. He would never drink again.

He reached into the bag a second time and pulled out the Captain's daughter. He looked down at the frayed rawhide lash with mixed emotions. He tightened his grip around the familiar smoothness of its leather handle and swung it easily through the smoky air.

He felt no animosity towards the object. If anything, the power of its punishment had at times allowed him to go on living. It was like an old friend, one who knew all of his dirtiest secrets yet still called him friend. "Thank you, but I'm through hurting the things I love, and finally, that includes me."

He tossed the cat o' nine tails onto the embers and watched tiny flames climb up the sides of the whip and run along its braided tails, eager diligent flames that sought to cremate all evidence of an old man's sins.

He turned and walked out of the smokehouse, closing the door behind him, leaving all of his demons trapped inside to suffocate. Lost in thought, he didn't hear the man coming up behind him until he spoke.

"Señor dos Santos."

Ignacio turned around and looked up at the towering figure of El Guapo's most trusted thug. The sun was in Ignacio's eyes. All he could see was NCM's silhouette and the movement of the giant's arm as he raised it.

"In Haiti, we say it's after the battle that you count the wounded." NCM was holding something in the palm of his huge hand.

"Mr. Mestizo," Ignacio said. He took the bird into his hands and choked on his tears.

The excited rooster crowed and clucked, telling his friend of his wild adventure and of his victory, and he asked about sweet mangoes, harems and the shade of a cashew tree.

DESTINY TAKES A BRIDE

IGNACIO SAT ON THE warm hood of his bus, sipped a cold morir soñando and surveyed the tattered remnants of Puerto Plata's merengue festival. The wind blew plastic cups, paper plates and neon adverts into loose piles along the street as if it had been paid to sweep up. Except for a few staggering zombies, the malecón was deserted.

"Looks like I missed a good one," he said.

He looked out over the water and watched it sparkle. It conjured up images of Spanish galleons heavy with cargos of silver pieces of eight, gilded pommels and bejewelled scabbards.

He thought about his visit to Don Camino's shoe factory and about his inability to find a girl who no longer worked there.

"Hey, papi, that's a funky bus," a female voice said.

Ignacio looked over at a teenaged couple as they passed by. The flirtatious girl was just becoming aware of the power of her sexuality, and her boyfriend gripped her hand with a jealous strength, his thick neck muscles bulging with veins and insecurity.

"Mucho gracias, señorita," Ignacio said, and raised his juice.

"Did you paint it yourself?" she asked.

"Come on," her boyfriend said, tugging her along. "He's just some old man."

The girl smiled an apology at Ignacio and walked on.

As he watched the couple fade away, he grinned to himself and thought back on his life. "Just an old man," he said, and chuckled. "An old man who once did the mambo with Marilyn Monroe, an old merenguero who wrote a hit song, an old gallero who raised a champion gallo."

He swirled the melting ice in his cup.

"And I'm still here, muchacho. Still here and still dreaming. I hope you will be as old one day."

Something winked at him from the far end of the malecón, its mystery and motive igniting his mood. He watched a barefoot girl emerge from a heat shimmer. She moved like a melancholy river, troubled and flowing. Morning light admired its reflection in the metallic scales of her skirt, and a playful breeze tried to steal a red rose from her dark hair.

Ignacio knew it was her, knew that it couldn't have been anyone else. He knew that they were both exactly where they were meant to be. From birth through all that they had suffered, fate had led them to that very moment. They were two forlorn vessels on a preordained collision course, both flying tattered white flags of surrender.

"Estrellita."

She stopped and looked up at him, surprised that other people still existed on the brutal blue surface of planet earth, that life had continued despite her grief. She blinked at the image before her: a neatly dressed elderly man and a hallucinating bus that had dropped out of someone's LSD flashback. She wasn't sure if they were even real.

"How do you know my name?" she asked.

Ignacio stared at her face, listened to her voice and reminded himself not to say anything that would make him appear to be insane.

It's not Sophia

"I saw you perform. You are so talented. I'm your biggest fan," he said, bowing at the waist and smiling.

"Thank you," she said, and turned away.

"Wait. Please. I have an offer for you. I believe in you, and if you'll let me, I can help you achieve your dreams."

She looked towards the water and spoke softly. "I'm afraid you're a little late. Dreams never come true, rainbows hold no magic and true love cannot defeat evil."

He could see her music dying on her lips.

She kept walking.

Say something!

"Estrellita Luminosa," he blurted.

His callous words jolted and weakened her step. They mocked her loss and desecrated her vigil. They were cruel words from a cruel song, one that never should have brought her joy or stained the flesh of a hand she would never hold again.

She turned her fury his way. "How *dare* you say that to me," she hissed.

Ignacio took a step backwards, his eyes widening in alarm. "Estrellita Luminosa," he repeated. "I wrote that song."

"Liar!"

"What? No. I did. My name is Ignacio dos Santos, and I'm a merenguero. I wrote that song…a long time ago…for my wife. Her name was Estrellita as well, same as you. I only tell you this so you understand that I know of what I speak, that I'm capable of helping you."

Her eyes brimmed with tears she refused to release. "But I thought you were dead."

"I was, chiquita, as dead as a man can be and still feel pain."

"Your song…you will never know what it has meant to me." She stepped towards him and took his hands into her own. "It has been an inspiration, an anthem."

"I am honoured. Do you believe in destiny?"

"I used to."

"Well, dreams are the beginning of a destiny we can create for ourselves. Don't give up on yours. Come with me—you and the Cinnamon Roosters. I've got a big bus, plenty of room."

"It's just you in that thing?"

"Just me and another cinnamon rooster. He can be our mascot. I think you will like him. His name is Mr. Mestizo, and he has crazy mambo legs."

She smiled before she could stop herself. "And what's ·in it for you?"

Redemption

"Fifteen percent," he said, holding out his hand. "What says you?"

She thought Jaragua, about how she had promised him that she would never quit on herself. She took his hand. "Deal."

"I always knew you had a voice, and now the world will as well. Shall we begin?"

"I have to say goodbye to someone first."

Estrellita turned away from him and walked towards the ocean. She sat on the seawall, took the flower from her hair and pressed her lips to its wilting beauty.

"Watch over me, Jaragua," she whispered.

She brushed a single tear from her cheek and dropped the rose into the sea. She watched the solemn waves gently coax her sacrament out into deeper waters, watched until the colour of her love sank beneath the surface, bestowing new and troubled songs upon mermaids and sirens.

Bachata

EPILOGUE

9:15 A.M.: WASHINGTON HEIGHTS, NEW YORK CITY.

ANTHONY DOMINGUEZ DROPPED THE phone into its cradle, blew out his breath and tilted back in his office chair. He pinched his earlobe and wiggled it vigorously. He had just spent the first two hours of his day on the telephone, and his inner ear felt liquefied.

There came an energetic rapping at the door, and a small lean woman entered the room. She was sharp and quick, and her translucent skin clung to her stringy muscles like crepe paper on a skinned rabbit.

"Mandatory break time. New rules. Fifteen minutes. You can't help anyone if you can't help yourself," she said. She placed a cup of coffee on Anthony's desk and refused to smile.

"I know the new regime, but I have to—"

"What you *have* to do is nada for the next fourteen minutes." She looked at her watch and arched her plucked eyebrows. "I will handle all calls, pat some hands, put out some fires, and don't worry, your beloved stress will be there waiting for you when this torture is over."

Anthony picked up the coffee and inhaled deeply. "Okay. I know you're right. I just don't know if I can even enjoy this without a phone under my chin and a pen in my hand. Smells great though, thank you."

"Caffeine junkie." She allowed one side of her mouth to curve slightly upwards as she closed the door.

Her name was Paula Perez, and she was a well-educated social activist in her mid sixties. Two decades earlier, she had left a convent in Argentina to cofound H.A.N.D. with Anthony. The acronym stood for "Help, Assimilation and Naturalization for Dominicans." The non-profit organization relied heavily on private donations and fundraising in order to continue its outreach programs. The charity assisted Dominicans with visas, green cards, access to social services, accommodations, employment, education, language courses, lawyers and addictions counselling. The grassroots group had grown from a one-bedroom apartment and three telephones to a highly respected organization that employed fifteen people and occupied the entire top floor of a renovated warehouse north of Washington Bridge.

Anthony stretched the complaint from his back, sipped his coffee and gazed out one of the industrial windows that ringed the room, original fabrications whose heavy frames lent the place an air of permanence, which he liked.

There was a light snow falling, and he looked out across the sullen Harlem River towards the grey tenement buildings of the Bronx. They looked humiliated, like boxcars full of living skeletons with shaven heads destined for winter camps and toxic showers. His gaze swept out over the Dominican stronghold of Washington Heights, and he considered how his compatriots were no different from all the other immigrants in NYC, carving an ethnic enclave out of the siren-drenched air and foreign bedrock—a place that felt like home.

The Italians had Little Italy; Puerto Ricans owned Spanish Harlem; the Russians had Little Odessa and Brighton Beach; African Americans ruled Harlem and the South Bronx; the Jews had Borough Park; there was Chinatown, Little Germany, Koreatown and, in one of the largest diasporas since the Irish had fled their barren potato fields for the grit and grind of Hell's Kitchen, the Dominicans had laid claim to Washington Heights, a.k.a. Da Haze, Little D.R., Santo Domingo II and Quisqueya Heights.

Anthony knew that the instinct to flock together had less to do with racism and xenophobia than with the comfort of familiar faces, music, food and language, and he was quietly proud of the part H.A.N.D. had played in easing the feelings of alienation that new arrivals often suffered. However, it was ironic that the organization never would have been born if not for the mayhem inflicted on the world by a murderous street gang. They had called themselves the Wild Cowboys, and during the eighties, they had terrorized the community, flooding the city with cocaine and violence. Quisqueya Heights had become known as Crack City, and it was the epicentre for drug distribution on the eastern seaboard.

He and Paula had been sickened by the collapse of their neighbourhood's family values. Seemingly overnight, prostitution, drug addiction, homelessness and brutality had eradicated all the good will that the previous generations of Dominicans had worked so hard to achieve. Suddenly, anyone with a Spanish surname or Dominican accent was being treated with suspicion and contempt. By the time the decent citizens left in the neighbourhood found their voice, he and Paula had begun their life's most important work.

Anthony leaned next to a bulky ornate radiator and luxuriated in the warmth that oozed from it. He had always felt confused by the reverse morality of criminal minds and how they believed that the world was theirs for the taking and not the building. It was so easy to release the animal within, believing that a willingness to kill—in order to drape oneself in shiny metals and expensive clothing—spoke of a survivor instead of a quitter. True power came from sacrifice, from doing what would make your children proud, when they were old enough to judge, old enough to emulate. Embracing hatred was simply a failure of the spirit.

He drained his cup and picked up one of the many self-help pamphlets that he and Paula had created together. He read the words emblazoned across the front: "ONE HAND: Language, Identity and Success." Their pamphlet informed the reader that it wasn't necessary to lose one's identity in order to adopt a new one, that language was the key to success and assimilation in their new home. Americanization didn't mean that an individual ever forgot their roots. If anything, the process forged nostalgia and patriotism. It was the reason why the Irish held their St. Patrick's Day parade so dear, the reason why Italians loved their food and Dominicans their music.

Anthony turned the pamphlet over and read the last passage aloud. "The Spanish tongue will always define you no matter how polished your English becomes. If Spanish is your heart and soul, if it is your body and blood, can you not spare a single hand for English? One hand that will be able to open so many doors?"

He dropped the red pamphlet onto a stack of yellow ones that educated the reader on STDs.

He looked at his watch. "Ten more minutes? This break stuff is harder than working," he mumbled.

He walked over to a wall of framed pictures and looked up at the images. They recorded milestones, captured emotions, confirmed existence and reminded him that he had led a good life, one he sometimes forgot had been his.

There was a shot of him and Paula smiling euphorically as they cut a blue ribbon they had strung across the entrance of H.A.N.D.'s first real office space. There was one of him looking fresher than he ever remembered feeling, his arm draped around Desi Arnaz's shoulders and his eyes shining with starstruck incredulity.

"Ciro's," he whispered, recalling the famous LA club where the photo had been taken.

Next in line was another one of him and Paula receiving a community service award from Mayor Ed Koch. There was one of a sunburned group of firemen and police officers at a fundraising BBQ one sweltering July weekend. And then a favourite: Anthony shaking hands with Sammy Sosa.

As usual, he tried to bypass the next picture, and just as predictably, he failed.

His gaze settled reluctantly on the faded black and white photograph, and he allowed the bittersweet memories it evoked to surface once again. The picture had been taken in New York City in the late fifties. It was a promotional shot for a merengue band he had played in. He looked at the image of himself as a young merenguero, his hair black and oiled, his teeth shockingly white, his treasured German accordion resting across his knees. Occasionally, he still heard the group's biggest song on the radio. It was their only hit, and it had changed everything for them.

"Estrellita Luminosa."

He stared at the photograph, at the man who wrote the song, the band's charismatic leader and Anthony's childhood friend. He wiped a nonexistent smudge from the glass. "Ignacio dos Santos, whatever became of you?"

Anthony had been at the hospital the day Ignacio's daughter had come into the world…and his wife had left it. He would never forget the look in his friend's eyes when they told him that she was gone. It wasn't so much what he had seen in them that disturbed him, it was what was no longer there.

He remembered Ignacio's inability to hold his own newborn baby girl, to even look at her. Anthony had helped him survive that horrible time in his life, watching as he slowly forged some sort of brittle peace with his innocent daughter, but nothing was ever the same after that.

Anthony sighed and thought about the last time he had ever seen Ignacio—twenty-five years ago. It had been at Sophia's funeral, and if the death of his wife had made his friend dream of madness, then his daughter's had awakened him to it.

He could still see Ignacio in his mind's eye: his shoulders hunched, his black suit jacket blowing out behind him as he walked away from Sophia's casket, walked away from everyone and everything he had ever known, away from the world and all it had done to him.

Nobody had seen him since.

"Stupid coffee break," Anthony grumbled.

He walked back to his desk.

Paula opened the door without knocking and pointed a red nail at the telephone. "You're going to want to get this."

He looked at his watch and grinned. "But I've got two minutes left. What kind of bully-boy operation you running here, buddy?"

"So start a union," she said, and jabbed her finger at the telephone again. "Seriously."

He twisted his mouth around his amusement and picked up the receiver. "Hands, do you need one?"

Silence

"Hello?" Anthony said, furrowing his brow towards Paula.

"Hello..." said the voice on the other end. "Um, can I speak to Anthony Dominguez, please?"

"This is he. How can I help you?"

The voice hesitated a moment before continuing. "My name is Maximo Caesar Ventura, and my sister's name is Lourdes, and Ignacio says to tune up your squeezebox..."

Merengue